Ordinary World

Jack T Canis

Published by Jack T Canis, 2023.

Ordinary World
By Jack T. Canis
Text copyright © Jack T. Canis 2023
Cover illustration, 'Ordinary World' by Danielle Farrington © 2023
Art copyright © Danielle Farrington 2023
Edited by Steph Warren (Twitter: @bookshineblog)
The moral right of the author and illustrator has been asserted according to the Copyright, Designs and Patents Act 1988.
All Rights are reserved.
No part of this publication may be reproduced, stored in a retrieval system, or transmitted, in any form or by any means without prior permission in writing of the publisher and copyright holders.
This is a work of fiction. Names, characters, businesses, places, events and incidents are the product of the author's imagination or are used in a fictitious manner. Any resemblance to actual persons, living or dead, or actual events is purely coincidental.

Author's note:

I hadn't planned on saying anything before letting you get into 'Ordinary World', but I thought there were a couple of things I ought to point out for you.

In case you missed the warning on the back cover – there's a lot of strong adult profanity in this book.

If you look very carefully you may find the Easter Eggs I've put into the text. There are six deliberate ones, a couple of them are quite obvious as long as you've got as an eclectic taste in music as I have. Two are very obscure. But if you're stuck and want to know, I'm on Twitter most days and would be happy to discuss them with you. @JackCanis.

'Ordinary World' stems from a dream I had many years ago. I have always known what the ending would be, it was just a problem finding the correct path to it. The novel was written with it being a standalone, although when rewriting the ending once again, as I attempted to find that correct path, I realised there was the opportunity for a follow-on story. Especially as I had come up with an alternative ending for 'Ordinary World' while writing it. I have, however, stayed true to the original concept I had in mind. I have already made some inroads into the second story, 'The Conduit', but I make no promises that it will be ready for publication until at least 2025. That said, 'Ordinary World' is quite complete without it.

I hope you enjoy 'Ordinary World' as it is an insight into my mind.

Chapter 1

Thursday April 8th 1993, early morning

Olivia's sixteen years of life to date had been unremarkable. Not unpleasant nor unhappy, but certainly not a burning orgy of thrills and delights either. She had always been demure and slight, with curly shoulder-length brunette hair, which she invariably wore tied up in a severe bun at the back of her head. Her physique had coined her the nickname of Olive Oil at school, or oily Olivia when the kids were feeling particularly unkind. It was an unfair reflection of early teenage hormone imbalances, as they oozed across her complexion. Just like every other kid in her school. But there's always one child that gets picked out from the crowd to deflect such ignominies from others. For Olivia, she was the hormone scapegoat.

Life at home was worse. School was a welcome relief and, for the most part, mild bullying by some of her peers was a breeze in the park. Whereas her father, Reg Buchanan, was a vile brute of a man and coarse of tongue. Once, he was well-built, but these days the muscle had turned to saggy fat that hung heavily around his overweight edges. When Olivia was younger, his most affectionate terms of endearment towards her were descriptions like,

'You're nothing more than a lanky streak of piss!'

Her mother, Phyllis, was of no help to her throughout her childhood, not because she was uncaring or lacked maternal instinct, but because her mother lacked any semblance of self. She was more a shell of someone who had once been. Olivia had seen photos of her mother when she had been probably not much older than she was now. She had found them stuffed inside an old cushion at the back of one of the cupboards in her mother's bedroom. Were they hidden deliberately for moments when her mother could steal back a memory of who she was? Or were they just long-forgotten memories, like the cushion seemed to be? They showed a completely different person: a vibrant, intelligent, beautiful-looking young woman, with her whole life to look forward to. Embracing the moment with friends now lost to time. Like the neighbours and Olivia's friends, she assumed that that woman had been beaten away after too many years of being married to her father and, in some aspects, this was probably true. But there were other factors that had made her mother the woman she was today. The empty, vacant shell with hollow, distant eyes, ringed by endless sleepless nights – so many wracked by the horrors of an infected mind. She knew the answer, thanks to her father, as to what was wrong with her mum:

'She's fucking mental, is her fucking problem. Fuckin' batshit crazy!'

Not a clinical diagnosis, but still accurate. Phyllis' mental deterioration had started shortly after Olivia had been born. Initially diagnosed with post-natal depression, but as her condition had worsened the doctors had referred her for a long stay in the local 'nut house' and there it had been determined that she was suffering from schizophrenia. They expanded upon this diagnosis a few months later and determined, after a particularly violent episode, that she was delusional to boot. Periods of experimenting with medications eventually found a suitable balance for her to function on a low level. But it meant that Olivia had never had a mother to look out for her, to nurture or love her. There had been fleeting moments of lucidity. At these times Phyllis would become the tender, nurturing mother Olivia craved. Brief encounters that would take Olivia's breath away.

Unfortunately, with the medications these moments became more distant by the day, by the month and by the year. Now her mother would sit staring into space for much of the day unless

ORDINARY WORLD

'urged' by her husband to 'get off her fucking lazy arse' and do something 'fucking useful', like burn his dinner. Olivia, used to these daily routines, was certain that once in a while that glimmer of the woman her mother had once been flickered into life and a little defiant smile crept into the corners of her mouth as she presented her husband with the charred offerings he had demanded. The smile would then be slapped away by his ire and she would be left confused upon the kitchen floor, until he had gone out 'to get a proper fucking meal', at which point it would be safe for Olivia to cradle her mother and help her to her feet, guiding her unsteadily to the sitting room sofa.

It's an amazing testament to the fortitude of the human condition, what a person can consider 'normal', and what they are prepared to contend with as part of their day-to-day existence. For Olivia this was her life: miserable, violent and loveless, but not lonely. She had two peers she could confide in. She would spend precious moments of sanity and happiness with them. And there was one other, older person who acted like a de facto guardian to her. Someone she couldn't remember not having in her life: her aunt, Morag. Phyllis' older sister, a good ten years her senior and someone who had not been in her mum's life for very long, because, being older, she had gone to make a life of her own. Aunt Morag had distantly maintained contact with her sibling. But she had only re-entered that life when she had heard of the ailments that so afflicted her younger sister and she had helped to raise Olivia in those very early years, until a confrontation with her father made it impossible for them to be in the same room, let alone the same house. It was odd really, Olivia just had to mention her aunty's name and the blood would drain right out of her father's face.

'Fucking mental witch, she is. If I'd met her when I married Phyllis, I would never have married the stupid bitch cos I would have seen how fucking mental the whole fucking family was!'

That said, Olivia knew that her father, bully and braggart that he was, feared her aunt and it often made her wonder, what had happened in that fight that had so unsettled him?

• • • •

Olivia was wrenched from a deep sleep by a visceral scream from somewhere in the house. Even before she was fully conscious, she was swinging herself up and out of bed. That was a scream she knew to react to. She had been disturbed many times by her mother's screams over the years and Olivia had come to know each one for what mood they meant for her mother. This was a scream steeped in fear and aggression. It was a dangerous scream - a scream that would lead to blood being spilled if she, Olivia, didn't rush to intervene. Olivia forced her eyes open, as she grabbed her dressing gown and stumbled hurriedly out of her bedroom. From downstairs she could hear the sound of a struggle and her father swearing. She broke into a run. Vigorously rubbing the sleep from her eyes, she practically threw herself downstairs, fearful that either one of her parents could be dead before she got to them. A memory shot unbidden into her head as she took the stairs three at a time: of the first time she had heard that scream. On that occasion, her mother had savagely attacked the new armchair that her father had just bought for himself, with a pair of antique, textile scissors. The chair had been eviscerated in the frenzied attack. Her doctors had pointed out what this could have meant had the chair been a person. Her mother had then spent a protracted few months interned at the local mental health facility, while they experimented with her medication and attempted counselling and analysis. Olivia and her father had taken the time to remove every conceivable sharp implement in the house and lock them safely away. It did make life inconvenient, to say the least, but better a little inconvenience than for her mother to end up slitting one of their throats during a psychotic break. It had been over a year since they had experienced such a violent episode from her and Olivia was surprised that such an incident could well be occurring right now, especially given how placid and docile her mother had been in recent months.

As Olivia ran to the kitchen, she could hear her mother's broken and cracked voice shouting at her father.

'Who are you? Why are you here? I know what you want! Who are you?'

Her father's bedside manner left a lot to be desired and clearly, as usual, he was only making the situation worse.

'I'm your husband, you stupid, fucking mad bitch!'

'You're not my husband!' her mother screamed at him, 'How did you think that disguise would fool me? Fool any of us? You can't have her! You can't have any of us!'

Olivia saw her mother backed into the corner of the kitchen, over by the cupboards on the back wall. The back door to the garden lay just to her right, her hands were proffered in front of her, palms open, as if trying to ward off Olivia's father. Phyllis stood partly slouched in her dressing gown, which was untied and open for Olivia to see her white, lace-trimmed chemise underneath. Olivia was momentarily hypnotised by the sight of her mother's chest heaving up and down as her lungs dragged great gulps of air in. Phyllis' pallor was livid, blotchy and sweaty.

'What the fuck are you on about, woman? All I want from you is for you to take your fucking meds! Before you go completely batshit crazy on us.'

Her father had sensibly placed their large, pine kitchen table between her mother and his ample frame. Olivia could see he had a bottle of her mother's pills in his right hand and several of them in his open left hand.

'I'm not taking your poison; do you take me for a fool?' her mother responded.

Her father started to edge around the table, thrusting his left hand towards her mother, as if the mere action would suffice in her accepting and consuming the pills. Her mother was having none of it though and she drew herself up to her full height, all five foot eight of it, and thrust her chest out as she once again shouted at him:

'Keep those things away from me! I have every right to kill you... it's self-defence. Everyone will see you are evil and trying to poison me.'

Olivia moved into the room more cautiously than her previous haste would have allowed. She walked slowly to the right of the table, keeping it between her and her father, using it as a psychological barrier for her mother to deduce that she was nothing to do with the evil creature trying to poison her. She inched her way down the side of the table, feeling the solidity of the smoothed, pine edge pressing into her left hip. She started to mirror her mother's stance, upright and with her hands placatingly held to the fore. As she moved, she glanced around the kitchen, taking in the lie of the land to ensure there were no obstructions nor potential hazards that could make the situation worse. She noted one of the kitchen chairs lay on its back on the vinyl tiled floor; presumably thrown there when her mother had reacted to her father's intention that she take her pills. The early morning breakfast array lay strewn across the table, probably jarred out of place when her mother leapt to her feet. She also saw that there was a carving knife on the counter near to where her father was standing. For a moment she wondered where it had come from, and why it might be out. Had her father become lax, given her mother's recent placidness? If so, could they be in for some serious trouble? She would need to ensure that both of them remained between the knife and her mother's outstretched hands.

Olivia looked back at her mother, who remained unmoved in her position by the cupboards. Her father was drawing breath to shout again and she knew she had to interject before he exacerbated the situation.

'It's OK, Dad, I'll look after her. You can go now.'

It came out more dismissively than intended; a hurried comment to try and get her father to back off so that she could calm everyone down. Her father, always quick to anger, immediately took umbrage.

'I'm not your fucking servant to dismiss at the click of a finger, Olivia. I am your father!' he turned his ire towards her, shifting his weight and his frame from behind the relative protection of the table. 'You don't get to say where I can go. I do as I damn well please.'

Wasn't that the fucking truth, Olivia thought, as she glanced at him. She took her eyes from her mother, fearful that maybe he would take out his frustration on her. It wouldn't be the first time he had slapped her for a minor indiscretion.

Her mother responded to the perceived change of antagonists in the room and started to move across the frame of the back door towards the sink and draining board - where the carving knife lay. However, Reg still blocked her path to that goal and she was wary of being assaulted by him. She paused, possibly considering her options. Whom did Phyllis believe was the biggest threat to her wellbeing?

Olivia forced herself to look at her mother whilst replying to her father.

'I wasn't *dismissing* you, Dad. I'm sorry if that's how it came out. I was just trying to let you know that I would sort mum's meds out, as I usually do in the morning.'

It was odd, now she came to think about it. Why was Dad trying to give Mum her meds? All of Mum's care usually came down to her – bathing, dressing, feeding, meds, all of it – so why this morning did he think to try and give his wife her medication? She would never understand her father. As she talked, she started to move towards Phyllis again, ensuring as she did that she came between her parents, so that her mother's attention would be drawn to her and away from her potential aggressor.

Reg's response was along the lines of what Olivia would expect from him. Capitulation in the form of permission – he could save face like this and still get his jibe in, presumably washing his hands of the whole situation while still thinking he was in control.

'Fine, you deal with her; you're both as bad as each other. I just hope I'm not still here when you start going bonkers like your fucking mother.'

He'd laid his position on the line, now there was just the matter of the pills he was still holding on to. Olivia saw out of the corner of her eye, her father glance at them and then back towards Phyllis. Olivia returned her attention to her mother once more. She suddenly became very aware as she stepped closer to her, that her mother was now holding the carving knife. How did she get it? In that moment when she'd been distracted by her father, had Mum made a lightning grab for the knife? It seemed inconceivable given how limp and lacklustre her mother usually was, primarily as a side effect of her pills. No matter, there was now an imminent danger with the knife and Olivia was in a prime position to be impaled by it. She moderated the tone of her voice to address her mother, calmly and quietly. Olivia spoke soothingly,

'It's OK, Mum, Dad's not going to make you take the pills, isn't that right, Dad?' It was a bit of a risk involving her father again, but if he did the sensible thing and backed-off she knew she would be able to defuse the situation. There was an uncomfortable grunt from her father. 'Isn't that *right*, Dad?' she prompted him.

'Yes,' he said grudgingly.

Olivia's eyes locked on to her mother's, insisting that she pay attention only to her. Her mother's eyes were watery and bloodshot, but slowly they started to focus on her.

'Who are you?' her mother asked more quietly, a new wave of consternation crossing her once-beautiful features.

'It's me, Mum. Your daughter, Olivia,' Olivia replied.

'I don't have a daughter,' her mother answered in a flat tone, 'I was *going* to have a daughter and we were going to call her Charlotte, but then things... happened...' her voice trailed off and her eyes started to lose their focus.

'Yes Mum, that's me. I *am* your daughter, the one you were going to have, but you called me Olivia.'

Olivia had been devastated the first time they had entered this cycle of denial, but she had been much younger when her mother had failed to recognise who she was. Now she felt safer because she knew where the conversation would lead, as she reaffirmed that her mother did indeed have a daughter. Olivia was eager to get to the part where her mother would hug her; it was one of those few moments in their lives when her mother seemed to come to life. There was, however, still the matter of the knife, a factor that was new to this dialogue.

'Let me see you; come to me!' her mother ordered.

Olivia moved closer to her mother, still wary of the threat posed by the carving knife.

'Yes. Maybe,' she said, looking Olivia directly in the face, searching, questing her features to find some recognition within her delusion of whom she was trying to connect with. 'How old are you?'

'I will be seventeen next week, Mum,' Olivia replied.

'You're exactly how I imagined you would be when you were seventeen,' her mother said and a smile broke through the consternation. Her mother reached forward and wrapped Olivia up in her arms, squeezing her tightly, a sense of urgency and desperation coming through to Olivia in that sudden contact. She let herself be taken up in the moment, savouring the warmth of the embrace; enjoying a lucid moment of love with her mother, knowing all too soon it would be gone. Being of a slight frame, her mother's arms were able to wrap all the way around her torso and shoulders, bringing the knife to lie against her ribs. Olivia could feel the point of the blade pressing down into her hip bone; slowly, she slid her hand down and round and was able to retrieve the knife from her mother's relaxed grasp. She then took the opportunity to reciprocate the embrace with a renewed passion.

Phyllis slowly drew back from her daughter, so that she could gaze with fondness up at her. Knowing the moment had passed, Olivia guided her mother to a kitchen chair and helped her to sit down. The tranquillity of the moment was shattered as her father's body suddenly appeared between them. Reg grabbed Phyllis by her hair and tried to shove her medication into her mouth. Her mother choked out a scream and pushed back at her attacker. Olivia was knocked into the table as her father shot past her, hurled bodily across the room. He slammed into the back door, his head connecting with the bottom pane of opaque safety glass that adorned it. At the point of impact there was the sound of tissue paper being scrunched, as the glass cracked, causing a shock wave of skittering patterns to ripple a path across the pane. For a moment, all was still; Olivia lay on the floor under the table with the wind knocked out of her. She watched as Phyllis calmly sat down and spat the pills out of her mouth. She then pulled her chair under the table and poured herself a bowl of cornflakes. Just a normal thing one does in the morning when you sit down at the table. She picked up a spoon that lay a good stretch from her, dipped it into the bowl and then stopped. Her eyes glazed as she continued to stare at the bowl. Olivia knew she had slipped from lucidity back into one of her catatonic-like states; there would be no reaction from her again for several hours, possibly even days.

• • • •

Reg sat on the sofa holding a cold compress to the back of his head with his right hand, his left clutching the remote control for the TV. Understandably, he didn't appear to be in a good mood. Olivia came into the sitting-room, dressed in her school uniform and putting some papers into her shoulder bag. She sat down in an armchair to the left of the doorway to strap on her shoes and address her father.

'I've spoken with the unit. They said Dr McIntyre would send someone out later or maybe they'd report it to the mental health team and get them to send an ASW round to assess Mum. Problem with that is, it could be any time between now and the end of the week before anyone comes. And Maureen's still on the sick.' Maureen was Phyllis' case worker with the mental health team.

She paused from her shoes as she spoke, and looked at her father. All she could discern was a thundercloud of hurt pride and frustration upon his face and when she mentioned Maureen, she saw a flicker of annoyance in his eyes. Maureen was her mum's fifth case worker in three years. Each one seemed to be either burned out by the time they received Phyllis' file or just a stop-gap agency worker. Either way, they didn't remain with her for long and there were always issues with getting anything done in the 'process' – there was a serious lack of consistency for Phyllis' care. Olivia sighed. The mental health team would send an ASW out sooner if they thought her father might have a tantrum at her mum, which ended up with either one of them in hospital, as had happened once before. But that was not the way to go. She looked at the TV screen; the new morning show was spouting words of pointless wisdom. She turned her wrist to look at her watch. It was already gone 10.00am, so, late for school again and she had been doing well this term. Mainly because mum had been so placid. Still, the school understood and made allowances; she had already spoken with the school's secretary to let her know that there had been an 'incident' this morning and that she was going to be late. That said, the headteacher, Mr Rawlinson, wasn't so understanding, and as her regular late arrival and absences affected his attendance records, perhaps he wouldn't be so forgiving. Olivia chanced her arm and enquired after her father's injury.

'How's your head, Dad?'

Her father's response was gruff, but not as unpleasant as she had been expecting. Being slammed against the back door had obviously knocked some of the bravado out of him. He huffed heavily before answering.

'Hurts like a bastard and there's a big lump, but it's not bleeding, so that's something, I s'pose.' He didn't look at Olivia as he replied, he just continued to focus on the TV, where an advert for sparkling dishes was wooing the viewer. 'I suppose you want me to stay in until someone comes to look at *her*?'

'If you don't mind, Dad. Yes, please,' Olivia felt sorry for her dad, even though she wasn't exactly fond of him. He'd had a tough morning and was feeling the consequences of his actions and temper. Probably grumpier than usual, because he had decided to try and help for once and just had it spat back in his face.

Olivia closed the front door behind her and, despite being late, dawdled her way to the cut-through to the high street and the bus stop. Her head felt fuzzy, there was a pain in the corner of her left eyeball and she knew that a headache was on its way. What could she expect? Wrenched from sleep by a visceral scream and then hurling herself straight into a warzone. It was surprising she even had the energy to go to school, let alone knowing a migraine was on its way. She paused as she turned right into the cut-through and, leaning on the wall for support, she drew in a long breath from the chill spring air. Eyes closed, a finger pressed into the pain spot in her eyeball, she slowly exhaled and then opened her eyes. Yes, that had helped; the pain in her eye had receded. She looked down the length of the alleyway - empty, a scattering of litter and a stain near her feet suggestive of the excesses of a Friday night on the town being violently ejected. She sighed: was this a picture of her life? An empty alleyway of rejection? She drew in another breath, more quickly this time, bolstering herself and coming to attention. If it was, there was a turning ahead and it led to better things. She strode towards it with determination.

Chapter 2

Olivia waited for Mrs Flint to finish on the phone so that she could log her attendance with her. She also wanted to clear with her that it would be OK to leave the school grounds during lunch break, as she wanted to pop home and check on her mum, and find out if the ASW had been in to assess her. Olivia stood in the doorway to the secretaries' office; Mrs Flint sat in her usual swivel chair by the window, arranging a meeting with a parent to discuss extra-curricular options for their son. Mrs Flint was a motherly figure within the school, to whom all the troubled students would go when they felt life was getting too much for them. She was a rotund, middle-aged woman with an ample bosom that seemed to meld with her midriff when she wore her oversized woollen jumpers. It was a bosom that had been nuzzled into by many a student for comfort. Mrs Flint shared the office with Miss Stirling, another matronly figure, who glanced up occasionally and smiled her supportive, 'poor dear' smile at Olivia. Miss Stirling absentmindedly tapped along to the songs on the radio that were playing softly in the background. The door to the adjoining office where Mr Rawlinson sat was ajar when Olivia had first arrived. She had seen Mr Rawlinson look up from the papers he was poring over and roll his eyes when he saw her. He had then made a marked act of looking at his watch and scribbling something on a pad of paper. Olivia smiled sweetly at him and then turned her back to lean on the door frame, thus obscuring him from her vision. *He's such a tosser*, she thought, turning her attention back to the radio as the DJ announced the current single from Duran Duran. She really liked this song and strained to hear it over the ambient buzz of the office.

Mrs Flint finally said goodbye to the parent on the other end of the line and turned to speak with Olivia. She nearly missed Mrs

Flint's opening remark to her as she was drawn into an 'Ordinary World'. How she longed to live in an ordinary world.

'Thank you for calling ahead, my dear,' she said. 'How's your mam now? How are you doing?' she asked, her head tilting to the side.

'Mum's quiet now, she's back into her catatonia, and I'm fine, thank you. Just a bit thrown; things had been going so well the last couple of months.'

'I'm not surprised you're *thrown*, dear. Your mother's episodes are hard at the best of times, let alone first thing in the morning and without any hint of one coming on. Honestly, I don't know how you soldier on! I would have been at a complete loss if that had been me; I'm, as you know, not a morning person.' She shrugged her shoulders, 'there's no way I would have been able to cope with that situation, I would have been too busy trying to work out where I had put my slippers and which foot they should go on.' She smiled deprecatingly up at Olivia, who returned the smile, knowing that Mrs Flint was a far more capable woman than she was making out, but appreciating the emotional support that she was receiving.

'I would like to go back at lunch time, just to check on Mum and also see if anyone's been out to assess her, if that's OK?' She suspected it wouldn't be a problem, but having just seen Rawlinson's expression, she needed to have official confirmation on her records.

'Of course, that'll be OK, my dear,' Mrs Flint said.

Olivia thanked Mrs Flint and left the office for her 10.30am class. She slipped into the room, Mr Coombes giving her a perfunctory nod of acknowledgement as he continued with his lesson. She glanced briefly around the room before finally settling on a seat next to her best friend Evie.

ORDINARY WORLD

Evie watched as Olivia sidled across the classroom to her table and immediately leaned over to whisper to her friend as she sat down.

'You OK?'

'Bit of a headache, but fine, really. Just an incident with Mum,' Olivia replied, as if Evie didn't already know that her mother would be the cause of her lateness to school.

'Do you want to talk about it?' Evie asked.

Olivia glanced up as Mr Coombes paused his lesson; he was looking directly at them and she could tell he was allowing them a moment, but that would be all he would be allowing them. Mr Coombes was a stern task-master, but he also understood Olivia's situation. He had sat down with her the term before last, with her grades sliding, and discussed her position. It had been during this conversation that Phyllis' plight had come pouring out in a deluge. Olivia had never cried about her life before and it had been a shock to her how much she had pent up on the matter. Even with her friends, she always kept a modicum of control. But sat there, with Mr Coombes, as he expressed his concern for her work, which he couldn't put down to anything other than something more pressing being the obstacle. *Home life*, he had said, *was often the most telling factor in a student's work*. Was there anything in her home life which was more pressing than her future? At which point Olivia had let it all out. Her mother's illness, her father's brutality, her despair. A massive tsunami of anguish and tears. Mr Coombes had been brilliant. She knew now that if she ever needed to talk, really talk, about her home life, he was her confidant. He understood the trying nature of illness in the family; his son was autistic and it made life difficult. He loved his son dearly, but that still didn't make it any easier when his son was punching him in the face. Olivia was quite surprised at how open Mr Coombes had been about his own home life and she could see his anguish as he had spoken about it. She knew he understood. In many ways it seemed that all her problems were scattered between her parents, whereas Mr Coombes' problems were all parcelled together in his son. Her mother was mad, her father violent. Mr Coombes' son was her mother and father rolled into one.

'Not now,' she replied to Evie.

Evie also looked up at Mr Coombes and gave him a cheery wink; he scowled back at her.

'Lunch?' suggested Evie.

'Nope, gotta go and check on Mum. Talk more after school.' Olivia signalled to Mr Coombes that that was the end of the catch-up by taking her notebook and pen out of her bag and settling to listen.

• • • •

As Olivia walked up the street to her house, she looked around. She had seen no evidence of Dr McIntyre's car parked in it. Nor did she see any of the other cars belonging to the case workers she knew from the unit or mental health team. Not that that necessarily meant anything, but she suspected no one had been out, nor was likely to, today at any rate. As she approached the entrance to her house, a subtle movement across the road to her left caught her attention. She looked up from her bag, where she had been trying to find her door key. The movement had come from the cut-through on the other side of the road. There, huddled in the entrance to it, was a large bundle of rags. They were piled into a cardboard box, which appeared to have been flattened by the weight of so many overcoats. She realised the breeze must have caused some of the material to flutter and this was what had attracted her peripheral vision. She was just about to move on, disregarding the event and the slight flutter that it had caused in her already highly-strung nerves, when the whole bundle shifted and a face appeared out of the crumpled clothing. It startled her.

The face was ghostly pale and somehow distorted. It was as if the left-hand side of the face had just melted away. She jumped at the sight of it. The more so when she realised the eyes within this face had locked onto hers. They were dark, densely dark, sat in hollows of shadows in a face that seemed to have slipped. They were intent on her and Olivia felt a sudden motivation not to be on the street any more. She picked up her pace and hurried towards her garden gate.

As she went she shot a hurried glance to her left, over the parked cars. The shambling mound of coats was no longer sat in its box. No, now it was up and moving. Moving in her direction and it was fast. *How could a shambling mound weighed down by so many overcoats move so fast?* she wondered in horror. Her pace picked up a notch. Her right hand rammed into her shoulder bag as it quested her door keys in desperation. She looked again, to where the mound had been moments before. It wasn't there, it was nowhere close to where it had been; the mound was now in the road, just over halfway across. Even at a sprint, Olivia couldn't imagine how that was possible. The mound was now on this side of the road, next to Mr Worthy's Ford Fiesta. Had she blinked? She hadn't seen the mound move and yet there it was – in a different place. She must have blinked.

She looked ahead of herself, her hand still scrabbling for the key. She could see her gateway ahead, maybe twenty feet to go now. She gave up all pretence that she wasn't scared and running for her life. She started to run, once more looking swiftly to her side to see where the transient was. The overcoats were no longer in the road, they had disappeared. Her head came round to face forward and she pulled up short as the mound appeared directly in front of her. Her momentum carried her forward into the wall of overcoats. She made no effort to stop, instead charging brashly into them, hoping to knock her potential assailant to the ground and leap over him to get to her house. She had underestimated her ability to charge down a full-grown adult.

Olivia slammed into a solid wall and was thrown backwards by the impact. Her nostrils were assailed by a stagnant odour that rammed itself into her sinuses, catching in the back of her throat and leaving an acrid stench in her senses. She gagged even as she fell away. Two claws, wrapped in what looked like grey, frayed bandages lashed out at her. There was no breath in her lungs to scream. To scream for help or to scream out of fear. The talons wrapped around her forearms – steel vices clamping into place and locking on, as the shuttle might do when it docked with the ISS. No room for manoeuvre, no chance of escape. She looked up into the face of her attacker; it was a face from the nightmares of the great horror writers of her age. She became fixated on the mouth as the transient started to speak. He drew in a great gasp of air with which to perform the task, but her eyes were drawn to where his face sagged. The flesh hung heavily down on one side, clumping together in a massive jowl that swung pendulously near the top of his chest. Heavy chunks of flesh wobbled inside a leathery sack and where it was exposed to the light, at the eye socket and the inside of the mouth, the flesh was grey and bloodshot like a steak that had been left to go blue for too long. At the corner of the sagging jowl there was an oasis of discoloured drool that slopped about the edges as it drooped past the transient's chin. A foul odour wafted from the viscous liquid and Olivia watched in horror as a long gloop slid over his puffy bottom lip and dangled, reflecting a grey-silver sheen to the oversized globule dangling at its end, until the strand could no longer withstand the pressure of gravity with the mere strength of surface tension any longer. The globule snapped free and plummeted right down on to her exposed wrist. It hit with a resounding and nauseating splat, leaving a slime trail behind as it eventually made its way to the pavement below. Olivia retched.

'Flurg! Flurg!' the transient shouted at her. His breath washed over her and she gagged anew, the stench of fetid meat curdled in her stomach. She pulled away reflexively and she suddenly found herself free of his grasp. Olivia took a step back readying herself for a dash to her gate and then looked back into the densely dark eyes of her assailant. The darkness was impenetrable and yet she suddenly felt a deep sense of anguish and loss from those tenebrous pools; the emotion hit her so palpably that it made her stagger. She brushed her fringe from her eyes and looked at the transient with fresh eyes. What she saw now was a shambling, comical figure to be pitied for its ugliness. She started to shake her head; *he probably just wanted some food or money*, she thought.

'I'm sorry, I don't have any change on me. But if you wait here I can get some from the house.' She tentatively leaned forward and patted the grotesque on the forearm through its coarse brown overcoat. 'Wait here!'

She ran past him, not certain if he understood her, nor even if she meant what she had just said. All she knew was that the safety of her home lay a matter of yards away and she now had the chance to access it. She bounded up to her front door, constantly checking over her shoulder to see if the transient was staying put or trying to follow her. She fumbled in her school bag for her keys, then jammed a key into the lock. The key turned and she let herself in through the faded and peeling apple-green wooden door. She was about to close it hurriedly behind her, when she heard her father's voice coming from the front room. She paused to listen, hoping this meant he was talking with a professional visitor and that her previous pessimism had been misplaced.

'Yes!' he said sharply to the unseen person. 'The new pills seem to be working; too bloody well, if you ask me. She could have killed me! I need more money for this. You said this would take no more than five years, it's been nearly fifteen; I want more money!'

Reg paused as he listened to whomever he was talking with. As Olivia heard no sounds other than her own breathing and the faint twitter of birdsong from outside, she concluded that her father was on the phone.

'Yes, I know,' he paused briefly again, 'yes, I said they seem to be working, much better than the last strain, which just made her a vegetable, but *so* much safer. These seem to have reactivated her talents, which is why I was nearly stabbed and she managed to hurl me across the room. And that's half the problem, isn't it? As she comes out of her stupor, well done, you've brought her closer back to her true potential, but she's also more aware, so she's going to start working things out and that ain't good for me!'

There was a longer gap, as her father listened intently to his caller.

'Yes, OK, normal arrangement. Don't know, she's not shown any signs whatsoever.' Reg listened again before responding, 'yes, I can do that, no problem.' Then he stopped talking abruptly and hung up the phone.

Olivia could see he had been pacing the front room as he'd been talking, the cord on the phone stretched so taut that the loops had disappeared. In doing so, he had come into partial view; a view which now meant he could see her standing in the hallway listening to his private conversation, hence the sudden cessation. The expression on his face changed rapidly from shock and consternation at her listening in, to one of annoyance and anger.

Olivia marched into the room; she had questions to ask of her father because she didn't like what she had heard. To her, it sounded like he had been experimenting on her mother and she wanted to know with whom.

'Who were you talking to?' Olivia demanded.

'None of your bloody business,' her father replied.

'It is when it concerns Mum,'

'And what makes you think it had anything to do with your mother?'

'I think that was obvious from your comments about her coming out of her stupor and hurling you across the room. Not to mention that stuff about her medication. So, what was that about? Have you been experimenting on Mum?'

Olivia was fuming. If her dad had been giving drugs to her mum that weren't part of her prescribed regime, that would explain her sudden change this morning and also justify her mother's paranoia that her dad was, in fact, trying to poison her.

Reg cleared his throat several times and Olivia wondered if he was preparing a plausible lie.

'OK, fine, yes, it was about Phyllis. I was talking with the locum, Dr Varjay. He's been sorting her medication for the last few months and he has been trying to tweak the meds to give her more lucidity.'

'And you agreed to this without consulting with me first? Does Dr McIntyre know?' Olivia's hands were balled into fists by her sides and she stamped her foot down as she asked the first question in her barrage. She was tilted at the waist, spearing her body towards her father in an aggressive and volatile manner. Reg, having already been attacked once today by a woman in his family, took an involuntary step back at the wave of rage being directed at him. He held up his hands in a placatory manner to ward her off.

'Yes, McIntyre knows, he signed her meds routine off to Varjay ages ago. You were ill when this all came about and your mother was getting home release after her last incarceration, so the meeting happened when I went to pick her up. Varjay was new to the team and came highly recommended from London, from one of the research labs attached to one of the hospitals down there. Can't remember which one. Anyway, he reckoned that if we wanted more from Phyllis, he could look into her current meds and see what new things were on the market and within the remit of the unit, and see if some subtle alterations to the regime would give her, and us, a better quality of life. That's all it was, nothing more than trying to improve Phyllis' state of mind.' He seemed to be almost pleading with Olivia at this point and she relaxed her stance, backing off from him slightly. Then she remembered his comments about money. Her features hardened again.

'So, why were you demanding money from him?'

'I wasn't 'demanding' money from him...'

'You were! I *heard* you.' Olivia's voice rose half an octave, 'You said you needed more money, in fact you said: I want more money! So, what was that about then?'

Reg paused; he was sweating profusely,

'Fine, yes, alright,' he said, stalling for a few more moments, 'the new drugs are... experimental... to a degree,' he added as he saw her about to interject, 'they're fine, they've been through clinical testing, but because they're so new, they are only being used on a trial basis. Anyone using them gets funding with their usage. Because of this morning's incident I wanted more of that money. I felt I had a right to it because she attacked me. There. Are you satisfied?'

'Not in the slightest,' Olivia shouted at her father. The man was incorrigible! Trust him to use her mother as a cash cow to fund his lifestyle. 'How dare you use Mum as a guinea pig. How dare you profit from her. You are utterly despicable! Only you could use Mum for your own petty greed.'

'It's not just for me, y'know; that money goes to paying for our food and our mortgage. I don't see you stumping up for any of that. And Phyllis sure as hell isn't a bread-winner in this family, is she?

It's about fucking time she paid her way.' His angry response may have been ill-advised.

Olivia was spitting with contempt for her father and couldn't speak she was so angry. She stood there, ramrod straight, fists at her sides, practically frothing at the mouth. Her face was scarlet with the pent-up frustration at her father and his behaviour. She struggled to get any words out and was shocked by what she eventually managed to say.

'You are such a complete cunt!'

She stormed out of the living room and then the house, slamming the front door behind her. Olivia was halfway down the road before she realised she hadn't even checked on her mother. She came to an abrupt halt and then took in her surroundings, remembering in that instant her run-in with the transient a mere twenty minutes earlier. There was no sign of him, presumably giving up on her ever returning. Suddenly she was gripped by an intense sense of guilt at misleading the poor deformed man. How many times must that have happened to him before, a promise of succour that never materialised? Just a desperate ploy to rid themselves of the freak. She sighed. She didn't have the time nor the energy to contend with that as well right now – maybe later. She glanced at her watch to check the time; if she went back now, she would be late for school again, but her mother came first. So, she slowed her pace and turned around. As she walked back, she came into view of the cut-through and she looked in, with a slight hope that the transient was back at his boxes, but there was no sign of him now, nor the cardboard box he had been sat upon. She hurried her pace and paused when she was facing the entrance of the cut-through. She stared hard down its length, but could see no sign of anyone in it, at least till the bend. She wasn't prepared to go and investigate further though. She recalled the transient's ghostly visage with its sagging jowl and she felt a shiver run down her spine.

She turned briskly for her house. When she got back in, her father was nowhere to be seen and she presumed he, too, had fled. How typical that he had, leaving her mother all alone in the house. True, if she was settled in her catatonia, she was probably safe for a few days from getting up and wandering, but there was still the more obvious factor of bodily functions and the like, that could prove discomforting at best and life-threatening at worst.

Olivia made her way to her mother's room and went inside. The room was empty; there was no sign of her on her unmade bed, nor was she in the adjoining bathroom. Olivia looked inside the wardrobe and saw that her overnight bag was missing. She went back into the bathroom and saw that all of her personal grooming things had also gone. She concluded that someone had obviously been from the unit and taken her in for a residential assessment. She returned to the sitting room, picked up the phone and rang the unit.

A quick conversation with the unit's team clerk confirmed her belief that her mother had been sectioned again. The clerk was unwilling to divulge over the phone any specifics and none of her doctors were available for conversation at the moment. Eventually, Olivia determined from the bureaucrat that her mother would be in for the foreseeable future and that if she wanted any further information then she would either have to make an appointment to see one of her mother's doctors or seek redress via the mental health unit. Olivia slammed the receiver down into its cradle. She stood for a few moments, fuming at the unhelpfulness of the clerk. She drew in a long breath, held it, then let it out. She glanced at her watch again. She was going to be late for the second time today. Well, good, she thought. Rawlinson could go fuck himself... as could the unit's clerk!

Chapter 3

Thursday April 8th 1993, early evening

'You called him a *cunt*?' Evie said in disbelief.

'A complete cunt, as it happens, yes,' replied Olivia.

'I wonder what constitutes an incomplete cunt,' Rhys mused, wondering if he would get a rise out of them, 'no clit, I s'pose.'

'Rhys!' admonished Evie. He gave her his roguish smile and she huffed, knowing she had yet again fallen into one of his little traps.

They were sat in Evie's bedroom on cushions on the floor; in the background the dulcet tunes of Radio 1 ran counterpoint to their conversation, as much to mask it as to provide entertainment. Evie's mother was a bit of a nosey parker and was wont to listen in on all of her conversations.

'In your best interests, of course,' Clarise would say whenever Evie flung open a door to find her craning to hear what was being said. Her mother was a small, plump woman with no real life nor interests of her own; she was downtrodden by Evie's father and Evie was a personal project and, as much as anything, she needed to ensure that Evie never fell from the correct path. That being school, university and then a wealthy, domineering husband, just like *her* life. Evie, like most teenagers, had other plans for her future and she was indulging one of those right now as she toked on the joint Rhys had just passed to her.

'About fucking time too, if you ask me,' said Rhys lying back into the cushions and watching as Evie took another drag and then vigorously sprayed the immediate area with Oust. 'I know he's your dad, but he's always seemed to be a cunt to me. I'm surprised you didn't let your mum just gut him and have done with it.'

He smiled his infuriating smile at Olivia, who was about to reprimand him for his comments. The boy was so irritating; usually spot on with his blunt observations, but annoying for having the audacity to openly vocalise them, often couched inside humour or over the top comments. Olivia just frowned at him and turned back to Evie, who seemed reluctant to pass the joint back to Rhys.

'It's alright, Evie, you keep it, I'm not really in the mood. Or, better yet, give it to O. Think she needs it more than any of us.'

Evie took another quick drag, without properly exhaling the last one, and then tried to pass it to Olivia, who just waved her hand at it.

'You know I don't, Rhys... not after last time.'

'O, my dear,' he said, imitating Mrs Flint's voice to a tee, 'you need to relax, have a drag, let it pass over you and chill.'

'That's the last thing I need; besides, last time I tried it, all it did was make me feel peculiar.'

'Peculiar's a good thing, O,' he said in his normal voice. 'That's what it does; it's kinda the point, y'know. Besides, skunk'll do that sometimes, especially if you're not used to it.'

'Well, I'm clearly not used to it and I don't *want* to get used to it.'

Rhys shook his head despairingly at his young friend.

'Once in a while you need a destresser; weed's good for that. Hell, you're all into meds; they use weed all the time as a medicinal for people in pain and stress. I was reading a journal about it last night; kinda kyboshes the government's view point on criminalising every fucking drug under the sun. So, having seen how stressed you were when you got into school today – both times – I'd say you really need a good destressing. Which is why I'm giving you a block for your birthday next week, some of the really good stuff, nice and smooth and not known for causing whiteys.' He continued on, brushing her attempts of 'no fucking way' to one side, 'we'll have a round then go to the Wheatsheaf, neck a few and then head down into town and hit a club. I'll see if I can score us some Billy or the like, to put a bit of pep into your step, missy.' He smiled his ingratiating smile, the one he knew Olivia found almost impossible to say no to.

She shook her head. She wasn't about to start bingeing with Rhys any time soon, especially not if her mum was in the middle of a delusional break and her father was behaving the way he was. She put it to one side and returned her attention to Evie.

'So, when can we go and see Phyllis?' Evie asked.

'I don't know. I'm going to the hospital tomorrow; I have an appointment with Dr McIntyre at 5.30pm, I'm hoping I'll be able to see her afterwards, so perhaps you could come with me?' She tilted her head towards her friend, who nodded and took Olivia's hand in both of hers, squeezing tightly. Letting her know that Evie was there for her, no matter what. Olivia's smile froze as she saw the expression on Evie's face change suddenly.

'You know how your dad said that thing about how he has food and a mortgage to pay? I've never really thought about it before, but what exactly does your dad *do* to pay for all that stuff? I mean I know what my dad does, sort of, he works in the city shuffling money about the globe and being paid stupid amounts of it for doing fuck all, as far as I can see. And Rhys' mum is a nurse at the hospital and his dad's a builder, but I don't know what your dad does. He never actually *goes* anywhere to work.'

Olivia sat back on her haunches as she took in Evie's words. It had never really occurred to her either, to question what her dad did for money. He got his carer's allowance and various other support payments for looking after her mum; she knew that he went out at various times of the day and night, and whatever he did had to be flexible for looking after Phyllis, but actually she'd never bothered to find out. She realised this was because she was relieved he wasn't there. She looked back at Evie.

'You know now I think about it, I really don't know. He goes to the pub and the betting shop a lot, so I'd guess he's a professional gambler; they have a weekly card game at the pub in one of the back rooms and we're never strapped for cash. I guess he must be quite good at it. Although, maybe he isn't and for all I know we could be behind on the mortgage and about to be turfed out by the bank. Maybe that's why he took money from the drugs trial and was demanding more. But I've never seen the letters from the bank – they're all addressed to him and he deals with all of that sort of stuff. It's what parents are supposed to do, isn't it?' she shrugged. Evie suddenly looked worried.

'Could you be about to lose the house? Would he tell you if things were really that bad?'

'He wouldn't tell me fuck all, not even when we were sat in the road looking at our stuff being repossessed. If anything, I s'pect he'd just leave me there and fuck off down the pub.'

Evie became animated. 'Right, we need to sort this out then.'

She stood up, spraying the room over their heads with a great gout of Oust, 'C'mon Rhys, get up!' she demanded as she pulled Olivia up with her free hand.

'What? Why?' Rhys replied not moving; he was clearly comfortable with no desire to move.

'We're going over to Olivia's to check out her father's paperwork. Do some detecting.'

Olivia promptly let go of Evie's hand,

'No, we bloody well are not,' she said.

Evie looked at her and Olivia saw Evie's jaw setting, the way it did when she became determined.

'Yes, we *are*. We need to look at your dad's accounts to make sure he hasn't gambled the house away. Make sure you have security, whatever that may be.'

'No, Evie, we're not. We're not rooting about my dad's papers. Apart from anything else they're *his* papers and he'd go fucking ballistic if he knew anyone had been rifling through them.'

'Well, then, we'd best make sure he doesn't find out,' she turned to Rhys and kicked his foot. 'Come on! Get up!'

Rhys was having none of it; he appeared more than content to fall asleep in the cushions, 'Nah, I can't be arsed to walk all the way down to O's.'

'Not even if it meant you'd be saving her life?'

'Oh, don't be so fucking dramatic, Evie,' Olivia interjected.

Evie's shoulders squared off at her friend, 'There's nothing dramatic about being evicted from your home, Olivia. And you said it yourself, your dad was most insistent about getting as much money out of the drugs people as he could. Sounds to me like he's desperate. So, are you coming or not?'

Olivia's initial resistance faltered. What if Dad was desperate for money because he had lost at cards? What if he owed some loan shark a ton of cash and was now being threatened with being kneecapped if he didn't cough up? A sudden cold hard lump caught in the pit of her stomach. It would be so like him.

Evie grabbed her wrist and tugged her towards the door. Rhys reluctantly stood up and followed.

'Come on, the pair of you.'

'Well, I *am* feeling peckish,' Rhys said.

'What?' Evie's expression was one of bemusement.

'The chippy's on the way to O's,' he replied, shrugging his shoulders.

'Oh! For the love of God, Rhys,'

Olivia felt herself being dragged out of Evie's house; her sense of objection having wilted with her own thoughts on how her father behaved. And yet, what Evie was suggesting was so wrong. They had no right to go and rummage through her father's papers.

Those were his personal and private things. How would Evie like it if Dad was to rummage through her diary and read it? It was the same thing, really. Olivia found herself on Evie's doorstep being pulled along by her friend's sudden crusade.

'Now wait a minute, Evie. Even if any of this is true, we still have no right to go through my dad's things. And as I said, if he finds out or catches us, he'll go fucking nuts. I wouldn't put it past him to clout all of us.' Olivia suddenly felt that clenching coldness in the pit of her stomach again, as she imagined her dad lashing out at Evie.

'He wouldn't dare,' Evie responded. Olivia didn't think she sounded convincing. 'He wouldn't hit me. Would he hit you?' her final question seemed something of an afterthought, based on what she knew about Reg and his relationship with Olivia.

'Oh, he'd very definitely hit me. I don't know if he'd wait till he'd thrown you out of the house though. And he may well just launch into all of us, especially if he's been in the pub.'

It was at this point that Rhys finally injected himself into the crusade, 'If he tried to thump either one of you, I'd stop him.'

Both girls stopped in their advance down the street to look at Rhys - the lanky boy who was all elbows and knees. They stared at him in disbelief and Olivia said, 'And how precisely would you do that, Rhys?'

'Simple. I'd fucking clock him one,' Rhys replied straightening his back and attempting to look like a veteran brawler.

Olivia didn't laugh; the images in her head precluded such humour, 'And after you'd clocked him and he had laughed at you, Rhys, what then? Would Dad give you a friendly pat on the back for being a good knight protector? Or more likely completely ignore your punch and then floor you. Then it would be a tossup between whether he'd come after us or be too engrossed in kicking you while you were down. He's a dirty fighter, always has been. And he's more than happy to employ that in his parenting skills.'

All of them were now stood in the middle of the path, Rhys and Evie both looking at Olivia. She could see the abject horror etched into their faces as they started to comprehend the kind of man her father was. She saw Evie's face set again and her heart sank.

'All the more reason, then, for us to go and look at his paperwork. Determine if he's about to lose the house. Or find a way we can get you away from him. Either way, I'm going to look into your father's finances.' And with that, she strode off down the street towards Olivia's house.

'Fuck's sake, Evie!' Olivia marched after her. Rhys gave a big huff and then followed.

• • • •

Olivia let the other two in through the front door. There was a bit of a tangle, as both Evie and Rhys tried to wedge themselves through at the same time, while Rhys was busy trying to drink the last of the pea liquor from his chips' tray. With the amount of noise the two of them were now making trying to get into the house, she feared her father would come storming out of his room and have a go. Perhaps not a bad thing, as it would put paid to Evie's half-baked idea about proving her father guilty of financial wrongdoing.

'Shhh!' Olivia commanded in a hoarse whisper. She bustled past them as they sauntered into the hall. She hurried to the kitchen, stopping briefly to glance in through the sitting room door and then look into her father's study. When she arrived in the kitchen and found yet another room deserted, she relaxed. The room was in gloom and felt cool; no evidence that he had been in recently to make his dinner. She glanced at the clock on the wall above the back door, 7.37pm. She made her way back into the hall where the other two were still milling about, uncertain whether the coast was clear and behaving rather sheepishly all round. Olivia called up the stairs.

'Dad?' there was no reply and there were no discernible lights on up there, 'DAD! Are you in?'

Again, there was no answer. That was a relief, but then where would he be at 7.30 on a Thursday night? Best answer would be, the pub. She wondered if he was there for just a few drinks or if the poker game would be on. Either way, she suspected they wouldn't be seeing any sign of her father much before midnight. They had a clear run at his study to check out the bank statements. She bustled over to Rhys and took his beige polystyrene chip tray out of his hands, before he could deposit it on the hall table. She held her hand out to Evie, who grabbed the last few crispy chips from her tray and then handed it to her.

'Right, Dad's study is the door on the left, just before the kitchen. You two go on in and I'll just get rid of these.'

Olivia moved briskly to dump their rubbish, before hurrying back to her father's study, disrobing her overcoat as she went, dumping it and her bag on the table opposite her dad's room. Stepping across the threshold, she saw the other two had already made themselves comfortable. Rhys, in her father's swivel chair in front of his rolltop desk and Evie in the easy chair in front of his TV. Rhys looked up at her as she came in.

'So, I suppose the question is, what is it we're looking for? And then, where will we find it?' He swung the chair back round from facing Olivia towards the desk, 'In here, would be my guess.'

'It's where Dad keeps all his personal papers, but...' Olivia suddenly felt uncertain again about rummaging through her dad's personal belongings. OK, it was true, Dad was a bit of a grumpy shit a lot of the time and, from her perspective, she wondered why he even stayed with them, because he certainly didn't seem to love her mother. She always got the feeling he put up with her out of habit. As for Olivia's own relationship with her father, again, she couldn't see why he stuck around. Perhaps so she didn't have to go into the foster system, although, she supposed if things ever did go tits up, she would just end up living with Aunty Morag. But given her dad's feelings about Aunty Morag, perhaps *that* was why he stuck around, to prevent her becoming like his sister-in-law.

'But, what?' Rhys said, breaking into her train of thoughts.

'But I don't know if we should be looking at any of it. We've always lived here and there's never been a problem about living here. So, I don't really think we need to be worrying about it.'

'Nonsense,' declared Evie, leaping up from her reclined position, clearly re-energised by her tray of chips. 'Not so very long ago you were worried the house was being repossessed!'

Olivia interrupted her, 'Actually, it was you who suggested that. Until you brought it up, I'd never even considered it. All I think about usually is Mum.'

'Exactly,' Evie replied, as if that was an end to it, 'C'mon, Rhys, let's have a look.'

Evie leaned over Rhys, gripped the bottom of the rolltop screen and pulled. It moved about an inch and then stopped. Evie's fingers lost their grip and her hands flew upwards, raking her nails over the wooden slats and breaking two of her nails. It was rather an anticlimactic gesture and left Evie looking deflated and in discomfort as she inspected her fingertips. Olivia presumed Evie was expecting it to whirr up into its recesses, exposing a ton of illicit paperwork, much as she had. Rhys gripped the bottom of the screen, gave it a push and, with some effort, it creaked up far enough for them to be able to look inside the desk.

'All looks rather dull, actually,' Rhys said, flicking at a couple of piles of receipts. He drew in a long breath, 'Oh well, better make a start then. Perhaps,' he continued looking over his shoulder at the two girls, 'you could have a look through the dresser and any other cabinets in here. You never know what old Reg might be hiding.'

'Porn,' both Evie and Olivia remarked at the same time. They glanced at one another and chuckled. The three of them spent the next twenty minutes or so giving Reg's paperwork and personal things a thorough sifting. After which time, Rhys had found nothing much of use and the girls had found, other than a stack of expected pornography, only one locked draw in the dresser.

'I know a bit about bank statements, mainly from when Dad does his accounts, but as far as I can see there's nothing particularly remarkable about them. Except for this.' Rhys held up two statements, one under the other, for the girls to inspect. Evie snatched them from his hand and pored over them. Olivia tried to see what it was by peering over her shoulder.

'That's a bit odd,' Evie said.

'What's a bit odd?' Olivia enquired.

'Well, first of every month,' Evie handed the sheets to Olivia and then leafed through a few more statements, 'five grand gets paid into his account. There seems to be no large payments out during the month, other than for utility bills. There's no mortgage or rent payments. Then, on the last day of the month, the account empties down to exactly £100 and the rest is paid out to the same account every month.'

'Savings account?' Rhys suggested.

'Could be, I suppose,' Evie replied.

'So, then there's nothing odd really about it at all. Perhaps Dad bought the house outright when he got it – so no need to pay out monthly. Presumably the monthly income is whatever he gets from the social for Mum and what he doesn't spend goes into a savings account. All sounds perfectly normal to me.' Olivia felt relieved that her dad wasn't up to anything stupid or crooked and maybe, just maybe, Evie would let the whole matter drop now. She didn't.

'Oh, but there is something odd. Who gets paid five thousand pounds a month by the social? That's, like, sixty thousand a year! If the social paid that kind of money out, no one would work. No, there's definitely something not right about it. But I can't tell where the money's coming from. The numbers in front of the payment suggest another bank account, quite similar in origin to the one it all gets paid into at the end of the month.'

'Perhaps he pays himself from one savings account to another then,' Olivia put forward.

'I doubt it. Who has sixty thousand quid lying around to just live off every year? Let's face it, O, this is very fucking odd. Besides, I sort of recognise the sequence of numbers for the end of the month account. Dad's shown me a lot of what he does in the city. I think he hopes I'll go into it when I finish school.' Olivia saw the shudder that ran through Evie's frame at the mere thought of working, let alone working in the city. 'Anyway, this looks like an offshore account.'

Evie turned to Olivia, 'Why's your dad paying money into an offshore account every month? Where's it coming from in the first place? If I didn't know better, I'd have said your dad was laundering money through his accounts.' Evie took a step back from her friend, as if the mere act would distance herself from any potential wrongdoing Reg was clearly up to.

Olivia let out a blast of exasperation, spittle-spraying Rhys, much to his annoyance.

'Evie, don't be so fucking ridiculous!'

'Well,' Rhys interjected, wiping the saliva from his face, 'if he is laundering money, it could be from money he's earned illicitly. Given that you said he's out at different times of the day and night, maybe he's selling drugs?'

'Fuck off, Rhys,' Olivia was starting to get really pissed off with her friends. She was also starting to get anxious about the mere fact that they were rooting through her father's private accounts and they seemed to be turning up anomalies that don't normally appear in your average person's banking. What the hell was her father doing? Whatever it was she didn't want to know, because it was making her feel ill.

Rhys looked visibly taken aback by her explosion. 'Sorry, O. It's just that it all seems a bit odd, like Evie said.'

'Well, if he was selling drugs, surely *you'd* know?' Olivia snapped.

Rhys shrugged his shoulders, 'Possibly, but I don't know all the dealers. Users tend to stick with just one or two dealers that they like.'

His attention shifted from Olivia to the locked dresser draw on the far side of the room. 'I wonder if there's an explanation in that drawer?'

Evie shrugged her shoulders, 'Well, we aren't going to find out, because it's locked.'

'Not for long,' Rhys said with a mischievous glint in his eye. He bounded over to the drawer, slipping something from his inner pocket.

'Hey! What are you going to do?' Olivia demanded. The last thing she needed was for her dad to come home and find his dresser drawer had been jimmied.

'Found this key in a little hidden drawer in the desk. I reckon by its size and shape that it'll fit right into that dresser'. He inserted the key and then pulled on the drawer, just as they all heard the front door slam shut.

'SHIT!' Olivia squeaked in a hoarse screech. 'Dad. Quick, get out! Both of you get out!'

Olivia started to panic as she heard the sound of her father lumbering through the hall, chucking his keys on the table under the coat hooks. She was flapping her arms at her two friends, both of whom appeared to be utterly paralysed with fear.

Rhys looked around frantically. 'How?'

Olivia looked back into the room, unwillingly taking her eyes from the door out to the hall. Her first inspiration was the sash window. She pointed at it.

'Through the window. Hurry!' she demanded in her hoarse screech. The coldness had returned to her stomach, although now she could feel it crawling up into her chest and gripping mercilessly at her heart. Fuck, she was going to have a heart attack. *Good*, she thought, *drop stone dead and then I won't have to face Dad*.

Evie was the first to react to Olivia's command. She rushed over to the window and swiftly slid it open. She looked over her shoulder at Rhys, who was still dithering by the dresser. She waved at him and mouthed urgently, 'Come *on*!'

Olivia took up guard in front of the door. Her only thought was to stall her father's entry. If he came in, she'd slam the door in his face. Rhys finally reacted to the situation. He shut the dresser and hurried over to the window. Outside in the corridor, Olivia could hear her father walking towards his room. She suddenly realised the lights were on and flicked the switch. Bad timing as Rhys was making his way through the more cluttered part of the room. He bumped into a table and swore from the sudden pain in his knee. Olivia heard her father's bootsteps falter. Everyone in the room took a collective sharp intake of breath and held it.

Olivia felt the air starting to choke the life from her, so long had she held it. But she dared not let it out, fearing even this would be enough to alert her father of their presence. She was desperately trying to hear where her father was going. But the roaring rush of blood that pumped through her head obscured all sounds. It was like listening to the sea rushing through a seashell. Outside in the corridor, her father started to move again. He walked past the door to his room and into the kitchen. Olivia breathed out. She flicked the light switch on again and turned to look back into the room. Evie was outside the window, leaning in, frantically ushering Rhys to get a move on. Rhys was doubled over the side table he had just walked into, clutching onto the stack of magazines that had threatened to topple from the collision.

Olivia rushed over and helped him replace the tower. Then she grabbed him and bodily moved him towards the window. Being an old house, the sash windows made it easier for him to slide through sideways. With an extra push from Olivia, he virtually fell out of the house. Behind her, Olivia heard the sound of the door to the room opening. She slammed the window shut, not caring whether she might inadvertently crush Rhys' hand in the process. She turned just in time to see her father swaying in the doorway, beer bottle in one hand, ham sandwich in the other.

'What the actual fuck...?' he said with an aggressive sneer curling his lips.

Olivia was surprised by the effect this question had upon her. The last hour or so had been far too extreme for her liking. Evie's argumentative and accusatory attitude had pissed her right off. The vast levels of guilt and shame she had felt rising as they deceitfully rummaged through her father's stuff had given rise to anxiety she had not asked for. And now, she had narrowly avoided her dad discovering their larceny and he'd had the audacity to be aggressive towards her. His greeting had tipped the balance on her nerves.

'What the actual fuck, *Dad*? *Really*? You forget to lock the back door. You forget to close your window.' Her voice kept rising half an octave with every statement. 'I'm going to bed in a house that's open for any opportunistic weirdo to creep into and rape me in my sleep. And you have the nerve to have a go at me!'

She was physically shaking, whether from the anger that had suddenly erupted out of her mouth driven from the depths of her belly, or because of fear at what her father might have done had he come in a few minutes earlier, she had could not fathom in this moment. She staggered towards him on legs made of jelly. She pulled herself to her full height as she pushed past him in the doorway, almost too rigid to walk as she tried to control her flailing legs. She grabbed her coat and bag from the side table and moved to the stairs. She risked a quick glance over her shoulder at her flabbergasted dad, who had pivoted unsteadily in the doorway as she'd stormed through.

'Good night, Dad. Don't forget to lock up again!' and with that she stomped upstairs and slammed her bedroom door shut.

She pressed her back to it and slowly slid down to the floor, her coat wrapped around her bag clutched in her arms – its weight lent a sense of protection. She slid to the floor because her legs no longer had the strength or rigidity to keep her upright. She stayed thus, listening to the sounds from below, still terrified that her father would stumble up the stairs with the view of knocking some sense into her. She listened and heard silence from below for several seconds. They ticked by and with each one she imagined what her father was doing. Bracing himself to come up here and knock seven bells out of her? Eventually she heard his door slam shut and then the TV came on. Finally, she felt she could breathe.

Chapter 4

Thursday April 8th 1993, late evening

Olivia waited behind her door, she needed the time to compose herself, but it also gave her father time to settle in his room, TV on loud enough to rumble through her floorboards. She wondered if he had turned it up deliberately by way of punishment, as it would make going to sleep a lot harder. But then, she had no intention of going to sleep, she was wide awake. Adrenaline has a tendency of doing that - preventing sleep. When she felt she was calmer, she planned to slip out of the house and go back to Evie's. It might be late in the evening for a house call, but she needed to get some things straight with her. This evening's escapade had been far too close to home for Olivia's liking. It might have been a fun idea for Evie to play detective, but the repercussions were not hers to own. Olivia needed to have words with her friend before the day was done.

• • • •

Evie's mother, Clarice, wasn't surprised to see her at all when Olivia knocked on the front door.

'They're up in her room, Olivia,' Clarice said, 'if you hold on a moment, while you're putting your things down, I'll get the refreshments.'

They're? Olivia thought. Had Rhys come back too? She waited patiently for Clarice to return from the kitchen with a tray covered in a veritable feast. She couldn't help smiling at it and thanked Evie's mum for her trouble.

'Oh, no trouble at all, Olivia. It's what mums are for,' Clarice withdrew back to the kitchen.

Olivia stood holding the tray and considered the statement. *So that's what mothers are for, is it?* In her life she had never realised it. She could hear a TV on in the sitting room; presumably Evie's dad was in there, listening to the end of the ITN news as it did a roundup of the financial markets. *Boring,* her brain instinctively said, spurring her to take the tray up to the conclave that appeared to be happening in Evie's bedroom.

'Thank Christ!' Evie said as Olivia pushed open the door with her shoulder and marched in. Rhys relieved her of the tray as Evie swept her up in a massive hug. 'I thought you were unconscious or dead or something.'

Olivia looked into Evie's face as she withdrew from her and held her at arm's length, presumably to inspect her for injuries. Any thoughts of having a go at Evie had been swept away with the hug. Olivia could see the streams of dried tears on her cheeks and the expression of worry upon her face. She suddenly found herself being embraced tightly again and she was starting to feel suffocated. She pulled away.

'I'm fine, Evie, really. A bit shaken, but fine.'

'He shook you?'

'No, I mean I'm shaken by events, is all. He didn't touch me, didn't give him the chance.'

'Well thank fuck for that,' Rhys said through a mouthful of tuna sandwich.

Olivia and Evie settled on the cushions on her floor, as Rhys sat on the edge of her bed, balancing the tray next to him. He continued to devour the spread.

Evie kept hold of Olivia's hand, 'And everything's alright with your dad?'

'Yes. He wasn't best pleased to find me in his room, but I blagged my way out of it. Waited until he was settled and then came round here.'

'I'm so sorry I went off like that, O. I never realised just how bad your dad is. I certainly wouldn't have intended for him to cause you harm, not for something that was really my doing.' Evie looked shamefaced and any residual thoughts Olivia might have had of berating her dispersed.

'It's fine, Evie. Honestly, just best if we don't go back in his room again any time soon.'

They both looked up as Rhys apparently started to choke on his sandwiches.

'Er,' he said as he suddenly saw two faces staring at him. Olivia thought he was looking guilty.

'Er what, Rhys?' she had a sinking feeling.

'Er, well. It's just that you might have to go back in his room quite soon,' he stuttered out.

'Why?' Evie and Olivia demanded at the same time.

Now he really was looking guilty, Olivia thought.

'Er, well, because,' he paused and then fumbled in his jacket, which he was still wearing. He pulled out a medium-sized grey metal box and presented it to them gingerly. 'Because I took this from your dad's dresser and he might notice if it's missing.'

'Rhys!' Evie's voice shrilled.

'For fuck's sake, Rhys!' Olivia responded at the same time, 'What possessed you?'

'I, I don't know,' he replied defensively, 'we were there to find something out about your dad. And then he came back when we hadn't really found anything. And this was just sitting there, calling to me, saying Rhys – Rhys, so I grabbed it before you dragged me out.' He paused again, before concluding, 'It was instinctive.'

He looked pleadingly at the girls, both of whom had a desire to slap him, which they did, from their positions on the floor.

'I'm sorry, OK?'

Evie was clearly the first to forgive him as she said, 'So what's in it then?'

Rhys looked at her for a moment, then over at Olivia, before looking down at the box and lifting the lid.

His face blanched, 'Bloody hell!'

Olivia and Evie both stood up and looked down into Rhys' lap to see what it was in the lockbox that had caused such a reaction.

'Bloody hell indeed,' said Evie taking a step back. Olivia refrained from expletives, but did let out a gasp. Rhys put his hand in and retrieved the object of their horror. Olivia noted that as soon as it was nestled into Rhys' hand his entire demeanour appeared to change.

'Well, whaddya make of this?' he said, hefting the sleek-barrelled pistol and waving it about the room. He held his arm out straight and leaned his head down onto his bicep, closing one eye and sighting down the length of the barrel. 'Your dad a hitman or somethin'?' Rhys asked Olivia, not taking his eye off the sight.

'Why does your dad have a gun?' Evie demanded of Olivia in a remonstrative tone.

'I... I dunno.' Olivia continued to back pedal, especially as Rhys was now twisting back and forth on the bed, waving the pistol about the room. 'Rhys! Stop doing that! Put it down this instant!'

Rhys' head reverted back to the upright and he reluctantly lowered the gun. Evie drew in a breath and then spoke to Olivia again, 'Sorry, I didn't mean to be so waspish, I just wanted to know why your dad would have a gun?'

Once again Olivia shook her head, waving her right hand at Rhys for emphasis, 'I have no idea. Rhys you need to put that thing away. In case it's loaded and it goes off.'

Rhys lowered his arm and then drew the pistol closer to him for inspection. The barrel was long and smooth, with a rich, dark metallic sheen to it that caused the low light of the room to sparkle enticingly along it. The barrel was supported by what seemed to be a second barrel underneath, yet this one had no opening for a bullet to pass out of. The trigger guard was solid, moulded into the body of the weapon. The trigger itself was thick and ribbed, making the sensation on the finger pleasurable. Rhys found himself stroking it. The handle was also a solid rectangular affair, with panels on either side of where the palm and fingers would rest. Each panel had a dappled effect to it, made up of hundreds of tiny four-sided pyramids, giving it a rough texture, yet improving the grip no end, thus preventing it slipping from a sweaty hand. Rhys turned it over several times, a frown starting to crease his features.

'Don't handguns usually have the magazine in the butt of the handle?' he asked of the girls.

'How would I know?' Olivia responded, 'I've never seen a gun before.'

'Of course, you have,' he continued dismissively, as he heard her interject that she should know if she had ever seen a gun before, 'on all those American movies you've seen. Guns galore in those films. And they always have a clip that springs out of the butt of the handgrip.'

'So?' said Evie.

'So, this one doesn't appear to have a magazine. It's solid. No ammo.'

This nugget of information seemed to make Evie less wary of the offensive object; she moved closer to Rhys and looked down at it. 'Maybe it's a replica?'

Rhys' shoulders sagged slightly at this suggestion and he started to nod. Yes, maybe that's what it was. 'Perhaps your dad's not a hitman after all,' he concluded sadly.

For Olivia, the idea that her father was a hitman was frankly ludicrous, but knowing the weapon that Rhys had been so free with a few moments earlier might not be dangerous after all was certainly a relief.

Rhys continued to look the weapon over before eventually grunting, 'Replicas don't have working parts; this one definitely does. Look, you can cock it, although that's the oddest hammer I've ever seen.' He placed his forefinger and thumb on a flat bit of metal that jutted from the back of the barrel, where the breach was. He twisted it and the spring he had expected in the butt suddenly shot out, catching his fingertips painfully.

'Sonofabitch!' he dropped the gun. The girls screamed as one. And everyone flung their arms over their faces as they expected the weapon to discharge and blow one of them to kingdom come.

There was a dull thud as the pistol bounced onto the carpet. It didn't discharge. But something did fall out of the breach. A long mercurial tube with what looked like a miniature yellow feather duster attached to one end. They all lowered their protection. The girls looked, first at Rhys in condemnation for nearly getting them killed, then down at the offending article that had spelled their doom moments earlier. Rhys sucked his fingers. He looked down at the pistol and the disgorged tube. He picked it up and inspected it. One end did indeed have a feather duster of coarse-stripped material, the other end had a short fine needle.

'Well, I'll be buggered,' he said.

The girls moved closer, 'What is it?' asked Evie.

'I think it's a tranq. I think the pistol is a tranq gun, y'know, like the ones they have at the zoo for putting down the lions when they need to give them a once-over.'

'A tranq gun?' Olivia quizzed, 'why would my dad have a tranq gun?'

Rhys and Evie both looked at each other over Olivia's head. Olivia looked up at them as she noted the silence. 'NO!' she said,

'No, he wouldn't.' Her face had scrunched up in her desperate desire for her negative to be true.

Rhys shook his head apologetically, 'I'm afraid I think he would. You did, after all, note just today that he is a cunt. A complete cunt to boot. So, working on that principle, I'd reckon your dad is just the kind of person to have a tranq gun for using on his wife.'

'No,' Olivia repeated, horrified with the prospect, 'the... the...' she was going to say bastard, but Evie got there first.

'Cunt?' she supplied, a little shocked at herself for using the vile word.

Olivia looked at the expression on Evie's face and started to laugh; a mixture of relief, horror and amusement at her friend giving rise to the only healthy way she could release her sudden turmoil of emotions. Rhys glanced at Evie, also shocked to hear her say such a word and then he, too, started to chuckle. Evie scowled at her companions' response, but eventually she too gave into the mirth and the tension of recent minutes was finally broken.

Rhys reassembled the pistol, with its load intact. He then placed it on the bed as he returned his attention to the lockbox.

'I was going to say,' Olivia said as she stepped over to him once more, 'was there anything else in there?'

Evie moved closer too. 'There appears to be only this,' Rhys responded, pulling out a folded sheet of paper. It looked old. The creases of the folds were well-defined and the edges of the paper had discoloured. He unfolded it carefully, flattening it out on the bedside table, and they all peered at it.

Rhys' brow furrowed again in confusion. 'Your dad's name is Reg, isn't it?'

Olivia nodded. They all knew what her father's name was. 'He's not known by any other names, is he?' Rhys peered up at Olivia, who shook her head emphatically.

'Anyone in the family by this name?' he asked.

'Not that I'm aware of,' she replied, 'but then, as far as I know, there isn't much family. Just Mum, Dad, me and Aunty Morag.'

Rhys started to get his roguish smile back as an idea formulated in his sordid little mind, 'So, who is John Fitzgerald Kennedy, then?'

'I don't know,' Olivia replied, suspicious of his question; she could see from his smirk that he was toying with something. 'Why? Do you know a John Fitzgerald Kennedy?'

'No,' he replied innocently, pausing to draw her in, 'but, I wondered if perhaps your dad might still be a killer. D'ya think he murdered this Kennedy guy and stole his house?' his grin practically split his face in two.

'Rhys! For God's sake,' Evie stated.

Olivia wasn't impressed either, 'No, I don't think he murdered anyone nor stole anybody's house.' She practically stamped her foot as she said this, although she wasn't certain if it was to emphasise her reprimand to Rhys or for her own wellbeing. 'Why on Earth would you even suggest such a thing?'

'Oh, I dunno. Maybe because your dad has a title deed for his house hidden in a lockbox. Locked in his study, with someone else's name stamped all over what is an official document. A document that gives rights of ownership to his house to the person named on the title deed. Add to that the fact that your dad doesn't appear to pay rent or mortgage on your place and... and, well, it all looks a bit fishy, really,' he concluded.

He trailed off and Olivia wondered if perhaps he was thinking he shouldn't have said anything at all, as he took in her own expression of shock and horror.

'It's certainly rather strange.' Evie said trying to alleviate Rhys' discomfort by moving the subject on apace, 'that your house would be owned by a dead American president.'

Both Olivia and Rhys looked at her sharply to determine whether she was joking. By the serious frown on her face, they deduced she was being serious.

'I think you're thinking of John F. Kennedy. His 'F' stood for Franklin,' Rhys corrected her.

'Actually, no,' Olivia said remembering her recent reading for school, 'She's correct. You're thinking of Franklin D. Roosevelt. JFK *was* John Fitzgerald Kennedy. But John Kennedy must be a fairly common name, I would have thought.'

She paused, then turned and left the bedroom. A few minutes later, she returned with a phone book, taken from the hall table. She was flicking through the pages as she walked.

'Here, look,' she said to them, 'there's at least a half-dozen pages of Kennedys in here and a pile of them have J or JF for their initials.' She looked up at them, not really certain what she had discovered from this inspiration.

Rhys nodded and his eyebrow rose slightly, as did the whole left-hand side of his face. 'Very true. Maybe...' he paused as he considered his thought, 'maybe we should call them?' He looked at Olivia for confirmation.

'Why?' she replied, confused by his suggestion.

'Well, if we call all the JFK's in the book, we could determine which of them were John Fitzgerald, but, more importantly, we could find out if any of them owned your house.'

'I'm not sure that's such a good idea,' Olivia responded, hesitant to be ringing strangers and asking them personal questions.

'Yeah,' Evie concurred, 'besides, even if we did find out that one of them owned the house, do we want to be reminding them? What if, for some reason, they've forgotten and then we go and remind them. Olivia might suddenly find herself turfed out. The whole point of this exercise was to ensure Olivia still had a house to go back to.'

Rhys looked crestfallen. The girls always shot down his best ideas.

'It was just an idea,' he said sullenly.

'Well, not a very good one,' Evie said sharply.

The clock on Evie's bedside table chimed the witching hour, as befitted its motif, and they all looked round at it.

'Blimey, is that the time?' Rhys asked standing up. 'I ought to be getting back. The parents are pretty lax with when I can be in and out, but I'll be pushing my luck a bit tonight. 'Specially as it's a school night. O?' he turned to her, 'I'd best walk you back to yours, but we need to get a wriggle on.'

Evie nodded, then looked over to Olivia, 'Well, you going to be OK, O? I don't think our investigations have done all that much to alleviate your worries.' She hugged Olivia by way of farewell. Olivia smiled reassuringly at her.

'It's fine. It's been a bit of fun really and it's taken my mind off Mum and all that's happened today. Although,' she paused dramatically, 'it has brought up some interesting questions that I have no idea how I'm going to answer.'

. . . .

Olivia thanked Rhys as she slipped quietly into her house. She watched him amble off back down the path to her gate as she closed the door, then went into the sitting room and sat down on the sofa. She stared at the blank screen of the TV directly in front of her and thought back over what they had discovered this evening. Could Rhys be right about her dad? Was he a hitman? Or just a thieving murderer? She shook her head in disbelief, a small chuckle emanating from her chest at the mere thought of it all. Yes, Reg could be violent, but he was a fisty kind of angry man and the most that would happen would be a single clout. To be fair to the old git, she thought, he didn't even do that very often. So, yes, he was a brute, but not a killer. As for stealing this house, it was more likely that he won it in a poker game than performing some kind of deception to relieve an unsuspecting homeowner of their rights. Her gaze moved from the TV over to the telephone and the book cradle nestled underneath it. *Maybe?* She leaned forward and then stopped. *Maybe not.* She looked at the phone book. *Maybe Rhys' idea wasn't so half-baked.* She leaned down and picked up the book, flicking through its pages once more as she hunted down the Kennedy section. Then, with her finger as a guide, she skimmed down the list till she came to the first J on the list. It was a local number. She could just ring it. And if worse came to the worst she could hang up. She nodded to herself. Yes, she could do that.

'Well, that was disappointing,' she said hanging up the phone after the first number she had tried had rung and rung and rung with no answer. She felt her heart calming down as she hung up; she hadn't been aware of how tense she had become. Taking her hand from the receiver, she looked at it and noted it was quite damp with sweat. She wiped it on her school pinafore and then picked up the phone again. She put it back in the cradle as she noted her heart starting to race again. *How silly*, she thought, *to get so anxious about ringing a complete stranger*. She tried the same number again.

'Do you know what time it is?' said a man's voice from the other end of the line.

Olivia squealed and slammed the phone down in its cradle. *No, this was definitely a bad idea.* She put the phone back on the table and the book into its holder. She looked at her watch – it was gone midnight. She shouldn't be ringing strangers in the first place, and certainly not in the early hours of the morning. She stood up and her stomach grumbled. She hadn't had chips with the others, even though they had both offered to buy her some. Nor had she indulged in the feast Clarise had supplied. She went to the kitchen and made herself a sandwich.

She noted the carving knife was still on the kitchen table where she had put it this morning after taking it from her mother. Neither of them had bothered putting it away, not now mum had been taken away. She picked it up and, in the light, she noted a tiny dark stain on its tip. Closer inspection showed a flaky dark brown, nearly black, residue on the tip. She remembered then how the knife had dug into her hip. She lifted her dress and inspected her hip bone. Yes, there was a small scab, where the knife had pierced her skin. She dropped her skirt back into place and took the knife to the sink to wash it up, along with Reg's lunch plate and her evening detritus. She then locked it up, almost reverentially, in the old cream metal cabinet at the end of the counter, where they kept all the sharps. She sighed and shivered. It was cold in the house. It was silent as well. She should go to bed, but there were things playing on her mind. The day's events seemed to be jumbling all over the place and she turned from the counter. She glanced towards the clock over the back door and then screamed.

. . . .

In her peripheral vision, Olivia espied two glowing, amber orbs of damnation, peering into the kitchen through the window.

'Fucking hell, cat!' Olivia swore at the neighbour's black fluffy feline that was sat on the windowsill. 'You didn't half give me a fright.' Olivia started to breathe more calmly, but still in fairly deep, ragged breaths. Even though she now realised what the glowing orbs were, she still found them very spooky. She went over to the window and opened it, letting the cat stick his head through for her to stroke. It purred and then meowed.

'No, I don't have any food for you. If you want food you need to go home and stop scaring the crap out of your neighbours.'

ORDINARY WORLD

The cat purred at her again, rubbed his head over her hand and then turned, leaping off the sill and disappearing into the back garden. Olivia could still feel her heart beating solidly against her chest wall. *Time for bed*, she thought; she'd had enough of today.

Chapter 5

Friday 9th April, 1993

Sleep was troubled for Olivia; from the start of the day, being wrenched from sleep by her mother, to the end of the day and the fright the neighbour's cat had given her, her nerves had taken a pounding. As such, sleep did not want to alleviate her of her strain. It was fitful and severely lacked the restful quality she so desperately required. She woke early from her fitful night's sleep, jarred awake by the dream she was having. As consciousness overwhelmed her, the dream slipped from her mind's eye; a shadow that passed without notice, but left a sense of foreboding in her deepest core. She sat upright and shuddered.

Downstairs, she found her father snoring in his easy chair in his study. The small room smelled of stale beer and sweat. Normally she would have opened the window, but after last night and her close call, she thought better of it. She dawdled over breakfast in a bit of a daze and, despite being up early, ended up nearly being late for school.

Her walk there gave her time to consider her day, which would be mostly taken up with lessons. But afterwards there would be time enough to come home, have an early tea and then take the bus out to the hospital and have the appointment with Dr McIntyre. She wondered if Evie would meet her there, or whether it would be better for her to just come home with Olivia and they could have tea together.

Her thoughts were suddenly interrupted, as she approached the junction at the end of her road, when she heard heavy-booted footsteps hurrying up behind her. She stopped and turned, wondering if it was her dad. But when she turned around, she couldn't see anyone behind her. The street was deserted. A few late cars still parked, but no pedestrians, not even a cyclist. Strange... she could have sworn she'd heard something. She shook her head and continued on her way. Crossing the road, she made her way down it and took a right turn halfway along, into the cut-through, which led to the high street. As she stepped into it, she glanced behind herself again, as she was convinced she heard a heavy, booted tread very close to her. But, again, there was nothing of note. She peered up and down the street she was leaving. There were certainly pedestrians now, but too far away to have made the footfalls she thought she had heard. She turned back to the cut-through abruptly and walked straight into someone.

'Oh! I'm so sorry,' she apologised, looking up into the gaunt features of an abnormally tall, lanky man. She faltered any further apologies, as she took in his peculiar-looking visage. His nose was large – too large for his face – bulbous with flaring nostrils and covered in a criss-cross pattern of tiny veins. His cheek bones were pronounced and seemed to suck his cheeks into his mouth, pressing them firmly against his jaw. The skin was pallid and paper-thin, highlighting the teeth set within his mouth, which were closely compact neat rows made up entirely of yellowing incisors. His ears were peculiar too, forming huge protuberances from the side of his head, yet elongated, with bulbous lobes that mirrored his nose, and sharp points at the top. Her gaze continued until it locked onto his eyes, sunken into the depths of his skull. Black orbs that reminded her of her fright the night before with the neighbour's cat. She took several involuntary steps back as his arms came up to encircle her frame. It might have been an instinctive reaction to steady her, or perhaps himself. But Olivia got a fleeting image of a praying mantis just before it decapitated its unwitting victim. She stifled a scream. After all, it was not this man's fault that he looked peculiar. And it had been *her* that had walked into *him*. His right hand continued to rise, up to the fedora that rested upon his crown. He gripped the brim and tugged it. Olivia found herself pressed against a parked car as the strange man spoke to her. Her right hand was laid across her mouth, physically preventing the startled scream from erupting. Her left hand was set against the car, giving her support and preventing her from falling after colliding with it.

'My apologies, miss. Entirely my fault,' the man said in a low rasping wheeze. He made no attempt to smile, nor any other action towards her. Instead, he turned briskly on his heel and marched off up the street away from her. She noted his stride was immense and he was gone from view in seconds. She continued to watch as she caught her breath. His face and shape had quite unsettled her, so peculiar did he appear. He looked like an emaciated elephant. She wondered who he might be; she had never seen him before and yet she was struck by a sense of familiarity. She continued to stare down the street in the direction that he had vanished.

Eventually, when she had finally calmed herself, she made her way down the cut-through and out into the high street. She had to run to catch her bus, so late had her little encounter made her, and once again she was out of breath as she threw herself into a seat.

· · · ·

'Sounds like a bit of a freak, if you ask me,' said Evie during morning break.

Olivia had recounted her two fright moments from the last twelve hours since she had last seen them.

'Is the circus in town?' Rhys asked. It was a serious question; he was fond of the circus folk that occasioned upon their town, if for no other reason than they always had an abundant supply of drugs.

'Not that I'm aware of, no,' Olivia replied. There had been none of the gaudy red flyers plastered on lamp posts and fences that usually announced the brief settlement of the circus in town.

Anyway, she wanted to change the subject; remembering both incidents was making her feel anxious and, with her appointment later, the last thing she needed was to be being anxious all day. She turned to Evie.

'So, are you coming home with me for tea tonight or will I meet you at the hospital?'

Evie considered her options, 'You could come home with me and have tea at ours and then I'll get mum to give us a lift up to the hospital. Saves fannying about on the buses that way, and way more comfortable in the car.'

Olivia smiled. She loved the way Evie seemed to be able to just get her mother to do whatever she wanted. But it was a trade-off, she realised. Clarice would do most things for Evie, but on the understanding that she always knew where Evie was and what she was doing. Clarice was more of a gaoler than a mother.

'Yes, I like that idea. Let's do that,' Olivia replied.

'So, what are you up to this evening, Rhys, as if I couldn't guess?' Evie said to their other companion.

'Wheatsheaf for a couple with the cousins, then town for a couple of clubs, score some Billy or an E and wake up in some bimbo's bed tomorrow morning's the hope.' He smiled at them, the kind of smile associated with an eighteenth-century dandy highwayman. Both girls laughed at him.

'And do these aging bimbos that you hook up with know you're only seventeen?' Evie asked scathingly.

'Some of them do, but apparently that's what the older ones are looking for, a bit of youthful exuberance,' he winked at them and gyrated his pelvis in their direction. Both girls turned their heads away in disgust.

'Rhys, really,' Olivia said.

'Tooooo much information,' replied Evie.

ORDINARY WORLD

As they got out of Clarice's car, Evie was giving her mother instructions about how long to wait. Olivia stood to the side, impatient to be getting in. It was 5.20pm and she had no wish to miss this appointment. Evie and her mother seemed to be talking for an infinite length of time and Olivia's attention was drawn to a car parked opposite. There was a woman sat behind the steering wheel reading a book and eating a sandwich. The window was open and Olivia could hear the radio playing, the chorus of the song that was playing, resounded with her in an unexpected manner: Marillion's Freaks.

Olivia was familiar with the song, although it had been years since she'd heard it last. She was jolted from the lyrics as she suddenly saw the woman look up at her. Their gaze connected, locking together like a shuttle docking with a space station airlock. The woman's eyes were dazzling, with an ambient ferocity unlike anything Olivia had ever experienced before. Rather than feeling panic or terror at such an event, Olivia suddenly felt a wave of peace wash over her. It started in the pit of her stomach - a warmth, a glow almost. Much like the angelic glow that seemed to emanate from the woman opposite. Olivia could see the light grow in magnitude, filling the gloomy interior of the car and lighting it up to a dazzling intensity. Olivia felt that brilliance pierce her stomach and radiate out through her entire being. The feelings of anxiety that had plagued her all day were swept away and she felt relaxed and at peace for the first time in, well, she didn't know how long. The moment was shattered as Evie grabbed her elbow and tugged her forwards.

'C'mon, or we'll be late for your appointment,' she said, ushering Olivia out of the car park and over to the mental health unit.

In the moment that Evie spoke, her words shattered the vision in front of Olivia. It was as tangible as a mirror breaking into shards and falling to the ground. She looked back to the woman in the car, but she had gone. The car was once more in darkness, the radio silent and the vehicle empty. Olivia drew in a sharp breath and hurried to keep up with Evie.

At the reception, Olivia appeared highly distracted and it was Evie who informed the assistant who Olivia was and about her appointment. They were then directed to the mental health wing, which Olivia knew all too well. Once there, they were checked through the security doors by a tall, blond orderly who then took them to a security desk to book them in. Olivia was inclined to pause by the desk for a few moments more; they had a radio on and it was playing 'Ordinary World' again. The stations were really hammering the single at the moment, but Olivia didn't mind because she found herself empathising with the lyrics.

Evie placed a consolatory hand upon Olivia's arm and guided her away from the desk and the music, following the orderly who accompanied them down the corridors.

'Wait in here,' he directed, peering at Olivia in a suspicious manner, she thought. She had remained distracted throughout the process, caught up in her thoughts about the car and that woman. 'Dr McIntyre's secretary will collect you when he's available. Although that may be a while. There was an emergency about half an hour ago and I doubt he's going to be free from that for at least another half an hour, maybe another hour.'

He glanced in through the door he was holding open, 'There are magazines in there and if you need refreshment there's the visitors' kitchen down the hall. Do I need to show you where it is?'

Olivia finally threw off the funk she had been in, focusing on the orderly's crooked tar-stained teeth. 'No, I know where it is. Been here before.'

He nodded at her, 'Yeah, thought you looked familiar.'

He ushered them inside then closed the door.

'Now comes the boring bit,' Evie said to the room. 'The waiting.'

She went and sat down in one of only three armchairs and picked up a magazine from the table next to it. She looked up at Olivia.

Olivia returned her gaze, suspecting that Evie was concerned she might be suffering anxiety over the enforced wait. But oddly Olivia felt composed and relaxed and she realised that this was what Evie saw as she looked at her, much to her friend's obvious surprise.

Evie tilted her head as she asked Olivia, 'Do you want me to come in with you?'

Olivia considered the question before answering, 'No, actually. Thank you for asking, but actually I'm feeling OK. I think I'll field this one on my own, if that's alright with you. I don't want you to think I brought you down here for nothing.'

'That's fine with me, I only really came to see Phyllis. Not into the boring psychobabble, and that part's probably best kept in the family anyway.'

Evie seemed relieved not to be going in, as far as Olivia could see. She went to sit down next to her friend. Evie passed her a magazine, which Olivia thanked her for and started to flick through, but she was distracted. She wasn't anxious anymore, but she did feel energised by her odd encounter in the car park. She was restless, too restless to just sit and wait in the room with Evie and a pile of magazines. She got up and went to the door. Evie looked up; concern etched into her features.

'Do you want a drink?' Olivia asked as she opened the door.

Evie shook her head, 'No, I'm fine, but I could get you one if you like?'

Olivia half smiled, 'No, I can get it myself. Besides, you don't know where the visitors' kitchen is, I do.'

Evie nodded reluctantly, 'Very true.'

'It's fine. I'll be back shortly.'

Olivia left the room and made her way out into the corridor, heading for the kitchen. She walked slowly; there was no rush now. Eventually, she passed a nurses' station and nodded at the two nurses sat behind it. Both looked familiar and they seemed to recognise her by the slight bob of their heads in her direction. The corridor split at this point into three more corridors; the one to the left took her to the toilets and the kitchen. She sauntered down it and was about to go in through the yellow-painted kitchen door when she heard conspiratorial whispering coming out of one of the patient rooms across the hall. The door, a familiar apple-green in colour, was slightly ajar and the ward was quiet, rather unnaturally so. In her experience of the ward, there was always noise. The bustle of orderlies and nurses; the crying and, quite often, shouting from the patients, but this evening all was still and this was what enabled her to hear the muted voices coming from the other room.

'*How's Phyllis doing?*' Olivia didn't recognise the man's voice. It sounded out of breath, as if the owner had just been running. It was the mention of her mother's name being spoken quietly across the void of the corridor that immediately drew her attention. Olivia wondered who could be asking after her mother so urgently. Olivia knew everyone her mother knew. She could count on one hand the number of acquaintances she had and none of them were men. Olivia crossed over to the door as swiftly and stealthily as she could. She leant against the wall to the side of it, so as to listen through the crack in the opening.

'*She's fine, as well you know, Stephen. I've been keeping you updated. You shouldn't be here – it's too dangerous. Both for you and for Phyllis. If they track you down then they'll find her and we can't be having that. Think of the baby, man. Think of your unborn child!*'

ORDINARY WORLD

Olivia nearly fell into the doorway. Her body felt instantly cold and she knew the blood had drained rapidly from her extremities as the hand she had resting on the door handle seemed to go numb with the chill. Her mother was pregnant? How was this possible? She pushed the side of her face flush with the wall, as if trying to drill her ear through it so that she could hear the conversation more distinctly. Perhaps she had misheard? Misconstrued? No, she had definitely heard correctly. Her mother was pregnant and Stephen, whoever he may be, was the father. She had to pry further, to find out what had been happening to her mother without her knowledge.

The second voice was that of a man's too. He sounded older than Stephen, although when she thought back on it later this could simply have been because of the authority that layered his tone. Olivia imagined a man in his fifties, in a beige raincoat, leaning into Stephen as he spoke.

'*I know, I know,*' Stephen replied. '*But I had to see them. I can't abandon them completely.*'

'*You're not abandoning them, Stephen. You're protecting them. We're protecting them. But if they come here, I don't know how much good I'll be in a fight. And if I'm here, they'll know I've been helping you, which defeats the purpose of me being able to help you any further. Not to mention the hell that would rain down on this place. You have to stay away!*'

The second voice cracked a couple of times as it spoke and Olivia wondered if it was the strain of talking in hushed tones or if it was something else that caused it to fracture so. Was it, fear?

'*I know that too, Simon. But I had to see them one more time. Just try, one more time, to try and get through to her. To try and bring her back. I don't know when I will be able to come again. I'm sure they're onto me...*'

'All the more reason why you need to not be here. You'll endanger them. I said I'll look after them. Let you know if anything changes,' Simon said.

There was a cessation of talk from the room and Olivia heard the muffled sound of movement. She darted in through the kitchen door, pushing it nearly shut behind her as she realised the people from the room were about to come into the corridor. Her heart was beating very fast all of a sudden, fearful that she might be caught eavesdropping on their very private and very intriguing conversation. She heard footsteps in the corridor and then the door opposite close, bumping quietly into its frame. She peeked through the crack in her door and could just make out the double doors at the end of the corridor closing. She was annoyed that she had missed a chance to see one of the men who had been talking. She supposed it must have been 'Stephen' that had left so hurriedly.

She stood in the middle of the kitchen, fists clenched at her sides, an enormous vacuum in her stomach. She wanted to fill that void by screaming. She had a sudden onrush of overwhelming emotions that could only be expressed through a visceral scream. She opened her mouth, but then closed it almost as quickly. True, a scream in this place wouldn't be amiss, but the ward was peaceful tonight and her screaming in the kitchen would undoubtedly draw attention. The kind of attention that she had no wish to draw at this time. She choked the response back down into her gut. She looked around the kitchen, not really seeing it, just staring with a blank gaze that washed over it as her mind reeled at what she had just heard. Her mother was being held here for her own wellbeing and yet now Olivia had learned that she was pregnant. By another man. A man who wasn't her father. A different man. *Who the hell was he? Stephen, apparently. But that didn't explain anything. Who the fuck was Stephen? How did he even know her mother? And, for that matter who the fuck was Simon?*

ORDINARY WORLD

She suddenly turned from where she was standing, staring unseeingly at the kitchen appliances and rushed for the door. She had to know. She ran across the corridor and grabbed at the door handle for the room her mother was in. She turned it, but the door didn't open.

'Fuck!' she enunciated for all the world to hear. She knocked on the door. She knocked again, without really waiting for a response to her first knock. Then she banged on it.

'Let me in!' she called. She started to pound on the door, rattling the door handle, 'Let me the fuck in!'

She shouted at the door that barred her passage, tears of frustration welling out of the corners of her eyes to spill down her cheeks. Her pounding upon the door lessened.

'Let me in!' she called more softly, as the sudden upsurge of emotion died in her breast and she found herself limp from the expended rush. She leant against the door, unable to gain entry. Unable to find out more about her mother's condition. She took a deep breath and attempted to centre herself. Calm herself.

She took a step back from the door. Well, obviously no one was going to open up to her, not in this place. There was a very good reason for keeping the doors locked, in case one of the patients decided to have a delusional break and charge into another patient's room. Or at the very least, hammer on the door demanding to be let in. She choked on a half laugh as she realised that was probably it. Simon, or whoever was in that room with her mother, probably thought there was a rampaging nutjob outside and the last thing he was going to do was open the door on the off-chance he might get attacked.

Olivia found her breathing returning to normal. She was becoming calmer. She wiped the tears from her face. As she did so, rational thought started to return to her as well. She was supposed to be here for a meeting with Dr McIntyre, he would know the intimate details of her mother's condition. All she had to do was go and have her meeting with him and ask him. Sorted. She was being stupid... what was it Rhys liked to call people in these sorts of irrational situations? Dunderheads. She wasn't entirely certain where that came from – the US, probably, given the quantity of shows he watched that were made in America.

She turned away from the door, returned to the kitchen and got herself a glass of water and then made her way back to Evie in the waiting room.

Evie looked up from her magazine when Olivia entered the room. Olivia detected a frown starting to crease her friend's brow.

'Are you alright?' Evie asked. Olivia nodded,

'Yes, I'm alright, thanks.'

Evie didn't appear convinced. She got up from her chair and stepped closer to Olivia, 'Have you been crying?'

'No,' Olivia replied too quickly, 'well, yes, maybe, just a little.'

Evie misunderstood the reason for those tears and took Olivia up in a companionable hug.

'It'll be fine, Olivia. Phyllis will be just fine. She always is, eventually.'

Further conversation was forestalled as the door to the room opened and a middle-aged woman stepped in, calling for Olivia to join her to go and see Dr McIntyre.

Chapter 6

'Pregnant? What on earth would give you that idea, Olivia?' Dr McIntyre seemed genuinely surprised.

'But... I heard...' Olivia stopped herself before she admitted to the head of the facility that she had been eavesdropping on private conversations.

'You heard what?'

Olivia hesitated, trying to think of something to fill the chasm she had been about to hurl herself into.

'I, I thought I heard dad saying something about mum being pregnant,' she glanced up at McIntyre out of the corner of her eye, as a thought sprang to mind, 'but he may have been talking about *when* mum was pregnant. You know, with me?' She felt bold enough to look McIntyre square in the face as this idea evolved into the open.

'Yes, that would make more sense now. I'm sorry, I just got the wrong end of the stick.' That was a phrase Aunty Morag was very fond of using, usually about other people.

Olivia felt Dr McIntyre's gaze, penetrating and analytical, as though she was being scrutinised like one of his patients. Perhaps she was being paranoid. Would he detect her sudden feeling that she was being paranoid and section her as well?

'Yes, that sounds far more likely.'

Olivia felt that with that one little sentence McIntyre had dismissed the whole subject. A wave of relief washed through her and she felt the tips of her fingers tingle.

'So, your mother is doing well. The new regime Dr Varjay has prescribed seems to be working very well. Phyllis has had several quite lucid moments during her stay to date. Although, the downside to the new drugs would seem to be a higher level of fatigue. I'm not sure if it's because of the drugs themselves, or a knock-on effect of your mother being more active for longer. She's not used to it, so it may just be her body's way of saying when it's had enough.' He looked up from the file he had been referring to as he spoke. He smiled an encouraging smile at Olivia.

'Will we be able to see her this evening?' Olivia was aware that her appointment was well past the normal, regimented visiting hours. They were in place for a reason. Continuity for the patients, among other things.

Dr McIntyre was nodding even before he spoke, 'Yes, I see no harm in that. I will get one of the orderlies to escort you to her room.'

Olivia nearly butted in that that wouldn't be necessary as she knew where her mother's room was, but she held herself in check. Having an orderly with her would, firstly, deny McIntyre the knowledge of what she had been up to prior to her meeting with him. And secondly, he might be able to explain who Simon was, when they went in and found him in her mother's room. In the end she opted for a discreet smile and nod of her head.

Dr McIntyre glanced down at his file, his hand pausing as it had been about to close it. She noted another frown cross his face, which settled back to its normal state as he looked back at her.

'There's a note in here that says you're questioning the new drugs we've prescribed, Olivia?'

Olivia was taken by surprise by the question as her mind had been elsewhere. 'Really?' she asked confused.

'Yes, apparently it says you're unaware of a regime change and need to know more about it.'

'Oh, yes, that. Well, as I give Mum her meds usually, I hadn't noticed any difference in her bottles. And yet Dad said yesterday that she's been on a new regime for a while now. Since Christmas I think.'

'About that long, yes. New Year, actually,' McIntyre checked the file for corroboration. 'I'm surprised you hadn't queried it before, to be honest, if you were concerned.' He continued to frown at her.

Was he judging her? Was he accusing her of neglect for her mother's care?

'Well, it wasn't until yesterday that dad had said anything about the pills being different. So, I didn't know to ask until then.'

Dr McIntyre sat back in his chair, steepling his fingers in front of him, Olivia wondered if he was preparing himself to psychoanalyse her. Given the way the meeting had gone so far, she was starting to feel very uncomfortable that he was beginning to doubt her abilities to handle the continued care of her mother. When she spoke to Evie about it later, Evie made a salient point: how many sixteen-year-olds had near sole responsibility for the care of their ill parent? And how many of them struggled far more than Olivia ever did? Evie said that if the shrink had a problem with Olivia, then he had a problem with Evie, because she'd be quite happy to go in and slap some sense into him. By the time she got home Olivia would be feeling much happier about things, but right now, as she sat under the spotlight glower of a man capable of dissecting a person's brain, metaphorically speaking, she was beginning to feel very ill at ease.

'I see,' Dr McIntyre's response was very noncommittal; he sniffed before continuing, 'the different pill bottles didn't give you a clue? I believe you tend to be the one who administers your mother's pills to her.' He leaned forward as he spoke. Olivia shrunk back into her well-cushioned chair.

'Er, well, yes. But the bottles are still the same as they've always been.' She paused for a moment as she scrabbled in her shoulder bag. She pulled out the Boots bag she had stuffed her mother's pill bottles into before leaving the house. She passed it over the desk to

McIntyre, 'You see, they're all the same as before. I brought them to ask just this.'

McIntyre emptied the bag on top of his file and sifted through them. His frown returned and he opened one of the bottles and poured the contents into the palm of his hand. 'Hmmm.' He did this again for two more of the bottles; each received an accompanying hmm. Eventually he put them all back into the Boots bag.

'Well, I can see why you might be confused or not know. The bottles are all the old ones from before the regime change, but the pills are definitely different. They appear to have been put into relevant or equivalent bottles. Which is a bit odd, if not downright bloody dangerous.' He looked up at her and she wondered if he was accusing her, but if he was, he didn't pursue it.

'Do you think this was your father? I only ask because none of my staff would have done this, and the pharmacist is highly unlikely to have done this. As you're bringing it to me, I would be inclined to discount you as a culprit, which only leaves your father.' His eyes were piercing.

Olivia could feel her blood boiling; her cheeks flushed and she had to grip onto the sides of the chair to prevent herself from launching out of it in rage.

'Yes!' she said, 'yes, it bloody well was my dad. The...' she nearly said that word again, but bit it back, '...the bastard.'

McIntyre was well aware of the dynamics in the Buchanan house and was clearly unperturbed by both the revelation and the response. He waited for Olivia to fully process the information.

Olivia settled back into her chair, already starting to calm down, 'I know why he did it. It was because of the change; it happened when I was ill. So, it was easier to do this than explain what was actually going on. Why he thought it necessary, I have no idea.' She looked at McIntyre who was nodding.

'I know your father of old, Olivia, and it's just the sort of thing he would do. Obfuscation is his way. No, I don't know why he would do this instead of just saying we'd changed the regime either. But he is your father and it seems to be his way. I suspect he felt there was something deceitful about the whole subject and therefore felt a need to hide it and his part in it. That said, I hope we've cleared it all up for you and that you are still happy with the new meds Dr Varjay is prescribing. If you need to know more on it, then you will need to speak directly with him. He is the authority on these things.'

Olivia nodded, 'No, that's fine. At least I know what's going on now.'

'Will you talk to your father about it?' Olivia wasn't certain if this was a leading question. Should she talk to her father about it?

'No,' she said shaking her head, what was the point? She sighed, 'No, I'll leave it.'

Dr McIntyre responded by standing up, and she thought she detected a slight inclination of his head as he did so. He made his way round his desk; clearly the meeting had reached its conclusion. She stood up and let him lead her outside to a nurses' station.

'Well, I'm glad we've resolved a lot of your questions, Olivia. One of the orderlies will take you to see your mother. And hopefully you will see that things are definitely improving for her.' With that he shook her hand and returned to his office.

• • • •

Olivia and the orderly picked up Evie from the waiting room before making their way to her mother's room. She was a little surprised when they turned right at the crossroad of corridors She knew her mother's room was to the left, she stopped so suddenly Evie bumped into her. The orderly turned to see what the problem was.

'You alright, miss?'

'Yes, fine. But I thought my mother's room was the other way?'

He shook his head with a slightly patronising smirk on his face, 'No, miss. The wards can do that though; they're a bit of a maze, so they can turn you on your head if you're not familiar with them. Your mother, Phyllis Buchanan, is at the end of the corridor. Second to last door on the right.'

To prove that he was correct, he led them up to the door and opened it, ushering them in for them to see Phyllis sat up in bed staring out of her window.

'Oh!' Olivia exclaimed.

'Oh, indeed,' the orderly replied. 'When you're ready to leave, just press the intercom button. We're on nightshift now, so a lot of the wards are locked and you'll need one of us to escort you through the security doors.' And with that he closed the door on them.

Olivia remained where she was, perplexed. *But?* She opened the door and could see the orderly walking back the way they had come. She closed the door again and looked round to see her mother smile vacantly at her. *But*, she thought. She shrugged her shoulders. Maybe the orderly had been correct, maybe she had been confused. She opened the door again and looked at the room opposite. It said 'Maintenance' on the plaque, the door was white; she glanced at the paint on her mother's door, it was also white – not apple-green. So, that was not the kitchen and this was definitely not the room she'd been eavesdropping at previously. She closed the door once more and finally committed herself to visiting her mother. Evie had already gone to her and was giving her a big hug.

· · · ·

ORDINARY WORLD

For most of their visit, Phyllis was drowsy but lucid. She was relaxed, with colour in her cheeks, and managed a few meaningful sentence exchanges with the girls, from asking after Olivia's schoolwork to how Evie's parents were. The visit ended when the girls decided there was nothing more forthcoming from Phyllis after she had been dozing for ten or so minutes. Evie called for the orderly who then led them back to the entrance. As they neared the crossroads of corridors, Olivia became more aware of her surroundings once more. She craned to look around the orderly towards the way she had originally been convinced they should have gone. She started to lag more and more behind the orderly, until, when he and Evie turned the corner, she was several paces behind.

She darted across the junction as quietly as she could. She stopped briefly in front of the kitchen door to her left, then moved diagonally across the corridor to the door she had been eavesdropping at earlier. She leaned into it, pressing as close as possible to listen. There was barely any sound from within. The beep, beep of a heart monitor and maybe just the faintest sound of breathing. No voices nor signs of other occupancy. She put her hand on the door handle and turned it slowly until she was certain it had reached its maximum turn. She then pushed gently. The door didn't budge. *Bugger it*, she thought. She glanced over her shoulder; there was no sign of the others. She didn't know what to do. She wanted to find out who was inside, but she could hear the others' footsteps fading. She needed to leave before she was found out. With one final frustrated fumble with the handle, she abandoned the door and moved as quickly and quietly as possible to catch up with Evie and the orderly. She turned the corner and they were nowhere to be seen. *Crap!*

Olivia hurried along the corridor. There was a T-junction at the end and they had originally come from the right, which would lead back to Dr McIntyre's office through a multitude of corridors and security doors. If they were being escorted out, she would need to turn left, which she did in haste and promptly bundled into the orderly who was coming back.

'Oof,' he declared as she collided with him.

'Sorry,' she uttered hurriedly.

'Where did you get to?' he said gripping her by the shoulders.

'Sorry,' she said again sounding flustered, which if she was being honest with herself, she was. 'I was really thirsty after the visit and as we were passing the kitchen, I thought I'd just pop in and get a swig of water. I thought I'd have time and still not have to hold you up.'

He looked down at her, an eyebrow rising in disbelief. He relinquished his hold of her shoulders, instead opting for an almost guiding restraint hold upon her left bicep. Olivia was fairly convinced he didn't believe her.

'Well, next time you should say and we would have waited for you. This is not the place to be getting lost nor straying from the set corridors. Even if the patients are locked down in their rooms now, there are protocols to adhere to. And if one of the more violent ones had been roaming the facility you could have been in serious trouble.' He looked very sternly at her and she suddenly realised the enormity of her decision for an unguided trip, even if it had only been a short one. She stammered another apology, feeling quite shaken all of a sudden.

'Fine. Your friend is waiting at the main entrance. I'll see you to her.'

Olivia was brusquely escorted out of the secure wing down to the main entrance, where the orderly finally relinquished his hold upon her arm. He didn't even bid them a good evening, before turning on his heel and marching back into the mental health wing.

'What happened to you?' Evie asked eagerly as she glanced past Olivia at the retreating back of the orderly.

'Nothing,' Olivia replied quickly, not wishing to talk about why she had deviated from the path, 'I just stopped to tie my laces and then you were both gone when I looked up again. Took a couple of wrong turns and then had to wait to be rescued, is all.'

Once again, Olivia wasn't certain if she was believed, but it did prevent Evie from pestering further.

• • • •

Olivia stood in her kitchen with her coat half off, staring down at a note on the table.

'*There's a casserole in the oven. It just needs warming. There are dumplings with it, unless you'd prefer rice. Feel free to eat it all or save some for your lunch tomorrow. I'll eat out.*

Dad.'

Olivia finally slipped her coat off and laid it over the back of one of the chairs. Dad had made a casserole? He *never* cooked. Olivia wondered if the bang to his head yesterday morning had finally knocked some sense into him. *Best not look a gift horse in the mouth*, she thought, another of Aunty Morag's sayings. She turned the oven on. She'd have the dumplings; she was too tired to bother with rice. She sat at the table mulling over the appointment with Dr McIntyre. Mum would be staying for at least a few more days, but he did think she would be released in time for Olivia's birthday next week. She felt quite happy at the prospect of Mum being home for her birthday; in years past this had not always been the case. There was also the possibility that Mum might be on a higher level of mental acuity, because of the new drugs. A birthday with her mother actually being able to say 'happy birthday' to her would be the best present she could dream of.

As she served her casserole and sat down to eat it, she switched on the radio and suddenly realised how late it was. John Peel's show had already started on Radio 1. She liked the Peel show: his taste in music was eclectic and she always enjoyed Captain Beefheart.

While she ate her dinner, Olivia's mind drifted. She had been thinking about the meeting with Dr McIntyre, but then something on the radio shifted her train of thought imperceptibly and she was back in the corridor listening in on the clandestine conversation between Stephen and Simon. Who were they? And who was the Phyllis they had been talking about? Obviously not her mother. But what were the chances of two women being on the same ward with the name of Phyllis? It wasn't a common name. Quite old fashioned some might say. If it had been Sandra or Jane, then she probably wouldn't have even thought to listen in. And then there was what they had been discussing. Stephen and Phyllis seemed to be hiding from a group of people. Stephen had even admitted to being hunted. Who hunts people in this day and age? Why hunt them? Were they criminals? But surely if they were criminals Dr McIntyre and his team would know and have informed the police. From what she had heard, it was almost as if they were hiding in that room with no one in the facility any the wiser to their presence. But that couldn't be possible. Could it? On top of that was the revelation that Phyllis was carrying a baby. Was Phyllis unconscious or catatonic, like her mother had been so many times in the past? Neither, surely, would be good if she was pregnant. Olivia had a thousand more questions to ask about them, but not a single answer. At least, nothing that seemed reasonable or logical. The mystery of Stephen and Phyllis plagued her thoughts for what was left of her evening.

As she lay her head down on her pillow, pulling her covers over her shoulder, she was still considering Stephen and Phyllis. It made no sense to her. Maybe, if she went back again during the day, she might be able to listen in again. Maybe even see into the room, if it was during normal visiting hours. Patients' rooms were usually unlocked so that they could freely gain access to the common room, where a lot of visitors would end up.

Visiting hours were fairly strict at the wing, but they were available every day and, as tomorrow was Saturday, it wouldn't be seen as strange for her to go and visit her mother again. Perhaps, if she did, not only would she manage to get some more fleeting moments of lucid comment from her mum, but she could have another crack at the mysterious room and its occupants. Yes, that was the plan for tomorrow. Visit the ward again.

・・・・

Not for the first time this week, her sleep was restless and fitful. Dreams disturbed her through the night. She found herself being pursued down endless hospital corridors, with junctions to multiple possibilities just out of reach. The overhead pinky-yellow neon light strips flickered and buzzed annoyingly, like they were filled with millions of angry hornets hammering at the flimsy captivity to escape. She glanced up as she ran under one of them and saw the black, hinged leg of a gigantic insect thrusting its way between the light cover and the case, using its chitinous limb like a crowbar to free itself and its hive. The sight of it spurred her on. All the while the heavy-booted steps pursued her. Ponderously slow though they were, the stride on them meant they were always nearby.

She turned a corner and ran straight into a door that had 'Kitchen maintenance' scrawled across it in toxic green spray paint. She fumbled with the handle, the sound of bootsteps getting closer. The anxiety started to pump harder through her veins. Her heart was racing. She nearly screamed in frustration as the door handle resolutely refused to turn in her sweaty palms. Desperate to get inside, she could feel the warm fetid breath of her pursuer upon her neck, blown there by the beating wings of the humongous winged beast that it rode. She grabbed at her petticoat and used that around the handle, finally managing to get it to turn. She forced her way through and then slammed the door, coming to rest with her back against it. She felt the pursuers bounce against it and the force threw her forward, but she found herself suddenly pulled back again. She realised her blossoming skirts – the skirts of the courtly dress she was now wearing – were caught in the door and the pursuer was pulling at the fabric on the other side of the door, drawing her back to it. She tore at her dress; ripping and rending at it until she had removed it, just as she found herself being squeezed through the crack in the door. She fell away and landed in a heap on the floor. Sweat pouring from her. Her heart pounded so loudly against her chest wall it was all she could hear. Thump, thump, beep, thump, beep, beep, beep.

She looked up as she realised the new sound wasn't coming from her. She looked up and saw a figure, crucified to the far wall; held in place by a myriad network of different coloured wires and tubes. They wore a patient's nightgown that flapped freely in a wind that didn't exist. Her eyes moved inexorably up the figure until she could see its head. The face was completely covered by what looked like a World War I gas mask, intubating the patient. The smeared eye pieces were dark and formless. But a growing sense of urgency told her to press forward. A growing sense of morbid fascination made her stand up to look into the void of those dusty crystal orbs. How she wished she hadn't. Peering in, she saw nothing at first. Just a tenebrous darkness that sucked her down into its void. And then, in a heartbeat, the eyes opened.

· · · ·

Olivia woke with a start and a stifled scream. Her heart was pounding heavily in her chest and she was sweating profusely.

She had a headache and her limbs ached as if she had spent the entire night in the gym. She fell back into her pillow, unable to move her legs because they were so completely entwined in her duvet. She closed her eyes in relief, then wished she hadn't. The eye pieces sprang to life in front of her and the eyes opened. Wide, staring terrified eyes. Blueish-grey eyes. Eyes that were just like hers, and they were terrified to the point of insanity.

• • • •

Saturday 10th April 1993

Olivia woke with a start. Her heart was pounding. She had a headache developing. She didn't feel rested at all, if anything she was more tired now than when she had gone to bed. She knew she had been dreaming and she knew she hadn't liked what she'd been dreaming. Those terrified, insane eyes haunted her waking vision. What was scarier still was that she had actually dreamed that she had woken up! She was now left with an overriding sense of foreboding and gloom. She sat up, rubbed her eyes and stretched, trying to ease the ache in her legs. It felt like she had been running all night. She sat back and listened to the house. She looked at her clock. It was still early and the house was silent.

She got up slowly, checking the house for evidence of her father, but there was no sign that he had returned last night. It begged the question, was he still in the pub or did he find someone else's house to go to last night? Olivia had never really questioned her father's fidelity before and, truth be told, she had no idea if he had any other female acquaintances. But, given his relationship with her mum was unusual and given what an utter bastard he was, it wouldn't surprise her to know that he messed around on the side. She supposed the reason she had never considered it before was because it had only been in the last couple of years that the comprehension of sex had even entered her vocabulary, let alone associated with her parents. She doubted much happened in the marital department between them. Her mother wouldn't have anything like a sex drive, given her medication, but Dad presumably had one. Evidence to suggest this hypothesis lay in his study and the stack of pornos Evie had found. So, those nights when he didn't come home, or when he came home very late, maybe he was with another woman. Olivia spat her toothpaste into the sink and turned on the tap. She watched the white froth lift up like a raft on the sudden jet of water, to spiral bubbling down the plug hole. Yup, that about summed up her feelings on the matter of her father's sex life.

Saturday morning TV wasn't thrilling. It was either news and sport, or the two main channels were geared around child entertainment. Neither really thrilled her, but she left it running in the background as she laboriously chewed her way through her cereal. She was somewhat adrift as to what to do until visiting hours commenced later this afternoon. She supposed she could do some schoolwork, after all she had been doing quite well this term in keeping afloat and she did want to do well in her A-levels next year, so she could stand a chance of going to uni. Not that she had any idea what she'd do at uni. Most of the time all she thought about was looking after Mum. But Dr McIntyre's comment to her last night that the new drugs might be just the ticket, suddenly reopened an ancient wish she had made years ago of being able to go to university. If mum really was going to be more mentally agile and less prone to her illness, then dad would be able to manage her. Especially if they pushed the mental health team to provide additional carers to help support and monitor home life. Olivia was suddenly buoyed up with the notion of attending university.

She picked up the phone book and skimmed through its pages, looking for numbers to the local higher education facilities. Maybe if she rang one of them and spoke to the admissions department, she could get a better understanding of what she would need to do. Her fingers slowed turning the pages. Then stopped. It was Saturday; none of the universities nor colleges would be open for that sort of phone call. She focused her attention on the page that she had stopped at.

J. Kennedy,

J. Kennedy,

J.A. Kennedy.

There were dozens more. She was taken by a sudden impulse. She picked up the phone and rang the number for J. Kennedy. The phone rang for twenty seconds and then that same male voice she had heard previously said,

'Hullo?'

Olivia launched herself into her mission before she could bottle out of it. 'Hello. Mr Kennedy?'

'Yes, that's me. Look you'd better not be trying to sell me something. It's Saturday morning, for God's sake, and you've just dragged me out of the shower.'

Olivia felt mortified, 'Oh, I'm so sorry, Mr Kennedy. I never meant to disturb you.'

There was a grunt from the other end of the line, 'Yeah, well, that's alright. Are you trying to sell me something?' he said gruffly.

'No. No, certainly not, furthest thing from why I was calling you actually.'

'Good.' There was a pause. It lengthened until Mr Kennedy spoke again, 'and the reason you called was?'

'Oh, yes, sorry, yes. I called because, and this may seem a little strange, but I was calling to find out if you owned my house?'

There was another pause. Olivia heard Mr Kennedy sniff loudly.

'Yes,' he said, finally breaking the silence, 'that does sound a little strange. And no, I doubt I own your house. I barely own mine. The bank owns most of it. So, I think it's unlikely that I have any ownership of yours.' He sniffed again, 'Was that of any help to you, miss?'

'It was. Thank you. Thank you. Goodbye.' Olivia started to hang up and then leant forward towards the receiver as she did so and hurriedly shouted down the phone before he could hang up at his end. 'Please, go back and enjoy your shower. I'm so sorry I disturbed you.'

She heard a gruff, 'that's alright', fade on the line before it went dead. The receiver was back in its cradle. Olivia took in a long breath and then held it. She let it out and felt herself calming down after the sudden adrenaline rush from her rashness. She looked at the next name on the list, also a J. Kennedy. Should she ring another J. Kennedy? After all she was actually looking for a J. F. Kennedy. So that would mean it was pointless ringing any of the other Kennedys if their initials weren't J. F. She skipped over a page and then started again.

'Hello, I was ringing to speak with a J. F. Kennedy?'

'Oh, that'll be my mother, but she's not in at the moment. Can I take a message?'

'No. No message. Thank you.'

Olivia hung up. That was the third J. F. Kennedy and not the one she was looking for. She glanced at the endless list and then realised as she went through them that she was going to get lost. She looked over to the telephone table. There was a cup by the phone base which had several pens and a pencil in it. She opted for the pencil. If for any reason dad was to look into the phone book and see she had crossed out a pile of Kennedys in it, he might start to suspect something. If she did it lightly, in pencil, she could rub it out when she was finished and he'd be none the wiser.

Olivia supposed she was quite lucky that all the Kennedys she had rung so far had actually answered the phone. She wondered if it meant anything in the grand scheme of things that it was the thirteenth Kennedy she rang who didn't answer. She put a little dot by their name. Then rang the next one. No joy there either. In the end, it took well over an hour to ring all the J. F. Kennedys in the book. Nearly all of them weren't John Fitzgerald and of those few that were, none of them had any idea about owning another house. When she had cleared the list, she came back to the three names that hadn't answered. One was just J. F., the other two were John F. Kennedy. She rang them again, but once more there was no answer. She huffed. Oh well, what was it that the great detectives always did at this point when the leads all seemed to have dried up? They got off their arses and walked the streets. That's what they did. Olivia went and got dressed. She wrote out the names and details of the three elusive Kennedys and rubbed out her pencil markings in the rest of the book. Then she slipped the paper into her jacket pocket and headed out of the house.

Chapter 7

Saturday 10th April 1993

All three remaining Kennedys lived on the other side of town. John Kennedy and one of the J. F.'s lived within a mile of each other; the final J. F. lived outside of town, beyond the suburbs. Olivia stepped off the bus and immediately found herself in a rundown area. Many of the shops that still remained open were scruffy and dilapidated. Most of them were family-run stores and bargain booze outlets. Beyond the occasional shop-orientated street, there were a myriad of tiny offshoots, roads, streets and alleys, that all looked as though they had been forgotten about as side-dressing for a Victorian novel on deprivation. It reminded her of sepia pictures she had seen in her history books of bombed-out London after World War II; kids in frayed hand-me-downs stood on piles of rubble staring out over the stark wilderness of urban desolation. She shook her head and went to one of the more salubrious-looking shops, a Tesco Express, and asked one of the cashiers if she knew where to find Durban Street. The tired, middle-aged woman happily took the time out from the drudgery of her everyday job to give Olivia explicit details on how to find it.

'Thank you...' Olivia said as she tried to extricate herself from further conversation. She glanced at the woman's name tag, 'Margaret.'

'You're welcome, m'dear, most welcome,' Margaret replied.

Durban Street was the same as every other street down here; two rows of terraced two-up-two-downs. The road itself was narrow and, with cars parked on both pavements, it made it extremely precarious to drive a car down the middle without removing several wing mirrors. With the cars parked on the pavements, it also made it difficult to walk a straight path down them. Had she been wheeling a pushchair she would have done better to have walked the road. Finally, she found John's house. It was squeezed into the middle of the left-hand side of the street. There was nothing remarkable about it. Nothing to make it stand out from the rest of the houses in the road. She had to walk up to the front door in order to check that this was the correct number; so many of the houses had no numbers at all and many that did, had not had the foresight to put their numbers on the gates that led to their front doors. Several times she'd had to walk a path hesitantly, for fear of being pounced upon by an occupier for trespass. But that was something else about this street and the others she had walked down. They were all deserted. No children outside playing. No pedestrians. No one. Not even birds seemed to frequent these foreboding streets.

    She knocked on John's front door with the old, tarnished brass knocker that was suspended upon an equally tarnished plaque. There was no answer. She waited a few moments, peering in through the grimy opaque glass in the door, hoping to see some flicker of movement to indicate someone was coming to answer her call. But there was nothing to discern beyond, merely an ominous gloom that seemed to enshroud the house. A gloom, she felt, that started to extend itself outwards: out into the porch and then out to envelop the pathway behind her. She shivered as a chill suddenly went down her spine. She glanced behind and watched as the shadows appeared to cluster into the tiny patch of grass that was well overdue a cut, huddled behind a low brick wall with ancient iron railings topping it. She glanced up. Up over the roofs of the parked cars, to the fronts of the houses on the other side of the road and then up again, past the overhanging wires for the telephone lines, to the skies that hovered low and impending above them. That was what had given the impression of the house's gloom extending over her. The clouds had become heavier and moved to obscure the sun from the day. She shivered again, turning back to the front door and tried the knocker once more.

As she walked back to the bus stop, Olivia had to admit to herself that she was relieved no one had been at home. She had never been to this part of town before and her first experience of it, other than Margaret, had been unnerving. She hoped she would never have to come here again. But she knew that John F. lived not far from here, so the probability was that she would have to continue her sojourn within the confines of a suburb that was disquieting for her soul. She looked at the timetables and then her watch. In the time she had till the next bus was due to take her to John F., she could just as easily walk it. Not that she knew exactly how to get there from here. She looked around the street until her eyes settled once more upon Margaret's Tesco Express. *They might sell street maps?* Olivia said to herself. And it could be useful for finding the other John F.'s place when she left the confines of this miserable suburb. She headed back to Margaret.

Once more at the bus stop, she leant upon the fixed, slanted, thin bench the bus company presumed was comfortable for waiting customers and flicked through the small, blue map book of the district. To get from here to John F.'s street took her across two pages, but she reckoned it would only take about twenty minutes and the bus wasn't due for twenty-five. She set off, clutching the map book against her chest under her coat like a shield to ward off the ills of this dour neighbourhood.

• • • •

The threatening skies followed her all the way to John F.'s road; occasional spots of heavy cold rain splattered on to her head and she berated herself for not thinking of bringing an umbrella. She turned left off the main road and down into John F.'s street. As she did so, a great gust of wind shot down out of the mouth of it, like the torrid breath of a demon, dragging with it all the aromatic stenches of hell. The force of the blast made her stagger and she closed her eyes to avoid dust or debris blinding her. She found herself back-pedalling, clutching her arms to her chest tightly to avoid being completely bowled over by the sudden expulsion. It was gone almost as soon as it had arrived and she found, as she opened her eyes, that she could walk forward unhindered once more. As she stepped into the street, the world around her lit up with glorious sunshine and, glancing up, she was blinded by the brilliance of a white April sun pouring its radiance down upon her. Olivia's mood shifted perceptibly with this sudden phenomenon. Her steps picked up and she strode briskly down the road to find John F.'s home. She was a little surprised, therefore, when she came to a pillared gateway, leading up a tarmacked pathway, which ran at an acute angle to the street. It was cobbled on either side and led to a glass portico at the base of a tower block. She hadn't been expecting one of her targets to reside in a block of flats. Although, as she stood there taking in the vista, she supposed any number of the previous Kennedys she had spoken to may well have been talking to her from a flat.

She opened the gate and walked towards the portico. On the right-hand side of the pathway, about two hundred yards from the entrance, there was a long row of cycle racks. Olivia saw a dozen or more bicycles, padlocked to them. At each end of the bike racks there were two larger vehicles covered by tarpaulins; judging by the shapes, she surmised them to be motorbikes.

She peered in through the glass-fronted door that led from the tiled portico she currently occupied, into a well-to-do looking hallway. It was carpeted – a faded jade. Scattered throughout were aspidistras in large pots upon tall, thin-legged, black tables. She turned to the panel to her right with rows of doorbells and cards under each indicating the occupier. John F. Kennedy lived in No.

ORDINARY WORLD

1. She pushed the bell and held it for several seconds. Then she waited. Nothing happened. There was no crackly voice asking who it was through the intercom. The main door didn't buzz and unlock. There was only silence. She let out a long sigh. Two out of three had given her no answers to her mystery. Was there any point trying the third one, given that he lived out of town? She hunched her shoulders and then thought of the first Kennedy she'd spoken to today. He'd been in the shower, maybe this one was too. *Give him another shot*, she thought. Her forefinger stabbed into the button again, depressing it long enough that the fingertip went scarlet and her first joint went white and achy. Behind her, she heard the door opening and someone coming out. She turned to see a faceless man stepping through. Faceless because he wore a black motorbike helmet and the sun visor was down, obscuring his face. His arms were held out as he shrugged on an armoured black leather jacket, with blue emblazoned shoulder pads. The man stopped his progress abruptly as he became aware of her presence and then removed his helmet, as he spoke to her. His opening comment was muffled by the action, but Olivia still heard him address her by her informal name.

'Oh!' he said.

'O?' she replied, 'Yes, how... Oh! Ooooh!' she finished.

He looked at her, bemused. Then reached forward with his free hand and removed her finger from the button.

'Yes, oh. Oh, as in you seem to be ringing for me.'

'Really?' Olivia responded, taking a moment to look at his face properly for the first time. He was a young man, early to mid-twenties, she reckoned, with close cropped black hair. His face was appealing she suddenly realised, especially when he smiled and the realisation caused her to blush.

'Well, that's my doorbell you seem to have murdered. So, I can only guess it's me you're after.'

'John Kennedy?'
'Yup, that's me.'
'John *F.* Kennedy?'
'Still me, yes,' he said with a smirk. 'So, what can I do you for?'

'Oh,' for a moment Olivia was thrown. She had been so caught up in the idea that she wasn't going to get an answer here that now she didn't know what to say. She looked at him and slowly became aware that he was still holding her wrist. She lowered her eyes to the contact and then back up to his face. She also realised that she wasn't all that bothered about the fact that he seemed to be still holding on to her. It felt warm and comfortable.

John's eyes followed Olivia's gaze down to her wrist and saw what she saw. He let go and then raised his eyes once more to engage with her.

'Yes,' Olivia continued, trying to remember why she was there. 'Well, this may sound a bit odd...'

She noted his eyebrow rise slightly as she said this. She envied him this ability. She had practiced and practiced over the years to get her eyebrows to move independently of the other one, but they seemed doomed to be conjoined, so instead of the inquisitive look she was going for, she always ended up just looking surprised. With his eyebrow raised in such a manner, Olivia felt he looked quizzical, which under the circumstances was quite reasonable.

'Well,' she started again, 'you see it all started with my friend, Evie, who became worried that I was about to be evicted from my house, because my father's a bit of a ...' she paused as the word 'cunt' materialised on the tip of her tongue. Given the handsome man in front of her, she felt the usage of such a despicable word could ruin any further contact. She didn't want that to happen, she realised. She felt a slight blush rising in her cheeks as she continued to look at him. The pause in her explanation and that word, which kept on resurfacing in her mind, was causing her to lose any aplomb she may have thought she had. She was getting flustered.

'Your father's a bit... what?' John asked, prompting her to carry on.

'He's a bit, er, a bit, well, not very good with money all the time,' she concluded hastily. 'So, we got it into our heads to have a look at my father's documents to see if his finances were actually OK and that we weren't about to have the house repossessed. Anyway, cutting a long story short, we found the title deeds for the house and they were in the name of someone else. Which is why I happen to be here, talking with you.' She finished, hoping this would clear the whole matter up. Which, of course, it didn't, because she had left some pertinent information out.

'I see,' said John frowning slightly. Olivia wasn't certain if this meant he did see and wasn't impressed with her actions of rifling through her father's personal and private papers. Which, now she came to think on it again, was a bad thing to have done. Or if, in fact, he didn't see and was just stalling for time. 'The name on the title deeds?'

'Yes?' Olivia said.

'Would that have been 'John F. Kennedy', by any chance?'

Oh, he was quick minded, she thought, 'Yes, it was. Although the 'F' was detailed.'

'I see,' he said again. And again, Olivia wondered if he did see or if it was merely a turn of phrase he liked to use. But he had already solved the 'name on the deed' information, so she was beginning to think that he did see. She smiled in response to his comment.

John suddenly pulled back the cuff of his jacket and inspected the watch on his wrist. His stature changed in that moment and Olivia noted a sense of urgency course through his physique.

'Walk with me,' he commanded, as he started out from the portico down the tarmac pathway. She dutifully followed, almost skipping in order to keep up with his brisk stride.

'Why did you come to my door, though?' he asked, 'You could have phoned. I'm in the book.' The sideways glance he threw at Olivia and the tone of his voice suggested to her that he had suddenly become suspicious of her intentions.

'Oh, but I did and I know you are... that's how I came to be here,' she replied. 'Only you didn't answer the phone when I called this morning... and...' she was breathing hard as they came to a sudden halt by the bike rack after their dash down the path. But this wasn't the only reason for her pauses, as it occurred to her that he had ignored his doorbell. He must have been in his flat when she had first rung. So, what if that was also true for the phone? Not that he didn't have the right to ignore these demands on his time, but...

'And?' John prompted once more as he laid his helmet on the ground and started to pull off the tarp from one of the vehicles, revealing a jade green super bike.

'Well, and,' Olivia paused, her attention drawn from the conversation for a second by the inherent beauty of the bike, 'er, I did phone you this morning, a couple of hours ago now. Maybe three, and then as there was no answer I came here to see if I could catch you at home.'

'I see,' his insistence on using this phrase in answer to every stage of her explanation was starting to grate on Olivia. 'Well, if you did ring two to three hours ago, I wouldn't have answered because I was asleep. I work shifts and as such my sleep patterns don't fit in with the world around us. As for my doorbell, well, truth be told, you weren't the one who murdered it. It doesn't work. But then, as I never have unexpected visitors, I don't need a working doorbell.' He stood up from the crouch he had been in to unlock the hefty chain that secured his bike to the tubes. 'Until now, it would seem,' he concluded, rolling the chain up and sticking it into a compartment under the seat of his bike. He moved to where he had thrown the tarp and started to meticulously fold it up into a remarkably tiny parcel.

'OK, so what exactly is it that you were looking to ask of me? Do I own your house?' he tilted his head slightly as he asked this second question.

'Well, yes, I suppose, although actually not directly, not at first, at any rate,' Olivia said.

'Really?' he seemed surprised by her response, 'Surely that would be the first thing to ask if you're concerned about being evicted?'

Olivia moved on with her explanation as she watched him put the remains of his tarp into the same compartment as the chain had gone.

'No, my first question was going to be what the 'F' stood for.'

'Oh, OK. Yes, I can see that would make sense.' Both his eyebrows rose as he said this, although it didn't make him look surprised, just emphasised his acknowledgement that her comment was sensible, she felt. Olivia started to feel more relaxed once more. His interrogation of her had started to make her feel quite uneasy.

'So,' she went on, 'what *does* the 'F' stand for?'

John looked at her with an appraising stare. 'Before I answer that, can I just clarify the situation?' Olivia nodded; it seemed only fair.

'Right, it's late Saturday morning and a rather attractive young girl knocks on my door to ask me what the 'F' stands for in my name. A particularly good-looking girl, whom I've never met before, I might add,' the corners of his mouth rose into what Olivia could only describe as a highly appealing smile. She felt her cheeks getting warm and she knew she was starting to blush. In all her life, she could not remember ever being called attractive or good-looking before. Unable to speak for a moment, fearing she may stutter or say something stupid, she merely nodded a response.

'OK, well as delightfully attractive young girls never come to find me, I'm starting to wonder what the catch is? If I tell you what 'F' stands for and it's not the answer you were looking for, are you going to stab me?'

Olivia was shocked by this turn of the conversation, although in hindsight she could understand how this thought might have come to mind. After all, her life had been filled with the uncertainty of violence from both of her parents. She had no idea what kind of life experience John had had. In a moment of judgementalism she concluded that, being a biker, he probably encountered a lot of people who would willing stab him for any number of reasons, one of those being that he was a biker. Although, and again this was with the aid of hindsight, he didn't look much like the kind of bikers she was aware of that dealt in that sort of lifestyle. His hair wasn't long, she couldn't determine any tattoos, he didn't smell of stale tobacco or weed – which she knew she did, on occasion, after spending time with Rhys and Evie – and he didn't appear to have any horrific scars from fights and brawls.

'Of course I'm not going to stab you, no matter what your middle name is,' she sounded appalled by his suggestion.

'So you say, so you say,' he countered, 'but what's in it for me?' he smiled a slightly lopsided grin at her. Now it was her turn to frown.

'I don't understand,' she said, 'what could be in it for you?'

'Well, the way I see it is this. Currently I'm getting quite late for work,' he glanced at his watch again and tutted, 'although if I put my chin on the tank, I could still make it in time. There's this attractive girl asking me to tell her my middle name. A name, I might point out, that I never tell anyone anyway, and given that she sought me out from the crowd of Kennedys that must live in this town, I get the impression that if I don't say the correct name, it could be the end for me. It's a bit of a Rumplestiltskin moment, if you ask me.' He smiled apologetically at her. 'So, I think to balance it out a bit, there should be something in it for me, especially with the threat of stabbage.' He continued to smile at her.

'I'm *not* going to stab you,' Olivia's voice rose an octave by way of emphasis.

'So you say, so you say,' he said again. His desire to repeat certain phrases had been getting annoying for Olivia, but in this moment and the way he had just said it, with a slight shrug of his shoulders and the rising of his hands, palms to the sky, made her inwardly chuckle. There was something of a jester in this John and she felt a surge of endearment towards him the longer they conversed.

'OK,' she said in response to his gesticulations, 'so what could I give you if you were to tell me your middle name? I don't have a lot of money on me and I need my bus pass to get me home. I'm not sure I have a lot else to offer you.'

'Well, that's where you're mistaken. You see, I think that if I tell you my middle name and I give you an answer that doesn't fit what you're seeking, it's highly probable that I'll get stabbed.' He held up his hand to prevent her interjection of a denial. 'And given the number of names there are that begin with F, I think it's also highly probable that the odds are against me giving you the correct answer. So, if I tell you, and before you stab me when it's wrong, I think you should give me a kiss.' His smile changed subtly to one that Olivia could only describe as roguish; it reminded her of Rhys.

'But what if you get it right? A kiss for getting it wrong,' she blushed more heavily as she stuttered the word kiss, 'seems expensive and I have nothing higher to give you if you get it right.'

'Hmm,' John rested his chin on his left fist, cradling his left elbow in his right hand and striking a pose of a man deep in thought, 'I s'pose you speak the truth there. OK,' he went on, dropping his hands to his side once more, 'so if I get it wrong, you can kiss me on the cheek. But,' and he paused dramatically at this point, a finger pointing to the sky, 'if I get it right, you have to kiss me on the lips. Deal?'

Olivia was in a quandary. She had never kissed anyone before, well, not like this anyway. She didn't know what to do; he was, after all, a complete stranger. A handsome and roguish stranger, a stranger that reminded her of Rhys in many ways, but still a stranger. She couldn't just go around snogging strangers, what would people think? What would she think, come to that? She continued to consider her options. John was indeed a stranger, but he had complimented her several times in a way that no one had ever done before. The best compliment she had previously received was being described as a lanky streak of piss by her own father. She had never considered herself to be pretty or attractive; those were the realms Evie lived in, not demure, gangling Olivia. She had no idea how long they had been talking for, but she felt like it had been an eternity and *not* an eternity of misery. Which is what she would have openly described her life to date to have been. She made a decision.

'Deal!' she said. 'So, what does the 'F' stand for, then?'

John seemed suddenly hesitant, 'It doesn't really stand for anything.'

'What do you mean?' she said suspiciously, her eyes narrowing, 'What do you mean it doesn't stand for anything. It must stand for something? It's an 'F' in the middle of your name.'

John nodded, 'You're not going to like the answer, but it doesn't really stand for anything. It stands for Fuckall.'

ORDINARY WORLD

'It can't stand for fuck all! It must stand for something... Is it really embarrassing like, like...' she paused for a moment as she tried to think of an embarrassing name beginning with F. She drew a blank and looked up at him once more.

'No, I mean that's what it actually stands for.' John tried to clarify, 'The 'F' in the middle of my name stands for Fuckall.' He stared at her hard to try and get his point across. Olivia stared back at him for several moments, until what he was saying came from another angle in her brain.

'OH!' this time her conjoined eyebrows rose in actual surprise. 'You really mean it stands for Fuckall.'

'Yes,' he said reluctantly.

'What kind of name is that?' she asked rather perplexed.

'It's a unique name and a joke. No one else is going to have a middle name of Fuckall, are they?'

'No, I suppose you're right, they're not,' Olivia seemed rather disappointed, John's revelation was something of a let-down, after all the foreplay leading up to it.

John looked at her and relented, 'It's not Fuckall.'

'What?' Olivia looked back at him, her eyes narrowed, suspicious of him again.

"F' doesn't stand for Fuckall, but it does stand for Fangjack. Which I can tell by the expression on your face is probably worse than if it had really been Fuckall.' John's face mirrored Olivia's in its level of despondency.

'Fangjack? What kind of name is *that*? That's not even a real word?'

'It *is* a real word.' John sounded perturbed by her disbelief, if not a little offended. 'But I can see you're not up to speed with cutting-edge tech theory. Which, in fairness, there aren't that many in the world who are. But in my line of work, Fangjack's quite a cool and amusing name to have.

'Fangjack is a type of jack lead, shaped like a wolf's fang. It's a hypothetical concept that many of the leading-edge tech corporations are experimenting with at the moment. The idea is that a base plug is surgically implanted into the back of the skull and then a Fangjack can be inserted directly into the cerebellum. The lead that runs from the jack can then be attached to any form of electronics. Thus creating a mind-to-machine interface. Like I said, it's cutting-edge theory and, at the moment, nothing more than science fiction. Because all the initial tests on it seem to have exploded either the electronics or the base point. They're a long way from getting it to human trials. But for my work, and other things, I'm known as Fangjack on the 'net; it's my handle on there. So, it seemed reasonable to make it permanent and legal and add it to my name out here in the real world, away from sci-fi tech and electronic information.' John finally finished his explanation. Olivia believed him. She felt sorry for him looking at the disconsolate expression on his face. Clearly, in his line of work, whatever that was, this weird nickname was important.

'So, I'm guessing that wasn't the name you were after, was it?' John said despondently, 'Be gentle when you stab me, I really don't do pain well.'

Olivia smiled at him and then impulsively stepped forward, kissing him soundly on the cheek.

John was taken by surprise and it was his turn to blush. He reached into an inner pocket of his jacket and pulled out a wallet. He flicked it open and turned over a couple of the inner plastic containers until he found what he was looking for. He presented it to her for her inspection. It was his driver's licence.

Olivia looked at the document. There, in official ink, was his name – John Fangjack Kennedy. She let out a little chuckle at such an oddity. As he pulled the wallet away and closed it back up, she caught a glance at the ID card that was in the pouch below his driver's licence. It caused her a moment of pause and to take an involuntary step backwards. It had his photo on it and in bold, solid, official print she'd seen four letters. She wasn't certain what she made of it. She knew the letters well. But they were synonymous with clandestine shadowy official corridors of power. This was why she had stepped away from him. GCHQ was where spies hung out.

John pocketed his wallet, 'You know, I really do need to be getting to work. Even with my chin on the tank I'm still going to be horribly late and my bosses don't take kindly to their employees not being at their desks when they're supposed to be.' His smile was full of chagrin; Olivia could well understand why he might feel that way.

'Can you come back tomorrow afternoon? Any time after four,' he asked. Olivia was startled by the question and uttered a haltering yes, before she realised what she was saying.

'Good. We can continue our conversation and it would seem I may have been mistaken when I accused you of a desire to stab me. For which I am most grateful, by the way. I'm wondering if I might be able to help you with your search for the elusive Kennedy on your title deed. My official work is that of an analyst, but my unofficial work means I know where to look for information that most people don't even think exists. So, it might have been serendipity that brought you to my door...' he looked at her, suddenly realising he had no idea what her name was.

'Hi,' he said to her in a very casual, offhand manner, 'I'm John, John Fangjack Kennedy. What's your name, beautiful?'

He smiled that roguish smile again as he held out his hand to her.

Olivia stuttered again and, again, she felt her cheeks explode with a very hot blush. They felt taut as the skin strained to contain such a massive outlet of blood into her system. 'Olivia, Olivia Buchanan,' she replied.

Chapter 8

Olivia glanced at her watch as she took her seat on the bus. With three changes, she was going to be lucky to get to the ward for the start of visiting time. Any delays or missed connections and she wasn't certain it would be worth trying at all. But she had a distinct urge to go to that other room in the wing and see if she could find out more about the mysterious woman and her gangster boyfriend. As the bus set off and she considered this, it occurred to her that getting involved with gangsters wasn't the most sensible idea she had ever had. But it *was* the most exciting one.

There was a woman sat on the bench opposite Olivia reading a glossy local magazine, and Olivia glanced at the back page story headline: '*Star-crossed lovers caught in families' feud*'. It brought to mind the clandestine party in the ward room she so desperately wanted to know more about. Could their story be a matter of star-crossed love set to the backdrop of feuding families? As yet, she had no idea, but it was far more romantic than the two of them being involved with gangsters, and probably a lot less dangerous too. Olivia's gaze slid across the page to the advert that had been placed next to the story. 'English National Opera proudly presents its Summer Extravaganza – *a retelling of Charles Gounod's Romeo & Juliet*'. She wondered if this had been deliberate on the editor's part.

The bus suddenly ground to a halt. Olivia looked past the woman and her magazine, down the corridor to see what the holdup was. She could just make out a long queue of traffic extending beyond the front of the bus and ending near some mobile traffic lights. There appeared to be road works, but as was often the case, no one was actually working. *Great*, she thought and looked at her watch again. Perhaps the Fates had been listening in on her internal dialogue and thought it would be funny to put a spanner in her works. She turned in her seat and looked out of the window in an effort to find something to distract her. It took a few moments for her gaze to focus on a strange apparition on the far side of the street.

She let out a little gasp of horror as she looked at a crouching man with no face. He had extremely bushy white sideburns, an oval head, but where his face should have been there was nothing. Just a blank, featureless expanse. The man turned his head to look back down the street from whence the bus had travelled. Olivia let out a relieved giggle as she realised her mistake. It was strange how the eyes could play tricks on the mind, she thought. The man's face was there, but his chin was so elongated and his nose so flat and unpronounced that it had looked like he had no face at all. Now that she could see him in profile, she actually thought he looked a bit like Great Uncle Bulgaria, the Womble. She also realised that he wasn't crouching; he really was that short. Perhaps, he *was* Great Uncle Bulgaria; the wombles were known to disguise themselves in order that they could venture into the wider world. She peered more intently at him in the hope of discovering wombles.

The man was very square of physique: a solid torso set upon stumpy legs. His arms appeared to jut out incongruously from his sides and his head was just as peculiar in shape. He wore an old-fashioned tweed longcoat and, judging by the glint of sunlight from his waist, she guessed that there was a pocket watch in his waistcoat. He was leaning heavily upon a gnarled and twisted lump of wood, which could have been a cudgel. It had a large, rounded tip, around which his right hand was clasped. The bus jarred suddenly as it started to move forward. It threw Olivia nearly off her seat and she scrabbled to right herself. She glanced back out of the window, questing the disappearing form of Great Uncle Bulgaria. She could just make him out. He appeared to have turned to face the traffic once more, faced towards her bus, in fact. He then tapped his walking stick upon the ground three times in quick succession before raising his arms up to the sky and yelling something to the heavens. Olivia half expected to see a bolt of lightning descend from the clouds and impact the head of the cudgel. The bus continued to move and Great Uncle Bulgaria disappeared from view. She turned back round to face the front of the bus and the woman opposite her.

Olivia let out a second gasp, her hand rising to her mouth to prevent a full-blown shriek erupting from it. The woman in front of her had a blank face. That is not to say her expression was blank, but to say that she had no face at all. Olivia continued to hold in her horror; she could feel her feet slipping upon the floor as she tried to move backwards further in her seat to escape the abomination in front of her. The woman opposite raised her head from her magazine, now resting in her lap and Olivia let forth a great gasp of relief followed by a slightly hysterical giggle. Of course, the woman had no face. That had been the top of her head. The woman was wearing a light tan hat that, when seen from above, was featureless. How stupid of her, thought Olivia– twice in as many minutes she had seen faceless people. Clearly her recent bouts of disturbed sleep, combined with her impulsive recklessness to pursue a more exciting life, was taking a toll on her nerves. Was there any doubt, given that her nerves were shredded because of the last couple of days dealing with her parents? With the last decade, in fact, of living with her mother and her troubles?

The woman opposite Olivia was looking at her with something akin to consternation upon her face and when next the bus drew to a halt the woman stood up and moved to another seat, away from Olivia. Olivia smiled after her apologetically, but the woman was not mollified and opted to move to the front of the bus, preferring to stand for the rest of her journey.

When Olivia arrived at the hospital, she still had three quarters of an hour before the end of visiting time. It was more than enough time to go and see her mum and then slip out and investigate the other patient. Her mother wasn't in her room, but in the common room. This was a major breakthrough, as Phyllis invariably remained in bed when at the unit for a stay, despite cajoling by the staff to give her a change of scenery. Phyllis was sat by the window staring blankly out of it. Try as she might, Olivia failed to gain any conversation or even acknowledgement of her presence from her mother. She sighed and sat back in her chair, she held her mother's hand between hers and just accepted the moment for what it was.

There was a crash from further back in the room. Olivia looked round hastily to see what had happened. One of the other patients was leaping up and down flapping at his crotch which appeared stained and steaming. As her vision expanded to take in more of the scene, she realised that a table with a tray of tea things had fallen over and the contents of the tea pot had fallen into the patient's lap. A commotion ensued, as other patients joined in, either whooping at the fun or screaming from the terror and the noise. Several attendants were on hand to calm the event down. Olivia sat back around as she felt a squeeze from her mother's hand and, looking at her face, she could see colour pouring into her cheeks and a small wisp of a smile break her lips. Phyllis turned to look at her daughter.

'Sorry, my love, I was distracted. That man is awful, you know. He's constantly picking on the other residents and he needed to be taught a lesson.' Phyllis' eyes moved up and around Olivia so that she could see the performance as it came to an end. Her smile didn't diminish, but her gaze came back to her daughter.

'Unfortunately, it has left me feeling extremely drained, my love. Could you help me back to my room, please?' Phyllis was attempting to stand, but Olivia could see how her legs trembled with the effort. She stood up and helped her mother back to her room.

Phyllis took her daughter up in a big embrace as Olivia helped her into bed, squeezing her so tightly that Olivia wondered why she had needed help in the first place. She felt the hug slacken and she moved to stand upright over the bed, only to see that her mother had fallen asleep. She smiled fondly down at her, bent once more and kissed her upon the forehead, before finally collecting her coat and bag and withdrawing from the room.

Olivia was ecstatic when she closed the door to her mother's room. Brief though their exchange had been, that was the most lucid she could remember her mother ever being. And the strength of that hug had been fierce. Phyllis had been a limp weakling for so long, Olivia had forgotten how steely her mother's grip could be. If she had been regaining her physical strength as well as her mental, then it was no wonder that Phyllis had managed to push her dad into the back door. She veritably skipped down the corridor to the residents' kitchen and the object of her alternative quest.

Arriving in the corridor, she was thankful to find it deserted. Although, as she moved into it, she could hear the sound of the kettle in the kitchen coming to the boil and muted conversation within. Not to be unexpected during visiting hours. She moved cautiously over to the patient's door and leaned into it, hoping to hear something telling from within. She leant one hand upon the door frame, ready to lift her foot off the ground and perform the act she had thought of while sitting with her mother earlier: to pretend she had stopped at the doorway to remove an obstruction from her shoe, should anyone inadvertently catch her apparently eavesdropping. She strained to hear anything from beyond the portal.

There was movement. She could hear a soft tread as someone moved about the room. She wondered if it might be the patient, finally awake and slippered. There was a click and faint hum and then a voice came out towards her.

'Thank you to the news team and now we continue with our list for this day, 'Regret' by New Order, which was new in this week...'

Three or four guitar riffs then wafted through the room to caress the wood of the door she was leaning up against. She was drawn in by it as the drums kicked in; she'd not heard it before and there was something melancholically soothing to it. A new voice, Simon's voice, suddenly cut over it.

'Thought you might like this. You always preferred this sort of music over anything else. Although, it has to be said, that if I was to listen to "the classics" I would prefer something by Puccini or maybe Tchaikovsky. They're what I would consider classics. Probably why they're described as classical.'

Olivia heard the footsteps pause, there was a scrape of a chair being dragged across linoleum and then a soft sigh. She imagined Simon sitting down next to the patient.

'Doctors say you're doing well, so's the baby. But still no sign of you coming out of this coma of yours. What are you doing, my love? What are you doing?' Simon's tone was most accusatory. 'I don't understand why you would think this could possibly help. It is damaging for you and surely it will only end up damaging your baby. We need you to snap out of it. I need you to snap out of it. Now!' Olivia heard Simon shout the last word and there was the sound of a fist slamming down on a table or dresser. Olivia nearly jumped out of her skin from the suddenness of it. She was amazed she hadn't fallen through the door in her jolt. She held her breath for fear her reaction might have alerted Simon to her presence.

'Hmm,' Simon continued, 'you are a one, my love. Stephen is all over the place, with you like this. If he's not careful he's going to get himself caught and it is definitely not the time for him to be taken back in. I fear he may be likely to do something rash, thinking he's protecting *the two of you. This is another reason I think it would be good if you came back to us now... you were the only one who could ever temper Stephen's outbursts. The two of you were a formidable team and that was before you fell in love with one another.'*

Olivia thought she heard Simon snort, *'Who could have imagined that love could so fundamentally and intrinsically change your talents? I have no way, no instruments to measure or calibrate for such an anomaly. It is immensely fascinating though. So, whaddya say, my love? Will you come back to us? Imagine the effect having a child between you would have? Unconditional love, I believe, is what parents have for their children – imagine the possibilities then, with a child. Just imagine.'*

Simon fell silent. Olivia was thankful that Simon had finally shut up. She really didn't like him, she had decided. She didn't like the way he talked to the patient. She didn't like his attitude towards her. He was condescending and downright rude. His accusations that it was her fault that she was in a coma were, well frankly, unhelpful at best. Olivia had no way of knowing how the patient had fallen into her coma, but once in one, as far as she was aware, it wasn't really just a matter of the conscious mind waking up. So his insinuation that she'd done it deliberately, merely to vex him, put Olivia's back up. If she ever actually got to meet Simon, she felt that she would be hard pressed not to slap him.

As Simon's silence continued, Olivia heard the kitchen door open and the conversation that had been muted before suddenly became much more audible. She hesitated for a moment as she saw a man and woman exiting the kitchen, both holding mugs. Then she remembered her plan and pretended to fumble with her shoe. She nodded at the man who had glanced her way, his head went back in acknowledgement and then he returned his attention to the woman who had stopped to continue their conversation. Olivia continued to fumble with her shoe, but then realised neither of them were moving on. She knew she couldn't maintain her pretence for long. She let out a sigh, placed her foot back on the floor and slowly made her way down the corridor, towards the double doors at the end.

She didn't risk a glance over her shoulder until she reached the doors. Then, surreptitiously, as she opened one of them, she looked back the way she had come. The man and woman were still conversing on the strain of caring for someone with a long-term mental health issue. Their progress out of the kitchen appeared to have halted completely, both sipping from their mugs. Their conversation was clearly riveting, as neither seemed willing to disengage and go back to their respective relatives. The woman's head shook as she disagreed with something the man had just said, and in doing so it brought her vision round to the end of the corridor, where Olivia was still pretending to exit. Not wishing to be recognised nor remembered for loitering, Olivia pushed hurriedly through the doors and stepped into the corridor beyond. As the doors shut, a wave of relief washed over her. She stood for a moment with her back pressed against the doors. Eventually, she walked further down the corridor until she came to a waiting area. She sat and waited. She checked her watch. She waited a full fifteen minutes and then headed back to the doors. She hoped that the two natterers would have moved on by now and she could return to her post. What she had been hearing from within had been peculiar and intriguing. Who was Simon to the patient? She had thought Stephen was the patient's partner, but Simon had kept referring to her as his love. Yet, she got the impression the baby belonged to Stephen. A coma patient with an incumbent baby, Olivia pondered, that surely couldn't be good. Could someone in a coma carry a baby to term? She had no idea. Maybe yes, but then how would she give birth? Caesarean perhaps?

ORDINARY WORLD

Olivia arrived at the doors and pushed the right-hand one ever so slightly in order that she could peek through the crack and determine if the coast was clear. But the door resolutely remained shut. *No, that's not right*, she thought, pushing against them again, both of them this time, trying to force them open. They remained barred. Olivia was overcome by frustration. She had started to get some really good information from that room. Not that she had any idea what any of it actually meant. But now she wasn't going to be able to find out any more. Visiting hours were over and there was no other way back onto the ward. She turned away from the doors, her earlier elation now dissipated by the frustration of simple mechanics.

'Dammit!' she said.

• • • •

It was early evening as Olivia walked briskly back home from the bus stop. The wind had picked up again and the sky was threatening the rain that had narrowly missed her earlier in the day. She was hurrying, in the vain hope of getting back without getting drenched. As she went, she considered her day. Olivia suddenly felt a wave of guilt wash over her as she realised that she was thinking about John and not her mother. Surely she should have been thinking about Mum, she thought. Not only was her mum the last person she had seen, but she was doing so much better, and yet... And yet it was John's face that she was remembering. It was his words to her that beat a steady pattern in her chest. It was John, she realised, she was excited to meet again tomorrow afternoon. The mixture of feelings now coursing through her made her feel dreadfully conflicted. Next week her mum could be home. Next week it was her birthday and she could possibly even have a small gathering at the house. Dad would obviously be a problem if Aunty Morag was there. But Aunty Morag would, of course, be there, because it would be Olivia's birthday. *Oh good*, she thought, Dad and Morag having a massive barny on her birthday with Mum there being almost well. How typical of Dad to ruin what could be a perfect day. Evie and Rhys would come, she knew, Rhys on the off-chance of watching a family brawl erupt. Evie, just because Evie was always there when she needed her. John's face slipped back into the forefront of her mind again. She wondered if he might be there as well? But why would he? They'd only met once. True, they'd kissed; well, if she was honest with herself, she had kissed him. And in effect it hadn't been more than a granny-style peck on the cheek. However, it was still the first time she had ever kissed a boy. And she was going to see him again tomorrow, under his invite no less. Although this was more of a business thing really, wasn't it? He was offering to help her with her search; it wasn't like it was a date or anything. She sighed, and then wondered if it was even appropriate for her to invite him to her house for her birthday? Probably not and he'd probably say no. But then, he had been the one angling for a kiss in the first place and he was the one that had invited her back to see him tomorrow. Plus, he had said all those lovely things about her. She remembered him saying that pretty girls never came calling on him. Not that she considered herself a pretty girl! And if he did come, he'd meet Evie and then that would be an end to it. Her brain started to melt into a maelstrom of melancholy at the thought of her initially conceived 'best birthday ever' turning into a hellish nightmare, as Dad and Aunty Morag had a fight with Rhys egging them on; Mum having a relapse and going catatonic – although her mind started to consider the possibility of a full delusional break and the carving knife sprung to mind with Dad sitting on the kitchen floor with a bleeding head. And then, just to wrap it all up, she'd find Evie and John in her bedroom snogging. She was just about to burst into tears as her mind completely rebelled against the possibility of her ever finding happiness, when the sound of booted feet broke the spell. They sounded as if they were hurrying up behind her. Like they had done before, only no one had been there. She jumped to the side of the pavement, up against the hedge of one of the houses in her street and swung round, brandishing her bag, bringing it round in order to batter the owner of the boots that had been stalking her.

'Fucking 'ell, Olivia, what the bloody hell?' yelled her father as he jumped back from the impending doom of a lady's bag to the face.

Olivia wilted. She was so relieved it was her dad. 'Jesus CHRIST, Dad! You scared me half to death!' With tears now freely running down her cheeks, she ran to her father and hugged him for dear life.

Reg could but stand there as the rain started to hammer down upon them. Both his hands were full of shopping bags and, even if he had been the type of father to embrace his daughter, he was incapable of it in this particular moment.

'Alright, there there,' he said, sounding uncomfortable with the sudden outlet of emotion from his daughter. 'What's this all about, then?'

Olivia carried on hugging her father, sweaty-smelling though he was. Bad-tempered, cantankerous bastard that he was, didn't stop her from wrapping her petite frame incongruously about his bulk. Eventually, her hair now plastered to the sides of her head because of the downpour, she slowly relinquished her grip on his waist.

'It's nothing,' she said.

'Nothing?' Reg said in disbelief. 'Nothing? There must be something to make you this bonkers, girl.'

'I saw Mum this afternoon and,' but she wasn't able to finish what she was going to say because of her father's interruption.

'Oh,' he said in a knowledgeable way. 'Well, that explains everything. You know your mother's bat shit crazy. So, of course, she's going to upset you. I don't know why you do this to yourself. You know you always get upset when you visit her at the ward. It's why I rarely bother these days, it's just not worth it.'

As he spoke, Reg started to walk up the street to their house, Olivia trailing behind him. She kept trying to say that Mum was doing really well, but he just kept going on about what a complete basket case she was.

When they were at the front door, Reg shoved a handful of bags at Olivia, who dutifully took them from him. He then delved into his pocket for the house keys, still berating his wife for the loony that she was.

'SHUT UP! SHUT UP, Dad! For fuck's sake, stopping having a go at Mum. She's doing really well. Whatever those stupid bloody drugs are that you've been giving her, they're doing the trick. She's getting better.'

Reg had opened the door, but now just stood in the porch, watching the rain bounce off his daughter's body as she tore into him.

'Now,' he began, but got no further as Olivia dropped the shopping in the doorway and ran inside. She ran to the bottom of the stairs in tears and started up them. She stopped halfway up and turned back to him.

'Don't be a bastard all your life, Dad!' she commanded of him and then fled to the sanctity of her bedroom.

Chapter 9

Sunday 11th April, 1993

Olivia woke later than she had done on previous days, but only because she was exhausted. Her dreams had been vivid and lurid again, so restful sleep had not come to her until the late hours of the night. She dressed quickly and made her way across the landing to the stairs. She had decided to go and see Evie; she needed to talk to her before seeing John. Evie was far more worldly and knowledgeable about boys and Olivia needed some guidance. She had just put her hand on the top of the bannister, foot hovering over the top step, when she heard her father's gruff tones ascend from the sitting room. He was on the phone again. He didn't seem to be pacing like the last time she eavesdropped on him; his voice was even and level and it made it easier for her to tune in to what was being said.

'Yes, it seems to have come on a lot faster than you estimated. Friday. Yes, that's right, Friday. I know, well it's obviously having some kind of effect given last night's little episode. Hmm. Couldn't say. Could go on like that for sixteen years for all I know... that's what's happened so far.' Reg's tone sounded disgruntled at this point.

'Yes,' he said with a heavy emphasis of unspoken sarcasm, 'I *know*. Yes, fine, but that said none of us want this dragging on for another sixteen years, do we? No, precisely. So, what are the suggestions then.'

There was a pause as Reg listened, Olivia suspected, to the suggestions.

'Really? Yes, I think trauma had been mentioned before. Will you arrange that or should I just get on with it? What? You'll sort it will you? Good. Make sure it happens then. Shall I keep up with the dosage? Really?' Reg sounded surprised, 'Increase it, you say? OK, well, you're the expert. We'll see what happens. But bear in mind the dangers I'm facing here,' he paused again as the other person obviously interrupted him, 'yes, and I got my head nearly caved in last time. God only knows what'll happen if *she's* anything like *her*. Younger, newer, probably pack a helluva punch. Yes, I know I'm being compensated above and beyond, but to be honest, most of the time I doubt I'm ever going to live to see my retirement. And I'll be wanting to make it an early retirement.' Reg paused again.

'Yes, I know you're older than me and also look forward to the end, but you've been in this from the very beginning, and as you originally said to me, this is your life. It ain't mine, or at least it certainly wasn't when you first came to me. I was happy doing what I was doing. This is my once in a lifetime gig and I'm getting to the end of it. So, make sure the trauma's a good 'un and let's get this thing expedited.'

Reg listened for several minutes to the voice on the other end before finally ending the call. Olivia moved back from the top of the stairs as quietly as she could, as she heard her father get up and move into the hallway. He disappeared into the kitchen, from where she then heard the sound of pots and pans being banged about. She took a deep breath before slowly walking down the stairs. She wasn't entirely certain what it was she had just heard her father talking about, but whatever it was she knew she didn't like the sound of it. She was fairly convinced it had something to do with her mother. All the more reason why what was said was not good. Upping dosages, trauma – sounded as though trauma was a deliberate necessity to be inflicted and it was being arranged for someone else to inflict it on her mother. This wasn't good, or sane, or rational. Why would her father be arranging for her mother to be traumatised? And yet, some of what he had said didn't seem to fit with this idea. She needed to talk with Evie and Rhys, if he was available, too. She moved more determinedly down the stairs and went into the kitchen, where she found her father with his shirt sleeves rolled up basting a chicken.

She stood in the doorway with her mouth open, whatever she had been about to say lost to the aether. What the hell was going on with her dad? He NEVER cooked.

'Ah, Olivia,' Reg said, looking up from the chicken, which now had his right hand stuffed up its bottom. 'Thought it might be nice to have a roast for lunch. It being Sunday and all. If you have any plans to see your friends, that's fine, just be home by one thirty. I'm hoping it'll all be serving about then.' He smiled at her in a manner most unbecoming, she felt. There was an eerie quality to it, as if he was trying to be someone else. It was almost as if he *was* someone else, pretending to be what he thought her dad should be like.

'OK, Dad,' she replied cautiously. What else could she say? She'd heard half of a conversation in which her dad seemed to be conspiring to do horrible things to her mother and he was acting completely out of character around her. Plus, there was her outburst last night with him; he had every right to be angry with her for the way she had spoken to him. Even though he deserved it for speaking that way about Mum, but then, he always spoke that way about Mum. So, she just didn't know. She needed her friends. 'I'll see you at one thirty then, bye.'

She left the kitchen; her dad muttered a goodbye as his hand went back into the chicken. She fled the house, not in fear, but in her urgency to get to Evie's and talk with her about what she had overheard. She hurried up the street away from the high street, over to where Evie's house lay on the other side of the park, which started at the other end of their road.

The weather was still blustery, but the rain had subsided in the night. Even so, her head was bent low to avoid the occasional drops of wet that seemed to be being carried by the wind and therefore she wasn't aware of the feet until she had bundled into them. She looked up and started to apologise. The middle-aged woman she had run into caused her to falter because of her appearance. The woman had an exaggerated, elongated face: oval in shape, but it looked like when it was being formed someone had grabbed both ends of the oval and pulled them until they had stretched to capacity. Atop this very long head, the woman's hair was silvery grey and textured just like a brillo pad. It was caught up in a severe bun, presumably, Olivia thought, because this was the only way for the wire to be kept in check. Her nose was long, sharp and beak-like, in keeping with her face. Her eyes were hollows in a wasteland of bone-white flesh, bloodshot and dark, the pupils dilated far beyond where they should be, squeezing the irises into minuscule tight thin rings around them. It was difficult to determine any colour in them, but a steely grey sprang to her mind. It was the woman's mouth that really forced Olivia to come to a grinding halt though; as it opened, she could see it forever expanding into an eternal abyss of hellish darkness, ringed around the lifeless lips by triangular teeth that glistened in the daylight. Olivia felt a sudden desire to scream, but was prevented from doing so by the woman, whose hand shot up and clamped like a vice over her mouth.

The woman spoke to Olivia in a harsh whisper, as her other hand came up and gripped her shoulder, preventing any thought of escape.

'You need to be careful, young lady,' Olivia nodded trying to utter an apology for running into her, but the woman continued, shaking her head as she did so, 'No. I mean you *need* to be careful, O-li-v-i-a.' The woman pronounced every syllable of her name precisely, extracting syllables where there usually weren't any, for heightened emphasis. How the hell did this woman know her name?

'Be *very* careful in whom you place your trust. Do I make myself abundantly clear, O-li-v-i-a?'

Olivia nodded her head, too terrified to speak, even if she could have done so through the hand clamped over her mouth.

'We can only do so much for you. You will have to learn to protect yourself, very quickly. We cannot be seen by *them*. It is too dangerous.'

The woman suddenly seemed to become aware of her predicament on the pavement, nervously looking all around herself. Slowly she withdrew her hand from Olivia's mouth as she turned to face her once more.

'Be careful whom you trust!'

The woman suddenly walked away leaving Olivia breathless, the smell of the woman's touch still upon her mouth. It reminded her of graveyards: moist air, damp dying flowers, old cut grass and fetid turned earth. She shivered and nearly threw up; bending over clutching her stomach, she retched. Tears budded in the corners of her eyes with the strain. She straightened up and looked over her shoulder to see where the woman had gone, but she had completely vanished. Olivia looked about the street; there were one or two late morning pedestrians coming out of the park entrance, well-dressed and presumably hurrying for church service, but none of them seemed to be paying her or her disturbing encounter any heed. She started to move away from the scene and hurried towards the sanctity of the park – the route to Evie's house and hoped-for sanctuary from all the weirdness that seemed to be starting to come her way. As she trotted in through the wrought iron gates of the park, she threw another glance over her shoulder. Her hackles had risen sharply as if someone had just walked over her grave and, looking back, she suddenly spotted the exceptionally tall man from the cut-through. He, too, had an exaggeratedly elongated face. He was standing several hundred yards up the street from the entrance, leaning on an umbrella next to a lamp post. He was watching her; he doffed his fedora in her direction and then turned smartly, heading away from the park, disappearing around a corner in less than a few strides.

Olivia ran.

・・・・

'**B**loody hell!' Evie exclaimed.
Olivia had told her a lot of what had happened in the last couple of days. Not all the details, but certainly a lot of it. Not least of all the part about her dad arranging an accident to befall her mum. 'And you've never seen this old woman before?'

Olivia shook her head and took another long sip from the tea that Evie's mum had made her. Evie shook her head in disbelief.

'And you saw the freak again, too? Do you think they're working together?' Evie suddenly let out a gasp, 'Huh! You don't think your dad meant for you to have the accident do you? I mean these two freakish people keep jumping on you... just you telling me that is traumatic enough, without actually experiencing it!'

Olivia shook her head again, she honestly had no idea, 'Why would Dad want me to have an accident? I mean, I don't understand why he'd want Mum to have one, but husbands and wives are often doing horrible things to one another, so at least that would make a kind of sense.'

Evie nodded, 'No, you're right, I think the freaks aren't connected with the intended accident. But it does seem strange that they're watching you, following you. But then you said the old woman gave you a warning. Perhaps she was warning you about the other freak.' Evie sat back into her pillows, shaking her head too. 'I really don't know. What if Rhys was right, y'know, about your dad being a hitman? Maybe he wasn't talking about your mum at all, maybe he was talking about his target.' Evie smiled a little with this insight; at least it took the focus off Phyllis.

'Target?' Olivia replied.

'Yes,' Evie started to sound sheepish as she explained, 'well, since Rhys mentioned it, I popped to the library yesterday and started reading up on famous hitmen. It seems they often talk about their intended victims as 'targets'.' She pursed her lips into a kind of smile and shrugged her shoulders when she received a disappointed and disapproving look from her friend. 'Sorry. Blame Rhys.'

'I will,' Olivia said.

Evie changed the subject, 'So you have a *boyfriend*.' She poked Olivia in the stomach with her forefinger.

Olivia immediately blushed and floundered to respond, 'I don't. No, I don't, I only met him yesterday. He's not a *boy*friend. He's just a boy who I met and we might become friends. But...'

Evie waited for her to continue, but nothing more was forthcoming. Olivia trailed off.

'But you'd like him to *become* your boyfriend? I don't see why not – he sounds perfect for you. Goofy, good-looking and you've already kissed him.' Olivia shied away at her friend's comments, but most of what she said was undeniable. 'So, what's next, babies or marriage?' She poked Olivia again as Olivia told her to shut up and took a swipe at her with a cushion.

'Oi, careful, I nearly spilled my tea, woman!' Evie reprimanded her friend. They both laughed, Evie's impression of Rhys had been spot on. Evie continued, becoming more serious and trying to give her woefully inexperienced friend some tips on how to corral a boy to her way of thinking.

When Olivia finally left Evie's, she was feeling a lot better about a lot of things. And she had some very useful tips on how she could approach John with a view to finding out more about him and his potential for boyfriend material. She went home, arriving just before 1.30 and headed into the kitchen, where she found her father laying the table.

'Good, you're here,' he glanced at the clock and nodded to himself, 'well, perhaps you could finish laying the table and I'll serve,' he said, dumping the handful of cutlery he had into the middle of the table. He went to the oven and removed the chicken for carving.

• • • •

Olivia felt the mood at the lunch table was strained. Not surprisingly really, this was the first time since she was twelve that they had actually sat down like this for a meal. Of course, there were often breakfasts, with Mum. But nothing so formal as this. Evening meals would invariably involve one of them, usually her, feeding Mum either at the table, if she was in a physical mood, or in her bed, while Dad sat and stuffed his food as quickly as possible so he could get to his room or the pub. It had been Mum's birthday, when Olivia had been twelve, when they had last all attempted a meal out together. It hadn't gone well. It started with her mum accusing the maître d' of being a spy; it really went downhill when she then accused the waitress of having an affair with her dad and the chef of poisoning her meal. They'd left shortly after that.

'Have some more stuffing, I made it from scratch... followed the recipe and everything.' Reg said to Olivia, thrusting the dish with the stuffing in it at her. She took it and spooned some out on to her plate, not that she'd finished the initial helping he had served her. She went to pass it back to him.

'No, you keep it,' he said.

'Not having any of your own stuffing, Dad? Isn't that a little suspect?' Olivia teased.

'Huh, what do you mean? No, no,' Reg sounded flustered, 'No, it's just stuffing gives me indigestion.'

Olivia was taken aback by his initial response and wondered if he was being defensive after her recent accusations towards him about Mum; she tried to clarify, to mollify. 'I only meant that saying, that if the chef doesn't eat his own food because he knows what went in it, then no one else should, cos it's poisoned or bad.' She realised even as she said it, it was the wrong thing to say. Too often Mum accused them of poisoning her, so it would obviously be a sensitive subject for Reg.

'Oh, don't you start,' he said his voice quivering. 'I'm not trying to poison you!' he added very defensively. 'It's indigestion, like I said. Don't have the fucking stuffing if you don't want it. I made it for you, but you don't have to eat it if you don't fucking want to!' He made to get up, but his thighs got stuck under the table and all he managed to do was knock over his beer bottle and the gravy jug. 'Fucking bollocks!'

Olivia got up and went to the sink to get a sponge. 'It's alright, Dad, I wasn't having a go. I was just trying to tease. Not a good idea, as it turned out. You stay put. I'll get you another beer.'

She tidied up, got Reg a second beer and patted her father affectionately on the shoulder. She shook her head as she went and sat down again. She had no idea who this man was any more. She gave him a tentative smile and forced a large mouthful of stuffing in. It seemed to mollify Reg and lunch continued in relative silence. Olivia cleared the table when they had finished, allowing her dad the opportunity to retreat to his room. It gave her time to consider further the overheard phone call and Evie's thoughts on it. Slowly her thoughts turned to this afternoon and her impending visit with John. She checked the time and decided that the last of the dishes would be fine for a soak. She parcelled the leftover food up and put it in the fridge, before going up to her room to change.

When she finally left the house, she was wearing an optimistic summer dress and cardie, as prompted by Evie. She had her coat to fend off the chill breeze and she cautiously made her way to the bus stop and the long wait for the Sunday service. As she went, she kept a close eye out for any freaks that might be stalking her, but she was thankful that none were evident. She was also thankful that the bus arrived on time. She settled on an individual seat and mentally prepared herself for her meeting with John.

Chapter 10

John had told Olivia to head around the side of the flats, go to the back and knock on the second window. The first was his bathroom, the second his kitchen-cum-sitting room. She dutifully did as he had requested and almost immediately she was answered by a curtain twitch. She saw a shadowy figure wave at her. He pointed back the way she had come; Olivia took this to mean for her to go back to the front door. She indicated as such and received a thumbs up, at which point the curtain fell back into place. Olivia went back to the portico, where John answered the door; he seemed slightly out of breath.

'Come in,' he ushered her through to his flat.

Olivia walked into a long and spacious sitting room which extended the full length of the apartment. Turning left on entry she could see the sitting room and off to her left, through a bar room style counter, the kitchen. Directly opposite the front door was another door, which was currently closed. The far end window opened out onto the expanse of lawn to the rear of the building, but she couldn't see this because the curtains were almost completely drawn shut. To the left of the window was a second doorway, which she guessed led to his bathroom. A third doorway led off from the right of the window in the adjacent wall, on the far side of the kitchen.

'Would you like a drink?' he asked.

'Sure,' she replied nodding her head and wondering where to put her coat once she had taken it off.

'I have wine,' he said matter-of-factly, 'girls like wine, I believe,' he smiled uncertainly, 'or cider, or...?'

'Cider,' Olivia leapt on this suggestion. Evie had warned her against heavy drinking and wine made her sleepy within seconds of imbibing it. Cider, though, she could drink till the cows came home.

He bade her sit as he went into the kitchen and got their drinks. He came back, sat next to her and handed her drink to her.

'So,' he hesitated and took a nervous sip of his beer. Olivia was starting to get the impression John didn't entertain girls in his flat very often. He shifted uncertainly upon the sofa, took another, slightly larger gulp of beer and then appeared to come to a resolution.

'Right, so, you would like me to help you find your landlord, then?'

'Well, you did offer,' she responded with a slight smile, clasping her as-yet-untouched glass.

'That I did, that I did. Well then, I'll just go and fire up the machinery and see what we can do about that.'

He stood up, hesitated as he considered what to do with his drink and then, with a slight shrug of his shoulders took it with him as he went through the door opposite the kitchen. He was in there for several minutes before finally returning, hastily stuffing what looked like a sock into his jeans pocket.

'Right, then, if you'd like to come this way, we'll see what we can find on your elusive landlord.' He smiled encouragingly at her and she rose to follow him to the next room.

She halted as he went in through the door, as she remembered something Evie had said to her. '*Don't, whatever you do go into his bedroom. All boys ever think about is* sex. *You go into his bedroom he's bound to take that as you wanting to have sex with him. Which is fine, if that's what you want.*' Evie had looked at Olivia at this point. Olivia seemed horrified at the prospect of sex and said as much. '*I'm not having sex with him! We're not even...*' she'd stopped abruptly at this point as she realised she was going to say, we're not even married. She knew how prudish this would sound to her worldly friend. It wasn't that she was prudish, merely that sex had never really been something she ever thought about. In fact, the only time it had really entered her head was when it had disturbed her thinking about her parents' sex life, or lack thereof.

'*Not even* married?' Evie had finished her sentence for her and stifled a giggle at her friend's expense.

Olivia addressed John as he walked into the next room, 'Is this your bedroom, John?'

'It is, yes,' he replied from within. There was a momentary silence and then he appeared in the doorway. 'Is that a problem?' he innocently enquired.

Olivia was on uncertain ground, 'I'm not sure. Only, we have only just met and yet here I am going into your bedroom. I want to make it perfectly clear I'm not having sex with you.' She blushed as she said this, feeling awkward at just using the word 'sex', let alone the turn the conversation had taken.

John appeared equally abashed, for he too started to blush, 'Farthest thing from my mind,'

Olivia looked at him and realised how true this statement probably was. She felt comforted by this and was about to advance into the room when John continued.

'Only all my equipment's in here and I was hoping you'd sit next to me while I looked as there may well be questions I'll need to ask of you.' He glanced behind him into his bedroom, 'I promise I'll keep my hands to myself. They're only needed for the keyboards and mouse.'

Truth be told, this sincere and honest statement left Olivia feeling both mollified and just a little disappointed. She wouldn't have minded if his hand had strayed a little bit. Touched her on the leg or the like, but then she had laid down firm boundaries and couldn't expect him to ignore them just because of a fleeting feeling on her part. She sighed to herself and then smiled at him. 'Good, then perhaps we should begin.'

Entering his bedroom was like entering another world. To the right of the doorway, nearly up against the far wall, was a large bed. Two thirds of the room was taken up by several desks set next to one another with monitors, keyboards, computer towers and other unknown equipment on them. And yet it was the bed that elicited her first comment:

'My, that's a big bed,' she said. Rhys' voice popped into her head, sounding like the wolf from Little Red Riding Hood, *all the better for having sex with you.* She inadvertently blushed profusely.

'Er, yes,' John said. Clearly it was not the comment he had expected as he blurted, 'I bought it with my ex, but never got rid of it as it's so comfortable.'

Rhys' voice came into Olivia's mind again and she was wishing they could get off the subject of John's bed. In an effort to distract them both from the bed, which did look very comfortable and seemed to be the only object that insisted on filling one's view, Olivia went and sat on a stool next to a swivel chair in front of the desks. John hovered uncertainly for a moment and then joined her, sitting in the swivel chair.

'Right then, so finding your chap shouldn't be that difficult. All we have to do is go to the HM Land Registry and type in the details. A few years ago we would have needed to go directly there, but the government departments have been scanning vast swathes of documents and uploading them into databases. Which for us techies has made life so much easier. Of course, usually this would take a few days and probably some money too. The government does like its opportunities of making an extra buck.'

John started typing on the keyboard in front of him. 'Right so John Fitzgerald Kennedy and what's your address?' he swivelled the chair around to face her.

Olivia gave him her address, 'Post code?'

'Oh,' Olivia faltered, she wasn't sure, she'd never really needed it before, 'er.' John waited patiently until Olivia suddenly let forth a muted shout and gave him a code. It seemed to do the trick.

'Well, here's a copy of your title deeds, and their records confirm John Fitzgerald Kennedy as the owner of your house.' He turned to her again, 'so when did you move in?' He turned back to the keyboard, poised to enter more data.

'About fifteen or so years ago,'

John swung round to face her, 'Really?' he sounded surprised; she said as much to him and he merely pointed out that, given her potential predicament, he had expected her to have lived there for no more than a year or two.

'Well, that's not a problem, if anything it might make things easier. If he's been registered as the owner for fifteen plus years, then we have a fixed point in time for him in the district. I'm going to do a quick search to find out if he's associated with any other properties on their database. It may take a few minutes. My equipment's pretty up to speed, but it's still not as good as the machines we use in work.'

John typed vigorously for a few moments, pausing on occasion and then flicking through with his mouse.

'Hm, interesting. Your landlord's quite the entrepreneur it would seem, at least in the housing market. Hmm,' the documents on his screen scrolled up more slowly as he took in the information. 'Interesting... he certainly likes your neck of the woods.'

Olivia looked at him, 'How so?'

'Well, it's not just your house he owns. There're five houses just on your side of the street. Yours is smack in the middle.'

'He owns number 64?'

John nodded as his forefinger clicked to continue scrolling.

'But that means he owns Audrey's house. That can't be, as I know it's hers. She's been there longer than we have.' She shook her head and leaned over to get a better look at the screen, placing her hand on John's thigh for support. He glanced at her and then her hand, she appeared not to notice and he returned his attention to the screen with a smile.

'Any other houses in our street?'

'Yes, three directly opposite and four more scattered the length of the road.' He looked over at her and she faced him. There was consternation on her face.

'Your records must be wrong. That would mean even the Burns' house is owned by him and I know they own their house.' She sounded adamant.

'The records aren't wrong,' John said matter-of-factly, 'and how certain can you be that your neighbours own their houses? Have you seen their title deeds?' his eyebrow rose in concert with his questions.

Olivia stuttered a response, 'Well, no obviously I haven't, but they talk about their homes and their houses. I... I just assumed, by the way they spoke about them that they owned them. Same as we did.'

'And yet you don't. And neither do they.' John returned to the screen as he let this sink in with Olivia. 'It does beg the questions though, why and how he owns all this property in such close proximity. His other properties are more scattered. He also has a dozen other properties throughout the UK in his name. Some of them look to me to be commercial, probably warehouses. Good. Right then. Let's see what else we can find out about him. Like where he might actually live now and who he voted for in the last election.'

'You can do that?' Olivia asked incredulously.

'*I* can; your average Joe on the street can't. But then, as I said yesterday, I'm good at this sort of thing, it's kinda what I do all day in work.'

John typed for a while, occasionally asking Olivia a seemingly innocuous question. Screen after screen of information scrolled past and most of it looked like gobbledygook to Olivia, until after nearly an hour John sat back in his chair and appeared to call a halt to the proceedings.

'Well, that was all very interesting.' He turned to face Olivia. 'Your landlord seems to be a very interesting person, for someone who doesn't exist.'

Olivia looked at him in disbelief, 'What do you mean, he doesn't exist?'

'Well, he has all the normal stuff to his name: bank accounts, electoral register, national insurance, even has yearly tax returns going back to well beyond those uploaded through the 'net to HMRC. And those are quite interesting in themselves because there's no mention of income from property lettings or sales.' He looked at her pointedly; it took Olivia a few seconds to understand the significance of his statement.

'Oh. But wouldn't he get in trouble with the tax office?'

'You'd think,' John replied, 'but it's possible he runs them through a company. In which case returns would be logged separately. And without a name I can't cross reference this theory with Companies House. But I'm sure given time I can find out. But that's not the really interesting thing about our Mr Kennedy.'

Olivia frowned, 'So what *is* the interesting thing about him, then?'

'Well, despite all this paperwork, it appears he doesn't actually exist. I found a birth certificate notification for him, although no passport; he even has a listing with the DVLA. But his fundamental paperwork is so pristine it flagged something with my professional inquisitiveness. I dug a little deeper, beyond what most officials would look for, beyond the obvious. And it's very clear that your John Fitzgerald Kennedy is a made-up person. I followed the birth certificate trail and discovered a death certificate for him for ten days after he was born. Doesn't that strike you as odd?'

'Well, yes, yes it does, if it's a real thing. But if he died ten days after he was born, how could he own my house? Or any of the other properties you say he owns?'

'Well, that's just it, isn't it, how could he? Because he's a made-up identity. Trouble is I can't determine right now if this is because he's a front for criminal activity or for something else, something more sinister.'

'What could be more sinister than something criminal?' Olivia was starting to get very worried. Especially as this made-up person owned the house she had lived in all her life. Evie and Rhys popped into her head with a look of *'told you so'* as they pointed at her dad.

Olivia paled and it wasn't lost on John. He misconstrued, 'It's fine, Olivia. I'll make sure you're safe. No one's going to be evicting you from your house any time soon. But I will need to do some more tracking. If it's criminal, I'll have to inform certain people who liaise with our office. If it's something worse, then I am honour bound to inform my office. As I said, it's kinda what I do.'

He placed a comforting hand on her knee, reciprocating her earlier contact. It sent a shiver through her, but in a pleasant way. Her eyes rose from her lap and looked past him to the other side of the room and she blushed as certain thoughts started to parade through her mind. John's other hand rested upon hers. He patted it and then turned back to his monitors.

'This may take a while and I'll need to concentrate. If you want to go and watch TV or something, have some food, whatever, help yourself.' Olivia detected a change in his temperament, he seemed to be very excited. Was this why he was so good at what he professed to do, because he got a thrill from it?

'No, that's alright, I'll stay,' she said. She wanted to find out more herself. Despite his assurances she was very worried, not least of all because she wondered if her friends had been correct all this time. Was her dad a hitman? Was all this down to him being part of a criminal organisation?

John went to work.

• • • •

'OK, I'm in,' he said. Olivia wasn't certain he was talking to her any more.

'Oh my,' he exclaimed after a couple of minutes, 'this network is fabulous. I've never seen anything quite like this before.'

He was typing all the while. Streams of code appeared on the screen in front of him, but none of it made any sense to Olivia.

'Blimey, this is active. Their defence grid is actively maintained. I'm going to need total silence, Olivia, and I'm going to need back-up.'

His typing became frenetic; the speed at which his hands travelled across the keyboard was truly phenomenal. He was muttering all the while, giving her a running commentary about things she had no comprehension of.

'Going to have to engage some bulldogs to back me up.'

'Need to make sure they can't track me or trace me back to this terminal. Need to employ anti-trackers. Bloody hell, this guy's good. No, no, there it is. Quick, dash down here, block him. Block him again, side step and through. Got you! Catch me if you can.'

'Fucking hell, he caught up with me, he is good. No, wait. He's not alone. That's not right, surely not. Tandem active? Block. Block. Backdoor. Block. Nope, to be this good they must be running a team. I can't do a team, I need reinforcements.'

All of a sudden, John slid his chair round to a second monitor and started typing on a second keyboard. As he did so, he leaned back to the first, punched some numbers in with his left hand and then flicked three switches on a box above the first monitor. 'Right, let's see how you deal with that, while I call in the cavalry.'

Turning his full attention to the second keyboard he pulled on a headset and started to talk into it.

'Hi, Alex? Good you're in work, excellent. Can I ask a wee favour of you? Marvellous, just running a blockade and need some back-up. Yes, I'm at home. No, nothing like that, just doing a favour for a friend. Yes. Yes, as it happens, she is a girl. Thank you, Alex, much appreciated.

'Are you locked into my pathway? Good, no, I see you. Good stuff. Right, we're going to need a lot of anti here, they've got a team running against me and they're fucking good. Never seen anything quite like it before. Yes, you've spotted them. Yup, now you're getting it. Yes, they're good, aren't they? Hmm, hadn't thought of that. Nope, not NSA, definitely homegrown, but where I've no idea. Right. We're nearly into their central core, can you bring up a battery of bulldogs. We need to keep them occupied while we deploy Fluffy.

'Oh, yes, that's right you don't know about Fluffy. Er, are you next to my workstation?'

There was a pause, 'Good man. Right, bring up my personal folders. No, I'm logging you in now. Right, got my folders? Good. Look for Pendragon. Open it, inside you'll find a file called Fluffy. Yup, you got it, she's a dragon. New kind, one I've been working on for the brass. Right, well we'll just say we took her for a test run and by the looks of this network and its defences it's going to be a doozy of a tester. Right, on my mark, upload her.'

There was another cessation in the commentary and the chatter John was having with Alex. All the while John was typing vigorously on both keyboards, flicking switches and sweating profusely, Olivia noticed. Under his breath in the pause, she distinctly heard him swearing.

'Right, Alex, three... two... one... Mark!'

Everything froze for a second and then John was typing again. 'Good man, well done. Fluffy's in. Now we just need to keep them distracted for a couple of minutes. You run counter, I'll run point.'

John continued to type. How his fingers, his hands hadn't seized by now with all the activity Olivia would never know. She had no idea what was really happening in the cyber world that John seemed to be living in, but she still felt the excitement – it washed over her in waves. The danger. The tension. The potential catastrophe that was impending if one of his keystrokes was misplaced. She realised she was starting to feel faint because she kept holding her breath.

'Got it. Extracting Fluffy now, getting her to bomb her way out. That should cause some issue for pursuit.

'Once she's clear I'm going to dump her in the Pacific. You cut the lifeline and then bug out. I'll take it from there. Thanks a bunch, mate, I couldn't have done it without you.' John's clipped, public-school accent became very clear in these moments. 'You're a star. And if it all goes tits up you were never there. If not, I'll give credit where credit's due. Cool, catch you on the flip side. Right, we're almost at zero mark.

'And you're... gone!'

Olivia thought that was it and she started to breathe normally again. But John was still typing, as fast if not faster than he had been moments before. Was it because he was now running a solo mission?

'Right. Lifeline's down, let's 'chute you into the Philippines. Now over to Australia. Cut that lifeline. And we're *not* out? Fuck me, they're still pursuing. OK, Fluffy we're not done yet.

'Olivia!' he almost shouted at her, catching her completely unawares, 'give me a country!'

'Er... Monaco?'

'Excellent. Fab choice, beautiful girl.' He typed.

'Right, three. Lifeline cut, over to Azerbaijan. Lifeline cut. Olivia?'

'Tunisia,' she said instinctively. She'd always wanted to go to Tunisia, the adverts on TV always looked like paradise.

'Fantastic! Always wanted to go to Tunisia, looks like paradise.' John said. 'Lifeline cut. Where we at? Four? And they're still on us. I don't believe it. They're good, I'll give them that. OK, Bolivia.

'Lifeline cut and they're still there, bastards! Mexico.

'Lifeline cut. One more should do it, no one's that good. Six, must be government.

'No, surely not.' John was sounding out of breath; there was sweat pouring off his head, which he intermittently attempted to swipe away with his forearm. 'Olivia?'

'England?'

'YES! England. Great, I nearly forgot. Seven. Lifeline cut. And they're still with me. I don't believe it. No one's that instinctive. How the fuck are they still in the game? Another one Olivia!'

'Iceland?' she was breathless herself and running rapidly out of ideas. She needed to keep ahead of the game if she was to help John in his monumental marathon against these unseen enemies. 'Congo,' she almost shouted it at him.

'Read my mind,' he said, as he typed. 'Nine and they're failing. About fucking time, I never thought I'd get away. Scrubbers in. Antis in. Bulldogs, release the hounds of war! Fuck yeah. Ten equals Tenerife. And... we're... out!'

John stopped typing for a second. Olivia held her breath – was that the end of the roller coaster or not? It was not it seemed, he started to type again, although more slowly than he had been.

ORDINARY WORLD

'Ten, fuck me, ten. Right, trail teasers to tail off. New Zealand. Ireland. USA. Peru. Germany. Russia. And we're dead in the water. Well done, Fluffy, you're safe. Well done, me. And fucking well done, Olivia!'

John stopped typing. He turned his chair round to face Olivia. He leaned forward, placing his hands on the stool, either side of her thighs. His shirt had dark stains of sweat on it. Sweat was still dripping from his head, which he flicked away distractedly as he spoke to her. His entire face was flushed and, had she not witnessed the fact that he'd been sat in a chair for the last hour, she would have been convinced he had just run a marathon.

'Ten countries before I lost probable pursuit. That's unheard of, young lady.'

He stared intently into her eyes.

'Ten. Baseline hackers and corporations can probably pursue up to four countries. Governments, you're looking at maybe six. Organisations like mine and those in other countries, between seven and eight. No one, and I mean no one, can track past eight, even with state-of-the-art equipment. It's not possible. The computations are just too vast for the machines. The only way is if your team is made up of instinctively intuitive people and there aren't any teams anywhere in the world like that, because the permutations to gather a team like that are impossible. It is just not possible to do that. Maybe in a hundred years it would be possible but right now, it's *not* possible! They pursued me for TEN countries, TEN! Im fucking-possible! And I laid down six trail teasers in case of forensic pursuit. I shouldn't have needed more than two. And I don't even know if six is enough.'

John's expression was scaring Olivia. He looked very tense, very angry, just a little bit scared and totally wired. Olivia realised she was sat there shaking her head. John took in a long breath, which he held for several seconds before exhaling.

JACK T CANIS

'OK, Olivia Buchanan. Just who the fucking hell are you?'

Chapter 11

Olivia was still coming to terms with the most amazing roller coaster ride of her life. One that had occurred in the bedroom of a young man and hadn't involved sex. To suddenly be confronted by that young man turning accusatorially to face her and doubt her identity was unnerving and hurtful. Her elation was blown away and she started to stand in order to leave, but found his hand upon her knee once more and it didn't have the same warm, comforting quality to it that it had had moments before. This was an authoritarian hand with a stony grip that commanded her to remain seated.

'No,' John said with an edge to his voice, 'you're not leaving until I know who you really are. I've just invaded an ultra-secure organisation on your behalf and, ignoring the basic laws of the various lands I passed through, I want to know if I've just committed treason for you. So, given that it's not just my job on the line here, but also very probably my freedom, you're going to answer some questions.'

The look on John's face left no room for discussion and Olivia sat back on the stool. She was feeling very scared now. The idea of treason, in her mind, suggested being taken out to the centre of London and publicly having her head removed from her shoulders. Decapitation seemed to be an ongoing theme in her psyche in the last few days.

'OK,' she said hesitantly, 'what do you want to know?'

She could feel her eyes stinging as tears tried to break free. Opposite her, John wiped his flushed face free of sweat with a flannel he pulled from beside his keyboard.

'First things first,' he said, turning back to that keyboard. He pulled up a new screen and entered some digits into it. 'Right, your name.'

'You know my name,' she said automatically. He looked round at her.

'So, we're going with Olivia Buchanan, then.' He turned and typed, his face still stern, distrusting. 'Any middle names?'

'No,' Olivia said quietly, looking down at where her hands were wringing the blood from her knuckles on the top of her knee.

'Address, we'll take from the title deed.'

Olivia responded automatically before John could look at the deed, '66, Fenella Fields.'

'OK, thank you. Date of birth?'

'Seventeenth April 1976.'

As he typed John did some mental calculations, then he stopped typing and turned back to her, 'You're only sixteen?' he said incredulously.

'I'll be seventeen at the end of the week,' she replied defensively. This almost elicited a smile from John.

'I thought you were older.' Did she detect a slight flush in his already overheated cheek? 'Happy birthday for the end of the week,' he concluded.

'National insurance number?'

Olivia had to think for a moment, then told him. John pushed a red button on the second keyboard.

'Hi, Alex? Good, you're still there. Yes, it was an exciting run. Yes, Fluffy excelled, she's safe and uploading as we speak. No, no idea. Er, can you run a couple of personnel checks for me, please? Yes, standard stuff. Thanks.'

He turned back to Olivia, 'What school do you go to?'

Again, Olivia told him what he required. 'OK, Alex, sending a file to you now.'

He pushed return and the file from the screen flickered for a moment. There was an uncomfortable silence that started to extend into an abyss of eternity for Olivia. Her stomach was knotted and she could feel the tears rolling unbidden down her cheeks. Her head came up as she heard John talk to Alex again; she swiftly wiped the tears away, fearing John might see her crying.

'Cheers, Alex. Do you have a photo?'

There was another pause then an icon started to blink on the bottom of John's screen. He clicked on it and a school photo of Olivia popped onto it. It wasn't a very flattering picture of her, but it was still her. John sat back in his chair and pinched his nose a few times in thought.

'Thanks, Alex, no, stay on the line. I have at least one more to run by you.'

John turned to face Olivia. 'Well, Olivia, it looks like you may well be who you say you are. Alex couldn't find any back doors or hidden lines of information tallying with you. Everything you gave me checked out. So,' he looked at her and saw her huddled down into a tight ball of anxiety upon her stool.

He sighed and his tone changed slightly, 'I'm sorry if I came across a bit harsh there. Only, from my side of things, I've just run a gauntlet with something that shouldn't exist. People and tech that are still to be considered science fiction, y'know, like my Fangjack. Out there that was mortal danger, not just for my programs but for my continued existence within the realms that I work. My bosses run this country. If I just did something to jeopardise that, then I could well just disappear. So, I hope you understand why I came across fierce; I was panicked. I was scared. But I am honestly sorry for making you that scared as well.'

He took her hands in his and tried to smile up at her. She responded slowly. She appreciated his apology, but she still resented the fact that he had doubted her. She tried to pull her hands out from his, but he held firm, squeezing them. She relented and left her hands in his. His smile was infectious, and there was still that little twinkle in the corner of his eyes that so reminded her of Rhys' roguish smile. Gradually she found herself acquiescing and she started to smile back. The moment was broken when John tensed slightly and spoke into his headset.

'Yes, Alex, I'm still here,' he sighed, letting go of Olivia's hands and returning his attention to the keyboard and monitor. 'OK, Olivia. Let's have a look at your parents. What are their names?'

Olivia shuffled her stool a bit closer to John; she suddenly missed the warmth of his contact. She needed comfort and having her leg pressed against his would have to do for now. Her voice cracked as she tried to speak. She took a sip of cider and then tried again.

'Phyllis and Reg Buchanan.'

'Good, Reg? Is that short for Reginald? And do either of them have middle names?'

'Yes and yes. Phyllis Anne and Reginald Arthur, although Dad never uses Arthur, doesn't like it for some reason.' John smiled at her and typed. 'OK, don't suppose you happen to know either of their national insurance numbers, do you?'

She knew her mum's better than she knew her own, because of all the forms she'd had to fill in over the years for her care. She rattled it off for him. As for her father though, she didn't.

'Date of birth for both, please.'

'Oh,' Olivia paused, again this was not a problem for her mother and she dutifully gave it, but her dad, she wasn't so sure when he was born. 'Er, I know Dad's birthday is the fifteenth of August, but I don't know the year. He's, oh I don't really know how old he is,' she suddenly realised. Of course, in their family no one ever really celebrated birthdays, they were usually quite muted affairs, because of Mum. John patted her hands, 'No worries, I have enough for your mother to draw up some details and I can always cross reference your father from them.'

He pushed a button and again the screen flickered. A few moments passed and then a stream of files downloaded into the bottom of his screen, pouring into a basket for Phyllis Anne Buchanan. 'Blimey,' John said. He scanned several of the files.

'Oh, Olivia.' He said with real compassion pouring out.

He turned to her, a tear in his eye, 'Olivia, I'm so sorry, I had no idea. You poor girl.'

He stood up and moved closer to her, giving her an immense hug. His arms wrapped her up completely and her head nuzzled into his chest. The wash of warmth and love that she felt from him caused a stopper in her mind to release and she suddenly found herself crying uncontrollably. It was such an immense relief. So many conflicting emotions, too many of them fear-related in the last few days; all the turmoil and heartache of years of caring for Mum, it all just came out. Out into John's arms.

Eventually it passed; she let out one or two small sobs and then pulled back from him. John looked down at her, worry and concern etched into his open features. He took up the sleeve of his shirt in the fist of one hand and dabbed away the remaining tears.

'Not now, Alex,' he said quietly into his headset.

Olivia smiled up at him, a sense of overwhelming relief consuming her. He looked down at her and his smile gradually broadened to split his entire face into a massive grin, that crinkled his eyes and made them sparkle. Neither of them were entirely certain how it went from that exchange of smiles to their lips locked firmly to one another. The hand John had been using to dab away her tears released his sleeve and cupped the side of her face. The kiss was enduring. There was a deep yearning inside Olivia with the connection of their lips and she threw herself entirely into the moment.

Olivia was lost. Overwhelmed by a tsunami of emotions so intense that she felt like she was drowning. She knew not all of the emotions in the torrent were hers. Somehow, John's passion and heartfelt compassion for her were amplified, pouring into her through their kiss. She was lost in the swell of a storm-tossed ocean. Drowning in their combined emotions. She gave in completely.

• • • •

Slowly she became aware of the babble in John's earpiece as Alex wanted to know what was going on and if his talents were still needed. They broke slowly from the embrace, still both smiling, and then John acknowledged Alex with a laugh.

'Yes Alex, you're still needed. I'm sending you another file... can you run a check on the man for me, please? Cheers.'

They parted completely from the embrace, although John's hand remained on Olivia's cheek and she still clung to his side with hers. John moved and sat back down, Olivia went to sit on the stool, but then found John pulling her onto his lap. She didn't object. With his arms around her, he was still capable of typing and it gave her the chance to look down into his face, stroking it affectionately and occasionally kissing him.

The incoming icon started to flash once more and John clicked on it. He perused the information that he was receiving and then Olivia felt his whole body tense as he straightened in his chair and leaned forward to the screen. She turned to look at it too.

'What is it?' she asked, previous concern flowing back into her soul.

'Well, it seems a bit odd. Reg is definitely here, and yet,' he paused, Olivia waited, wondering if it was a dramatic pause or whether he was trying to find a kind way to put something horrible to her.

'And yet, what?' she finally prompted. He continued to look at the screen, flicking between documents and reports. Finally, he sat back and looked at her. He put his arms round her small waist, as if to catch her if she fell from what he might say.

'And yet, he doesn't seem to be here from about fifteen years ago.'

'What does that mean?'

'It means Reginald Arthur Buchanan was born on the 15th August fifteen years ago, having been someone else prior to that. But who that someone else was, I currently have no idea.'

His face had taken on that stern quality that she didn't like. Her hand went automatically to it to try and smooth the sternness away. He didn't object, instead turning his lips to her hand and kissing it. Her expression took on a sternness of its own as she processed the news. Evie and Rhys saying 'I told you so' came back to mind.

'There must be a reason why he changed his name. People change their names for any number of reasons, all of which stem from hiding who they used to be. He might have done something really heinous in his past and is hiding from it for shame. Or hiding from it to prevent arrest. He could have committed fraud and be hiding on his ill-gotten gains, although most people who do that usually flee the country, rather than set up family in the West Midlands. He could be hiding because of a need for protection. Perhaps he was a grass and the police set him up with a new identity, although they usually flag these files with certain clues for us to find – not on purpose, you understand, just that they make mistakes and we know what we're looking for. I can't do anything more on it from here at the moment, though. I'll either need to go into the office and do it, or get Alex doing a check until I do.'

He spoke into the headset and Alex dutifully started the deeper scan of Reginald Arthur Buchanan. 'Actually, Alex can you get Patricia on the line for me? I need to report the organisation to her. No, I'll take any flack until I know it's clear, then I'll name drop you.' There was a wry smile on his face as he said this.

Olivia remained upon his lap, as John made a formal call to what she presumed was one of his bosses. He informed Patricia that he had been doing some home testing on the new Dragon program and that, whilst running some basic routine sub searches, it had picked up an anomaly and pursued it. He said the Dragon had performed well beyond expectation, but that it had also flagged this organisation to him. He was sending her a file now via the encryption line. Patricia seemed satisfied with his explanation and told him to leave it with her. He hoped this would be an end to it, but as he expressed to Olivia, in his line of work it probably wasn't.

Fluffy was still uploading information and would be for another few hours. There was little more that could be done on this front, the same with the questions about Reg. He powered down his machines and then turned his full attention to Olivia, who was still sat on his lap. She was disinclined to move; he wasn't inclined to move her. They looked at one another for several minutes, just looking - eyes caressing the surfaces of their souls. Olivia's heart skipped in her chest and she leaned down, brushing her lips against his. His eyes closed and he pressed his mouth to hers. Olivia heard the roaring of dark ocean waves rolling in the back of her mind. She felt the swell lift her up and once more she let herself go. The broiling black clouds that enshrouded the ocean of her mind split asunder, revealing the heavenly beauty of a star-filled void.

• • • •

They lay in each other's arms, entwined on the bed, under a sheet. They were naked. Olivia's head rested upon his chest. She stroked his arm and he caressed the small of her back. She wasn't quite certain how it had happened... one minute they were sat kissing in his chair, the next he had stood up and was carrying her over to the bed. After that, it was just a blur of intense sensations: passion, a moment of exquisite pain, then a shooting stab through her brain. There were stars. A brilliant flash, like a flare bursting in the night sky. She had noted, in that moment, a look of concern from John and then they had dissolved into one another.

As she lay there in his arms, she imagined the warm fuzziness of it all, but at the heart of it there was still that moment of pain. It didn't really matter. She had all too willingly succumbed and now she was lying in a man's bed. Naked. Having had sex with him, and on a Sunday evening no less! She wanted to feel those sensations again; they were apocalyptic in her mind and in her body. She sat up, running her hand down his chest to his waist and below the sheet. He gasped and smiled, his own hand reaching up to cup her breast, the other moving to her buttocks and pulling her onto him. They made love again. It was slower this time, the ardent passion having ebbed. Now it was an experience of getting to know each other on a far more intimate level than the previous urgent need for satisfaction. Olivia's mind danced and disappeared into a world of imagination. Sparkles of light danced in her vision and she let forth a scream of such delight that it rattled the monitors on their stands.

• • • •

'I'm not sure what to do. About you, I mean,' John said to Olivia. She looked at him in surprise.

'I think it's a bit late now, isn't it? You seem to have done quite a lot with me this afternoon,' she smiled coquettishly.

John snorted, 'Ain't that the truth, but in part it's this afternoon that concerns me.'

Olivia gave her best not-surprised, quizzical look.

'Knowing what we now know about your dad, I don't know how safe it is for you to go home,' he looked genuinely concerned.

'I've lived with him for nearly seventeen years and he hasn't done me any harm...' she paused. That wasn't really true and she could see from John's expression he was reading her body language and coming to a similar conclusion, that this was a lie. 'Well, a little harm, then, but he's my dad and it still stands that I should go home. It'll be suspicious if I just don't go back.'

'I suppose, but I'm still not happy about the idea'

'Thank you,' her face beamed and she nuzzled into him. 'And you were right about one thing.'

'Really? What was that?'

'This bed really is comfortable.'

He smiled, 'Don't change the subject, I'm serious. I'm concerned about your safety,' he pressed his fingers onto her lips forestalling an interjection, 'but I accept that you feel you need to maintain a sense of normality. So, if you're going home, then I'll take you home. And whenever possible I'll be there to give you a lift.'

Olivia was taken aback by his expression of gallantry and then her brow furrowed as another thought struck her, 'This wouldn't just be an excuse to see me more often, would it?'

He held up his hands in surrender, 'Dammit! You're a smart one, you've seen right through my cunning plan.'

Olivia slapped his shoulder, 'Don't tease me!'

He chuckled, 'Yes, it may be true that this way I can get to see you more often, *but* it does also mean I can keep you safe when you're out and about. Ensure you get home, even if I think that might be the most dangerous place you could be, frankly.'

He drew in a deep breath before continuing, 'I'm also going to spend a bit of time looking more into both your dad and JFK, see what's really going on there and whether they're connected in some way. It would make sense that they were connected, given that neither of them really exist – they're both fake identities. I'm just hoping your dad's original identity was nothing to do with organised crime.'

ORDINARY WORLD

Olivia felt her heart flutter at the thought, a flutter that was exacerbated by John's concerned look.

'As a final precaution, I think I'll get a copy of my flat key cut so you can get in should you need a safe house to flee to and I'm not about, for whatever reason. Here would be best for you as no one else knows about it. But if you can't get here, is there anywhere else you can hide out? A friend?'

Olivia considered her options for a moment, obviously there was Evie, but Dad would know to go there in a trice. Aunty Morag's was where she normally went when she had to escape Dad and his vile behaviour.

'Most likely Aunty Morag,'

'Two women are no match for Reg if he's as brutal as you've made out,' John started to say, but Olivia cut him short.

'Oh, have no fear, Aunty Morag is most formidable and Dad is terrified of her. No clue as to why, but I know she has a power over him. I'll be perfectly safe with my aunt.'

John still didn't look convinced, but Olivia was getting bored of all this serious talk. She wanted some more fun before she really did have to go back home. She placed her hand over his mouth.

'Enough! I think it's time for us to take your bed for another spin.'

And with that she leapt upon him.

Chapter 12

John dropped Olivia off at her house late evening. Her summer dress, delightful though it was, was highly unsuitable for riding pillion on a superbike. John had given her a selection of hand-me-down leathers, which he said suited her. On the ride over to the house, Olivia had clung tightly to John's midriff. She was quite nervous of being on the bike, fearful that it would fall over at any moment with the two of them trapped under it. But John's confidence and then the actual journey changed her mind. She could understand John's passion for his bike – it was so exhilarating. She was loath to dismount when they finally arrived. It was snug clinging to his back and she was enjoying gripping onto him. It kept flooding her mind with recent memories of clinging onto him at his flat. That inimitable closeness with him inside her. She sighed when he patted her clasped hands, indicating it was time to dismount. She swung off and then stood next to him as she fiddled with the strap on her helmet, eventually letting her hands drop away in resignation that she was never going to be able to get the damned thing off. John removed his gloves and then lifted his helmet off, smiling at her, laughing at her. She slapped him on the shoulder,

'It's not funny!' she said stamping her foot on the pavement like a petulant toddler. John's expression turned to a fake frown, even though he was clearly still laughing at her.

'It is kind of funny from where I'm sat,' he replied. She slapped his armoured shoulder again. 'Come here, my pretty wee thing and I'll have it off you in a jiffy.'

Olivia leaned down and he unclipped her helmet. 'The clip's easier if you haven't got your gloves on,' he said smiling at her as she tossed her head about, loosening her hair that had flattened inside the helmet. 'If I take your lid, you might as well hang on to the leathers for now. They may come in handy when I pick you up tomorrow.'

Olivia noted how commanding he suddenly seemed to be, taking charge of her life. She quite liked it when she thought about it later. Someone was actually there for her and looking out for her; it was something of a novelty, just as long as it didn't become overbearing.

'And what makes you think you'll be picking me up tomorrow? I have school, y'know?'

'And I have work in the morning. But I thought we should meet up in the afternoon again. I'll pick you up from school and we'll go back to my flat. Wouldn't you want to do that?' he asked. She thought he looked crestfallen at the idea that she wouldn't want to spend as much time with him as possible.

'Yes,' she said, 'I would like to do that. Would we be spending all our time at your flat in your very comfortable bed?' her head tilted knowingly as she said this. She saw him blush under the lamp light.

'There are other things that we could do there, other than spend time in my bed. Although, I'm not adverse to the idea of spending the afternoon in bed,' he looked up at her, perhaps trying to gauge her reaction to this suggestion.

She couldn't help smiling at him. Oh, it had been glorious, especially the second time. She felt a knotting in the pit of her stomach near her pelvis and a sharp stab ran through from the back of her head into her left eyeball. That first time had been mixed though. A real moment of pleasure-pain. She rubbed at her eye with a gloved finger, hoping the pressure would alleviate the pain.

'What other things? And yes, I could be tempted to your bed... it is very comfortable after all.'

His fake frown returned for a moment and then she noted the expression settled into a more serious one, 'Well, not that I'm wholly keen on pursuing it, because we have no idea where it's going to lead us, but there is the matter of your father and whatever information Fluffy spews out.' He took her other hand in his as he said this.

'Yes,' she became serious as well, 'yes, there is that, isn't there? We could be working on that, I s'pose. Or we could avoid it altogether and just lie in bed.'

'Both options are viable,' he said with a slight crease of his lips, his eyes twinkling in the orangey light from the street lamp. She knew which of those options he preferred and, truth be told, she agreed with him on this. She wished she could go back to his flat right now and just curl up in a ball in his bed, with him wrapped around her. She sighed, feeling a rush of melancholy swamping her. Her heart ached at the thought of him driving away without her.

John obviously detected a drop in her mood as he kicked the stand on his bike and dismounted. He moved over to her and took her up in his arms, and there was a rather comical accompaniment of creaking leathers as he embraced her. His hand came up and brushed stray strands of hair from her face and he leaned down and kissed her softly on the lips. Olivia was aflood with emotion when he did this. A warmth burst in her womb and flowed down to her loins, her neck tingled and she felt the hairs on the back of her neck stand on end. Her mind reeled, filling her head with wave after wave of crashing light. Christ alive! His simple touch made her feel like a goddess. She pressed up into the kiss, wrapping her arms around him once more. She clung on for dear life, never wanting the moment to end. But, of course, it did. There was a lingering moment as their lips started to part, when she quested them feverishly once more and he relented, letting the kiss prolong. Olivia wished they were back in his bed; she so desperately wanted to feel him inside her again. And to think, an hour before they had joined together, she had been adamant that she wasn't going to have sex with him, ever.

The moment ended, John finally withdrew and she was left yearning his warmth, his protection, his soul. He stroked her face once more.

'I'll pick you up from school tomorrow, so you'll need to take your new leathers with you. I'll bring the lid,' he said lifting up the helmet he had removed from her a few minutes earlier. 'Then we can go back to mine, have some dinner, perhaps, and just do whatever it is you need to do.' Olivia nodded.

'We will need to look into your dad further. I will have some information from Fluffy by the early hours of tomorrow morning – her upload should be finishing about then. And I also think it might be best if I can spend as much time with you as possible, at least for now, until we determine how safe you are, given what we know about the man who owns your house, the organisation he's with and the missing past of your dad.'

Once again John looked stern and concerned. Olivia wasn't worried though; she now had a knight to protect her from all the ails of the world and, she realised, she also had a lover in that knight. It was the perfect tale, like the ones she used to read when she was younger.

'And what about after that?' she asked.

'After what?'

'After tomorrow afternoon?' she was fearful again that they would undoubtedly have to part company.

'Unfortunately, Tuesday I'm in work all day. There are a lot of briefings and whatnot, plus that should probably be enough time for the shit to have hit the fan over my little escapade earlier. I could be in for a bit of a roasting, so I definitely hope Fluffy has come up with something useful… it might be what'll save my bacon!'

'So, I won't see you Tuesday?' she sounded plaintive.

'No, sadly not. Will you be alright? I am worried, knowing what we do, that things might not be as safe as they once were for you. But you will have my key by then, so you can always come to mine if you're feeling unsafe.'

'Oh, I'll be fine on that front – Dad will just be Dad, after all. I doubt he'll suddenly turn into an axe-wielding maniac overnight, no matter what we know. And I need to make sure the house is set for Mum's return from hospital. She should be getting out Thursday or Friday. And then, oh!' she suddenly remembered Saturday. Saturday was her birthday. Saturday was the day that she hoped she might have the birthday of her dreams.

'Oh?' again the sound of concern in his voice.

'Yes, Saturday it's my birthday,' she informed him.

'Yes, so it is.'

'I was supposed to be having a small gathering, because Mum will be home and she might be more her old self.' She looked at him intently, 'You will be there as well, won't you?' she almost begged for fear her family gathering might put him off.

'Of course, I'll be there. Perfect opportunity to meet your parents, although it's a little soon in our relationship for that sort of etiquette.' He winked at her as he said it.

'Good,' she responded.

For the first time since they had arrived, she looked over her shoulder at her house. It was very late, she had school in the morning and she really needed to get in and sort her things for that. She needed to go to bed. She flushed at the thought; *to sleep*, she reminded herself. Although her mind told her how much more she wanted to not be in her bed any more. Only John's. She looked back at him. She didn't want to be away from him for a second. She made up her mind, hard though it was. She kissed him affectionately upon the lips,

'I'll see you tomorrow, after school. And the week can pan out from there. Goodnight, John.'

'Goodnight, Olivia,' he watched her disappear up her garden path and into the shadows of her doorway. He heard the door close and then he remounted his bike, slipped his helmet on and drove off into the remains of the night.

• • • •

The house was dark, cold and empty. Olivia went into the sitting room and turned on the lights. She heard the rev of a motorbike from outside and she looked through the windows just in time to see John's tail light zip off into the night. There was a strange zigzag after-glow trail of red light from it. She blinked and all was darkness again. She sighed and placed her hand onto her lower belly as another wave of maturating warmth swept through it at the thought of John and her afternoon with him. She stood at the window staring longingly into the night. She sighed again and then drew the curtains closed. She wandered over to the TV with the thought of turning it on, but then decided against it. She noticed the telephone table seemed in disarray. There were several roughly scrawled notes, tottering on top of one another, threatening to fall on the floor. Olivia looked through them. There were half a dozen that said Evie had called throughout the evening for her. The last one had a note scribbled under the word 'EVIE!!!!!!!!!!!!' saying that her dad was fed up of the stupid cow's ringing the house and that he was going out. Probably wouldn't be back and that he'd made a chicken and stuffing sandwich for her, which was in the fridge.

Olivia laughed - out loud. It was a wonderful release for the emotions that had been building inside her since John had left. She went to the fridge and got the sandwich out, along with some milk. It was just what she needed. She took it to her room and ate while she prepared her uniform and books for the following day. She pulled a large backpack out of her wardrobe in order to accommodate the biking leathers and everything else. She started by turning out her shoulder bag, with a view of laying everything on the bed to be ordered into the backpack. There was an unexpected clunk as the last object fell from the bottom of her bag.

Crap! she thought, she'd forgotten all about the box; the one Rhys had taken from her dad's dresser. She picked it up and turned it over in her hands. She supposed she ought to put it back. But something was stopping her. Was it the thought of her dad shooting her mum? Or was it the thought she had just had of shooting her dad in the event of him trying to traumatise her mother?

She sat down on the end of her bed and opened the box, looking down at the offending pistol. Tentatively she placed her fingers on the barrel and ran them up and down its cool surface. What would happen if she didn't put it back? Or if she only put the box back? *How often did Dad look in the box?* she wondered. Would he confront her if either were missing? After all, that would mean he would have to admit he had a gun in the first place. Would he be prepared for the potential repercussions of such an admission? Especially knowing his preponderance for avoiding difficult issues. She remembered the pill bottles.

Her hand coiled around the butt of the pistol and she hefted it out. Mirroring Rhys' approach to how to hold it, she sighted along the barrel and all of a sudden, she was taken by a sense of power. She imagined Simon standing on the other side of her bedroom patronising *his* Phyllis. Simon changed to the scary old woman with the wire for hair. And then she saw her dad, raging about how insane his wife was. She sighed. *Sod it*. She threw the gun back onto her bed and then hurried downstairs with the box. She replaced it in the dresser before returning to her bedroom to stare at the gun.

A number of thoughts came to mind as she continued to look at it, various scenarios of how a gun of any type could be useful. Her thoughts resolved and she picked the gun up, placing it into the bottom of her shoulder bag.

'Better to have it and not need it than to not have it and need it,' Aunty Morag's voice intoned in her head.

She was tired and she still needed to get everything stowed away in her backpack for the morning. In the end she just grabbed armfuls of the things on the bed and stuffed them roughly into the pack. She'd just have to wade through it tomorrow whenever she needed something and hope for the best. She placed the backpack by the door and her shoulder bag on top. Time for bed; it had been a long day.

After a long day she had hoped sleep would come to her, but it refused. There were too many thoughts. Too many feelings, not least of all what had happened with John. That was foremost in her thoughts, but then there were other things, like the men who didn't appear to exist. The man who owned their house and now her dad. And what about that scary weird-looking old lady, how did she know Olivia's name?

When finally she did fall asleep, it was restless, filled once more with lurid and vivid dreams. She struggled with unconsciousness as her mind seemed to be constantly shouting blasts of exploding light into the backs of her eyes. She disturbed on a number of occasions because of pain that would stab excruciatingly into her left eye. More than once, she rolled over and found herself half-awake pressing into her eyeball with her fingers, trying to make the pain dissipate. She got up at this point and went downstairs to the medicine cabinet. Her head was throbbing rhythmically, pulsing a lance of fiery pain into her eyeball; she needed relief. There was an array of strong prescription drugs in that cabinet – true they were supposed to be for Mum, but right now Olivia didn't care about protocols, right now all she wanted was for the pain to stop. She knocked back two of Mum's strong codeine tablets and then made her way dizzily back to her bed. After a little more tossing and turning, the codeine finally kicked in and Olivia slipped into welcome sleep.

• • • •

Monday 12th April 1993

When she woke in the morning it was only because of the insistent nagging buzz of her alarm and she felt exhausted and lacklustre. Olivia rolled over and slapped her hand down on the alarm button, almost intent upon rolling over and going back to sleep. She lay on her back for several minutes until she finally found the energy to get up. She prepared for the day in a listless manner, dragging her exhausted frame about upstairs until she was dressed and ready to descend for breakfast.

She was unsurprised when there was no evidence of her father in the house. He had made it perfectly clear he would be out, if Evie was going to be ringing every five seconds. Evie! Dammit! What would she be thinking? Her, Olivia, having gone to a strange man's flat and then never returned her calls. Well, she was up early, so she would be at school in enough time to catch Evie at the gates and they could catch up then. But, Olivia halted her train of thought, did she want to be sharing her new experiences with Evie? Evie's experiences with boys, which she often shared with her, were quite graphic and seemed more about how Evie got what she wanted from manipulating boys with sex. Or, at least, the prospect of sex. Now that she really started to consider her conversations with Evie, she wondered if her friend had ever had sex with any of the boys she purported to see. Lots of snogging, a bit of groping, maybe a couple of handjobs, but nothing more than that. Olivia suddenly realised that of the two of them, she may well now be the most sexually experienced. *The most emotionally advanced of the two of them*, she thought with a satisfied smile. She wasn't certain how this would affect their relationship, because Evie had always been the leader on most things. She had been a confidante and protector as well, but Evie did like to be in charge and the expert on any given topic. Sex and relationships had always been her masterclass. With that in mind, and the fact that Olivia wanted her experiences with John to remain between just them, she wondered how she would explain and describe her time spent yesterday. The more she thought about it, the more John kept invading her mind and the more she wanted to be with him again. She didn't want him to be in work and her in school, she just wanted to be with him. Wrapped up in his arms, curled up in his bed.

Olivia opened the blinds in the kitchen and was startled to see someone in her back garden. There was a distinct figure, bent over the end border and they appeared to be trimming the hedge. Oh, she realised, taking in the frills of the apron and the woollen skirt, along with the physiology of the figure, it was Mrs McKilliecuddy. One of their neighbours and someone her dad had managed to finagle to come and do odd jobs in their garden to keep it vaguely maintained. *He* was never going to do it. In fact, her dad had a number of the local neighbours who would come in and do odds and ends in their front and back gardens, ensuring they remained manageable and in good order. This was another thing that she had never considered before and wondered now whether her dad paid them, bribed them or blackmailed them to perform these thankless jobs on his behalf?

Olivia was about to head for the back door when Mrs McKilliecuddy suddenly stood up from the hedge and turned around. She waved at Olivia.

Olivia stepped back hurriedly from the window and stifled a scream. Mrs McKilliecuddy had a blank face. Not like the woman on the bus, nor like the extremely short man outside the bus. He had a face if you viewed it from the correct direction and the woman on the bus had merely been a hat until her face had come into view. Mrs McKilliecuddy was neither of these things. She really *was* a blank face. There were her greying, curled locks framing her face. There were her ears, sticking through her dangling hair. But other than that, there was no face. This time Olivia could not justify any reason as to what could be happening other than the simple, unassailable fact that her neighbour had no face. There were no eyes – merely the faint hollows of where the sockets could have been, skin stretched tight over the hollows. There was no nose – just a hint of an oblong bump somewhere near the middle of the oval of the proposed face structure. There was no mouth – just a flexing of fleshy tautness that seemed to undulate with the wind. Other than these hints of what could have been, had the Creator decided to complete their work on this human, it was utterly featureless; no creases, nor wrinkles. She was faceless.

Olivia backpedalled to the other side of the kitchen, hand over her mouth to hold back the scream she so desperately wanted to utter. She could see Mrs McKilliecuddy's hand drop and she moved out of view as she tottered up the small lawn to their back door. Olivia stood petrified at the back of the kitchen, one hand over her mouth and the other pressing into her eye as the shaft of pain had returned. The feeling of warmth that had permeated from the centre of her belly down into her loins only hours ago was now replaced by a chill watery feeling that sank into her legs and threatened her ability to remain standing as shivers ran through her thighs and calves. She waited as she knew her neighbour was advancing on her back door. She was terrified that it might be unlocked. She hadn't checked it last night and Dad was awful at remembering to lock up when he went out. Olivia made a decision and ran on quivering legs for the door to slam her body against it and keep her neighbour out, if it wasn't locked.

'Hello? Is anyone in?' came a call from outside. 'Is that you, Reg? Olivia?'

Olivia leaned onto the door, holding the door handle in the locked position. She was close to panic, fear ripping through her. As Mrs McKilliecuddy rapped on the outside of the door, the vibration of the knock rippled through the woodwork and pounded into the side of Olivia's head where it rested upon it.

'Hello? It's only me, Audrey. Audrey McKilliecuddy. Anyone there?'

It gradually occurred to Olivia that she was hearing a voice. A voice needed a mouth to vocalise it. That would mean Mrs McKilliecuddy had a mouth, even though she had quite evidently not had one a moment or two before. Olivia was struck by a sudden impulse, one that went against the grain of security and protection. She flung open the door, ready to retreat into the kitchen and retrieve a frying pan from the rack or to flee completely from the house through the front door. She was horrified by what stood before her and let out a scream. The searing pain in her eye became so agonising that all she could see was brilliant white light.

Olivia fainted.

Chapter 13

Olivia was aware of people hovering near her, talking. She was starting to come back to the world, but something one of the voices said made her body cease its wake-up call and instead remain dormant as her mind and her hearing listened in on what was being said in hushed whispers.

'What the hell did you *do*, Audrey?' Reg demanded.

'I didn't *do* anything, Reg,' Mrs McKilliecuddy sounded defensive. 'She opened the door, looked at me, with what I can only describe as a look of horror on her face, screamed and then fainted dead away. That was about when you came in.'

'Dammit all! Maybe I gave her too much,' Reg snorted as he said this.

'Too much?' Audrey asked.

'Yeah, well, I was all for toning it down, but orders is orders. And she said to up the dose. So I did, and now this. Fuck's sake, Olivia, if you'd just done what was expected of you at the time then none of this would have been necessary and we could all have just gone back to what we wanted to be doing.' Reg expelled a hefty sigh.

Olivia tried desperately to remain as still as possible. This was horrifying information imparted by her father. What the hell had he done to her? There was a tickle in the back of her throat, which had been nagging at her since she had started to come round. Probably an after-effect of her screaming. She tried to swallow it away; she needed to hear more of what they were saying.

'There, there, Reg, calm down. Maybe Olivia's just a late bloomer.'

'I think you're thinking of tits, Audrey,'

'Fuck's sake, Reg, do you have to be so crude?' Audrey sounded mortified.

'Tits aren't crude, Audrey. You have them, she has them,' Olivia imagined her dad pointing down at her as he said this. 'But tits aren't her problem, are they? It's...'

Whatever 'it's' was, Olivia was never going to find out now, because at that moment the tickle took control and she started to cough. The adults' conversation ceased abruptly and she found herself being pulled up and supported into a sitting position on the floor. Mrs McKilliecuddy was kneeling next to her, arms supporting her shoulders. Olivia's eyes were open before she had time to consider why she shouldn't open them. But looking at Mrs McKilliecuddy all she saw was the wrinkled face of a late middle-aged woman radiating deep concern for her wellbeing. She looked round and saw her dad crouched in front of her, holding a glass of water, which he promptly shoved towards her in what she could only imagine was his attempt at a caring bedside manner.

Olivia took the proffered glass and took a swig, without even thinking. She had already swallowed when suddenly she thought, had he dosed it with something? Dad was dosing her with something? Why? He'd had orders to do it, but from whom? What the hell was going on? Had they been really talking about her, because she knew Dad was dosing Mum with the new drugs? Would he be dosing her with them too? But why? *She* wasn't schizophrenic? She coughed again and then found herself being lifted up on to a chair by the adults.

'There, there, me lovely,' said Mrs McKilliecuddy, brushing Olivia's fringe out of her eyes. 'How you feeling now?'

Olivia shook her head. She needed to get away from here, find out what Dad was up to, what he might have been doing to her. She needed to ring John; he'd know what to do and he would protect her too. Perhaps John had been right last night, maybe she wasn't safe to be with her dad after all. But then, how could her dad have found out about her snooping around in his life? She couldn't ring

ORDINARY WORLD

John from the house, she would need to go to a phone box, or maybe Evie's, but certainly not here. She straightened in the chair and batted Mrs McKilliecuddy's hands from her shoulders.

'I'm fine, thank you, Mrs M. I just took a bit of a turn, that's all. Haven't been sleeping well, too worried about Mum is all.'

She glanced at her dad, but his expression was inscrutable. She continued, 'Been having bad dreams and one of them seemed to come at me just as I opened the door. It was all just confusion and being half asleep. I'm sorry if I caused you to worry.' She forced a smile for Mrs McKilliecuddy who seemed suitably mollified by her explanation.

Mrs McKilliecuddy looked over to her dad, who merely shrugged his shoulders.

'Are you well enough for school? I can ring the office and tell them you need a day off. But you shouldn't be worrying about Phyllis – she's doing grand and should be out on Friday, all being well. You can stop worrying now, Olivia.'

The last sentence was almost a command from her dad and she wondered if he was trying to lay down some kind of subliminal mind trip on her. None of anything in recent days made sense and now to discover that the man she thought of as her dad may be someone completely different and that he might have been poisoning her, was just a little too much for her. She had to hold it together long enough to get out of the house and to the safety of John's arms. Then she could let it all go and hope John could solve the problem for her.

'No, Dad,' her voice faltered as she said 'dad', 'no, I'm fine. Tired, but fine. I'll be alright for school and I really ought to be getting on or I'll be late. Don't want to be late on a day when there's no reason for it,' she concluded, standing up and looking to go to the sitting room, where she'd left her bags.

Her dad stood back from her and let her make her way, slightly unsteadily, from the room. He followed her, waving at Mrs McKilliecuddy to stay put.

'If you're sure, Olivia? I don't mind if you need to take the day off. Perhaps go to the park and get some air, rather than going back to bed, if nightmares are a problem. Don't force anything.'

Olivia stopped and looked back at him. There had been a genuine tone in his voice that had caught her attention and looking at him she realised he really did appear concerned. This just didn't sit right; it was a total juxtaposition from the idea that he was poisoning her. Had she imagined what they had been saying? Had she misheard? Misinterpreted? She shook her head again to try and clear her mind.

'Well, if you're sure. I should be around most of today, no jobs to do today. So, if you need me to come and pick you up from school at any point, just go to the office and get them to call me, OK?'

Olivia couldn't help but smile, this was so unlike Dad. Everything about him in the last few days had been so unlike Dad. This genuine concern, his cooking for her... his *cooking* for her! Was that how he'd been poisoning her? Had he been slipping something into her food? But no, that couldn't be it, they'd both eaten Sunday roast together. An image of Dad shovelling too much into his mouth yesterday lunchtime came to mind: the sliver of chicken that dangled from the corner of his mouth, gravy dripping down his chin and the horrendous mastication noises that had slurped from him as he had consumed mouthful after mouthful. So, that couldn't be it. She shook her head again trying to clear it of the sound of sloppy, soggy mouth noises. She wished she hadn't shaken her head, as all it did was make her feel dizzy. Her hand shot out and braced against the wall, to prevent her falling. Her dad was instantly there to support her,

ORDINARY WORLD

'I'm fine, Dad, really. I need to get to school.'

She hurried to the sitting room, grabbed her backpack and left the house. 'I'll see you later, Dad. Might be going to Evie's after school as we have a project we need to be getting done,' she lied glibly. Her dad nodded, she gave him a tentative wave and then fled the house.

• • • •

Time was getting on as she hurried to the high street via the cut-through, where, just up from the bus stops, there was a small bank of phone booths. She went to the nearest one and picked up the receiver, placing a pile of coins on top of the box as she did so. The phone was dead. She looked at it and realised why. *Bloody vandals*. She grabbed her coins and went to the next booth, this was working. She breathed in relief; gripping the receiver in the crook of her shoulder with her head, she rummaged in her jacket pocket for the piece of paper that had the elusive Kennedy details written on it. She stabbed urgently at the keypad and let the phone ring, jittering up and down, anxious to hear John's voice. Anxious for him to answer and to be able to come and rescue her, as she knew he was so keen to do. As she jittered, as she listened to the phone ringing and ringing, she nervously glanced about the street. It was full of early morning traffic, plenty of pedestrians hurrying on their commute. Those shops that hadn't been open first thing to catch the early shift workers were now going through their routines of opening up for the start of the week's trading. There was no sign of her father or Mrs McKilliecuddy having followed her. There was also no sign, thankfully, of the freaks. Although - she peered more closely at two people who were hovering near the corner of one of the roads off from the high street. Wasn't that the woman from the bus the other day? The two people walked around the corner and disappeared from view. She drew in a long, ragged breath; she must have imagined it. They were quite a distance from her and she had to admit, even putting aside her horrific vision of Mrs McKilliecuddy this morning, she hadn't been sleeping well and her nightmares could possibly be playing on her mind now. The phone continued to ring out. *Fuck! He must have already gone to work.* She hung up the receiver and then looked around the street again. There was nothing untoward out there. She shouldered her backpack more securely and then headed off at a fast pace for school.

• • • •

Evie was chewing her nails as she leaned against the wall just inside the school gates, when Olivia finally arrived. Morning bell was sounding as she hurried in and Evie's face lit up at the sight of her. They met on the dash through the main yard to the entrance.

'Well?' Evie said slightly out of breath from her morning smoke.

'Well, what?' Olivia replied, suddenly uncertain about telling Evie anything about anything. She wanted John all to herself and everything else that had happened too. She needed to sound off to someone though, but she had been hoping that was going to be John.

'How did it go with your mystery biker?'

'Well enough,' Olivia blushed uncontrollably. Evie wasn't naïve and jumped on the blush.

'So, it went very well then? You snogged him, didn't you?' Evie was able to nudge Olivia as they made their way down the hall to their first class.

Truth be told, Olivia *had* snogged him, so she would probably be safe to let Evie have that, she didn't need to know about anything else. Olivia nodded, possibly a little shyly, and she wasn't disappointed with Evie's reaction as she skipped around her calling her a devil, a minx and a sex kitten. Olivia wasn't entirely comfortable with any of those terms, nor indeed the attention it seemed to be drawing from other members of the faculty. Eyebrows were distinctly raised from some of her peers.

Olivia was distracted through her lessons as she thought back over what she'd heard while lying on the kitchen floor. Her dad had dosed her with something, because she hadn't done something she was supposed to have done. *What the hell!* Her dad was giving her some kind of dope or medicine because of not doing something. What was it she was *supposed* to have done? There was something expected of her and it should have already happened, but what? What could she have been expected to do and hadn't, causing Mrs McKilliecuddy to suggest she was a late bloomer? Something in her physique, obviously, although not her breasts, apparently. What is a young teenage girl supposed to have done physically, naturally, that she hadn't done, that would cause her dad to slip her medicine? Well, at least, she *presumed* it was medicine – it couldn't be poison, otherwise she'd be feeling ill all the time. She assumed the medicine was designed to force whatever it was into happening. Well, it wasn't her periods, because she'd been having them since she was thirteen, much to her surprise and horror when it first happened. Dad knew about them, as he'd had to help her with her first ones. So, it wasn't her breasts and it wasn't her periods... *what the fuck was it?*

• • • •

The rest of the day went tediously slowly for Olivia. She failed to hear any of her teachers as she pondered all the strangeness that had been happening in her life since her mum had been sectioned. The end of school couldn't come quick enough for her and she practically ran to the changing rooms where she slipped into her leathers. In hindsight, she realised perhaps rushing into the new garments wasn't the brightest idea she'd ever had. The jacket was ok, a snug fit and she realised why John thought it suited her. But the trousers were awkward. They bunched at her crotch, forcing her thighs apart and causing her to waddle like a duck as she walked. The cuffs, even when zippered shut, kept catching on every little protuberance, tripping her on more than one occasion.

Outside the true effect of this became apparent as everyone on the yard started to whistle, crow and laugh at her. Duck calls followed swiftly. She started to blush vigorously and tried to hurry as best she could to the gates. Normally she wouldn't have paid it much heed, but today she was feeling fragile. Too much had happened and she hadn't had any time to process any of it. As she neared the gates, she was assailed by a wave of relief as she heard the now-familiar roar of a motorbike. John's green monster slewed to a halt a few feet from her. He kicked out the stand and dismounted. He removed his helmet and strode straight for her. He winked at her as he approached and she could feel her cheeks ache with the strength of the grin that had erupted on her face at his approach.

The crowd had become muted by this sudden turn of events and all waited to see what happened next. They were not to be disappointed. John slid one arm around Olivia's waist, his right hand came up to her face to embrace it. He leaned down into the kiss, pulling her into him. Olivia was too shocked to react at first, but the softness of his touch to her lips melted her and she readily succumbed to the moment. She didn't hear the crowd's reaction and wasn't aware of it until John was pulling away, taking her hand and leading her to the bike. The crowd was whistling again, but it was far more upbeat. Wolf whistles, cat calls and a huge amount of whooping. Olivia could discern Evie's voice rising above the cacophony and she was clearly thrilled for her friend.

'You go, girl,' Evie let out a whoop of her own.

John spoke to her out of the side of his mouth. 'I may have overdone it a bit there, but I got the impression you needed a pick-me-up. Right, when we're on the bike,' he said passing her the helmet she'd worn the night before, 'hang on real tight, cos I'm going to crank it for these plebs.'

Olivia was grateful to slide into position behind him. She rested her head on his back and gripped him for all she was worth. She felt his hand comfortingly on her forearm for a moment before the bike started up. It gave forth a mighty roar, as if they were upon a mythical beast. Olivia's imagination had them astride a vast green dragon - akin to the beasts of the romantic fables she used to read - belching flame and incinerating the 'plebs'. John revved it and held the bike in check as the back wheel spun for a second or two. Then he declutched and the bike rampaged across the road out of the school's view and onto the bypass. They left in a cloud of smoke, as befitted riders of a mighty dragon. In the wing mirror, Olivia could see Evie leaping up and down. Rhys was running up to Evie, arms flapping, clearly not knowing what was going on. Olivia was thankful that she had obeyed John. As they shot from the kerbside her heart leapt into her throat and her head was nearly snapped from her neck by the force of the bike's forward momentum.

Once they had left the school and its minions in their dust, John eased back on the throttle. The rest of the ride was quite sedate compared with the overly dramatic departure and Olivia was both relieved and disappointed. Relieved at still having a head attached to her body and still being sat on the bike. Disappointed that they were no longer flying on the dragon. Her heart slowly recovered its normal tempo and by the time they arrived at John's flat she felt utterly exhausted.

Chapter 14

'Right, let's get you out of those leathers,' John said, turning to her as he closed the door to his flat. He started to unzip her jacket.

'Well, I can see what's on your mind,' she said with a whimsical smile.

His hand paused and he looked at her, blushing slightly, then cleared his throat before he replied.

'Don't think it hasn't crossed my mind,' he paused, 'but I really think we need to talk about a few things first.'

Olivia followed his unconscious gaze as he spoke to her. It led straight to his bedroom door, which was closed. She wondered if this was a deliberate act before he had left to pick her up, a psychological boundary that said 'No', in order that they could deal with the real and the scarier topics that needed to be dealt with. She had no wish to talk about any of it at the moment. The exit from school, that sense of flying over the town on dragonback had cleared her mind of all the weirdness of recent days and she knew that the only thing she needed right now was him. She needed that deepness of bonding with another human being. One she thought might just adore her. All the rest of it would still be there in an hour. She would be better able to contend with it after she had had her own brand of medication. She needed the stars again.

John continued to unzip her. She raised her hand to his chest and placed it dead centre. She rubbed at it through his exposed blue shirt, him having long since unzipped his own jacket. Her fingers slipped in between the buttons of his shirt, evading the loosely worn tie. 'Is there nothing I can do to change your mind?' she said tilting her head to the side with a coy smile.

He paused again, placing a hand over hers, 'I'm sure there are plenty of things you could do to change my mind, but I think it would be best if we stayed on track for now.'

She slipped her hand from under his and stroked it down to his belly, curling a finger in the soft hairs that resided there. She could see his resolve wilting. Looking down, she could also see that that was the only thing that was wilting, judging from the strain coming from his leather trousers. He was shaking his head... was he saying no to her or was he just trying to convince himself? She wondered. Her other hand came up to reside on the front of his trousers, cupping the bulge, she blushed profusely as she did so. While she knew what she wanted, she was still a novice at this sort of thing. Her prudishness, for want of a better word, still held sway in her mind and she could hear a voice telling her that what she was doing was unseemly, the act of a harlot. She was baffled as to where that voice stemmed from, but she knew the voice was wrong; it didn't understand her need. John pulled her jacket off and practically ripped her shirt off with it.

• • • •

'*You* are a very bad, bad girl,' John said through gasps for air, as she slid down to lie on top of him. She could feel the warmth of their recent lovemaking exuding from his naked chest. Their sweat mingled. Olivia could see the sparkles and stars starting to fade from the back of her eyes. The bright lights of before had burst inside her mind as they had last time and she had felt it like a wave crashing over the rocks of her mind. She had suddenly felt totally alive, like a goddess again; she could do anything. Her mind was alive with possibilities. She remained straddled over him, her head upon his chest that rose and fell as he continued to recover from her exuberance. She felt him gradually slide from within her and this saddened her, for as it left, so did the final stars and her sight returned to normal.

'Does that mean you don't like me anymore? If I'm a bad girl?' she asked innocently.

'Oh, far from it. I've always wondered what it would be like to be with a bad girl,' he replied.

'And your verdict?'

He chuckled, 'I can quite honestly say it's the best thing to ever happen to me.'

He sucked in a deep breath of air and suddenly moved, rolling her off him. He rolled on top of her, pinning her arms to the bed and sliding between her thighs. 'And bad girls need to be punished,' he continued, lowering his head to kiss her.

They remained in bed, with him 'punishing' her, for another hour.

She adored every second of it, until the pain returned to the back of her eyeball. She tried to ride through it and, even when the lights came on again and the monitors rocked on their stands, the pain remained. Intensified, even. She screamed. The scream changed to one of abject agony as a lance of consuming fire shot through her head and her eye seemed to swell with heat to the point of exploding.

· · · ·

She stood on the edge of a vast chasm. Above her, the roiling clouds blackened and blossomed, cycling through formations of foreboding darkness. As the fire speared her mind, the clouds split asunder, evaporating before the heat that threatened to boil her brain. Leaving only a blanket of the void, a night sky with no stars. Darkness so overwhelming, so oppressive she could no longer breathe. Her chest seized under the effort to drag a single molecule of air into her crushed lungs. The breath died in her throat and she toppled forwards into the abyss of the tenebrous chasm.

She couldn't even scream. Atmospheric pressure crushed her chest, gripped her throat and forbore the ability of her body to function in its subconscious capacity. She was stifled. No breath. No life. No scream. Only the pain in her mind as it tore through her synapses. White electrical brands searing a new road through her consciousness.

• • • •

Monitors fell from the desks and a glass on the bedside table shattered.

• • • •

She came to slowly. John was cradling her, stroking her cheek. As she focused on his face, she could see the furrows of worry upon it. She reached up a hand to stroke them away and suddenly she found herself pulled up in a hug so tight, she could barely breathe.

'Thank fuck, Olivia, you had me so scared. I thought I'd killed you.'

Slowly he relinquished his hold, letting her slide back into the cradle of his body. She lay there utterly drained and yet everything around her seemed totally crystal clear. Pristine, as if only just created. There was a glimmer, a shine to everything, even John, who looked as though he had a halo of heavenly light encasing his entire being. She smiled up at him.

'You could never harm me, John.'

'But are you alright? You screamed and passed out on top of me. What did I do?'

'It wasn't you, silly. My head was suddenly filled with light and bursting stars. And I got a sharp pain in my eye, but I've had it before. It's OK, just something that's happening at the moment. Probably due to poor sleep. I've had headaches from that before,' she paused for a moment and John peered down at her frowning, 'although not quite like this.'

She smiled up at him, a radiant smile that melted his frown away, 'But it's fine. I'm fine. In fact, I'm better than fine.' She stroked his cheek, wiping away the last of his concerns.

'So, I don't need to take you to the hospital?'

'No. Of course not. A passing aberration is all.'

John sighed with relief, as Olivia looked around curiously.

'What happened to your monitor?' she glanced over his knee at the floor by the bed. 'Actually, what did happen? Is that glass from your monitor?'

Olivia was referring to the shattered drinking glass that was strewn close to the face-down monitor.

'I'm not entirely certain,' John replied, craning his neck around to view the devastation, 'I think we may have been a bit too enthusiastic and it vibrated off the desk, knocking the glass off at the same time.'

Olivia looked back at him sheepishly, 'Sorry, do I owe you a new monitor?'

He shook his head, chuckling softly, 'No, no, it's fine. It was old and I'd been thinking about upgrading it anyway. Don't you worry your pretty little head about it.'

• • • •

Olivia got up from the bed. She immediately wished she hadn't. A wave of coldness washed over her, her vision lost focus and her mind seemed to start doing cartwheels filling her body with sensations of nausea and dizziness. She staggered forwards, glancing as she did so into the mirror on the opposite wall in an attempt to bring her eyes back into focus. What she saw did nothing to improve her sense of wellbeing as she could see that all the blood had drained from her face and extremities. She let out a short gasped 'Oh!' as she swayed forwards and started to fall. John turned abruptly when she said *Oh* and was in time to catch her before she plummeted to the floor. He laid her back on the bed, the concern immediately returning to his features.

'Right, that's it, I'm taking you to the hospital. I said I'd protect you and that goes for protecting you from yourself as much as from others.'

Olivia struggled to sit up, but her vision was blurred and the pain had returned to her eye. There was a brilliant shaft of light slicing through her mind and exiting through her retina. She was a little surprised that John didn't comment on it. She didn't want to go to hospital, though. She didn't like them, for obvious reasons, given how many she'd been in over the years with her mother.

'No, no, it's fine John, really. I'm fine.'

'No, you are not!' He said adamantly.

'I am,' she said faintly, she was starting to have difficulty hearing what he was saying because of the additional noise she heard that was drowning him out. It sounded like the radio was on but out of tune, nothing but hissing white noise. 'Can you turn the radio down, please?'

John looked bemused, 'The radio's not on, Olivia?'

'Oh,'

John bent over her and touched her forehead, she slapped his hand away, 'I'm not feverish,' she said petulantly, 'Just tired. Too many nightmares, not enough sleep, too many moments of seeing things that aren't there, nothing to worry about.' Her voice slurred slightly as she finished.

'You're seeing things?' John asked incredulously, he stood upright and moved to his front room, 'Right, that's definitely it. I'm calling in some favours, you're going to get seen to right now!'

Olivia called after him, 'But I'm fine, the only reason I've been seeing things is because Dad's been poisoning me.'

John's progress out of the bedroom halted, he spun around, 'He's what? He's been doing what?' He was almost shouting.

'Well, he may not,' Olivia wished she hadn't said anything at all, now she just seemed to be digging herself into a bigger hole, her father along with her, 'I overheard him saying something, and I think I misunderstood. I think he's been doping Mum, not me. But my headaches are just because of lack of sleep.'

John stood looking at her on his bed, Olivia saw him come to a conclusion as he turned once more and marched into his sitting room. She heard him pick up the phone and dial. Then she heard a long, muted conversation, none of which she could make out because the white noise obliterated everything.

When John returned he seemed determined yet more relaxed, 'I've pulled some strings and we're going to a government run clinic about forty miles from here. We're just waiting on the taxi, which should be here in the next fifteen minutes. So, that gives us just enough time to get you dressed.'

Olivia didn't resist as John took command. She presumed it was fifteen minutes later when she found herself in a taxi driving through the late afternoon streets enroute to a government run clinic, so they could stab about in her brain and determine whether or not she was going mad or just having migraines. John was attentive throughout the journey and filled her in on what to expect.

"The clinic is run by a Dr Eckstein, he specialises in brain chemistry, so if anyone can work out what's giving you headaches, it should be him. They'll also run blood tests to do a tox screen, so we can see if your dad's been dosing you with anything. So help me God, if he has,' John's face flushed at this point and Olivia saw his fists clenching. She placed a calming hand over his fist and smiled up at him, her head was clearing. The bright lights were diminishing, the white noise abating, even the pain in her eyeball was subsiding. She almost felt like her old self, but she knew it was too late to ask John to turn them round and forget about the clinic. *Besides*, she thought to herself as she sat back into the taxi's bench seat, *it might not be such a bad idea to have a poke around in my head... maybe there is something untoward going on in there.* She took a sharp intake of breath, *maybe I am my mother*. Schizophrenia was inheritable after all.

· · · ·

Olivia wasn't inclined to lie on the gurney so she could be pushed into the MRI scanner, but both Dr Eckstein and John had said there was nothing to worry about. If she felt like falling asleep then that was fine, just as long as she didn't move. Olivia doubted she would fall asleep, being pushed into a tube that seemed to close in on her and suck the air out of the environment leaving her short of breath didn't seem relaxing enough to induce sleep. She held her breath and tried to control the rising panic. And then she felt John's hand in hers and heard him whispering calming words to her. The tension in her chest subsided and, listening to what he was saying, she slowly started to breathe more normally. The panic gradually ebbed from her body. After a while she realised that just lying there allowing the machine to do its thing was quite relaxing and she could understand why the suggestion had been made to fall asleep. But despite being in the MRI for twenty minutes or so, sleep eluded her and then she felt the jolt as the gurney was being withdrawn and she was able to sit up. John embraced her,

'See it wasn't so bad after all,' he said with an encouraging smile. It didn't stop her from slapping him on the shoulder.

ORDINARY WORLD

Dr Eckstein stepped over to them and addressed Olivia, 'It'll take about an hour to collate the information, along with the results of the tox screening. In the meantime I'll show you to the Aftercare Room where you can get refreshments and rest. I'll be back with you later to go through what results we may find.'

John helped Olivia off the gurney and then they both followed Dr Eckstein out of the MRI suite and down through the corridors of the clinic to the Aftercare Room. He opened the door and ushered them in. Olivia was just about to step inside when she had a sudden urge to glance over her shoulder, back down the corridor they had just come along.

'Oh!' she gasped.

'What?' replied John taken aback, but he had no time to gather a response from Olivia because she had dashed off back down the corridor. 'Hey! Wait! Olivia?'

Both he and Eckstein started to pursue her as she disappeared around a corner. John came to an abrupt halt as he went round after her, because he ran right into Olivia, who was now standing stock still in the middle of a corridor. An expanse of pristine, brightly-lit whiteness extended before them, with a multitude of doors on either side and a T-junction at the end. Eckstein came round the corner moments later, a dash through his clinic clearly not being his forté.

'Olivia? What is it?' John moved round to stand in front of her, probably as much to gauge her expression as the possibility of preventing her from charging off again. Olivia looked up at him bemused.

'It's... I don't know, I must have been mistaken.' She craned her neck around John to continue staring down the corridor.

'Miss Buchanan?' Dr Eckstein puffed, 'Could you explain yourself, please?'

Olivia turned round to look at him, the look of puzzlement still clear upon her features. 'I thought I saw someone.'

'Well, that's always possible, the clinic's staff are often to be found within the corridors,' Dr Eckstein replied.

'Yes, obviously, but no, I mean I thought I saw someone I saw on the bus the other day.'

'Really?' asked John, 'Who?'

'Great Uncle Bulgaria.' Olivia said, without thinking about the potential consequences of such a statement.

'Great Uncle Bulgaria?' John repeated, 'The *womble*?'

'Yes,' she said,

'No,' she concluded as she looked up at John and it dawned on her how ridiculous she was sounding. Dr Eckstein interjected.

'You saw a *womble* on the bus the other day?' he scribbled something down on the clipboard he was carrying.

'No!' Olivia was starting to get frustrated.

'But you said,' John started.

'I know what I said, but I didn't see a womble on the bus. He was outside, I was on the bus.'

Dr Eckstein scribbled something else on the clipboard. This wasn't helping, nor was her explanations, she realised. She needed to start again before they locked her up.

'Wait both of you. And for God's sake stop writing things down, doctor.'

Both John and Dr Eckstein took an involuntary step back from her, perhaps from the shock of her command, but maybe also just to give her some room to breathe.

'OK,' Olivia started again, 'On Saturday, when I was out looking up the Kennedys I was on the bus. It got held up in roadworks and to pass the time I looked out of the window and saw a man, who I thought *looked* like Great Uncle Bulgaria, the womble. It was his nose that made the connection with my memory to the wombles. Anyway, just now when I looked back up the corridor I could have sworn I saw him walking across the junction, but when I got up here there was no sign of him.'

She looked at her companions to see whether her explanation had mollified their concerns about whether she was going mad. The gentle nod of Dr Eckstein's head and the smile on John's face indicated for her that this was indeed the case.

'Ah, yes, well that would make more sense,' Dr Eckstein said, crossing out his scribblings.

John looked over to the doctor, 'Does anyone fitting the description of Great Uncle Bulgaria work here?'

Eckstein shook his head slowly, 'Not that I'm aware of, but then Olivia's recollection of the womble and mine could be completely different. Could you describe the man for me, Miss Buchanan?'

Olivia paused while she considered his request, 'Well, he was unnaturally short, had very stumpy legs and his arms were similarly stumpy, seemed to just stick out of his torso really, as if he didn't have suitable joints for them to bend normally. But it was his face that was so distinctive. His ears were enormous, kind of like an elephant's and his nose was very broad and flat, which was why I thought he looked like Great Uncle Bulgaria.' She looked at the doctor hopefully, but saw him starting to shake his head once more.

'No, no, definitely doesn't ring a bell with me. None of my staff fit that description.'

'Could it be a patient?' John suggested.

'Well, it could, I suppose, except no patients would be in these corridors right now. You are an exception because of circumstances; normally this section is out of bounds for most patients, unless accompanied by a senior member of staff.'

They continued to stand in silence for a moment, before Eckstein finally suggested that they should return to the Aftercare

Room and that he could go and look at the results of the tests. In the meantime, perhaps it would be for the best to forget about wombles.

• • • •

Olivia stood by the window of the Aftercare Room and looked out over the expanse of the front of the clinic. It was set back from the main road, nestled in private grounds and unless you knew it was there no one would be any the wiser. John pottered by the counter where the refreshments were to be found. The silence was becoming uncomfortable for Olivia and she suddenly turned round on John,

'Go on then. Say it. Say what's on your mind!'

John dropped the cup he had been tinkering with out of surprise. He turned round to face her and she couldn't discern his expression. Despite his attentiveness in the taxi and then when she had been in the scanner, John's disposition had seemed somehow *off* since they'd arrived at the clinic. Her imagination had been creating all kinds of possibilities to explain it, and most of them suggested that he had become scared of the loony he'd inadvertently started shagging and was trying to find the nicest and quickest way to escape.

'OK,' John took a deep breath, 'I'm scared, Olivia. Scared that you might have inherited your mother's illness and that there's absolutely nothing I can do to help you. I don't know enough about the illness other than it's incurable. And I'm scared for you, because I don't want you to have to go through that, especially not alone. And I don't know if I'm the best person to be the one to help you, but I want to be the person who helps you, but I don't know how. So, basically, I'm scared.'

His head was downcast throughout his profound explanation and it rather took Olivia by surprise. In many ways it mirrored exactly what her imagination had been suggesting to her and yet, it also wasn't. This man, whom she had known for barely 48 hours was trying to commit himself to her care even though he was terrified of what that care might entail. It was so the polar opposite of her dad that she couldn't contend with it and promptly burst into tears.

'Oh, Olivia, I'm sorry, I'm so sorry, I never meant to make you cry.' John hurried over to her and swept her up in his arms. He promptly held her at arm's length as she started to laugh through her tears. 'OK, now I'm confused.'

Olivia shook her head and gasped for breath as she tried to rally her wayward emotions.

'I'm confused as well, John. I have no idea what's going on with me anymore. It's only been in the last couple of hours that I'd been wondering, like you, if I was turning into my mother. And since thinking that, I'd noticed how distant you seemed to be. And yet there you are worrying about me in a way that my father has never cared about my mother. It's all just so opposite and strange.'

John pulled her back into his embrace, 'Sorry, if I've been distant, I just didn't know what to think and then you started talking about seeing wombles on the bus and I really thought you were becoming delusional – like your mother.'

'Yeah, well, who wouldn't think that, if someone turned round saying they saw wombles on a bus.'

The two of them started to laugh in tandem. It seemed to do the trick for them, as they settled back from the embrace with smiles.

'I think the best we can do is wait for Dr Eckstein and see what his scan results have to say. We're probably worrying ourselves over nothing. As you've said in the past, it's probably all just down to a lack of sleep and all the stress you've been under these last few years with your family life. Families can be wearing at the best of times. I know.' John's face became serious for a moment and Olivia realised in that moment that she knew next to nothing about John, but he seemed to know everything there was to know about her.

'Your family's difficult?' she asked. Olivia instantly realised she'd asked the wrong thing, as John's body language completely shut down.

'You could say that, yes. Which is why I have as little to do with them as possible.'

'Sorry, I didn't mean to pry,'

'No, it's fine. Just a touchy subject, is all.' He smiled at her again, starting to relax, 'What a fine pair we make, Olivia. We would do well to stick together.'

They sat in companionable silence after that, holding hands, gazing at one another from time to time, lost in their thoughts. Olivia considered his last comment: *We'd do well to stick together.* She would be very happy with that, no matter the outcome of her test results.

• • • •

They were sat in front of Dr Eckstein's desk in his office. Behind the desk was a floor-to-ceiling bookshelf filled with professional books pertaining to the brain. Directly behind Eckstein, as he sat in his chair, the wall was covered with accolades and testaments to his years of study and research. It all looked very impressive to Olivia and instilled a confidence that if anyone could work out what was going on in her head it would be Dr Eckstein.

'So, Miss Buchanan, I've now had time to go through the scan results and also the preliminary findings in your bloods. Firstly, I think you would like to know that we haven't found anything untoward in your tox screen.' He glanced up at her before continuing.

'What about the brain scan?' she said impatiently.

'Ah, yes. The scans. Well, John did inform me of your mother's condition, I think he was concerned that you may have inherited some of her *traits*. However, and it should also be noted that scans alone can't determine schizophrenia, there are things we can look at in the brain to determine a possibility. A couple of those anomalies include different volumes and activity in the temporal and frontal lobes of the brain, generally seen as less grey matter. But as far as can be determined from your scans both areas are well within the normal bounds for a sixteen-year-old. If anything I would say that your frontal and temporal lobes show a higher than average amount of grey matter, which bodes well for your future, young lady. All in all, I would say your brain is very much a work in progress, but it is also healthy with good prospects.

'As to what may be causing your headaches and sleeplessness, that I think might have more to do with the stresses of your life, which from what little John has said to me, are many and great.' He pursed his lips and looked fiercely concerned as he stared down his nose at her.

'Perhaps, what you might consider to combat these two encircling issues, and by that I mean each is most likely caused by the other and as such each causes the other to worsen in a never-ending and ever-decreasing circle. What you may wish to consider is a period of respite. Get away from your family environment, which is wholly unhealthy for you and, for want of a better way of putting it, take a holiday. A long and extended one at that.'

There was a pause and Olivia started to feel uncomfortable under Dr Eckstein's gaze. She wanted to say something, tell him how impossible it would be for her to just up and go, leaving her mother's care to her father. There was school to consider; how would she afford such a holiday? Where would she go? Aunty Morag's? She found herself blushing and shaking her head at the doctor. She noted his lips suddenly compressed into a thin line at her rejection.

'But as that is clearly not a realistic option I'm going to prescribe some medication for you. Something for the headaches and something to help you sleep. Combined hopefully they will see you through so that you can return to a normal restful sleep pattern, which I believe is as much to blame for your headaches as the stress you're currently undergoing.' Dr Eckstein pursed his lips once more; clearly he despaired for Olivia's situation.

'John can pick them up from the pharmacy while you wait for your taxi home. I recommend you just take the time to sit and rest, young lady.'

Olivia concluded that this was one recommendation from her doctor that she would be unable to countermand. She would do as she was told.

Chapter 15

Tuesday 13th April 1993

It was gone midnight when the taxi dropped them outside of John's apartment block. They stood in the cool night air as the taxi drove off and John turned to Olivia,

'It's too late to be taking you home now; best if I drop you in school tomorrow on my way to work.' He seemed matter-of-fact about this, turning to make his way up the path to the flats. His progress was halted by Olivia's hand on his arm.

'Absolutely not,' she said as he faced her.

'Eh?' he was surprised by her response.

'It's one thing for you to pick me up from school and quite another to be dropping me off the following morning.'

By the expression she could see on his face, she knew she was going to have to explain further.

'Everyone'll have their own ideas of what we may or may not get up to once we'd left school, but if I turn up in the morning on the back of your bike, everyone's going to have confirmation of their seedy thoughts. So, no, you won't be dropping me off tomorrow. You can take me home, either now or in the morning.' She ensured her final sentence mirrored his earlier tone of matter-of-factness.

John glanced at his watch, 'Tomorrow morning it is then; too late to be taking you home now. Especially after the evening you've had.' He looked down at her, expressing a thought that had clearly just popped into his mind. 'Are you ashamed of what we've been doing, Olivia?'

'No. Why would you ask that?'

'Because you don't want it confirmed with your friends at school.'

'No. It's just none of their business what I do when I'm out of school and with whoever I do it with. And right now I want to keep my private life private.' There was a fierceness to her tone and her stance was not dissimilar to the one she had adopted with her father at the end of the previous week when she had confronted him about his phone conversation with Dr Varjay.

John started to nod, understanding creeping in. 'OK, I can see that. But for now I think you should stay here, at least for tonight. I can take you back to yours in the morning. It'll be early, mind, but probably not a bad thing, if you want to be getting ready for school. Are we OK?'

Olivia looked at him for a moment and relaxed. She nodded and then slipped her arm through his, leading him in through the gates to the portico.

• • • •

Olivia looked at the bottle of pills for insomnia that John had handed her shortly before they had retired for the night. Yes, she would love to have a night of dreamless sleep, but she wasn't entirely convinced tonight was the night she wanted to start on her pill regime. To start with, the suggestion was that she should take the pill half an hour before going to bed, and the other recommendation had been that the pill would make her drowsy for anything up to eight hours after consuming it. She didn't have eight hours before she needed to be compos mentis to be astride John's emerald dragon again. She threw the bottle into her shoulder bag and then slipped into bed next to John. This was very odd; she was getting into bed with a *boy*. To sleep, well that was the plan, assuming her body allowed it. It wasn't even her bed, not that the bed was a stranger to her, obviously, but... She shook her head and accepted the embrace from John who pulled her down under the covers, before turning off the light.

ORDINARY WORLD

'You alright, Olivia?'

'Uh huh,'

John kissed her on the forehead, 'I hope you can sleep. Wake me if you need me.'

He kissed her again before wrapping himself around her. Olivia envied his ability to almost instantly fall asleep, while she lay there feeling exhausted by yet another day of experiences, and totally failing in this one simple task.

While she waited for sleep to envelop her, she thought about her day. It had started with horror and a revelation. Her father was doping her and yet she now had evidence to counter this affirmation. Dr Eckstein's tox screen had shown nothing untoward in her system, so what had her father been talking about? She couldn't fathom it, she must have misheard, it must have been a reference to her mother's meds. But that was another thing: if she was to think on her mother's situation, hadn't her dad arranged for some awful trauma to happen to her mother? She must be mishearing things – that would make more sense than her father plotting against his family. If he didn't want anything more to do with them the easiest thing, surely, would be for him to just walk out? None of it made any sense. Her mind slipped away from such unpleasant thoughts to events later in the day. Her ride upon dragon's back... if only that had been true. For a moment there, she had felt like a fabled queen soaring across her kingdom. Why couldn't her dreams be more like that, when she finally slept? Why did she have to be pursued through endless corridors by giant hornets? That wasn't pleasant at all.

Her mind skimmed over her time at the clinic, most of it seemed to be a repeat of her dreams, endless blistering white corridors that blinded her. An image popped into her head of Uncle Bulgaria walking with a cane across the T-junction. It was most definitely him. She hadn't imagined him and as she went back over the image in her head he glanced surreptitiously her way. He looked directly at her! Was this her imagination or had he really done that, but in the moment she hadn't noticed? She went back over the scene again, and yes, once more he glanced her way. She was convinced this is what had happened, but where was he actually looking? Was he looking at her? He seemed to be, in those brief moments before he disappeared around the corner, but his gaze slid, as he did, and it looked like he was looking at John, at which point the corners of his mouth had twitched upwards. Olivia flinched and looked over at John who was snoring quietly. His face didn't belie any sense of hidden intrigue on his part as he slept, even so, suddenly his embrace felt more like a prison than a region of security. She gently extricated his limbs from about her body and shuffled over to her side of the bed. He mumbled in his sleep as she did this and then rolled over, clearly unaware that she had removed herself from his protection. No, she was being paranoid again, her mind *was* playing tricks on her, she was seeing enemies at every turn now and maybe distortions of what was real to boot. She sighed, plumped her pillow and lay down into it, desperate to stop thinking and just let sleep consume her. Her memory shifted again, now they were stood outside John's flat, the taxi was driving away. As they turned to go in through the gateway she noticed car lights out of the corner of her eye. Was that odd in such a quiet side street, especially at that time of night? Probably not, but her memory of the lights caused her to linger longer on the vehicle they belonged to as they switched off, the car parking up for the night. She thought at the time that there was something familiar about the car, but only now as she lay in a half-doze did it occur to her why. Wasn't that Rob Burns' car? He still lived with his parents, even though he was in his late teens and the Burns' lived a few doors down from her house. Why would Rob be parking up in John's street after midnight? She looked more closely to see if she could discern who was driving. Through the angled opaqueness of the windscreen, with the aid of the street lamps she suddenly saw Rob Burns peering back at her - with no face.

She jolted awake. Her heart was racing, sweat beaded her brow.

'Fuck!' she said to the darkness. More dreams of horror, *thank you brain*, she thought as she started to calm herself. She rolled over nesting herself into her pillow, curling up under the covers in a protective embryonic position. She closed her eyes and tried to think of something pleasant from her day – John slipped into her vision as she remembered the sensation of *him* slipping into *her*. And then the pristine white brilliance entered her mind as well, although thankfully the blinding lance of pain was absent. It was an exquisite white light that saturated her vision and her mind.

She awoke to find herself lying in a bed. She could see the outlines of her legs under neatly turned-down grey blankets, practically strapping them down, so taut were they. She looked around and could see she was lying in what appeared to be a hospital's private room.

The blinds were open over the nouveau style, white plastic-bordered window; beyond, all she could see was darkness of a starless night sky. There was a voice speaking, '...*released from their second album '(What's the story) Morning Glory, it reached number two in the UK singles chart and is one of the band's most popular and enduring songs, 'Wonderwall' by Oasis.*'

Oh, Olivia thought, as the guitar intro started. It sounded strangely familiar, almost haunting in quality and yet, as the vocals started, she knew she'd never heard this song before. In fact, she had never heard of the band either, which was strange because she listened to the radio whenever she could and was fairly up on the bands of the UK scene. Olivia knew she was dreaming and yet she could hear the music sonorously clear in her mind. What a fabulous dream. Another voice cut into her delirium and she was not best pleased to recognise that it was Simon. That man was the end! What? What did he just say? Was he being condescending again? No, she started to listen to what he was saying. Simon wasn't talking to the patient, he wasn't even talking to her, he was talking to someone on the phone. He had his back to her and his hand to his right ear, and he was clearly talking as if on the phone. But where was the phone? She couldn't see him holding anything. Was he just talking to thin air?

'No. No, I disagree, I don't think we can wait any longer. Time to retrieve her. Her condition is unchanged and I'm beginning to fear for the baby. Send a retrieval team; we'll have to remove the baby when we're back. If we can save her in the process, that's all well and good. If we can't, we'll just have to learn as much as we can from dissection. Yes, bring them in now. No, Stephen's not here. No, it won't be an issue. He's in the wind, but he'll be back. When he does, we can retrieve him too. He won't be expecting anything, especially if the ambush is set at one of the shuttle stations – he seems to think he can move through them with impunity. It'll be an easy takedown. No, well, I suppose. But no, if he causes an issue, we just tell him most of it... that his wife and child are back at the facility. He should come quietly enough. Yes, we can prepare for that eventuality. I'm aware of his volatility, but he's not as powerful when she's not consciously with him. Good. Yes. Now.'

Olivia was incensed, she wasn't quite certain why. But whatever and to whomever Simon had been speaking, he clearly didn't have the patient's best interests at heart. Nor her baby's, for that matter. He was supposed to be their friend. He was supposed to be Stephen's friend. Yet there he was calling for a retrieval and *dissecting* the patient. It was immoral, grotesque, inhumane.

The scene changed abruptly and there were half a dozen people all crammed into the small hospital room. She could hear Simon's voice somewhere outside the room giving instructions. There were two people in white lab coats standing at the end of the bed looking at a clipboard and Olivia could also see three individuals, she could only presume to be men, in black, armoured riot gear. They were all armed with automatic rifles and there was a cage to the right of the bed, just large enough for a small human to be crammed into. She could also determine brass clamps attached to the side of the cage, with red and black wires running from them down into the base of the underside of the cage. She turned to look up at the three armoured men. One of them was leaning over her with what looked like a silver metal collar, which he was attempting to place around her neck.

Olivia became suddenly very scared. A tight ball of anxiety gripped her in the belly and it tried to ram its way up her oesophagus to lodge in her throat. She was having none of this and tried to fend off the man with the collar, lunging her arms up to push him away.

The pristine white light that had cloaked her vision at the start of the dream suddenly coalesced in front of her, searing through her forehead and blinding her. When her vision cleared, she could still see the armoured men, but they lay in a crumpled heap on the far side of the room. The two people in white lab coats lay unconscious next to them. She turned her attention towards the cage and watched as it crumpled in on itself. It started to glow, from a dull red, to orange and then to a white so bright she had to close her eyes. She could feel the heat of that white light tingling on her eyelids. The heat faded, as did the light that threatened to blind her even with her eyes closed. She blinked and opened them. The cage no longer existed; it was a slowly cooling molten puddle on the floor. Or, perhaps more accurately, *in* the floor, for it had burned a hole right through the plastic tiles and down into the room below. She could just see the curve of the wall, that same nouveau, white plastic-embraced window and the essence of darkness that lay beyond the glass. She turned to look at Simon as he walked in to see how his operation was going. She was horrified by what she saw. He had no face. Reminiscent of Mrs McKilliecuddy, his face was not there, but there was movement on the blank canvas, as if there were multiple faces attempting to vie for the space. Olivia screamed.

She woke up. She was sweating profusely. Her covers were entangled about her making it almost impossible to move. The room was gloomy, early dawn shadows casting an unholy light into her waking nightmare visions. John tried to prop himself up on his elbow, a hand fumbling towards her in his half-wakefulness, to be laid upon her side as a comfort until his mind became conscious enough to contend with her predicament.

'Olivia?' he mumbled, using his free hand to rub at his eyes, 'Are you alright? Did I hear you scream?'

She sat back into her pillows, propping herself into an upright position and pulling the covers up to her chest as the sweat started to cool on her skin, leaving a chilled sensation. She sighed and then drew in a long breath.

'Yes, yes I'm alright. Just another nightmare. Nothing to worry about. Go back to sleep.'

John didn't go back to sleep, instead he forced himself upright in the bed and moved over to comfort her. She found his warm arms encircling her and for a moment she wanted to shrug them off as an image of a collusion between him and Uncle Bulgaria came to mind. But then she relented and took comfort from his embrace. They remained thus for some time, as Olivia slowly recovered from her nightmares and atrocious sleep, and John took the opportunity to fully awaken.

Olivia sat at John's breakfast bar as he served her a mug of tea and made them both some toast.

'Do you want to talk about your dreams?' John asked.

'Not really,' Olivia replied quietly, she didn't fancy going over the shards of memory that would insist on leaking into her waking hours. There were more than enough opportunities for her conscious mind to apply new visionary horrors without holding onto those from the bliss of sleep. 'Can we talk about something else, please?'

'Sure,' John replied as he placed a plate of hot buttered toast in front of her, but his hand failed to relinquish the plate as he looked at her. She looked back at him and she thought she detected confusion in his eyes. *Is he struggling to find a safe subject?* she wondered, *one that won't immediately turn me into a total nutjob?*

'What did you have in mind?' John opted for her to make the conversational decision. *Probably a wise decision*, she thought.

'Oh,' she had a sudden thought, 'What about Fluffy?'

John's eyebrows rose at the name, and there was a gentle nod of his head, 'Yes, I could talk about Fluffy and what she's uploaded. Who knows, some of it might actually help.'

John brought his plate over to the bar and sat on a stool on the other side, opposite her; he talked between mouthfuls as he expounded upon Fluffy's upload.

'Fluffy seems to have connected with a history record node. She downloaded most of what was on there, I think. Most of it seems to indicate that the organisation I infiltrated was set up in the 60's. Someone has been scanning old files into it for years. The records are woefully incomplete – huge chronological gaps – but there's plenty here to be getting on with. The newest file that seems to have been created, about three years ago, has a partial blueprint of their active defence system. And it's fascinating.'

John looked exuberant as he started talking about it. Olivia tried her very best to look interested, but it made little sense to her and she could feel her eyelids drooping.

'It's a bit of an oxymoron, but the defence system is simplistically complex. It's created using interlocking diamond matrices. So, if one zone is attacked, all the adjacent zones can help. And, what's really exciting about it is that it's three or four dimensional. Most stuff we do on the 'net is linear, so while I'm following a single pathway, they're countering this from multiple sources. It's incredibly advanced, and explains a lot of how they did what they did. In fact, I'm amazed we got out at all.' John was literally bouncing on his stool as he looked at her. His beaming smile subsided noticeably as he acknowledged her expression.

'I'm sorry, this isn't exciting for you, is it? Only me, and a few others.'

'Like Alex?' Olivia said helpfully, trying to assuage the sudden guilt she felt for not being excited with him.

'Yes, like Alex.'

'Or,' she frowned hoping she'd remembered the name correctly, 'Patricia?'

'Hm, not so much, Patricia. She'll be more interested in the outcome than this technical stuff.'

He continued with what Fluffy had also discovered.

'The organisation seems to have been founded in 1965. Back then it was a private charitable research facility looking into what I can only describe as very advanced theoretical research. They were looking at genetic manipulation of cells to prevent inheritable mental disorders. Way, way, way ahead of its time. Now I'm not a geneticist nor a biochemist, but by my reckoning the initial foundation for the organisation's research was at least a decade ahead of the rest of the world. The genetic manipulation theory at any rate, the actual concept for utilising genetics for something as complex and specific as the human brain and inheritable mental disorders and we're looking at being thirty years at least ahead of their time. We're talking about science fiction theory here, like my

Fangjack, and that's probably only about ten years, maybe twenty, ahead of the game. And still only a conceptual hypothesis.

'In fact, the one thing I've discovered for certain, looking through all these files, is that they seem to be running about a decade ahead in the scientific fields over the rest of the world on basic concepts and about thirty years ahead on potential hypotheses. Which makes it all the more interesting that no one seems to have heard of them before and that they don't technically seem to exist past 1976.' John slapped his hand down on the breakfast bar for emphasis causing Olivia to jump, so engrossed in his explanation as she was.

'They clearly *do* exist because we've accessed their databanks. But I can't understand how such an organisation has gone unrecognised for so long, especially given the kind of research they've been engaged in. There are other files that looked like formulas and experimentation notes, but again, these have no consistency and massive chronological gaps. Plus, not being even remotely clued up in the biochemical field, none of it means anything to me, anyway.'

'But how can your Fluffy have gained all this information if where it came from doesn't exist? It's like John Fitzgerald Kennedy; he owns my house, but doesn't exist. I don't understand how this is possible.'

'Basically, it's smoke and mirrors, my lovely,' John smiled at her knowingly, teasingly, because he obviously had some ideas on the subject and suspected she had not a clue in return. She tilted her head at him, to encourage an explanation. 'They all exist in principle, but some, like Mr Kennedy, only exist on paper. I'm not sure about the organisation, though. I would imagine they have offices somewhere, perhaps in one of those warehouses that your landlord purportedly owns. But, no one can see what's in front of them because it's camouflaged – the smoke. Or they're distracted to look elsewhere – the mirrors.'

'I think I understand, I've seen several films with this sort of thing in it. Thrillers, that sort of thing.' She looked at him enquiringly.

'Yup, those films are quite informative really on how the world works, even if they didn't intend them to be. The thing I don't understand is why this organisation would need a front man like John Kennedy and then not have him affiliated with a variety of shell companies. If you dig hard enough you can get straight to them. Seems like something of an oversight on their part, I'd say.'

'Yes, I suppose,' Olivia wasn't certain. Surely Kennedy's fake involvement was enough, she would have thought. After all, they had lived in the house for at least fifteen years and, until now, had been none the wiser. 'Was there anything else Fluffy found out?'

'There was one other file, as it happens, entitled MENTAT. But I can't access it. It's heavily encrypted and very securely sealed. I'm running a few algorithm-cracking programs on it now, but none of them seem to be making much headway. I do wonder if some of the holes in the chronology of the history could be explained by them having been uploaded into this folder. I'm wondering if we may have stumbled inadvertently on the organisation's superior project – it would explain the encryption – but it was in the history node, so perhaps it was an old project that's been mothballed? Until I can access it, we're not really going to know anything.'

He sighed; after his initial excitement, the rest of it seemed to be a bit of a let-down.

'Well, we know Kennedy's fake, but he does own a number of properties across the country in the organisation's name. So, we probably know places where the organisation might have a physical presence. Seems like something to me. Perhaps we could go and visit some of them and see if there's anything to be found out from them?' she looked enquiringly at John.

'Hm, seems a bit of a long shot. And it could also be dangerous, given the fact that they have remained hidden for so long and so desperately tried to stay out of view. If they do exist at one of these sites, I can't imagine them taking kindly to us snooping about. I'm not really a field agent, Olivia.'

Olivia looked disappointed with his response, 'Well, perhaps I will go and have a look then; if you don't want to come, that's fine. I can get a coach to wherever they are. I don't really need to be anywhere the next couple of days because Mum's not due back until Friday.'

She stood up, as if to start her quest right away. John jumped up with her, putting his hands on her shoulders.

'Now wait a minute. You can't just go off wandering the countryside by yourself, there's no telling what kind of people you'll run into. If they're half as paranoid as the people I work for, you'll disappear in a trice.'

'Then, perhaps it would be a good idea for you to come with me, make sure I don't disappear.' She smiled sweetly at him and gave him an affectionate peck on the cheek.

He looked at her long and hard, 'Fine, but it'll have to wait until tomorrow. I can't get out of work today; I have to be there for the briefings. Besides which, my programs may have had some chance at breaking into that file and it'll give us a chance to prepare properly for a jaunt about the country.'

She looked at him disparagingly, but it *would* be much easier if John was there, not least of all because he had transportation.

'Fine, you can pick me up tomorrow morning from my house. Eight a.m., on the nose.'

• • • •

John's departure from the front of Olivia's house was muted, given that it was still early morning. None of the dragon's roar today. Olivia watched him go from her front window and suddenly felt very alone and despondent. Once more she'd had no real sleep and the images that had plagued her the night before kept seeping into her mind's eye. She drew in a deep breath and held it longer than was probably good for her. When she let it out she suddenly felt very dizzy, not the best idea she'd had in recent days. She let out a shorter sigh and then compelled herself to get herself ready for school. No need for the big backpack today as John wouldn't be out of work until late. It took longer to ready herself as she bumbled about in a bit of a daze. She had to let herself back into the house twice before finally making her way to the cut-through, because she had forgotten something. Dad was in for a change, she could him snoring up in bed from the bottom of the stairs. She made no attempt to wake him, thankful that he was effectively out of her way.

Olivia's walk to school was haggard, she was so deeply tired. She felt like there was a fog in her brain, which slowly descended over her eyes, bringing with it a leaden weight that was insistent on shutting her eyelids every few minutes. She stumbled into several people and a lamp post on her walk to school and was quite amazed that she didn't get run over. She felt bemused, given her feelings of elation yesterday afternoon, as she lay in John's arms and felt like nothing could ever faze her again. Fleeting vague images of her dreams persistently popped into her head: the most notable was that of Simon with no face; it was replaced on occasion either by Rob Burns or Mrs McKilliecuddy, also faceless. She stopped near where the minibuses dropped off the school children from outside town and took a moment to rub at her face and eyes, trying desperately to regain a semblance of wakefulness. When she looked up from the pavement and started to consider what seemed an endless walk of a few hundred yards to the front gates, she saw the woman from the bus, at the corner of the street with that man again. She was positive it was her this time.

It startled her, especially as the woman seemed to be looking directly at her. Their eyes locked for a moment and it appeared to Olivia as though the woman suddenly became desperately afraid, because of the harrowed expression that leapt to her face. The woman turned abruptly on her heel, grabbed the man's elbow and dragged him around the corner. Olivia remained where she was, leaning against the lamp post, staring after them. Time passed, and she saw Rhys running up to the gates to catch up with a group of lads who welcomed him as a comrade. Then she saw Evie slipping out of her mother's car and going into the yard through the side gate; she was craning her neck, looking all over the place searchingly and Olivia suspected Evie was looking for her. Olivia's surveillance was disturbed as three boys from her year walked past her and gave low whistles, presumably in recognition of her amorous display yesterday. One of them started to make a remark about working girls and lamp posts, but was immediately hushed by his friends. Perhaps they had seen the aggressive look that had erupted on her face. She was too tired to be diplomatic or to try and ignore such things anymore. They hurried on and she turned her gaze back to the corner where the woman had disappeared. As she did so, Olivia saw the woman ducking her head round it. The woman looked briefly down the street in her direction, spotted Olivia looking at her and immediately dived back around the corner.

Olivia knew the woman was there and looking for her. She couldn't understand why the woman would be searching for her, following her? Why? An intuition told her to go and find out. Olivia pushed herself off the lamp post and started to march up the street to confront them. There was no thought in her mind that such a confrontation might get ugly, might be dangerous. She wanted to know whatever it was there was to know. She strode past the school gates and was immediately deflected from her passage by the assistant head teacher, Mr Barnaby, who stepped out in front of her.

'I think you'll find school is this way, Miss Buchanan,' he said authoritatively.

She looked up at him, surprised by his sudden appearance. By the look on his face, she knew he wasn't in the mood for any excuses on her part as to why it was more important for her to ignore the bell and march off down the street. She became annoyed by his interference and turned her ire towards him instead. She started to say something, but then found Mr Barnaby clutching his temples in apparent agony. She forgot everything she had been about to say, she forgot about the woman from the bus and just went to him. Olivia supported his weight as she saw his knees starting to buckle and helped the man stagger into the school grounds. With some effort from her own exhausted muscles, she settled him on a bench.

'Stay there, Mr Barnaby, I'll get the nurse,' she didn't wait for a reply, merely running to the office to get Mrs Flint to find the school nurse.

• • • •

They were all sat in the nurse's office: Mr Barnaby, Olivia, the nurse, Mr Rawlinson and Mrs Flint. The nurse had attended to Mr Barnaby and he was sat on her couch looking extremely pale. He kept avoiding eye contact with Olivia.

'I don't know,' he said in answer to Rawlinson's question. 'One minute I was talking to Olivia about coming into school, the next there was this blinding flash of pain right in the middle of my head that shot out through the sides of it. I couldn't think, I couldn't breathe. It felt like my head was going to explode.'

Olivia noticed him glance surreptitiously at her as he said his final sentence and look sharply away when he realised she was looking at him. She felt like he was blaming her for giving him a migraine.

'Well, how are you feeling now?' Rawlinson asked.

'Better, thank you. The pills Janine gave me seem to be working. The main pain went pretty quickly, but it left me feeling very woozy. The headache seems to be fading too.'

'Good. Think you're alright for work?'

The school nurse looked disapprovingly at Rawlinson, 'I would counsel against Mr Barnaby working any more today. And, if we're being honest, I would highly recommend someone drive him to his GP's straight away for an emergency appointment. A flash headache like that could be a precursor or warning of something far more serious. I would recommend him having an x-ray or scan, personally.'

She stood with her fists on her ample hips, just daring Rawlinson to gainsay her. Rawlinson took in her stance and the fierce glower upon her face and threw his hands up into the air.

'Fine. Fine, whatever you think best, nurse. But with two down with the 'flu and two of my supply teachers not having turned up, we're a bit shorthanded.' This appeal to the nurse fell on deaf ears as she rose a finger to point at Rawlinson and opened her mouth to back it up.

'No,' Rawlinson capitulated, 'of course, you're right, nurse, and I bow in deference to your knowledge in such matters.'

Olivia smirked at Rawlinson's discomfort. He clearly noticed this out of the corner of his eye, because he turned his thwarted ire onto her instead.

'You appear to be late for your lessons, Miss Buchanan. It will be duly noted on your records. Now I would suggest you run along before there's more to be added to those records.'

Olivia was of a mind to punch him, but instead she turned to Mr Barnaby and placed a hand on his forearm. 'I hope you feel better soon, sir.'

Mr Barnaby flinched at her touch, but managed to croak out a thank you to her, before she left.

Chapter 16

Evie pummelled Olivia's arm in her excitement when she slipped into class. Evie was beaming from ear to ear and wanted to know all about John and their relationship, but she had to be content with a warning from their teacher that she could find out about it in detention if she wasn't quiet. Olivia found Evie's persistence through the day irritating; she really didn't want to divulge too much about her new boyfriend. It made her smile uncontrollably when she thought of John as her boyfriend. In the end, she gave Evie some titbits on riding on the back of the bike and what an excellent kisser he was. The cherry on top for Evie was the discovery that John was in his mid-twenties with a really good job, at which point, Olivia noted how her friend's mood changed subtly and she realised that Evie was envious of her.

My god, Olivia thought, *Evie's envious of* me!

It had done the trick though, because Evie left her in peace after lunch as she contemplated Olivia's new status in the grand scheme of things. The afternoon passed quickly enough and Olivia was able to slip out of school unnoticed to go home and look forward to a long boring evening without John. Although she could plan and pack for their outing tomorrow.

Olivia was highly distracted during the walk back home due to the constant buzzing in her ears; in fact she wasn't entirely certain it was in her ears, it felt like it was in the front of her head half the time. It was that same white noise she'd heard yesterday in John's flat, but every so often, if she concentrated rather than trying to rub it away, she thought she could discern words.

'Sorry,' she said to a middle-aged couple she bumped into because she wasn't paying any attention. The woman gave a faux smile by return, the man a mere grimace.

'*Honestly, the youth of today, always in a hurry, never looking where they're going, no consideration for their elders.*'

Olivia rounded sharply on the woman, 'Look! I said I was sorry... I have a lot on my mind at the moment. It's consideration for my elders that's half the problem!'

The couple, who had already progressed several yards from the initial collision, turned with bemused looks upon their faces to look back at her. Olivia stared hard at the woman, as if daring her to say more.

'Young lady,' the man said, 'I don't know what kind of drugs you're on, but kindly keep them to yourself. Come on, Eileen,' he took his companion's elbow and swiftly turned on his heel, marching them both away from Olivia.

'*If she is on drugs she could be dangerous, the sooner we get out of here the better. If worse comes to worse, I can always shove Eileen at her to get away.*'

'You horrible old man!' Olivia shouted after him, 'I'm not on fucking drugs. And if I was you, Eileen, I'd get away from him as soon as possible.'

Eileen glanced over her shoulder at Olivia; she looked both shocked and confused by her outburst.

'What's she talking about, Winston?' Eileen said to her companion as he continued to drag her away.

'No idea, m'dear, no idea,' he responded, '*better check to see if that guttersnipe's swiped Eileen's purse, when she walked into us. It's the kind of ploy pickpockets use to distract their victims.*'

'I did no such fucking thing! How dare you, you... you old CUNT!'

Olivia stood fuming in the middle of the high street swearing after Winston. It was only once they had ducked around a corner that she started to calm down. She rubbed at her ears, the buzzing was getting more and more insistent. She drew in a ragged breath and then realised the scene she had made in public, as there were many by-standers gawking in her direction and several more were hurrying away from her – perhaps they too thought she was on drugs and was a danger to their continued existence. Instead of feeling abashed, Olivia felt her temper rising again, *well, fuck the lot of them*, she thought as she turned and set off on her way once more. That buzzing was getting really annoying now.

It was only as she was nearing the cut-through that something made her pay more attention to her surroundings: the buzzing was subsiding and she had started to push beyond its irritation. She distracted herself further by thinking about what she might need with her on her jaunt tomorrow. Suddenly, the hackles on the back of her neck flared, sending a chill down her spine. Her hearing had picked up a rhythmic, steady beat behind her, one that she recognised – boot steps. She paused at the entrance to the cut-through and looked back the way she had just come. Were her ears playing tricks on her again? Had they merely switched from that frustrating buzzing over to something more tangible? Something more familiar?

There were a few people about, mainly school children – it was that time of day – but no sign of any booted follower, no sign of her dad rushing up to scare her half to death again. She turned back to the cut-through and headed into it. She had gone a hundred yards or so when she heard the boot steps echoing off the high wooden fences on either side of her. She picked up her pace. The pathway bent to the left about fifty yards ahead; it would give her a chance to look back and see if anyone was actually following her without being suspicious. She arrived at the bend and glanced back down the lane. That was when she saw someone.

They were tall, well over six foot, but arched and angular like an ancient willow. Their head was bent down, looking at the pavement in front of them as they walked. They wore a black leather fedora, the brim obscuring their face. They also wore a heavy-looking, black, leather longcoat that hung to their ankles and barely stopped above their black steel toe-capped boots. Olivia's stride faltered as she saw them and she gasped at such an odd person. Her sharp intake of breath triggered a reaction in the fellow, because his head came up all of a sudden and she was able to see his face. He wore silver, mirrored, wraparound sunglasses that stood out against the pallor of the skin that covered his blank face. He had no mouth and no nose. No creases in his forehead, no discernible ears. And if he had eyes, they were completely hidden by his wraparounds. His head was pear-shaped, the jawline an extended rounded point of that inverted pear. She watched as the point appeared to distend and she realised that it was moving to allow the mouthless aperture to open. She remained frozen in a half-step, watching the face warp and melt as a maw revealed itself. The fleshy skin, that had once concealed it, peeled apart with a sticky elasticity, strands of slowly melting plastic stretching endlessly, gaps opening as the strands snapped apart, exposing the darkness of a void within. She could detect triangular teeth beyond the strands, just like those possessed by the wire-haired old woman. Olivia was stuck, horror and sickening fascination gluing her to the spot. The glue was suddenly dissolved as a fetid breath shot from the cavernous maw, swiftly followed by the feral hoarse scream of a banshee. The sound wave hit her like a tornado, rocking her where she stood. An ancient chill of deep fear washed over her – a justified fear of what lay in the darkness beyond the sanctity of the village. Finally, she expelled her own held breath in a reciprocating scream and she turned and fled down the cut-through.

Straight into another man, whose hands came down and gripped her firmly about her shoulders. Hands that were like the talons of an eagle. Ribbed, multi-jointed, greyish-green in hue. The fingers ended in claws, silvery-grey in appearance, that seemed to both reflect and absorb the light cast from the late afternoon sun. They were as hard as steel and pierced through her coat and into her flesh, clamping her in a vice that would not be easily broken. She could feel the bones in her shoulders being ground unpleasantly against one another by the force. Olivia looked up into a face identical to the one she had just seen. She screamed again and lashed out with a foot into her attacker's shin. Her hands came up, clasped together and she shoved her attacker in the sternum, smashing her foot into his shin repeatedly. To her surprise, he relinquished his hold, stumbling backwards as he gripped the sides of his head. His mouth opened, in similar fashion to his compatriot's and it exhaled a noisome stench and a low, keening moan.

Olivia looked beyond him, questing an escape route through to the end of the cut-through, but despite pushing him off her, he still blocked the passageway. What she saw over his shoulder plunged her into a well of despair; for there, at the entrance she saw the shambling transient who had accosted her days previously. Even were she to get past her tall assailant there was another potential foe blocking her path to freedom. Her only choice was to retreat back the way she had come, but as she reached the bend in the path she found herself pincered. The first freak had closed the gap on the bend rapidly and the second freak, despite his apparent consternation was advancing on her. She turned back to face him, making her stand at the bend in the path.

She glanced around because she could hear the first figure making a swift approach from behind. She turned back in time to see an apparition descending upon her with a preternatural speed, his longcoat changing in appearance as he came towards her, arms held out to catch her. Now he looked like a great, winged beast. A horror from ancient folklore. An angel of death come to reap her soul.

A horrendous icy lump settled in the pit of her stomach, weighing her down. It sent watery electrical sensations of cold down into her legs, immobilising them. And it was in that moment of utter terror that she saw the transient raise his arms parallel to the ground, hands clenching as if he were gripping the air in front of him. He stepped forward – and vanished – she couldn't believe her eyes. He vanished! And then he was there again, right in front of her, just behind her assailant. The transient's hands clenched again, this time not on empty air but perfectly placed to grip the freak's shoulders. In that moment, Olivia watched as the transient's face melted and started to slide, even more so than it had appeared the first time she had seen him. *Did he just wink at me?* she wondered. And then, as before he vanished, as did her assailant. One moment they were both in front of her, blocking her only means of escape, the next they were gone. As if they had never been.

She turned to see where the first willowesque freak had gone to, having felt his presence nearing. He was very close to her now, but it wasn't his proximity that caught her attention, it was the sight of the transient suddenly appearing at the kerb's edge a hundred yards behind her and pushing the freak he had grabbed into the road. There was a squeal of brakes, a heavy thump, the sound of splintering glass and the screech of rubber being forced along tarmac against its will. She watched as her assailant spun through the air to disappear from view as a Volvo slammed into him. The transient disappeared into the maelstrom he had created.

Her attention was distracted by this only momentarily because her vision was immediately obscured by the first freak as he hove into view. Once more eagle talons were thrusting towards her, a noisome fetid stench washed over her and the chill tingled through the pit of her belly and down into her legs. Her head filled with an agonising pulse of pain that threatened to rip her skull apart. The terror that consumed her, boiled out in one last ragged scream. A soul scream, from the depth of her being.

She felt herself falling. Falling endlessly backwards. Olivia heard a crash and the sound of wood splintering. Still, she was falling; she must have fallen into the fence and was now continuing her plummet to the ground. She waited for the impact with the pavement. For what little air she had left in her lungs, after two screams, to be knocked from her. It never came. She heard a scuffle and a grunt from in front of her.

She opened her eyes.

She was standing upright in the middle of the cut-through, facing the way she had come from. Glancing behind her, she could see a gaping hole in the fence on one side of the passage. Two leather-clad legs dangled from the jagged edge of the hole, the rest of the body obviously hanging upside down from this snare point on the other side of the remaining fence. She was confused, and rightly so, for there now appeared to be a third freak stood a few feet from her, with his back to her. He held a gun in his right hand and a silver collar in his left. She knew enough from the movies to know that it was a pistol with a silencer on it. As for the collar... she had seen it before, in her dreams. Any further speculation was suspended as she realised who the man was facing. It was the tall lanky freak she had bumped into, in this very cut-through, several days earlier. The freak still held his umbrella, which was resting point down on the floor. His other hand was raised, towards the freak with the gun, in a beseeching manner, as if to ward off the influence of the weapon. Maybe to suggest surrender? But then she watched as the freak closed his eyes and pushed his hand forward. Her attacker seemed to jump upwards and backwards, arms flailing, his gun thrown to his side, the collar clattering to the pavement, skittering down the walkway and bouncing off the brick wall that housed the fence. He continued to fly backwards, over

Olivia's head. She hunched down as he passed, although there was no need. He continued on his trajectory until he hit the fence with a crunch. Several of the planks buckled and split under the impact. He fell heavily to the ground.

When the third assailant tried to stand up, the umbrella-freak advanced on him, stepping around Olivia and shielding her from her attacker. He brought his fist downwards, as if he was thumping a tack into a board. Olivia's attacker's head slammed to one side and he sprawled in front of them, motionless. The freak took in the scene for a moment and then turned to her, gently grabbing her by the upper arm. His long, distended fingers wrapped completely around her woefully inadequate bicep and she saw the fingertips come to rest upon the base of his hand. Those fingers really were freakishly long.

'Come, Olivia,' he said in a quiet and calm voice, 'we must leave now, before others come. I will see you safe.'

She found herself being led at pace down the path and out into her street. But instead of heading to her house, he led her away from it – down to the end of the road and over into the park. She tried to resist as they went past her house, but his quickly-spoken explanation soothed her concern and allowed her to continue with him. Peculiar though it was.

'They will look in your house first; it won't be safe there until later. Miriam will look out for you as she foresaw this. She will know when it will be safe for you to return.'

They walked swiftly into the park, leaving the main path almost immediately and cutting across the grass to the manmade hills to the right. They came to a small copse, pressing beyond the first trunks. There was a chain-link fence within the copse which had a number of signs on it, indicating it to be private property beyond and warning of the danger of electrocution. Olivia tried to resist, but all aspects of her mind disagreed with her decision-making and overrode her, allowing the freak to lead her deeper into the wooded area, through a concealed break in the fence and beyond, into a shielded culvert hidden by bushes.

• • • •

The culvert was dark at first, but as they made their way deeper into its recesses Olivia started to see a glimmer of light. She presumed it was coming from the other side, the exit back into the park, so she was quite surprised when they entered a circular room off to the side, which looked more like someone's sitting room. There was a circular dining table in the middle, with a floral-patterned tablecloth. Upon this was set an antique oil lamp and a vase of daffodils. Directly ahead of her was an old, dark wood kitchen bureau and to her left, a settee. To her right she could see a closed oak wood door and just before that, a dark wood table. Sat at the table was the weird old lady that had accosted Olivia previously. The freak that had been guiding her here offered her a seat on the settee and then went and stood by the entrance, whether to suggest her way out was barred or that he was a guard against intruders, she wasn't certain. She looked at him for a moment then turned her attention to the old woman.

'Are you Miriam?' she asked.

The weird old woman nodded. Olivia continued to stare at her then back to the tall man. No one spoke. It was eerily quiet and Olivia didn't like it one bit. Not least because she couldn't tell if she'd been kidnapped or not. Finally, the unending silence was too much for her.

'What the hell is going on?' she demanded.

The tall freak looked at Miriam, who returned the stare. After a moment he nodded and then came and sat down on the settee. He turned to face Olivia and looked at her with his deeply disturbing eyes. Olivia thought they looked mournful. He spoke in a coarse whisper of a voice, that reminded her of the scales of a snake as they scraped across a rock.

'We didn't always look as we do now, Olivia. Once upon a time we were normal people like you and your friends. But we made a choice, because we were dying. We agreed to a contract with people who wanted to help us, wanted to help the human race, so they said. We believed them. I can't speak for all of us, but I believed them because I wanted to. Because I didn't want to die and anything was better than that. In some ways, the cure *was* better than dying because I gained from it, we all did. But it came with a price.'

He paused. Olivia wondered if he was remembering another time as a faraway look passed across his distended features.

'We are survivors. Not of our illnesses, but of their experiments. We number few compared with those that went through that first phase of trials. You could say we are the lucky ones, because they *did* cure us; we didn't die from our diseases. But most did. Most of us died, and not because we were ill, but because the experiments took a heavy toll. A few of us survivors remained with them. You've seen them. The three men who attacked you in the cut-through just now. They were triplets and among the first of us to come through the experiments. There are one or two more you may have seen over the years. Whether you realised it or not. And then there are us, those of us who survived the experiments and didn't stay with them. We left, although not with their permission. We fled their facility thanks to your parents, who were the best of us. Your mother and father were survivors too, but of the second phase of the experiment. Your mother suffers still, thanks to their regime of drugs that have altered her over the years. Her deficiency, her penalty for the success of their experiments is that her mind was warped, unlike us who merely had our bodies warped.

'We've been watching you for a long time now. Longer than you realise. You have started to notice us recently, which says where you are in all this. At least to us, even if you don't know it yourself yet. But *they* have also been watching you. Nurturing you, while they continue to experiment on your mother. They are desperate to see her come through her mind warp and come out the other side. It would mean they were finally close to their goal. And, we suspect with this new range of cocktails they have been pumping into her over the last few months, that finally they may have achieved that goal. She is brighter than she has been in a long time, maybe since it all began. Is she not?'

He stopped and gave Olivia a penetrating glare; she felt that he was specifically asking her to confirm his theory based on what she had witnessed of her mother's recent change in lucidity.

'But there's more to it than that. There's you, Olivia. You are the culmination of their experiments. Experiments designed to enhance the human race, enhance the human mind. You are their ultimate goal. Because you are the product of two of their greatest specimens. Your mother and your father. With you proven to have taken the next evolutionary step, they will be able to make more of you. The superhuman race that they have striven for, for over three decades now.'

Olivia stared back at him. She could feel something in her belly, a sensation that started small as she listened to him, then grew in intensity. It grew to ball up into her chest. It rose into her throat and eventually exploded from her mouth as she opened it, when he paused for a second time.

Olivia laughed. It was a deep, guttural laugh that encapsulated everything he had just explained. She laughed so hard her sides ached and she started to gasp, struggling to catch enough breath to fill her lungs to oxygenate her brain. She became dizzy and light-headed and still she laughed. Everything he had said was clearly delusional. But his final statement, that she was the culmination of a superhuman experiment, was so utterly ludicrous that she just couldn't help herself. It did, ironically, take a superhuman effort to bring herself under control. Several minutes passed before she was able to actually speak, dragging in great gulps of air in order that she might perform such a simple task.

'I'm superhuman?' she stated incredulously, 'If you really had been watching me for all this time, then you would be well aware of the fact that there is absolutely nothing superhuman about me. I'm a fucking mess most of the time! I can barely hold it together! I can look after Mum or I can do my school work, but I can't do both. If I was superhuman that would be a piece of piss, right? As for anything else, I'm barely holding it together and I'm suffering for it. I have headaches – blinding headaches. I can't sleep; I have horrible nightmares; I'm losing my hearing and I'm starting to hallucinate.'

She stopped, breathless, with this final revelation. She *was* fucking starting to hallucinate – it was the only explanation for what she had been seeing in recent days. The only explanation for the three abominations that had just attacked her.

'Fucking hell, I'm hallucinating!'

She said this by way of confirmation to herself. Fuck, if that was true, was it just because of poor sleep or had she inherited her mother's illness, after all? Oh god, she was just beginning to live her life, she was just beginning to think that maybe there was a life beyond caring for her mum and living with her dad. What about her future? Her sudden hope to fulfil a dream and go to university? What about John? She had a boyfriend now, a fucking boyfriend for fuck's sake. She had never before considered the possibility and now she realised that maybe she was more like her mother than she could have ever dreaded. And here was this freak telling her she was the culmination of a superhuman experiment – the ultimate human. What a fucking joke!

ORDINARY WORLD

The tall man remained impassive throughout her diatribe, waiting patiently for an opening to continue.

'Yes, Olivia, you are superhuman.' It was a quiet confirmation of the man's clear delusion, as far as Olivia was concerned. He really believed it; she could see it in his eyes.

'Ha! If I was so superhuman, then surely I would have been able to deal with those triplets who attacked me? Instead, I did nothing but try to run and that didn't go very well until you turned up and threw them through the fence.'

She frowned at him for a moment as she recalled the incident, 'How did you do that, by the way? You never actually seemed to touch them.'

The tall man inclined his elongated head at her and she got the impression he was bowing to her.

'I only did what you had already done, Olivia. I followed your lead. You were the one who threw the second one through the fence, by the time I got there my involvement was fairly arbitrary. Albert had phased the first into the street, you had dealt with the second, I finished the third one off, but it was you who had dismantled them; immobilising them with your banshee wail.'

She shook her head at him, 'I did no such thing. It was you... Albert?' she asked suddenly. He said Albert had *phased* one of them, what the hell did that mean? 'What's phased?'

The freak looked at her in a discerning way, tilting his head, as if gauging how best to respond.

'Albert,' he started, 'was the man who removed the triplet who had grabbed you. He is one of us, one of the survivors, although to look at him you might doubt that. Unlike Miriam and I, when we use our powers now nothing more happens, the damage has already been done. But when Albert uses his powers he continues to warp and melt. I believe this is one of the reasons he chooses to live apart from us.'

The freak's features took on a saddened expression, 'Phasing is a power that Albert possesses and one I have no idea how he does it. I don't know if he just moves faster than the human eye can detect or if he hops through space like those space ships you see in fantasy films, like Star Wars. I really don't know, but the theory behind phasing is that you take two linear points in space, fold that space so the two points are touching and then you step from one point to the next. It means you can travel vast distances in the blink of an eye. It's truly amazing.' The freak seemed genuinely awed by Albert's ability.

Olivia sat back into the cushions of the settee; no, that couldn't be what she had witnessed, that was impossible. Like the freak had said, it was the thing of fantasy, like Star Wars. Her mind revolted against the possibility, in the same way it had revolted against his conviction that she was superhuman. She changed the subject,

'OK, then how did you manage to disarm the last one without touching him? How did you manage to throw both of them through the fence, again, without apparently touching them?'

Again, he shook his head, 'No, it was you,' he repeated quietly. 'I don't know how it manifests with you; it manifests differently with all of us. Some of us have to say the words, others have to gesticulate – like I do – some go deaf with the sounds of a thousand oceans crashing into their minds as seas crash over rocks. But however it manifests, when this happens our minds can project into the physical world and affect it. Whether that is as simple as making a blade of grass wither or lifting a man off his feet and hurling him through a wooden fence. Your mind is now the strongest thing on this planet.'

Olivia didn't know how to respond to this final statement, it took her back round to the whole superhuman thing. She started to laugh again. She gently rocked back and forth as the laughter erupted out of her. She noticed, through the tears that streamed from her eyes, that the tall man was looking at Miriam again. He nodded, stood up and took his station by the door once more. Miriam suddenly replaced him on the settee next to Olivia. She felt the old woman's chilly touch as she placed her withered hands over hers. As the arthritic gnarled fingers curled around her hands, she felt the mounting hysteria that was threatening to overwhelm her drain away. A wave of angelic calm settled upon her and she looked deep into Miriam's eyes. It was like looking into the galaxy. She could see stars, billions of them. She could see nebulae and spirals, her mind drifted in the endlessness of it, calming her. It soothed her.

Miriam finally spoke to her and it was in that moment that she realised that Miriam's lips were not moving. Her jaw was not operating as one would expect it to when someone spoke. Miriam's mouth didn't move at all and yet Olivia could hear the words, clear as the sounding of a bell, in the heart of her mind. She felt the words in her head. She heard them in her ears and she felt the accompanying emotions of those words in her chest. They reverberated through to the very core of her being.

Chapter 17

Olivia balked at the invasion into her mind by another being. It was one thing for her to have been hearing things that probably had a rational explanation, like when the house creaked and settled, but left her feeling like there was someone else in the house when there obviously wasn't; it was quite another to have a voice in your mind which might actually be real. She was terrified; she screamed and as she screamed, her mind flooded with the brilliant pristine solar brightness that had been the precursor of her recent headaches. Only this time she felt a physical quality to the light. It had weight. There was a heaviness to it like a blanket. And it slammed through her mind cleansing it of anything that wasn't her. She sat back exhausted into the settee, feeling the lumpiness of old springs and clumped stuffing digging into her back and legs. There was silence beyond her, but she feared opening her eyes. For one, once she did the headache would start to rear its ugly vicious head, for another she wasn't certain she was quite ready to face her new companions.

Her breathing eased and, probe though she might for the first inklings of that headache, nothing seemed to be forthcoming. Tentatively she opened her eyes a crack to peer into the room. What welcomed her sight caused her to open her eyes fully. The room was in disarray.

Miriam lay slumped against the far wall, her chair a shattered remnant of its original self; her desk on its side with all its papers strewn to the four corners of the circular room. The oak door next to where Miriam had sat was buckled, a great crack splitting its central panel. The dining table, with cloth and vase, lay up against the base of the oak door; the vase was nowhere to be seen, but fine, sandy dust covered the floor and many surfaces leading away from her. The flowers were just shredded and burned petals strewn about. As for the tall man, all she could see of him was his legs and comical toe pincher boots sticking through the entrance way. She stood up, confused. What had happened to them? *Did I cause this?* How could she have caused this? All she had done was scream. She felt a chill of realisation course through her body, as the blood drained from her extremities. She looked around the gloom, which was gradually brightening. Not, as she had first thought, because her eyes were becoming accustomed to it, but because the oil lamp that had been on the dining table had set a number of fires after it had broken on the floor and the table cloth was starting to roar with the aid of the splintered kindling of the table.

She jumped up and ran to the varied pockets of fire, stamping them out before the place turned into an inferno. Whether this would have been likely, or whether this was just her imagination she had no way of knowing. But safety first. Once there was nothing but glowing embers, she hurried over to Miriam and half carried, half dragged her to the settee. There was no visible damage to her. No signs of bruising upon her exposed flesh. Nothing to indicate how she had become unconscious. Olivia laid her out on the settee and propped her head up on one of the arms, before turning her attention to the tall man. He was starting to stir and she heard just the slightest moan from him. She went and sat cross-legged on the ground next to him, knowing he was far too big for her to manhandle to a piece of furniture, had there still been one intact for him to sit upon. She lifted his head and placed it gently into her lap, where she then stroked his forehead as a mother would for a fallen child. It was only as she was doing this that it occurred to her that this was her opportunity to escape. Odd that, despite everything that had recently transpired, she didn't feel in danger here. She wasn't a captive, so there was no reason for her to try and flee.

ORDINARY WORLD

The tall man's eyes opened and she had the opportunity to watch them change colour and shape as consciousness returned to him. His eyes focused upon her and he smiled a crooked grin.

'That's lovely, Olivia,' he croaked in his rasping voice, 'for just a moment there I was a young boy again. My mother stroking my brow after falling from the apple tree in our garden.'

Olivia was mildly disconcerted by his grin as it reminded her all too much of a shark's smile, for his teeth were unnaturally pointy. And there seemed to be far too many of them.

He sat up and rubbed his temples, his eyes watered and a tear or two slid from the corners of his eyes. He dabbed them away with one of his immensely long fingers.

'You need to stop screaming, Olivia. At least until you have a better control of your talents.'

Olivia frowned at him. His expression changed and she realised that he understood.

'Ignoring for a moment what I said about the superhuman stuff, suffice to say the experiments, along with a battery of specially designed drugs, were implemented upon those of us who had certain chemical wiring within our minds. Distinctly abnormal wiring. So, people more prone to psychosis or mental instability. Our brains were far more susceptible to the program and therefore far more susceptible to change. With the experiments and the training that the organisation implemented, we were better able to utilise those areas of our brains that have lain either dormant or unexplained since man first started to be more than a hunter gatherer. We can manipulate the world around us with the power of our minds. TV and the like would describe it as telekinesis or telepathy, but those are just words to try and explain what is ostensibly magic for the uninitiated. Our minds can tap into the natural energies of the world created by background radiation, the sun's radiation, as well as manmade energy. We can then utilise that energy in a physical manner, so we can move objects, talk to one another, see into the past or the future. We can do anything our imaginations can contrive.

'But for us in phase one of the experiment it came at a cost. Whenever we developed a talent, our physical bodies rebelled against it and we warped. Even now, when we use a power, like Albert does, or we develop a new one, something physical may distend and become abnormal. This is particularly true for Albert, less so for the rest of us; the worst of our physical warping has already occurred. For those survivors of phase two, they found it accentuated their original psychoses, their mental instabilities, which is why they are less survivors than we are, because most of them just went so mad they could no longer function as human beings. There were a couple that managed to stay anchored in some part to the reality of our world. Your mother, Phyllis, is one of them, but they, too, suffered mental incapacity. Hence, your mother's frequent bouts of schizophrenia.

'What I was trying to say about you and your screaming was this. That you have transcended all of the obstacles of the other survivors. You do not warp physically and you do not appear to be suffering abject mental collapse. There is a distinct talent you have for defence when you scream. But it is untamed and immensely powerful. The devastation in this room is clear evidence of it. I am OK, although I do have a pounding headache from being knocked out, because I have talents of the mind and they shield me to some degree from similar mind assaults. Miriam is the same, but,' he paused for a second as he glanced at the still-unconscious Miriam upon the settee, 'I fear because she was mid-speech with you when you let rip, she may have taken a much heavier assault upon a relatively unprotected mind. I can only hope that once consciousness returns, she will not be insane.'

ORDINARY WORLD

He pursed his lips rather sternly at Olivia and she felt totally ashamed that she might have caused an enduring injury to an elderly lady.

The tall man continued, 'The scream is a powerful weapon, especially if it comes from the core of your being. It's visceral, bestial and perhaps the most devastating of the powers and talents we possess. Not all of us have the power of scream. But, in its higher elements, you can crush or melt steel, break bones or outright kill someone.' Again, his expression was stern as he emphasised the severity of an untamed power.

Olivia stared at him disbelievingly and then she started to shake her head again. *No, now wait a minute, he's saying that I did this with the power of my mind. But that's just science fiction... impossible. Unless none of this is real and I'm having a psychological break, because I've inherited my mother's schizophrenia.*

She felt a tentative prod in the front of her head; it was like a finger had been pushed ever so gently into a soft cushion. It disappeared almost as soon as it had appeared. The tall man spoke.

'That was me. I was showing you the point from which to reach out, should you wish to communicate non-verbally. And yes, that is precisely what I am saying, you did this with the power of your mind. And no, I don't believe you are having a psychological break, although it is possible that you've inherited your mother's schizophrenia. And, of course, that said, as a possible part of the delusional break, that you're not having, but could be having if you wanted to believe that, then I, as part of that delusional break would indeed be urging you to consider that you weren't having one, so I as an illusion within that break would remain constant and alive within it. Bit of a mindbender, wouldn't you say?' he smirked as he finally sat up and leaned against the wall.

'This is insane!' Olivia said in exasperation.

It would make sense that if the tall man was part of a delusion that he would be able to read her thoughts, as he just so obviously had done, because he was a figment of her imagination. What was her best course of action? Accept that she was going mad and go to the unit to be assessed. Or continue blithely on until something really bad happened to her or to someone else, hoping against all odds that she was actually just fine and this was all part of some elaborate dream?

'*Or* you could accept what we've been telling you and listen to how we could make things better for you, and your mother, in the long term.'

'You would say that– you don't want me to dismiss you from my dream.' Olivia was a bright girl and she was aware of a lot of the effects of delusional schizophrenia, having cared for her mother for so long. Was it any wonder she was now having mental issues of her own?

'Yes, that is quite possibly true,' the tall man agreed with a hint of chagrin. Olivia could feel him entering a quandary. 'I'm not sure I know how we can progress from here. You have two options currently: either you accept this to be the truth, or you accept that you're having a psychotic break. Neither are actually very good. At least not in the short term.'

He looked over at Miriam, 'We need Miriam, to be able to progress. I think she would be able to give you something to work with to try and resolve your conundrum.'

He stood up. He was a little wobbly and Olivia held out her hand to steady him.

'Thank you. There's a lot I haven't told you, we haven't told you. But what we've already said seems to have caused far more distress to you than we could have envisaged. None of which was our intent. We were merely trying to give you some insight that would hopefully help you progress in your path and maybe also protect you and your mother from them. Until Miriam awakens, I think we need to wait. You stay here and think. I'll tidy up and then go and get some nourishment.'

Olivia was going to object about him tidying by himself, but he seemed adamant that she should sit and think on her predicament. She could also watch over Miriam while she did so.

• • • •

Olivia sat and waited with Miriam as the tall man left the den in search of 'nourishment'. He returned about an hour later with two bags from the local corner shop and promptly handed her a packet of custard creams. It wasn't what she'd expected. Truth be told she had no idea what she'd been expecting, maybe a haunch of venison recently killed on the plains. Or maybe a couple of squirrels from the park. The tall man busied himself in the next room, once he had prised the oak door open; she guessed it was a kitchen. He came back in and placed a tray of tea things on the now upright dining table and poured a cup for Olivia.

'Shouldn't she have woken up by now?' Olivia asked him, as she took the cup and saucer. She was concerned the old lady might never wake up and that somehow it was her fault. 'Perhaps we should take her to the hospital?'

The tall man looked down at her and then glanced at Miriam. He shook his head. 'We're not the kind to frequent hospitals; besides, it appears she is coming to her senses at last.'

He moved back to the table and poured another cup of tea. He then ladled half a dozen spoonful's of sugar into it before bringing it back to Miriam, who was stirring. Olivia helped her to sit up.

'Thank you, Hiram,' Miriam said to the tall man on receipt of the tea. She then craned her neck round laboriously to look at Olivia. 'Please don't scream again, Olivia, at least not when we're conversing.'

Miriam's voice cracked as she spoke and she took a long gulp of the scalding tea, which seemed to revive her further.

'I... I'm sorry, I didn't know,' Olivia stuttered.

'No, you probably didn't,' she glanced at Hiram and nodded, 'Hiram's filled you in a bit then. So now you'll know better.'

Olivia nodded her head then shook it, she still hadn't the faintest idea what was really going on.

'I guess. But none of what he said really makes sense. In fact, most of it just sounds like a science fiction story. I can't believe any of it.'

Miriam nodded sagely, 'I understand your scepticism, young lady, but it's all true. We need you to believe us.'

Miriam stared intently into Olivia's eyes, who became uncomfortable with the attention.

'Why do I need to believe you. Even if it's true, then surely there's nothing for me to fear. I am a superhuman who can do anything with my mind. That kinda makes me invincible, doesn't it?'

Miriam's smile was condescending, 'Not really, we all have our frailties – invincible is not the same as invulnerable. And what it *does* make you is a target. They've been watching you longer than we have and now that you seem to be coming into your own, they will be very keen to retrieve you. Whether to harness you for their own ends or to dissect you to find out how your brain works now. Then they'll attempt to synthesise that knowledge into creating lab-born entities that they'll have full control of.'

Olivia paled at the mention of dissection; it was just like her dream all over again.

'If I'm in so much danger I could go to the police,' even as she said this, she knew that was a pointless argument. Miriam nodded, as if she had read Olivia's mind. Olivia frowned. Had the old woman read her mind? Or was she also a figment of Olivia's potential delusion, in which case Olivia was just talking to herself.

'No, my dear, we're not delusions. You're not talking to yourself and yes, I'm reading your surface thoughts. It is my forte, along with prescience. But we do need you to believe us.'

'Why do you need me to believe you? Surely if you can see the future, you must already know how I feel, how I will feel about all this, and your continued pressure for me to believe you suggests to me that I'm never going to believe you.'

'I can't see the future, as such, at least not very far into it. But I do gain foreknowledge of it and of potential outcomes. But where you're concerned, my dear, it all becomes very hazy. I could see, for instance, a number of contexts where you were attacked in the cut-through. Hence, I suggested Hiram attend to you this afternoon, on the off-chance one of those potential outcomes occurred. But as to your thoughts and feelings, especially on this matter, I have no clear understanding how you will ever feel. Hence my insistence for you to give us a chance.

'And as to why I need you to believe us, that is so you will trust us.'

Miriam smiled at her; it wasn't a warm smile. But then, given Miriam's appearance, Olivia wondered if the woman was capable of exuding warmth. It was in that moment that Olivia remembered Miriam's previous words to her, 'be careful whom you trust'.

Miriam nodded, 'Yes, that can also apply to us, which is why I'm going to add this to the pot in an effort to gain your trust. We have an agenda. We need you to believe our story, not just because it's true, but because if you don't you will fall foul of dangerous people and be totally unprepared for the consequences. When this happens, our agenda fails, because we need you in peak performance to thwart *their* agenda. They wish to control the world, to forge a new way of life where they are the lords of the land. They will accomplish this through their advanced technologies and utilising their new breed of humans to dominate the rest of the world. We want you to be the spanner in their cogs, to end their experiments and to end their plans. Because when that happens, the rest of us survivors will then be able to find peace. Not least of all because they won't be hunting us anymore.

'So, we have a vested interest in you believing this wild story of science fiction. You would be our saviour.'

Miriam slouched back into the cushions of the settee, clearly exhausted by her explanation. She had paled appreciably during it and Hiram immediately refilled her cup with tea and a mountain of sugar. Miriam was most grateful and sipped at the cup.

Olivia sat in silence staring at Miriam. What was she supposed to think? How could any of this be real? How could any of it be true? And how could she, a seventeen-year-old girl from a disturbed, dysfunctional family in the West Midlands, be the saviour of these freaks. No, not freaks. They were the victims in all of this, if anyone were freaks it was the Organisation, those faceless arbiters of the heinous experiments that had warped and dilapidated their trusting, hopeful clients. And for what? So that she could be their saviour, be the saviour of all mankind?

'No,' Olivia said, 'no. I can't possibly believe any of it. It's all just so farfetched.' She had a sudden thought, a thought that clearly trumped anything Miriam had to say.

'Hiram said,' Olivia continued, glancing at the tall man, 'that I am the culmination of my mother and father. That the experiments drove everyone from phase two insane and my mother to her schizophrenia? Even if that's true, then I still can't be this wonder person you seem to want me to be, because while my dad's a bit of a bastard, he certainly isn't mad. So, what you say can't be true.'

Olivia stared boldly at Miriam, daring her to counter her argument.

Miriam gave Olivia her condescending smile as she replied, 'Your dad? Do you mean Reg, my dear?' Olivia nodded, 'Oh, but Reg isn't your father, my dear, he *killed* your father. Reg is an imposter.'

• • • •

Olivia sat with her mouth open. She had opened it to respond, but nothing came out. She wasn't certain how long she sat like that, but when she finally closed her mouth, it was very dry and her throat felt as though it was sealed shut. She looked around and found the cup of tea Hiram had made for her ages ago. Cold though it was, it was just what her throat craved to make it work again. She turned back to Miriam whose expression had barely changed since her utterance.

'My dad isn't my dad?'

'No,' Miriam's head shook from side to side negligibly.

'My dad *killed* my dad?'

'Yes,' Miriam's head nodded ever so slightly.

It was like Rhys saying her dad had killed the owner of their house to steal it. That had been ridiculous, this was ridiculous. Of course her dad was her dad! And he wouldn't kill anyone.

'But everyone knows my dad. Everyone knows my dad is my dad.' Olivia was trying to marry it all in her head at the same time as countering the fantastical hearsay Miriam was spouting.

'Of course they do, my dear. That's because when he arrived in the area with your mother and you, he said he was your dad. So why would anyone doubt that? Stranger things happen every day. It also helps when a number of your neighbours and friends are in league with your dad and the Organisation.'

'Oh, now you're just having a laugh at my expense. If that's the case then there's this massive conspiracy surrounding me.'

'Yes, my dear, there is, because you are the centre of their universe.' Miriam seemed unperturbed by Olivia's disbelief.

'Ha!' Olivia was inclined to laugh again, but there was no mirth or hysteria to back it up this time.

She stood up and walked around the room. Every so often, she had a thought that she considered might counter anything or everything Miriam and Hiram had said. Each time, she then heard another voice cancel it out. The more she thought about it and the more she considered her life to date and in particular recently, the more she began to wonder if what they were saying could actually be true. A lot of things would make more sense if Miriam wasn't lying. But – but, how could it be true? How could her mum be the outcast of a medical experiment? How could she, Olivia, be some kind of super-powered mental warrior? And yet, when she thought about three of the occasions when she had screamed, when she had opened her eyes there had been devastation. John's bedroom, the attackers and this room. And yet, when she had screamed when the cat had scared the crap out of her the other evening, nothing had broken. She stopped pacing.

'I screamed at the neighbour's cat the other night, nothing broke, how do you explain that?' she pointed at Miriam as she said it.

'Depends, my dear, *which* other evening. We've only just seen your power coming to the fore in the last couple of days. It's quite probable that when you had a fright from the cat, you were not awakened. Trust me, if you scream with any intensity now, you will cause havoc.' Miriam grimaced as she spoke, and Olivia wondered if that was because she was remembering her recent unconsciousness.

'Have you been traumatised recently or lost your virginity?' Miriam's gaze was incisive.

Olivia's immediate response was, 'Of course I've been traumatised!'

She swiftly followed it up with some stuttering, 'That's none of your business.'

'Hm, I didn't mean the attack by the triplets, but you have answered my question adequately. Sex appeared to be a far more useful opening to your powers, from what I had seen of your future. So I can only presume the incident with the cat predates your first foray into adulthood.'

Olivia's mouth opened once more, and once again she could utter nothing but stutters and a short expletive. She started pacing again. It was all too much for her. Her mind was starting to suggest possibilities to her if it was true. The things she could do if she could use the power of her mind. It would be just like all those movies and comics Rhys used to show them when they were younger. And if it wasn't true, then what? Who were Miriam and Hiram really? And why did those three men try to attack her? Well, there was an obvious answer to that. Young girl walking an isolated route, gets jumped by three men with evil intent. She should thank Hiram for saving her from a probable rape.

'I can pass on your thanks to him, although it wasn't a rape attempt. I have a couple of ideas as to why they attacked you. The first being to retrieve you for the Organisation, although it seems a rather heavy-handed way of doing it, when Reg could more easily have just drugged you and brought you in quietly. Which brings me to my second idea, which is that they hoped to force your abilities out of you. I suspect they're getting impatient to see what you're capable of. If they confirm your talents, then you will be of value to them. In fairness, I think your talents may have deliberately been lying dormant to protect you from them. But they can't lie low forever. As you develop physically, so you develop mentally. Your acuity is becoming exponential as you near the end of your teens. If your talents don't find an out soon, you will implode. And no one wants that, least of all you.'

Olivia was feeling swayed by Miriam's constant confirmation of her unknown abilities and yet there was still the unlikely, wholly improbable, nature of it all. She needed to go home. She needed to talk with John. He was sensible. He would know what to make of it all. He could dissuade her of all this madness.

'Yes, my dear, that's a good idea. Talk to John. You can discuss it with him tomorrow when you go with him and discover the Organisation's facilities. I think you need tangible physical evidence for you to make an informed decision on this matter, Olivia. Find their facilities, listen to whatever John is able to dig up on them and use him as a sounding board for all your other doubts. But do be very careful if you enter their facilities, because if they realise it's you, they will apprehend you. And if they don't, they will kill you and your friend, John.'

As Olivia took in the very real possibility of being murdered by an unseen enemy, Miriam concluded with a reminder.

'Be very careful whom you put your trust in, my dear. Whichever path you choose to follow is yours alone to tread, but for everything to work out for the best… you need to choose wisely.'

Chapter 18

Hiram escorted Olivia back to her house. It was late evening now and Olivia was jumpy despite her guardian. Hiram, however, seemed to be at ease, twirling his umbrella as they strolled down the street, and told her that Miriam had seen no cause for alarm for their journey and that he couldn't detect any inherent dangers. He bade her farewell at her door, waiting for her to enter her house and close the door.

Once inside, Olivia went straight to her room. She needed to pack for her day out with John, but more so, she needed the quiet to think on her conversations with Miriam and Hiram. As she assembled the items she felt would be relevant for her adventure she found the tranq gun in the bottom of her bag. *Bollocks*, she thought, *if only I had remembered that thing*. It might have been useful earlier, but it was of no use to her buried in the bottom of her bag. She picked it up and considered it for a while before coming to the conclusion she needed easier access to it and a more constant reminder of its presence. She stuffed it into the inside pocket of her jacket.

By the time she settled for another disturbed night's sleep, she was no clearer in her head on where her life could possibly be going. But one thing she did before climbing into bed was to stick a chair under her door handle, just in case her dad *was* out to get her. Perhaps it was the thought of her dad as a killer and working for a shadowy organisation intent on turning her into a controlled super-soldier that made her ability to sleep nearly impossible. She disturbed at the slightest sound, even when she recognised them as the usual creaks and moans the house would make of an evening. She had no knowledge of where her dad was tonight, but surely if he was out, it was a good thing. Before all this had started, she had often thought that, because it meant he wouldn't have the opportunity to belittle her or be angry with her. With the knowledge that he was out and that her door was barred, she decided to take one of her sleeping pills and eventually drifted into a fitful sleep, once more plagued by Morpheus' demons.

• • • •

Wednesday 14th April 1993

As is always the case when you sleep poorly, the best sleep comes at the end, when you're supposed to be waking up. This was the case for Olivia and, as such, she was late waking. She slammed the front door behind her and hurried down her street heading for the cut-through. She could feel the nagging urgency in the pit of her belly to get to her destination as soon as possible, an overriding sense of guilt flushing her actions because she had overslept. She turned left into the cut-through, advanced at pace several feet and then came to a sudden halt. She looked ahead of her. There was something wrong. She couldn't place her finger on it. She turned around and looked back the way she had just come. No, that wasn't right, there was something definitely wrong, but what was it? She could hear the voice of urgency thrumming in her head. She needed to be getting on; she needed to hurry so she wasn't late.

'Shut up!' she cried aloud to the voice in her head.

Surprisingly, it had the desired effect and the voice became muted, but not silent. She could still feel it nagging at her. There was another voice, though, that spoke to her telling her things weren't correct. She walked back to the entrance, looking right, back to where her house lay, then directly in front of her at the house that lay opposite. That was it! There was a house in front of her that shouldn't be there. She had always turned *right* into it; the cut-through should be on the other side of the street. And yet it wasn't. Doubt seeped into her mind... surely she was mistaken.

ORDINARY WORLD

It was obvious she had naturally turned left into the passageway, and left was the only way she could possibly go. And yet... and yet, she had an intense sensation that this was wrong. She turned back again to view the path and it was then that the muted voice leapt upon her indecision and screamed at her to run.

She ran.

Headlong up the path for fear of never making it to her destination on time. She ran round the bend in the path and only just prevented herself from falling into the chasm that stretched across the entirety of the path between the fence lines. She teetered for a few agonising seconds on the precipice and in those seconds she wondered how she had never noticed the abyss before. She caught her balance and took a couple of steps backwards to provide safe standing, away from the edge. She looked into the chasm and saw a swirling endless void of darkness filled with the brilliance of the cosmos. It wasn't dissimilar from when she had looked into Miriam's eyes: swirling wonders of galaxies, suns and billions of planets. Something caught her eye to the left side of the chasm; there was an unwalled room, a single tiled pathway leading from a closed apple-green door to a statue bolted to the floor. It was a figure dressed in a surgical gown, flapping in a breeze that didn't, that couldn't, exist. The figure wore an astronaut's helmet and she knew it was her. The room was spiralling towards an impenetrable disc of blackness and as it did so she could see the room being torn apart, tiles ripped from the floor. They were all sucked into the black sink hole. In a matter of moments everything had been torn from its position and individually sucked into the centre of the dark.

Olivia felt herself being sucked into the black hole along with everything else in its vicinity. The only thing that saved her was the hand that grabbed her shoulder, spinning her around. She came face to face with the leering visage of Albert. Her relief was palpable.

'Where are you going?' Albert said.

It surprised her because it sounded so clear in her head, a dulcet Yorkshire accent when she knew that Albert's speech was slurred and unintelligible. She watched his sloping lips as he spoke again and it was then that she realised he was speaking to her with his mind. 'Wherever you are going, I'm to take you there.'

Not for the first time today she stuttered a response, 'I... I don't know where I'm going.'

'But you know that you need to be there now,' Albert filled in the rest of her unspoken sentence.

'Yes. Now.'

'Hold tight,' Albert smiled his lopsided smile at her as he took hold of her wrists.

There was no flash. There was no sense of rushing wind. There was just a complete absence of any sensation at all. Olivia blinked. One second she was in the cut-through, the next she wasn't. Albert was nowhere to be seen. She appeared to be in the park. It was dark, cold and dewy. She heard the rustle of leaves in the trees above her and felt the early dawn breeze caress her through her nightdress. She shivered. A predawn light bloated the horizon, lending an eerie glow to the parkland that surrounded her. There were sounds, all of them muted: the sounds of small creatures stirring in their dens and of others, nocturnal creatures, scurrying to find their sanctuaries before day ascended. She drew in a breath and her nostrils chilled and moistened with the intake. She let out the breath through her mouth. In the gloom she could see her breath take physical form, an off-white cloud of breath. She could feel the cool dampness of the dew settling upon her, slowly soaking into her nightwear; it became ensnared about her as it clung to her moistening body. It was chilly and she shivered again. Looking around her surroundings, she could see the street lamps starting to shut off for the night. One here and one there, as she watched and waited, wondering if she was dreaming still, the lights started to go off alternately as dawn's light strengthened. Every breath she took was moist and cold, it chilled her lungs and made her cough. She hugged herself against the cold and rubbed her upper arms to try and gain some warmth. Olivia slowly turned around and around as she took in her surroundings, her circumstances, and finally came to the conclusion that, no, she wasn't dreaming. She really was standing in the park, in her nightdress in the dawn of a new day.

Running seemed like a really good idea. For one thing it started to warm her up, for another it got her out of the park and towards her house that much more quickly. It took a matter of moments to open the gate to her house, jog up the path and get to the front door. She paused in the porch, glancing nervously behind, back to the street to check to see if anyone had seen her, check to see if anyone was following her, but other than the first few utterances of chirps from the dawn chorus line warming up their little voices there was no sign of life. She leant over to the left-hand side of the porch and pulled up the loose tile that had been there for as long as she could remember. From under it she took out the spare key and let herself in.

Before closing the door she looked out to the street once more, but there was no one around. She replaced the key and then closed the door behind her. With her back pressed against the door she shivered once more; entry to the house had not granted her renewed warmth. It was cold here too, although at least it was a dry cold. She paused to listen to the sounds of the house. It gave her comfort and a moment to consider her confusion of how she had ended up in the park. The last thing she remembered was tossing and turning in bed, desperate to fall asleep, the next she was stood in the park by a bench, feeling cold, wet and physically drained, as if she had just run a marathon. She made her way up to her room, turned the handle on her door and pushed it open. But it didn't open. Instead it jarred her hand and wrist painfully and remained resolutely ajar. Something was jammed against it and prevented her from opening it. She stood for a moment shivering in her soaking nightgown, rubbing her sore wrist. *What the fuck?* She was having enough issues without having to contend with her door playing silly buggers too. Then she remembered that she had stuck a chair under the door handle before she had gone to bed. She slipped her arm through the gap in the door and felt around for the door handle. Yes, there it was. Her chair. But... but how the hell had she managed to prop it back under the handle on leaving her room? Unless she'd climbed out of her window. In her sleep? *Dear God!*

She fumbled the chair free and walked into her bedroom, where she stripped off her drenched nightdress and slipped under the covers. There was a fading warmth to them, enough to make her feel secure as she wrapped herself into a nest within their embrace.

Olivia felt exhausted, drained. She snuggled into her nest and prayed for restful sleep. The last thing she noted as she drifted off was the sight of her window, firmly locked shut.

. . . .

Olivia woke with a start. Her alarm was going off. She fumbled an arm out from the comfort of her covers, which then flapped ineffectually in the vicinity of her bedside table as her hand quested her alarm clock. Finally silencing the annoying, insistent buzz, she drew her arm back into the warmth of her cocoon and lay there, half awake, trying to remember her dream, trying not to fall back to sleep.

She was so tired. She had thought she would be excited this morning. Excited to see John. Excited by their adventure together. But her head felt like it was filled with fog. Her limbs were sluggish

ORDINARY WORLD

and she felt a general malaise to her whole being. Was it any wonder? She'd had so little sleep and what she'd had was fitful, filled with bizarre dreams, most of which she couldn't recall. Except for the last part where she had awoken in the park and run home. It was then that she realised she was naked. The only time she had woken up naked in bed was when she slept at John's. She threw back the covers and slipped from her bed, questing her nightdress. It was where she had left it in her dream, crumpled in a pile on the floor by the side of her bed. She picked it up. It felt wet, cold, unpleasant. She dropped it aghast. *No, no, that part of the dream couldn't be real.* She looked down at the offending article and then picked it up again. It was still cold; it was still damp. She could smell sweat and the scent of grass upon it. A sudden thought made her look at the soles of her feet. They were grass-stained and muddy.

'What the actual fuck?'

Olivia threw her nightdress into her laundry basket and slowly, sluggishly got dressed. All the while trying not to think about the nightdress. She made her way downstairs. As she passed her father's bedroom, she could hear him snoring. Odd that she hadn't heard him come in, considering how she had disturbed at every sound last night. Especially odd because Dad was never subtle about his entrance to the house. And yet maybe she hadn't been in the house when he'd come home. *No*, she thought, *I was home. I was asleep, dreaming. That's why I didn't hear him come in.* She slipped downstairs quietly and had a nominal breakfast. There was no hunger to it, merely a knowledge that she needed sustenance if she was to stand any chance of staying awake through the day.

John arrived just before eight, and she had the front door open before he could get to it. Yes, she was keen to see him, but she feared he would ring the bell and disturb her father. She didn't want to see her dad, at least not yet. She had been unable to resolve any of the information Miriam and Hiram had given her yesterday. The idea that Dad had killed her real father and was just a stand-in still seemed to be surreal conspiracy fantasy. Maybe John would have some answers, or maybe their quest out would answer all of them.

'Morning, beautiful,' John said as he came up the path, helmets in hand. 'Not ready yet?'

He referred to the fact that she wasn't in her leathers. *Bollocks*, she'd forgotten all about them in her daze. She shook her head and ushered him in.

'Quietly, John. Don't wake Dad.'

He nodded and slipped in through the door. She could see he wanted to give her a hug and kiss, but with the helmets in hand it wasn't going to happen. She was momentarily relieved. Why? The fog in her head was making everything feel distant and she realised she wanted it to stay like that. Was it a defence against all that she now knew? If it stayed at arm's length, would that ensure that it was all just fiction? Maybe, or maybe she was just feeling low from so much disturbed sleep. John deposited the helmets on a chair in the hall and then turned to her with his arms coming up for a cuddle. She beckoned him with a flick of her head and then went into the sitting room. He followed. His arms had dropped and in a quiet voice he asked,

'You alright, Olivia?'

She shrugged her shoulders, with a slight shake of the head to accompany the gesture. John responded by lifting her chin gently with his hand, so that they made eye contact.

'What's wrong?'

Olivia drew in a long breath and held it, before finally releasing it slowly. 'Bad night's sleep again.'

She suddenly didn't want to tell him about yesterday. She didn't want to tell him that some deformed people had saved her from some faceless freaks and then taken her back to their secret lair. She didn't want to tell him the fantastical story they had then told her. She certainly didn't want to tell him that due to the eugenics experimentation of a shadowy organisation, her mother was mad, her real father was dead and she was the ultimate human in evolution. She nearly started to laugh hysterically as these thoughts tumbled through her head. Instead, she drew her shoulders up and braced herself mentally. Today they were supposed to be going to find the properties that John Fitzgerald Kennedy owned about the country. Or, at least, those closest to here. She doubted they would get to London or the Highlands. But there were a few in the Midlands that they could investigate. Maybe they'd even find John Fitzgerald Kennedy, even though he appeared to be a fiction too.

'I'm fine, John, just tired. I'll finish getting ready and be back down in a moment.' She feigned a smile for him. She wasn't certain if he believed her smile or not, judging by the frown he returned to her.

'We can do this another day, Olivia, if you're not up to it.' He had grabbed her hand as she passed him, turning her around and preventing her exit from the room.

'No, no, it's fine. Just a little ragged around the edges, but nothing I'm not used to, what with caring for Mum.'

Reluctantly, Olivia thought, John let her hand go and allowed her to ascend once more to her room where she struggled into her leathers.

When they were outside by the bike, John pulled out a map and laid it over the seats. Olivia could see the West Midlands detailed on it and a number of small, red-inked circles.

'JF has two properties in Birmingham and one in Wolverhampton. These are the closest to us and I thought made the most sense for initial investigation. I did a little digging last night and most of the addresses I've got seem to be non-residential. So, if there is some sort of facility then I'm hoping it'll be one of these.

Although, if I were a charitable organisation running cutting-edge experiments into mental health, I would have thought London would be the best place to have a facility. But then, who am I to say.' He flashed her a cheeky grin.

Helmets on, map stowed in the map pouch on the petrol tank, they mounted up. John patted her hand after he started the bike up, telling her to hang on, and off they went, north towards the motorway and Birmingham. Olivia hung on to her knight in blue emblazoned black armoured leathers – they were like his crest and reminded her of a forlorn heroic knight from her childhood stories. There was a comfort there that she had forgotten. Her head rested on his shoulder blades and she watched the world whizz by her visored vision. It was hypnotic. It was soothing. It was dangerous. She fell asleep.

The bike wasn't moving. Olivia could feel it leaning to one side and John was calling to her from a long way away, distant and muffled. She could feel someone slapping her arm. She suddenly jolted upright, totally awake. Fucking hell, she'd fallen asleep on the back of a moving motorbike. With her position altered, John had just enough room to slide off the bike and hop backwards onto the hard shoulder. He moved towards her and flipped her visor open.

'Olivia! Are you alright?' There was deep concern in his voice.

'Yes, no. I, I don't know,' she looked at him and then to her sides. They were on the hard shoulder of a motorway; the traffic was thundering by them and all of a sudden, she felt extremely vulnerable.

'I could feel you slipping off the bike. You weren't responding.'

'I think... I think I fell asleep,' she bowed her head, ashamed, knowing how immensely dangerous that could have been for her and probably also for him.

'Jesus Christ, girl,' John actually sounded angry. It was the first time he had ever been angry with her and she didn't like it.

'I know,' she said before he could continue, 'it was stupid. But that's what happened. I'm obviously more tired than I realised and the bike was so comfortable it just drifted me off. But I'm awake now. We can get on. Get off the side of the road.'

John stared at her; she wasn't certain what he was thinking and the helmet prevented her from seeing his expression. His cheeks were squashed up, causing his eyes to be unnaturally wrinkled. He could be laughing or he could be scowling, she just didn't know. She could feel herself starting to get angry in return.

'Well, come on then. Let's go!'

John remained standing to the side for a few moments longer. He still didn't respond and she still couldn't tell what kind of mood he was in.

'There's a service station about five miles ahead. We'll stop there,' he said, sliding back onto the bike and starting it up again. She gripped the sissy bar at the back of the bike, resolute in not giving him any form of satisfaction. There was a long pause as he waited on the traffic and then he punched it. She was amazed she didn't fly off. As it was, her buttocks ended up resting on her hands and she had to try and shuffle her way back onto the seat as they zipped through the traffic. Yes, he was definitely angry, she concluded.

· · · ·

It took no more than two minutes, maybe less, for them to reach the service station. Clearly John wasn't taking any chances on her falling asleep again. He pulled up in the car park and waited for her to dismount. Standing by the machine, they both removed their helmets and looked at one another. Olivia detected John was struggling between emotions – it was clear as day upon his face. She didn't feel like saying sorry, even though her actions had been perilous. It wasn't her fault she was so tired that she actually fell asleep in the most unlikely place. Maybe she should have taken his suggestion before they left the house to leave it to another day. But she hadn't thought she was that tired, that such a thing was possible. They remained looking at each other silently for several minutes. Olivia thought he might be calming down, but it was only a feeling. She wasn't certain.

'I'm sorry,' she forced it out, but her jaw ached as she said it. She wasn't really sorry. The reaction she received was unexpected. Olivia thought they were about to have their first argument. Instead, John gathered her up in his arms and hugged her for dear life.

'No, no, it's me. I should have realised you weren't up for this trip. I knew how keen you were for it. But I should have been more adamant about waiting. I know your sleep's been bad the last few days. Although, God only knows how you managed to fall asleep on the back of my bike... just goes to show your exhaustion levels. I'm sorry, Olivia, I put us both in danger there and I'm sorry I was angry with you. I was just so worried, that was all.' He continued to crush her in his arms. 'It's not the first time I thought I had killed you.'

This final addendum came out as a whisper through her hair, his mouth close to her ear. She realised he was referring to Monday's moment of passion. She let him hug her. How silly boys were sometimes, she thought. Truth be told, though, she liked this moment. Someone liked her enough to be angry with her for the sake of her wellbeing. It was unheard of. She wished they were back in John's flat, in his bed. She was safe there. Loved. And there were stars in her mind. Eventually, John released her, locked the bike and took her into the services where he bought her a proper breakfast.

Olivia let her vision slip away from the xanthous globules that trickled from the corner of John's mouth down on to his chin - as he shovelled a large forkful of fried egg and toast into his mouth -

over his shoulder and out of the window behind their booth. She could see the heavy looming clouds that haunted the horizon from where they had just been. She glanced over her shoulder towards the horizon of where they were heading, azure clear skies filled with a warm sunny glow of delicate promise – it brought her mind back to the gooey lumps of egg yolk that had adorned her boyfriend's face a few moments before. She allowed herself a half smile, as she wondered if the skies were trying to tell her something.

Chapter 19

Olivia could tell John still wasn't convinced that they should continue, but she said that breakfast had perked her up and then jokingly added that her nap had done her the power of good. He'd frowned, but she had skipped to the bike and he'd harrumphed. They now stood in front of a chain link fence on an industrial estate on the west side of Birmingham. Beyond lay a number of interlinked squat red brick buildings with boarded-up windows. It might have been a motor mechanic's workshop once upon a time. Now it looked derelict and forgotten. There were a number of official signs defaced with graffiti tags attached to the fence, mostly indicating private property. Down by the padlocked gates there was another sign, old and damaged, which said the property was for sale or leasehold. There had been a phone number to call for interested purveyors, but most of that had been ripped off. Pritchard and someone were the people to call. The azure skies that had promised so much as they'd had breakfast had skittered away from them the closer they had come to Birmingham, always tantalisingly just out of reach. Instead grey, overcast skies, hinting at rain in the breeze, greeted them upon their arrival at the industrial estate. They seemed more befitting for the place and the sombre mood the weather now instilled in them.

'Well, if this ever had been a facility, it's long since been abandoned. But then, by my reckoning the organisation went out of business in the seventies. And this place looks like it hasn't been used *since* the seventies.'

Olivia was inclined to agree, 'Where next?'

John sniffed as he pulled out the map and had a look. He pointed to a second little red circle, close to the one they were at now. 'It's in town, so I suspect it's an office or maybe a house.' He glanced at her and she nodded.

They turned to head back to the bike, but Olivia paused as she thought she had seen a shadow move between two of the squat buildings behind the fence. She focused on the spot, but saw nothing else. She shrugged her shoulders dismissively; it was probably a rat. She shivered and followed John.

The second property was indeed an office. An old Victorian townhouse that had been converted, probably back in the sixties, into a range of offices. There was a large brass plaque in the porch indicating the occupants. John's summation of it was that the rent must be high, as all the businesses seemed to be architects and solicitors. Scanning the list, none of them had a J F Kennedy as a partner. But one did stand out from the rest – Pritchard and Wright, solicitors.

'That can't be a coincidence,' John said as he placed his finger under the label for Olivia.

'No, wasn't there a Pritchard and somebody back at the mechanics?'

'There was,' John opened the porch door for her, 'worth asking if they know a J F Kennedy, don't you think?'

Olivia nodded and stepped inside. It was a gloomy interior with no natural light to speak of and only one strip light, which flickered intermittently. They walked the hall until they found another board on a tripod at the bottom of some stairs. It indicated Pritchard & Wright could be found on the second floor. They ascended, walked another lengthy red-carpeted corridor and eventually found a solid white-painted door with Pritchard & Wright stencilled into a glass topper. John knocked. There was no answer. He turned the handle, which creaked, objecting to being disturbed, and pushed the door open. It creaked too, on ancient hinges in dire need of oil.

Inside they found a tidy little atrium-style office with a long desk to their left. Two doors stood in the opposite wall and to their right was a kitchenette. They could hear someone humming in there and the sound of a kettle coming to the boil. They waited. There was a clinking of spoon on china and sounds of water pouring. A few minutes passed and then a young girl sashayed her way out of the kitchenette with a mug in her hand. She was quite startled by their presence and let out a small squeal of surprise, nearly dropping her mug.

'I'm sorry, I didn't hear you come in,' she said as she attempted to mask her fluster. 'You don't have an appointment, I believe.'

She dabbed at the coffee that had spilt onto her knee-length dress and then put her mug down. She moved around to stand behind the desk.

'How can I be of service?'

John paused, he had been taking the lead until now, but Olivia wondered if he was as stumped as she was on how to proceed. The silence lengthened. Olivia stepped in.

'The property at Lanyard's Hill, the old mechanics shop, I think it was? We were wondering what the history was on it? We're looking for similar properties for the possibility of setting up our own motor shop.' Olivia smiled convincingly and the secretary nodded briefly before going over to one of several grey metal filing cabinets.

'Lanyard's Hill, you say? I can't say that I'm familiar with it.'

'There was a sign on the gate indicating that this firm represented the property, but there was no number.'

'Hmm,' the secretary opened the cabinet and sifted through a packed draw. 'Oh, yes, Lanyard's Hill, so it is.' She drew out a thin beige folder and opened it.

'Well, there doesn't seem to be much here, it has to be said. Hasn't been occupied since 1983. Yes, it was a mechanics shop for about two years. It seems they were the only tenants. Purchased in

1976. We do indeed represent the interests of the property.' She looked up at them with a slightly embarrassed smile.

'If there haven't been any tenants for so long, does it mean the buildings are in need of substantial repair?' John interjected, following Olivia's lead.

'I would imagine so,' the secretary responded.

'I don't think we're in a position to conduct a major renovation, we were hoping to just move in, so to speak.'

Olivia spoke almost cutting John off, 'I wondered if one of the partners was a Mr John F. Kennedy? Your solicitors sounded familiar when we saw the sign and I distinctly remember a John F Kennedy associated with the firm.'

John nudged her with his elbow, although she wasn't certain if it was a congratulatory nudge for slipping that in or a warning not to push their luck.

The secretary paused sifting through the meagre sheaves of paper within the folder. 'No,' she sounded distracted, 'no John F Kennedy working here. Although he may have been here years ago, I'm relatively new to the firm.' She leafed through to the final page and scanned it.

'Oh, how odd.'

'Odd?' both John and Olivia said at the same time.

The secretary looked up at them, 'Yes, according to this final page the property is owned by a John Fitzgerald Kennedy, but there seem to be no contact details for him. Just a note indicating all enquiries need to be fielded to Mr Pritchard.'

'Is Mr Pritchard in? Would it be possible to speak with him?' Olivia asked.

'He is in, but usually it's by appointment only.' She bowed her head apologetically.

'We're only in town this morning, is it possible we could see him?' Olivia pleaded.

'Well,' the secretary glanced at the left-hand door. Clearly there was some trepidation on her part. Perhaps Mr Pritchard disliked being disturbed? Olivia could imagine a solicitor being rather stern and intimidating.

'Please?' Olivia pressed. The secretary drew in a deep breath and nodded. She walked to the left-hand door and knocked. If there had been a response, Olivia didn't hear it. The secretary opened the door and stuck her head round it, there was a brief exchange, most of which Olivia couldn't hear. She heard the last comment, however, as the secretary opened the door fully.

'I'll be right out,' said a rich baritone voice.

Moments later a portly man in his late fifties, early sixties, entered the office. He strode over to them and offered his hand, first to John and then to Olivia.

'I'm Jonathan Pritchard. I hear you're interested in the Lanyard's Hill property.'

He was a forthright man and Olivia did feel a slight hint of being intimidated just by his manner.

'We are,' John said. Olivia noted how he took a slight step to one side, shielding her from the solicitor. She wondered if it was instinctive or deliberate.

'Well, that property isn't currently available I'm afraid. Too dilapidated, needs a lot of work before it's fit for purpose. I'm sorry if we wasted your time, Mr, er...?'

'John Fastjack,' John lied smoothly. Olivia masked a smile at the ease with which John had managed that.

'That is a shame... it certainly had potential. Would it be possible to talk directly with the owner? See what works are required?'

'Impossible,' Mr Pritchard said drawing himself up to his full height, a mere five-and-a-half feet. If he felt intimidated by John's height, he certainly didn't show it. 'All dealings have to go through us. The owner is never to be disturbed.'

'I see, yes, well, understandable, I suppose,' John seemed rather disappointed. 'How about having a viewing? See for ourselves what works might be required?'

'The property is far too unsafe to allow the general public into it, I'm afraid.' Olivia thought the man was starting to look a bit sweaty with John's persistence; she saw a chance to nip in with a question of her own.

'I take it he's still alive, then? The owner, I mean,' Olivia asked, peering around John.

Mr Pritchard's expression was one of total surprise, 'No, I mean, yes, of course, he's still alive. What a peculiar question to ask, miss.'

'Not peculiar, solicitors often deal with estates on behalf of the deceased. And it is an old property, so there is always the possibility that the original owner might not be alive anymore.' Which Olivia surmised he wasn't, given the solicitor's first instinctive response.

'Er, no, quite,' said Mr Pritchard, then rallied, 'Right, well, as I said, the property is not up for sale, nor for lease currently. If you would like to leave contact details with my secretary, we can always inform you when the property becomes available. Pleasure to meet you, sir,' he shook John's hand again, tugged his forelock at Olivia, 'Miss.' He turned to retreat to his own office. Before he left, he held out his hand to his secretary.

'I think it's for the best if I take the Lanyard Hill file for my private files, Miss Kelly.'

'Whatever you think best, sir,' Miss Kelly replied noncommittally. She flipped the folder shut and handed it to him. Pritchard then stalked into his office and closed the door.

John gave some fake details to the secretary before they left the offices. Outside the main building they looked at one another.

Olivia's heart was racing; that had been quite exciting, like being a spy in one of those old movies. They walked back down the street to the bike. Olivia glanced up over her shoulder as they were about to turn the corner, as the hackles on her neck had suddenly pricked up and sent a small shiver down her spine. It took her a moment to acknowledge what she was seeing. Mr Pritchard was stood in the bay window of his office, net curtain held slightly open and he was watching them depart. When he noted her looking at him, he promptly dropped the curtain and disappeared from view.

At the bike they felt they had the opportunity to talk.

'So, that was all a bit odd,' John opened. Olivia nodded.

'Lanyard's Hill is supposedly up for sale, but no one's willing to part with it.' John summarised.

'And the owner's dead,' Olivia concluded. John looked at her quizzically.

'You're sure Kennedy's dead?'

'Well, no, but the owner's dead and Kennedy was the only owner we know of for the property. So, possibly Kennedy's dead. You said he was dead, ten days after he was born.'

'That I did. It all seems a bit odd, if you ask me. Right, then, shall we try the third property? See if we can glean anything from that.' Olivia nodded and buckled her helmet on.

· · · ·

The third property lay on the outskirts of Wolverhampton. It was a rather unexpectedly leafy suburb and all looked very pleasant. Not quite how Olivia had imagined Wolverhampton. John pulled the bike up in front of a pair of black wrought iron gates, set into a pair of well-built red brick pillars. Beyond lay a gravel drive that led through a very overgrown park. At the end of the drive, about six or seven hundred yards away, they could just make out the side of a large house. The only window they could see was boarded over. After dismounting the bike, they walked the perimeter of the property. The wrought iron railings stood to about five feet in height, mortared into a brick foundation which was at least two feet in height. Beyond the railings were thick hawthorn hedges, interspersed by the occasional tree. It was nearly impossible to see beyond the fence line.

Eventually John huffed, 'Sod this, hold my helmet, Olivia,' thrusting his helmet at her.

He walked back the way they had come, about fifty feet to where one of the trees had grown over the railings. He climbed onto the brick wall and grabbed the overhanging branch. Using the railings, he scampered up and pulled himself onto the tree branch. He then shimmied along it to the trunk and disappeared from view. *Great*, thought Olivia, *now what am I supposed to do?* She waited for her knight to do his knightly duty and was becoming quite impatient when she finally heard the grunt of a man struggling to climb a tree. He appeared moments later as he crawled down the branch and dropped to the pavement next to her.

'Well, that was interesting,' he said with a smile. Olivia got the feeling he was deliberately withholding whatever it was he had found to tease her. She refused to take the bait. John looked at her and raised an eyebrow.

'Not interested in what I found out?'

'I am, but I'm sure you'll tell me in your own sweet merry time,' she said with a glower. He chuckled. Oh, boys were so irritating sometimes!

'OK, well, it's abandoned like Lanyard's Hill, but I did find an original notice for it. Looks as though it was a private mental hospital before it closed. I could see in through a couple of the windows and all the furnishings still seem to be in place. No idea how long it's been disused for, but inside, or at least what I could see, didn't seem to be in bad nick. Almost like it gets used from time to time. There were some outbuildings, which I didn't investigate, but one of them looked like a guard hut, so I'm wondering if it might have some security on it at night to prevent squatters and vandals.'

He looked at Olivia, 'All said and done, though, I have no idea where this leaves us.'

Olivia returned his look: no, to be honest, neither did she. She shook her head at him, 'No, I don't know. There are three properties that belong to Kennedy – four if you include our house – that we've been to. Two are abandoned and seem to have been for decades and one is used as offices, by a solicitor who represents at least one of the abandoned properties. As for John Kennedy, he may well be dead from a legal perspective as well as being a figment of legal imagination.' They continued to look at one another, lost on what to do next. John's stomach rumbled.

'I'm hungry. Let's get something to eat and then head back to my flat. We can talk more about it there.'

. . . .

They were sat on John's sofa pondering the limited discoveries of the day. If the Organisation was still functioning somewhere – and John felt it must be, given its presence on the 'net – then it certainly wasn't happening in the Midlands. But, as he pointed out, the Organisation could be very small by now; operating on the 'net didn't require the vast areas of space it once might have done. So that left one property in London and two in the Highlands, that they were aware of. John thought he might be able to do some searches in work to try and determine the type of property that was out there.

'We're bound to have satellite footage of London, maybe we'll have some of the Highlands too. That would make it easier.'

Olivia was horrified to learn that her government might have been taking photos of their country from space and said as much. John chuckled, 'That isn't the half of it, my love.'

He stopped, as she gave him a piercing look.

'Did you just call me your love?'

John paled slightly and nodded, 'I did,'

'Did you mean it?'

John looked at her askance, then started to smile, 'You know, I think I did.'

Olivia leaned forward and kissed him.

Chapter 20

Olivia was aglow as she made her way to her front door that evening. The stars had returned, her mind had flooded with glorious white light and washed all the anxiety and confusion from her. Her buzz slowly ebbed though, the closer she got to the door. She could hear her father's voice long before her key went into the lock, he was shouting that loud.

'Well, where the fuck is she? I had the school on at me earlier because no one had told them she was having a day off. They were all nice as fucking pie about it, that patronising cow, Mrs Flint. Blamed it on her mother they did, but were saying it'd be nice if we'd told 'em like! Fucking cow, who the fuck does she think she is anyway, the fucking queen? I haven't seen her since yesterday. They lost her on the motorway... they reckoned he was clocking two ten, no way they'd be able to keep up. That boy's a fucking nutter. Trust her to link up with a fucking nutter. No. No. Yes, alright. I'll wait in, hopefully she'll turn up eventually. We obviously can't get the police involved. I blame you, you insisted on forcing the issue and now look where we are. Yes, I know I wanted it over and done with, but you're the one that calls the shots. Fine! Yes, I'll let you know when I see her.'

Olivia stood with her key in the lock, her hand on the key. She couldn't bring herself to turn it. She also couldn't just stand there all night – the wind had picked up on the way back, buffeting the bike and worrying her that they would end up in a ditch. Rain was starting to bounce off the path behind her. The porch lit up as a bolt of lightning shredded the clouds behind her. No, she definitely couldn't stand in the porch all night. She sucked in a lungful of damp, metallic air and advanced into her house. Her dad came into the hall as she closed the door, and there was no time for her to breathe out, let alone say 'Hi', before her dad launched into her.

'Where the fuck have you been, young lady? I've been worried sick! You don't just disappear for a day without a by-your-leave, without telling someone where you're going.' He looked down at her attire, 'And when the fuck have you been riding around on motorbikes? Is this Evie or Rhys' doing? Do they have bikes? Well, not on my watch... do you know how fucking dangerous they are? Do you know how many people get killed on bikes every year?!'

Olivia noticed that with each question her father advanced a step closer to her until she could feel the spittle spray over her face, along with the warm fetidness of his breath. Not quite the fresh breath of air that she had experienced earlier on the back of the bike. Something snapped in her head as her father yelled at her. For the first time in days, she had been feeling at ease with herself and he had just blown it completely out of the window.

'Shut up, Dad!'

He stood there with his mouth open, his jaw slowly rising until his mouth was closed. Reg shut up.

'I've been out with a friend. I forgot to tell school and I'll fix it with them tomorrow. As for you, well, I'm just not so sure any more. So, stay out of my way and everything will be fine till Mum comes home on Friday. We all want it to be nice for her, and then Saturday's my birthday and obviously we'll be wanting that to go well. Especially as my friends and Aunty Morag will be there.' She smiled sweetly at him, pushed past and headed for the stairs. Her heart was pounding, her head was pounding. Too much again. She needed to lie down.

Reg watched her to the bottom step of the stairs and then something obviously snapped in his head too.

'Where the *fuck* do you get off speaking to me like that? I'm your fucking father. You owe me respect. You owe me the decency to tell me where the fuck you're going to be if you're thinking of bunking off school. And don't you *dare* threaten me with the suggestion of Aunty-fucking-Morag. That evil harpy will be lucky if I let her in the fucking street, let alone my fucking house.'

Reg was fuming, saliva spraying across the hallway. His face was puce and a vein in his forehead was pulsating like a cockroach hiding under a pancake. His hands were balled into fists and he was shaking them in her face. Olivia suddenly felt very scared that he was going to batter her within an inch of her life. She made to dash up the stairs, but felt one of those fists grip her painfully around her bicep. He spun her around.

'I haven't fucking finished with you yet,' he hollered.

She saw his other hand rising and feared the incoming slap, which would probably knock her senseless. She defended herself the only way she knew how. As she spun around, her other hand came up and slapped him around the face, then she screamed at him. The hallway was lit up by a dazzling flash of lightning arcing across the heavens outside. The lights in the hall went out. There was a shattering of glass throughout. Her palm never connected with anything, but she felt his hand relinquish its hold upon her arm. There was a solid thump and then a crash, as something heavy impacted with something wooden. She heard a grunt, then silence. Moonlight washed in through the window on the stairs briefly, the storm outside having torn holes in the clouds. The moonlight was the only illumination in the hallway – its presence fleeting, but long enough for Olivia to see her father lying in a crumpled heap. He lay under the remains of a side table that had buckled with his impact into it. He was clearly dazed; he might even be unconscious. Olivia paused her flight up the stairs, considering tending to him. Then she thought, *fuck it*. She'd had enough of his weird behaviour and violent moods. She ran up the stairs in the dark and went to her room. Once there, she discovered the lights wouldn't work, but there was enough ambient light to see by. She packed her backpack swiftly and then went back downstairs, past her recumbent father, and back out of the front door. The wind caught it as she fled, banging it shut, causing one of the panes in the upper part of the door to crack. She ran through the increasing storm. When her father was violent, there was only one place she ever went to escape. It had been a while since she'd visited, but she knew she could count on safety there.

• • • •

The house was in darkness as she approached. A lightning strike in the woods behind the house silhouetted it, leaving a dense black shape in her vision. It sent a shiver down her spine, as it reminded her of the house from Psycho. Olivia stopped at the gate, suddenly uncertain about her decision to come here. *No, it was the right place to come, it's just your mind playing tricks on a dark and stormy night*, she thought. She pushed the gate open; it squeaked as it always did. It was deliberately left like this so that forewarning was given of a visitor's approach. Olivia rang the bell and waited. Her hair was drenched and she was cold from the weather. She rang again, this time holding the button for several seconds. Her impatience was rewarded by a light going on upstairs, which shone down into the hallway. She could just make out a shuffling shape stumbling down the stairs, arms akimbo, presumably as they attempted to drag a dressing gown on. The shape glided to the door, which then opened a crack. Olivia could see the silvered chain that prevented ingress without permission. A tanned, stern blank face peered through the crack at her. Olivia let out a squeak, until she realised that the gloom of the doorway precluded accurate vision.

'Olivia!' it said, startled by her bedraggled appearance, 'what brings you to my door at such an ungodly hour? As if I couldn't guess. Wait a moment,' the voice concluded.

ORDINARY WORLD

The door shut and Olivia could hear the sound of the chain being unfastened. The door opened again, wider than before, and Aunty Morag stood there in all her elder glory, a practical and warm dressing gown pulled tight across her bosom. Aunty Morag was a solid woman in her late fifties; her skin was leathery and still held the tan of decades of travel in foreign climes. She ushered Olivia into the house, leaning on the door to fend off the wind. She immediately replaced the chain and then slipped an arm around Olivia's waist, guiding her to the kitchen at the end of the hall.

'Kitchen'll still be warm and I can put the kettle on,' Morag said. Olivia allowed herself to be guided, it was a well-established custom now.

'So,' Morag began, as she pointed Olivia to a chair and went to the counter to sort out the kettle. 'I take it your father's been a brute again. Although,' she glanced over her shoulder as she put the kettle into its stand and flicked the switch, 'having had a phone call from him earlier this evening, I'm wondering if he wasn't within his rights to be cross this time.'

Morag turned, folding her arms and looked sternly at her niece. 'It's not like you to bunk off from school. What's that all about? Reg sounded genuinely worried and he must have been to ring me. Thought you might have come to see me. He says you've been acting strange recently. Going off without a by-your-leave, arguing with him, calling him some disgraceful things to boot.' Morag's right foot started to tap on the tiles. It appeared to Olivia that Morag disapproved of whatever it was her dad had been saying about her.

'I didn't bunk off, well, not deliberately. I meant to ring the school this morning, but I forgot. Dad said I should have had a day off yesterday, because I'd had a bit of a turn. I just took it off today instead. I went to see a friend that's all. Anyway, this isn't about me, it's about him!' she finished crossly.

Morag harrumphed, 'Did he strike you again?'

Olivia could see her drawing herself up to her full fighting height – it never went well for her dad when Aunty Morag learned he'd been hitting his family. She wondered if her aunt gave him a taste of his own medicine, maybe that was why he was so scared of her.

'Nearly, he went to, but I hit him back first,' she said defiantly.

Morag smirked, 'Did you now? Did you? Well, well, how the worm has turned.' Her head shook from side to side in disbelief, and she was still smirking. Then she stopped herself, her expression becoming stern again.

'However, young lady, it isn't right or proper for you to be hitting your father. It's not right or proper for him to be hitting you or Phyllis either, but that's just the kind of man he is. I wouldn't be at all surprised if that's a parenting, spousal technique he learned from his father and grandfather. He's of that generation, y'know. Doesn't make it right though. But we need to have a little understanding, especially as I think he was probably quite overwrought today, with you gone and everything.'

The kettle pinged. Morag turned and pulled down a couple of mugs from the hooks at the back of the counter and made them both tea. She brought the mugs to the table and sat down.

'Do you want me to have a word with him?' Morag's eyebrow rose.

Olivia shook her head, 'No. It might just make things worse. As you said, you and Dad don't have the best relationship. Can I stay here with you? At least for tonight? It'll give him time to calm down. Although, if I could stay for a couple of days...?'

Morag shook her head, 'It's fine for tonight, my dear Olivia, but I think it best if you return tomorrow to prevent further repercussions. I'll phone Reg while you drink your tea and let him know where you are. Don't want him getting any more worked up.'

Morag stood up to go to the phone, but paused when Olivia tried to speak.

'Er, er,'

Once more Morag's eyebrow rose, 'Yes, m'dear, is there something I should know?'

'Er, well, it's just that when I left the house, I think dad might have been unconscious.'

'Drunk again, was he?' Morag declared, the disapproving glower returning.

'Er, no.' Olivia was looking into her tea feeling rather ashamed now, especially for leaving her dad on the floor untended.

'No?'

'No. As far as I'm aware he hadn't been drinking at all. The reason he was unconscious was -because – of me,' she finally blurted it out.

Morag's full attention was on her now, 'What did you hit him with?'

'Just my hand, but he fell backwards into a table. I think he might have hit his head on it as he went down.' Olivia looked up all of a sudden, a terrible possibility coming to mind. What if she'd killed him accidentally? She'd seen it happen in movies before. People being pushed into tables and downstairs. And then the perpetrator trying to escape prison for murder or manslaughter. She felt the blood drain from her face and a chill ran through her entire being. She might go to prison. She started to tear up in panic.

Morag clearly spotted the signs of an imminent panic attack coming on as she hurried over to her niece and pulled her to standing.

'Now, you just pull yourself together, young lady. None of those what-ifs that I can see charging through that over active imagination of yours. You're going to take your backpack and your tea up to your room and make yourself at home. While you do that,

I will ring Reg and, if there's no answer, I will go round and check on him. At the end of the day, I suspect the worst that will be wrong is that he'll have a bump and a headache. He's probably in that little room of his, even as we speak, drinking himself into a self-pitying stupor.' Aunty Morag's explanation mollified Olivia and she found herself calming down. Dad was a brute, it was true, but he was made of solid stuff. Even a bang to his head wasn't likely to keep him down for long. But then she remembered this wasn't the first bang to the back of his head he'd had this week. What if that first bang had weakened his skull and her bang had exacerbated this and ended up being the killing stroke?

'Mum threw him into the wall last week and he banged his head. What if he hit the same spot?'

Morag prevented her from saying more, curtailing Olivia's obvious rising anxiety at her father's imminent demise.

'Stop it, Olivia. You will do as I have said and I will ring your father now.'

There was no gainsaying Aunty Morag when she employed this tone. Olivia hung her head, turned and picked up her mug and backpack. She made her way up the stairs to the room that had been hers in those first two years of Olivia's life, when the family had lived with Aunty Morag.

She left the bedroom door open so she could listen to determine if there was a conversation, or if her aunt was going to have to go out and brave the storm. Possibly to go to their house and dispose of a body. It's the kind of thing Aunty Morag would be likely to do, rather than phone the police. She heard her aunt in the sitting room, speaking to someone. Which meant her father was still alive. She put down the skirt she had just taken from her pack and crept out to the landing, leaning over the bannisters to try and hear more clearly the conversation below.

ORDINARY WORLD

'Yes, she's with me. I'll keep her safe till tomorrow. I've advised her to return to your house then. Presumably after school. Yes. It does seem that way. So, what happened? I see. I see. And you're sure about that? She seems pretty convinced she struck you. I see. Just like Phyllis? You're sure? Definitely? That's excellent news. Yes, things are progressing. Progressing very well. Well, yes, obviously, less so for you.' Olivia thought she heard Aunty Morag chuckle at this point.

'No. NO! The arrangements will stand as far as that's concerned. You're already doing better out of this than any of us ever expected. True, true, but as it stands, you're getting no more than previously agreed. Yes, I'm aware, but no. Good. Yes, you're right about that. Not sure, we'll think on it. But, maybe this weekend. They'll both be together then. That might be the best time for it. Yes, there does seem to be an end in sight. Good, so you'll behave yourself, then? We don't need you rocking the boat just as we're coming into the harbour, do we? No, precisely. Good, well I'll see you on Saturday then. Olivia will be home with you tomorrow afternoon and hopefully Phyllis will be back on Friday. You're picking her up or are they delivering her? They are. OK. Good. See you Saturday, then.'

Olivia could only guess that Aunty Morag was speaking with her father. After all that was whom she said she'd be calling. But some of the conversation seemed very peculiar. It had the same peculiarities to it that some of her father's phone conversations had had, that she'd heard this week. Olivia didn't know what was more peculiar, the fact that her father and Aunty Morag were being amiable about meeting on Saturday for her party or the arrangements that they were talking about. She retreated back into her bedroom and sat on the edge of the bed. What could it mean? Saturday, she felt was the key. Maybe they were talking about arrangements for her party? Maybe they were safeguarding measures for when mum would be home? That would all seem reasonable. But what was it about these arrangements that meant Dad was doing well out of them? Money. Obviously. It was always the money with him. She guessed that whatever arrangements were being made, Dad was being paid to do them. How fucking like the old money-grabbing bastard.

Aunty Morag knocked on her open door, 'You alright now, Olivia?'

'Yes,' she replied with a yawn. Morag looked at Olivia's half-unpacked bag. Then over to where her tea remained untouched. She tutted. Morag came into the room and proceeded to unpack the rest of Olivia's belongings.

'I think Dad's having me followed,' Olivia suddenly blurted out, 'I don't think he trusts me.'

Morag stopped hanging up Olivia's leather jacket in the wardrobe and turned fully to face her.

'And what makes you say a thing like that, young lady?'

Olivia looked up from her lap, took in Aunty Morag's disapproving glower and then looked back at her lap. 'Because of something he said on the phone earlier. He said 'they lost us on the motorway,' which means someone was following us, if he knew I was on the motorway with... with my friend.'

Olivia was watching Aunty Morag out of the corner of her eye and she saw the eyebrow rise imperceptibly when she faltered.

'I see,' Morag said, 'well, I'm sure he does trust you, but it's clear that he worries about you. In his own way, brutish though that may seem. As to having you followed, I can't imagine that's the case at all. It's possible you misheard what he said or it could just have been that someone he spoke to during the day while trying to track you down happened to have seen you on the motorway. I'm sure it's nothing sinister.'

ORDINARY WORLD

Aunty Morag placed Olivia's backpack into the bottom of the wardrobe, a few items left inside and laid out her school uniform over the corner chair. She then moved over to the nightstand and picked up the mug.

'Time for bed, young lady. Your father is fine. He has another lump on his head, which I'm sure he deserves. He's as surly as ever, but other than that he's fine. He reminded me that Phyllis will be being dropped home on Friday and it's your birthday gathering on Saturday. So, I think it's a very good idea if you go back home tomorrow, after school. Your mum will need you to be settled for her return. Plus, I'm sure there are some things that'll need doing in preparation of your mum's return. Then we can all look forward to your birthday. Yes?'

Olivia nodded, clarity over the phone conversation coming from her aunt's words. She yawned again. Aunty Morag patted her on the shoulder, turned on the bedside light and then left the room, turning off the main light and closing the door behind her, with a final farewell.

As Olivia drifted off, a thought occurred to her. How would someone know it was her on the back of a bike on a motorway if they hadn't seen her before then? She had a helmet on.

Chapter 21

Thursday 15th April 1993

Breakfast was a very serious affair for Aunty Morag. 'The most important meal of the day,' she always declared. Olivia awoke to the smells of a banquet being prepared downstairs. It was always the same when she stayed and she often wondered whether, if she were to live here permanently, she might lose her gangly, lanky frame and become a vast balloon of a woman due to the importance Aunty Morag put on food and portion sizes. Having abluted, she made her way down to the kitchen where she found Aunty Morag slaving over the cooker. Two places had been set at the kitchen table and Olivia sat down and took a sip from the tall glass of orange juice set at her seat. There was steam rising from the spout of a tea pot hidden under a particularly garish tea cosy. She had little time to consider it before Aunty Morag placed an overloaded plate in front of her, with a dour good morning and enquiry as to how she had slept.

'Morning, Aunty,' she replied. She sounded surprised when she continued, 'Actually, I think I slept really well. The best I have in weeks. I guess I was just so exhausted it happened naturally. No dreams, just sleep.'

She looked down at the food. Eggs, bacon, hash browns, fried tomatoes, mushrooms, black pudding, haggis, sausages, baked beans and two slices of toast. Her stomach felt overwhelmed just looking at it. She knew Aunty would have a go at her if she didn't polish off at least two thirds of it, but the idea of it made her heave. She was never one for breakfast; it always took her ages before she was hungry after waking. She looked up at her aunt, who stood next to her, fists on hips, tapping her foot.

'Thank you, Aunty.'

Aunty Morag seemed appeased; good manners never hurt anyone. Morag went and served her own breakfast and then came and sat at the table, where she proceeded to pour two mugs of tea.

'Will you be alright today?'

Olivia sighed as she tackled the plate of food, 'Yes, I'll be alright.'

'Good. Straight to school after breakfast then, and then straight home after school. I doubt your father will be much of a problem. Surly, maybe, but not a problem. I would think he'll probably sulk until the weekend, so will keep out of your way.'

She sipped her tea as she held Olivia's gaze. Olivia nodded. She imagined most of what her aunt had said would be true. She knew what her father was like. Olivia gauged how successful her attempts at polishing off breakfast were by the gradual expression shift on Morag's face. When her lips were merely a thin, severe line Olivia knew she could desist, which was good because she thought she would explode if she ate another mouthful.

Morag said goodbye to her at the door and Olivia made her way reluctantly to school. She would much prefer to spend the day with John again but, unfortunately, he had work this morning. By the time the school gates loomed into her vision she was close to missing the bell and hurried in, to be grabbed briefly by Rhys and Evie who had clearly been hovering for her arrival. A quick 'I'll tell you at break' and they were in for assembly.

• • • •

'Was it Phyllis?' Evie opened when they finally convened to catch up on Olivia's absence.

'Was what Phyllis?' Olivia replied confused.

'Yesterday's absence. Has Phyllis taken a turn for the worse? She is still going to be out for your birthday, isn't she?' Olivia wasn't certain where Evie's true concern lay – with her mother's health or for her having a good birthday.

'No. No, she's fine, the hospital's still going to be dropping her home tomorrow.'

'So why weren't you in school, then?' Evie persisted.

Olivia turned her face away as she suddenly felt her cheeks getting warmer. Was she embarrassed? Ashamed?

'I went on a road trip. With John.'

'Oh, aye?' Rhys' tone seemed to be dripping in inuendo. 'Is that what we're calling it now?'

He winked at her, his whole upper body going into the action. He then looked up over their heads around the yard – most of it was obscured by the gym – behind which they had decided to settle for their quiet catch up. He removed a wrinkled Jiffy bag from inside his jacket and sparked up a rollie.

'Rhys!' Evie slapped his shoulder and then turned back to Olivia, her eyes narrowed, presumably because she had seen Olivia's blush. 'What kind of road trip? Where did you go? Romantic picnic, was it?' Olivia felt that even Evie's tone was suggesting something more to the event than a picnic. She blushed more heavily, definitely embarrassed.

'Birmingham. And Wolverhampton.' She stuttered out.

'Birmingham and Wolverhampton?' Evie's voice rose an octave, 'I wouldn't have said they were particularly romantic locations. Although,' Olivia saw Evie's eyes shift focus as she remembered her own experiences of the cities, 'although, Birmingham does have a good array of shops.'

She looked more intently at Olivia, 'Did he take you shopping? Because that's romantic. I always get the boys who go out with me to buy stuff for me. How do you think I manage such a varied wardrobe on the pittance Dad gives me for an allowance?'

'No, it wasn't anything like that,' Olivia wasn't surprised at her friend's expectations; if anything, she suspected they were more her mother's indoctrination into how a young girl should behave. How they should develop in order to snare that wealthy older man to look after them.

'No, we went to find properties,' she realised even as she said it how Evie was going to take it. Rhys' immediate response was typical as well.

'Ooh er, looking for shagpads are you? You dirty little slut!' he smiled roguishly at her.

This time Olivia felt her face explode with the heat of embarrassment, 'NO!'

'So, you're not looking to move in with John?' asked Evie. Did Olivia sense relief in her voice?

'No!' although the idea was definitely appealing, just not something she had considered yet. She had only known him a few days, and yet their relationship seemed to her to have been in existence for a lifetime. She rubbed her cheeks to try and hide her embarrassment.

'You remember John Fitzgerald Kennedy?'

They both nodded.

'Well, John discovered that he owned a number of properties other than our house. Some of them were in Birmingham and Wolverhampton. We went to check them out.'

'Why?' Rhys said frowning; it seemed an honest query.

'Because I was hoping we might be able to find him so I could talk to him about our house.'

'Oh, OK, fair enough,' Rhys nodded and took a long drag from his rollie.

'And did you?' asked Evie, 'Find him, that is?'

Olivia shook her head, 'No, and it all became a bit odd really.'

'How so?' Evie asked eagerly.

'Well, one of the properties had this solicitors in it and they seemed to be in care of one of the other properties. But when we enquired about it and Mr Kennedy, the solicitor got all hot under the collar about it. Saying that it wasn't fit for people to see. He even kind of admitted that Mr Kennedy was dead. Or at least that was the impression I got from him.'

Evie had turned her full attention to Olivia now, and even Rhys was paying attention.

'The guy who owns your house is dead? Do you know how?'

'It was her dad. I told you, he's a hitman,' Rhys interjected, Olivia couldn't detect any joking in his tone though, which caused a sudden knotting of anxiety in the top of her belly.

'No, nothing like that. Just something he let slip suggested to me that Kennedy's no longer alive.'

'Well, that could be a good thing, right? It probably means that he won't be about to evict you.'

'A relative might, though,' Rhys put in unhelpfully. Evie's eyes rolled up to look at the heavens in disbelief at Rhys' crass response. Without looking at him, she slapped his leg.

'Ignore him!' Over her shoulder, she said, 'Rhys shut up.'

'But they could! Bowen's family got evicted last year from their house because the landlord died and his daughter decided she didn't want a family living there now that she was in charge. Wanted to posh it up and move a professional couple in,' he protested.

Evie rounded on him, 'Rhys! Shut the fuck up!'

Rhys was about to defend himself further, but then saw the subtle thumb jabbing that Evie was doing in Olivia's direction. 'Oh! Oh, yeah, right.'

He craned around Evie to look at Olivia, taking the opportunity to flick his rollie stub into the gutter. 'Yeah, well, that was Bowen, not you, obviously. I'm sure that won't happen in your case, O.' He smiled weakly.

Olivia smiled back, 'It's fine, Rhys. Evie,' she said turning her attention to Evie and laying a hand over hers. 'I don't think that's going to happen in our case. I don't think there are any relatives. That's why the solicitor's dealing with it all. And he's in no mind to rock the boat. So, we're fine.'

'Good, but if it did ever happen, you know you can always stay with us, if you don't go to your aunt's.' Evie placed her other hand over Olivia's and squeezed it reassuringly.

Olivia nodded.

'And that was your day, then. Trekking around looking at buildings. Not very thrilling, I have to say. Not very romantic either,' Evie looked despondent.

'Given how sexy you look in all that leather, O, when did John ravish you?' Rhys was incorrigible.

Olivia blushed on demand now, it seemed to her. She looked away from them trying to hide it.

'My god!' Rhys leapt off the wall he'd been lounging on throughout their conversation and walked round to face her. 'He did ravish you, didn't he? I know that look anywhere, you dirty little minx.' Rhys was beaming with his discovery. Evie appeared shocked by Rhys' revelation. She pulled on Olivia's hand to make her look at her.

'Is Rhys right? Did you have sex with John yesterday?'

Olivia couldn't contain it any longer, and why should she? John filled her mind with stars and she said as much. Rhys whooped. Evie, however, was quiet. Withdrawn even, Olivia thought. Her hand had been taken from hers. Olivia looked into Evie's eyes, but couldn't read what was in there.

'Yes, it's true. It's fabulous; he fills my mind with stars. I feel fantastic with him. Like I've never felt before, with anyone. I'm delirious with him, so much so that I passed out on him the other day.'

'You passed out?' Evie said shocked, and possibly worried too.

'The other day?' Rhys said accusingly.

Olivia blushed again; she had no control it would seem. She addressed herself to Evie, trying to ignore the whirling dervish prancing about in front of her.

'Yes, scared the crap out of him too. But my mind was overcome by this brilliant white light, it's all I remember, and then I woke up with him, in his arms. He looked so worried and he said he thought I died.' Olivia couldn't help the embarrassed smile that erupted on her face as she spoke of the moment.

'My god, O. Stars? White lights? Passing out?' Evie looked dreadfully concerned, 'Don't you think this is actually quite serious? It doesn't sound healthy to me.'

'Apparently you're not the only one who thinks it's not normal. John was that worried he took me to see a government doctor. But it was fine. I had a scan, we talked and the doctor put it down to a combination of poor sleep and migraines. He gave me some pills if I needed them.' Olivia looked at Evie daring her to gainsay a professional. She continued on her offensive, 'Well, what's it like for you? Have you never had stars before?'

Olivia knew this was not what she should be asking her friend, because it would force her to either lie or admit that she wasn't the sex vixen she had always portrayed herself as. But she didn't care, she had the upper hand. For the first time in her life, she was becoming the person in control of her life. Of her actions and her emotions. Was this what it was like to be a superhuman?

'No, O, I've never had stars,' Evie responded sullenly.

• • • •

Evie remained aloof from the trio for the rest of the day, even eschewing their group at lunchtime. Olivia wondered if her friend felt awkward now she was the only one not to have had sex. Especially after all the time spent insinuating that she had. Rhys was good enough company, though, through lunch, even if he did insist on trying to garner sex tips from her on how John performed. Olivia finally ditched Rhys by the gates and managed to get a quick goodbye half-smile from Evie as she went the other way. Walking home, her thoughts were occupied by Evie and how she might make it right with her again. But there was no undoing the sex part and that was what seemed to have put Evie's back up. She gradually became aware of the boot steps that were following her. Her heart skipped a beat in horror as she neared the cut-through, thinking the faceless triplets were about to strike again. She turned sharply, hand raised to ward them off. But, instead, there was only a couple of cadets, hurrying towards the park end of town for muster. She let out a big sigh. Checked to make sure there was no one else and then headed for home. She felt a gentle prod in her forehead, just behind the skull. She stopped. She'd felt that once before. She looked around, but the cut-through was empty. The prod occurred again. Olivia concentrated on it, placing her fingers to her forehead.

'I wasn't certain if you'd let me speak to you like this, Olivia. But it was better than trying to catch you up. You already seemed rather spooked.' Hiram's voice washed over her mind. It was a very peculiar sensation, but not wholly unpleasant.

'Are you following me?' she demanded. She stood still in the middle of the path. Walking and talking seeming too complicated. It occurred to her afterwards that if anyone had seen her stood there like that, they would think her deranged, pressing her hands into her head and having a conversation with an empty pathway.

'I am. As I often do, I might add. Just ensuring your safety, Olivia.'

'Thank you... I think.'

'You're welcome. I'll be back here if you need me, at least until I know you're safely home. Such as that is.'

Olivia determined a distinct inflection in Hiram's tone and she wondered if he was referring to her pretend father. A consideration she herself hadn't thought about since Tuesday evening.

'I was, sorry,' Hiram's voice was almost a zephyr in her mind.

'Can you stop doing that now, please? It's making me want to scream.'

Hiram left abruptly. Olivia remained standing in the alleyway, massaging her forehead. The most the conversation had done was to remind her of the possibility that her dad wasn't, in fact, her dad. As she considered everything she knew about him and their past together, she finally concluded that Miriam and Hiram were clearly mistaken. Barring the moments when it seemed they were talking to her mind, for the most part there was nothing to corroborate what they had to say. A lot of conspiratorial mumbo jumbo. Besides, her mother wouldn't have stood for being in a house with a man who wasn't her husband for all these years.

She started to walk on. And then she remembered last Thursday morning, when her mother had blatantly stated that her dad wasn't her husband. It wasn't the first time either, but then there had been times when Mum hadn't recognised Olivia either. Could it be that her mother wasn't delusional? Could it be that her dad had been drugging her to believe all sorts and that her mum had desperately tried to fight against all this to tell the world, only for it to fall on deaf ears? She stopped again, as she entered her street. She was beginning to doubt a lot of things, not least of all her own grip on reality. Did she dare go back to her house? Her dad might be there. If he *was* her dad, that was. She half turned around. Where would she go if she didn't go home? Aunty Morag's? No, she had been adamant that Olivia return home. But then, Morag didn't know about the possibility of him not actually being her father. She did know that Olivia believed he was having her followed, but had dismissed that too. Why wouldn't she, though? It was all so farfetched.

She turned back towards her house. She could go to Evie's, but Olivia wasn't certain of the welcome she would receive now. Or there was John? Definitely not Rhys, though. And then she remembered why Aunty Morag had been so insistent that she went home – Mum. Mum would be home tomorrow and Olivia needed to be there for her. With Mum coming home, things would be different in the house; there would be another focus for her dad, for one thing. She took in a deep breath, steeled herself and set her sights on home. *For Mum*, she thought.

Her dad was in the hallway when she came in through the door. His presence took her aback. It hadn't given her the moment of dread she had thought she was going to experience, trying to find out if he was even home.

'Oh, good, you're back,' he said, turning round at the sound of the front door.

'I've been organising your mother's things. But now you're here you can make sure I've done it all as she would like. You seem to have a better idea on how she likes her things. I had wondered if she might prefer to have some of her old objects and stuff out in her room, now she seems to be a bit more of her old self. So, there's a pile of stuff I've taken from the back of her wardrobe – cushions, throws, a box with some ornaments and trinkets in it – and put them on the end of her bed. I was hoping you could sift through them and see if there were any bits she might prefer to have out now.'

He didn't look at her the entire time he was speaking, instead glancing about the hall or looking over her shoulder.

ORDINARY WORLD

'I bought fish and chips for tea. Yours is in the oven keeping warm. They didn't have any haddock, though I know you prefer it. But cod's nice. So, well.' He trailed off. He cleared his throat. 'So, having tidied and whatnot, I thought you might like some quiet time to sort out your mother's things before she gets back. That being the case, I've arranged to meet some friends at the Harp for a couple of beers. Don't wait up, I've no idea when I'll be back.'

And with that, he collected his coat from the hooks by the door, shuffled past her, trying not to touch her and, from Olivia's perspective, seemed to flee the house. During all of it she had said not a word. Her father had appeared very sheepish and he had definitely avoided any eye contact. To be honest though, she was relieved he would be out for the night. She hung up her own coat on the hook next to the one just vacated by her father's, then dropped her backpack and went to the kitchen where she retrieved her tea. She took it, and her backpack, up to her room, before going into her mother's room to sift through the things her dad had laid out.

Chapter 22

Olivia had siphoned off a few of the ornaments and placed them strategically around her mum's room. She placed a throw and a shawl she knew were her mum's favourites over her rocking chair and was now going through the cushions with a view to placing a couple on her bed, before packing everything else away. She just couldn't fathom her father at the moment. He seemed to be all over the place. Olivia was beginning to seriously wonder whether he should go to see the doctor for the bumps he'd taken to the back of his head in recent succession. She'd heard of people having complete personality shifts from blows to the head. Was that what had happened to her father? If so, some of it seemed to have made him more considerate. In which case, maybe she wouldn't suggest a doctor's visit; she didn't want a doctor curing her dad of his improvement.

Her hand hovered over the lumpy, faded red cushion she had in her hand. This was the cushion that had been hidden at the back of the wardrobe – the one with the photos stuffed into its heart. She flipped the cushion around until she found the tell-tale slit in the seam. She prised the Velcro apart and slid her hand inside, through the old, clumped stuffing, until it closed around the familiar shapes of the photos. She pulled them out and fanned them over the bedspread.

There were half a dozen faded photographs of a time lost to her mother. Static memories of a person that no longer existed. Olivia cast her gaze over each one in turn and then back again. Pausing on her favourite, which was of her much younger mother half stumbling down some sand dunes, hat in hand and laughing. She wasn't certain if the photo showed stormy weather in the background or whether it was just the picture itself that was clouded by age. It mattered not; it was the focus of the picture that always caught Olivia's imagination. She moved on reluctantly to the photo next to it on the bed. Her gaze continued on and then stopped abruptly. She grabbed a photo and pulled it closer to her face. It was of a large group of people, standing and sitting in rows. They were all smiling, big honest happy grins of delight and joy. Truly a happy and momentous event for this group. Her mother was there in the middle of the second row, where she always was whenever Olivia had glanced at this photo in the past. But this time she recognised someone else. A tall, gangly figure on the far right – no need for a bench for *him* to be seen over the heads of those in front. He looked funny in a gawky kind of way, all elbows and knees, but it was his eyes that had attracted Olivia to view this person more closely. She knew those eyes. She recognised those eyes. That was Hiram.

'Hiram!' she said out loud.

'Yes?'

'Get outta my head!' she half screamed in fright.

She heard the fading whisper of a sorry as he left her mind. *No*, she thought.

'No! Wait! Hiram, come back, please? I'm sorry, you just startled me.'

A rather tentative enquiry came back to her, 'You're certain? I only came in the first place because you called so urgently.'

'I did?' Olivia sounded surprised.

'You did.'

'How did I manage to call you?'

'Easy, you thought of me and called my name. When I spoke to you earlier, that prod you felt at the front of your brain, that was me requesting entrance. In this case you kinda kicked in the door of my mind and commanded me. Which was why I answered.'

'I'm sorry, I had no idea. I don't know how I did that.'

'No, I suppose you probably don't. We had training, after all. But that's not an issue, my dear. I can show you the ropes.'

'Thank you,' Olivia sounded genuinely grateful. There was a pause.

'Was there something specific you required of me?' Hiram finally broke the silence.

'Oh, yes, I suppose there was. I wondered if this really was you in this photo I found in my mother's things?' she halted, how was Hiram going to see what she was looking at? He wasn't in the room... he possibly wasn't even in the street. She felt a gentle prod in the back of her head, near the base of her skull.

'If you let me in here, then I will be able to see what you are looking at.'

'Really?'

'Yes, really,' Olivia detected a smile in Hiram's voice.

'I'm sorry, I don't mean to doubt you, but this is all just so unbelievable. So fantastical I can't get my head round it. OK,' she said concentrating. She thought she detected a feather tickle her mind; an inside brain itch that she couldn't scratch.

'Ah, yes, that is indeed me. In my more attractive youth.' Olivia detected a forlorn sigh. 'That photo depicts the happiest day of my life. I believe it probably was true for all of us. By then we had all come to terms with our various diagnoses for our enduring mental incapacities. But on the day that photo was taken we had all been accepted onto an experimental program that promised to change our lives forever. It would cure us of our mental issues and make better people of us.'

Olivia heard the sigh again, 'Well, in part the promise was kept. We were cured of our respective ailments. And it certainly changed our lives forever. Although, for some, that came at the expense *of* their life. For the rest of us, it came at the expense of our physical selves, except for a very rare few. Your mother was one of those rarities. As was your father,' Olivia felt her gaze being drawn to a self-effacing young man in the front row, sat directly in front of her mother. The young man was pleasant to look at and had a boyish grin upon his features. Her eyes focused intently upon his face and she became aware of how her sight almost seemed to hone in on the very facets of his face picking out even the minutest of details. Startling slate grey eyes pierced the ground between them and the camera lens. Olivia wasn't certain what she felt looking at this stranger. Her father. A man she had never seen before, even when looking at this photograph, because all she had ever really seen was her young mother, in happier times. Did she feel sadness? Loss, for never having known him? All she thought she felt was an emptiness. A void of feeling for a man who should have been the person to have brought her up, instead of the brute of a man that had. No, she thought, there was nothing there for this man.

'It is to be expected, Olivia. Don't berate yourself for having no emotions for someone you've seen once in a photograph. It's not your fault that you were never allowed to know him. It was *theirs*.'

Hiram changed the view swiftly, Olivia wondered if this was more for his benefit than hers.

'Those three on the left near the end of the back row. Those are the triplets you had the misfortune of meeting the other day. Innocuous-looking fellows, aren't they? Not so now, rapacious killing machines they are now. I think the experiments changed more than their physical selves; it warped their minds as well. And, I think, the Organisation considers them to be among their finest conclusions to their experiments.' Olivia heard the tut in Hiram's tone as she looked at the three fair-haired young men who grinned inanely at the camera.

'And finally, the chap on the left of centre, in the chair next to your father. Jon Kennedy, son of the chief scientist on the project. He was the third person in the group who took the experimental warping in the same manner as your parents. I suppose it was because of him that the programme happened in the first place. His father was desperate to create a normal life for him. It did happen, I believe, he had a wife after all this, but it ended tragically. Although I believe their son survived. No idea what became of him though, he was but an infant when his father went completely over the edge.'

There was that forlorn sigh again, but Olivia wasn't paying attention at this point, she was hung up on the name. Jon Kennedy.

'John Kennedy?'

'Yes, Jon,' she wondered if Hiram's eyebrows had raised wherever he was.

'I've been looking for a John Fitzgerald Kennedy this week. Would that have been him? Only I had the distinct impression he had died in infancy.'

'Ah, yes, that would have been his older sibling. Had both physical and mental incompatibilities. Managed to survive a full week, or might have been two, I can't remember. I learned about him from Jon in the early days of the experiment. Sad really. His parents had been devastated, so when Jon was born they thought their prayers had been answered. And then it turned out Jon was deficient too. Mentally corrupted, Jon described it as.' Hiram fell silent. *Lost in the past?* wondered Olivia.

Slowly, she shuffled the photographs together and then shoved them back into the cushion. She was undecided on whether to leave it on the bed for her mother or to hide it back in the wardrobe. She had no way of telling what effect these pictures would have upon her mum's potentially still fragile mind.

'Are you still there, Hiram?'

'I am. Sorry, got lost in the past there for a moment. Was there anything else I can help you with?'

'No, not at the moment, I don't think. But I would like to try this again, soon. If you can help me with my,' she paused, *what are they, powers? Talents? Gifts?* '...abilities, show me a way to use them safely, I would be very grateful.'

'It would be my honour and my pleasure, Olivia,' she knew that Hiram had a sincere look about him, wherever he was, and imagined him giving her a courtly bow. She thought she heard a faint chuckle.

'I think you are learning things innately, Olivia. Those impressions you have, go with them. Follow them and expand upon them, for they are your mind and your intuition working in harmony. They see the truth that most others do not. Miriam was correct, you are indeed the greatest sum of all of us. And on that happy note, I will bid you farewell. I hope we will meet properly again soon. Perhaps, after your birthday?'

'I hope so too, Hiram. Yes, perhaps we could meet in the park on Sunday?'

'It's a date, then. Just ping me when you're ready and I will meet you by the pond.'

And with that, Olivia's mind suddenly felt lonely and devoid of life. How strange it all was. For a moment she contemplated trying to reach out to John. After all they had more of a connection than anyone, but then she thought better of it. What if she actually managed to connect with him and he was on his bike? She might cause him to crash and then where would they be?

• • • •

She could hear that song again, Wonderwall. She'd asked people at school if they'd ever heard of a band called Oasis, but no one had. Rhys was in the know about that sort of thing, he was big into his music, and yet he hadn't heard of the band or the song. It seemed strange given that she'd heard it on the radio. But when had she heard it, she couldn't remember and now here it was, playing again.

The music faded, as if it was being deliberately turned down and then it was superseded by a voice. She recognised the voice. She didn't like that voice at all anymore and she feared that the voice would come into view and she would see that it belonged to a faceless head.

'If Mohammed won't come to the mountain, then the mountain will have to come to Mohammed,' the voice chuckled. 'Maybe our efforts were a little pre-emptive, my love. There seems to be more life left in you than I had imagined and your little stunt has at least shown us that you're not as dead as you would want us to believe. Turns out it stimulated the baby inside you too. All the scans show a vibrant child once more developing within you. But if you're that determined to stay in this dingy hospital room, who am I to gainsay an expectant mother?

'But we can't have you here all alone. There's no telling what trouble you'd get yourself into. So, we're coming to you. We've bought the hospital. For all intents and purposes nothing has changed for any of the regular visitors and staff. Other than that this section is now undergoing long put off renovation. And by that, I mean this section is now an extension of the facility you and Stephen so wilfully abandoned in your haste to leave your family. You can't see it yet, but we're making this whole room entirely about you, my love. As for Stephen, when, if, he returns, well, there'll be a lovely surprise for him, and not just a new-born child for his paternal instincts to get all riled up about. I think, in the long run, your little stunt has advanced our cause no end, my love. So, thank you for that. Although the families of the wardens you slaughtered may not be so wholehearted in their thanks, but they knew what they were signing on for and their death-in-service package should be enough to quell any disquiet or irrational demands for inquiries. There's nothing that you can do *that we can't polish over, my love. So perhaps it's time for you to wake up and smell the roses.'*

She could hear footsteps receding and then what reminded her of a Star Trek door sliding open and then shut again. The music didn't come back on.

• • • •

Friday 16th April 1993

Olivia had a strained breakfast with her father the following morning. Their conversation was brief and reaffirmed that everything was set for Phyllis' return that afternoon. She was tense today, not just because of her father's unpredictable presence, but also because she realised she had mixed emotions about her mother's return to the family nest. She was excited at the prospect of having a potentially better and more lucid mother. A mother of old, before the illness and the battery of containment drugs had taken a full grasp of a fragile mind. But she was also anxious at the possibility of that lucidity slipping, of fading away like so many false hopes before. The idea that this time it would be different, this time it would be better. This time it would be different from before. She feared her mother settling in and then reverting to her delusion that no one was real. It was at this point that Olivia wondered if what she really feared was that the things she had been told *were* truly real. And if her mother was becoming more lucid, would her reaction to a false husband be, in fact, the truth? Could they be in for a rollercoaster ride of the illusion shattering, but with only her understanding what was happening, as the pretenders maintained their falsehoods and disguises, forcing Phyllis back into her shell, or worse, the mental health residential unit.

Olivia hurried to school. She was happy to hear the booted footsteps today, for she knew it was just Hiram keeping an eye on her. She reached out for him, but only met silence. She tried harder, stopping in the middle of the road unexpectedly as she attempted to thrust her mind out searching for the lanky man. But all she heard was a buzzing in her ears and then a loud beep of a car horn that made her jump out of her skin. She looked up and apologised to the driver as she realised she was holding up traffic. She hurried onto school, puzzled by the lack of response. She must be doing something wrong. Perhaps she wasn't being instinctive enough. After all, last night had been an accident and she couldn't really remember the process involved that had connected her mind with Hiram's. By the time she arrived at school, she had a headache from all the forced effort of her failed attempts and she resigned herself to the fact that she would have to wait for Hiram to connect with her.

She was jolted from her introspection by an excitable Rhys, who spent the day going over the plans for the after-party party. Evie seemed to have thawed a bit as well, which was a blessing for Olivia. She had no wish to spend the day with a surly and withdrawn Evie. That said, her friend was still not as forthcoming as she was usually wont to be. But she did confirm for Olivia that she still had every intention of being at her house for 3.30pm and the start of the gathering. She had no wish to miss out on what could be Olivia's best birthday ever and she was anxious to grill John about his intentions towards her best friend.

The trio walked together part-way back to Olivia's that afternoon and for a while it felt like old times. When they parted company, Evie still had a smile upon her face, even if Olivia felt it seemed a bit forced. Rhys left them on the understanding that, come midnight tomorrow, if he had linked up with some tasty bit of 'milf' then the girls would be on their own. They parted company and Olivia hurried on back to her house to await the imminent arrival of her mother.

Chapter 23

Friday 16th April 1993

Dad was in the sitting room when Olivia came home. He appeared on edge, although that was to be expected with Mum's imminent return. She did wonder if any of it had anything to do with their own strained relationship... she suspected that didn't help. She felt the same - on edge. Olivia hung up her coat and bag and went into the kitchen and made two mugs of tea, which she took into the sitting room, passing one to her father. He looked up from the TV and she heard a gruff thank you, before he returned his attention to the screen. He kept checking his watch and glancing out of the window.

'Trust the nuthouse to be late,' he said suddenly, more to the aether than to her she felt.

Olivia sat down in the armchair by the door and hugged her mug as she waited. She looked at the TV, but she couldn't focus on it. There was just a blur of random images; people were talking, but about what she knew not, nor cared. She started to glance out of the windows every time she heard a car door. In the end, she stood up and walked to the window, watching, waiting impatiently for the next event in her life to happen. It came eventually, in the form of a unit minibus, which pulled up outside the wrong house. Two men got out and then helped Phyllis out of the bus and into a wheelchair. The driver wheeled her to the front door while the other one carried Mum's overnight bag.

'They're here,' Olivia said moving briskly out of the room for the front door.

Reg was slow to rise. He took a hefty swig of his tea, scalding his lip in the process. He swore, slammed the mug down on the table and then made a slow approach to the front hall. The door was open when he got there and Olivia was in the doorway talking to the orderly who had wheeled Phyllis up the path.

'Thank you, we can take it from here. Dad's had a full rundown of expectations and an update on medication.' Olivia helped her mum out of the wheelchair and supported her through the door. Her father waited for them to go into the sitting room, before moving forward, collecting the overnight bag and unceremoniously shutting the door in the driver's face.

Olivia helped Phyllis to an armchair in the sitting room, Phyllis walked slowly, but upright. Olivia was uncertain if her mum's apparent frailty was due to the meds or something else; her dad may well have been informed, but as yet he had failed to pass on that information to her. Phyllis sat down with a soft sigh and looked about her sitting room. She nodded to herself and then turned to Olivia.

'Olivia, my darling,' she said, grasping both of Olivia's hands in hers, 'come stand before me so that I can get a good look at you.'

Olivia dutifully stood in front of her mother and gazed down at the eloquent stranger that had entered her house. Phyllis took several minutes to analyse the girl that stood before her and Olivia was becoming uncomfortable under the scrutiny. She forced a smile to ease the disquiet of those penetrating eyes.

'Yes,' Phyllis eventually said, 'you are exactly as I imagined you would be, were I ever to have a daughter. It's amazing how the mind and body works, isn't it, my darling?'

Phyllis beamed up at her. Looking into her eyes Olivia could see none of the previous cloudy haze of delirium, yet here she was talking like she had in the recent past... not quite here in the real world.

Her father had moved into the room while Olivia was being scrutinised. He'd thrown the night bag into a corner and then turned to stand staring down at his wife. He waited until her attention shifted to him.

'Reg,' Phyllis said by way of a greeting. It was said with no feeling; a single word with a hint of ice to it.

'Phyllis,' the word snapped out, almost like a reprimand.

Phyllis turned her full attention to her husband.

'Yes, I remember you, Reg,' there was that coldness again, 'I remember you completely.'

Olivia was aware of a steely glint in her mother's eye as she spoke to her dad. The coldness between them belied the eighteen years the two of them had been married. She felt that the tension in the room was growing and she had no way of knowing where it would lead. One thing was certain, there was no love lost between the spouses: a sad state of affairs caused, no doubt, by her mum's enduring illness – at least for anyone looking in on their lives.

Olivia was beginning to consider the truth that lay behind this ice sheet, despite her own doubts on what was real and what wasn't, the strained relationship between her parents could be best explained by what she now knew. *Now*, she believed her mother had been telling them the truth for a very long time, but no one had listened, because it could all too plausibly be explained away by her fractured mind casting shadows onto reality and obscuring the truth from her. Phyllis was showing distinct signs of being a wholly different person under her new meds, so surely her father should be happy? But then, was he ever? Could he be happy knowing his wife was becoming more her old self, an old self that, according to Miriam, was aware of Reg's true identity.

'Completely, you say?' Reg replied.

'Completely,' Phyllis emphasised. She placed her fingers to her temple and jutted her jaw out at Reg. Olivia was aware in her peripheral vision of Reg taking an involuntary step backwards, his face paling.

'No trouble now, Phyllis... we can always send you back to the unit if you're going to be a problem.'

'DAD!' Olivia rounded on him, 'Mum's barely through the door and you're already threatening to send her back?'

'No threat, only a promise. Promises are all we have after eighteen years, isn't that right, Phyllis?'

Her mum seemed to sag noticeably back into her chair, her features softened and her hand fell back down to rest on the arm.

'Indeed, Reg, indeed. I've been thinking in recent days of how it's almost time I fulfilled a long-made promise. Maybe you can help me with that?' she glanced up at her husband.

'I don't know what you're talking about, Phyllis. Clearly the meds haven't had the miracle effect we had hoped for. You're still a rambling lunatic.'

Olivia rounded on her father, and therefore couldn't see her mother's reaction to his comments.

'Fuck's sake, Dad. If you're going to make this harder than it needs to be, might I suggest you leave.' Olivia had squared off to her father and she could see a dangerous glint in his eye. She was all too aware of where that glint could take him, but in the past, no one had ever stood up to it. They had always cowered before his impulsive rage and then taken the brunt of it. She watched as the glint faded, her dad looking at her in surprise. He pulled himself to his full height, thrusting back his shoulders and straightening his back. Olivia readied herself for the incoming slap.

'Perhaps you're right, Olivia, perhaps you're right. I'll go and leave you to your mother's care. I'll be back later. Once I know she's asleep and no longer a threat to this family.'

And with that, Reg strutted out of the sitting room and then out of the house.

Olivia couldn't believe the change in her dad. She sagged, letting out a huge sigh of relief. She had been so tied up in the anxiety of the moment, so expecting the ringing sting of a slap to her face, that she didn't quite know what to do with herself. Her legs were like jelly and she eased herself down onto the pouf that sat near to her mother's armchair. Tears came unbidden to her eyes and rolled down her cheeks. Cheeks she could feel were red with blush, a lovely change from the red of an oncoming bruise. She smiled uncontrollably and then started to laugh. She had no understanding of what was happening to her, let alone her family. It was all changing and she didn't know if breaking the equilibrium of limbo was for better or for worse.

'Come here, dear,' Phyllis said to Olivia, leaning out of her chair to take Olivia's hands.

'Oh, Mum,' Olivia snuffled through her laughter and tears. She practically launched herself into her mother's arms and wrapped her up so tight, so fiercely in a hug, she feared she would snap her mother in two.

She felt her mother willingly reciprocate the hug, a hand coming to the back of her head to stroke her hair. This was what she had always dreamed of; this was the ordinary world she had craved. A day when she could openly let her emotions wash out of her in a cathartic tidal wave and her mum would be there to help mop up the flood. She suddenly felt immense joy at being so upset.

She lifted her head from her mother's chest and laughed up at her, 'I'm so happy you're home, Mum.' She buried herself back into her mum's chest and savoured the seconds before she knew it would all come crashing back to normality.

'There, there, love,' her mother crooned, 'it's for the best your father's gone for now. There are things I need to tell you. Things I can only say now and without him eavesdropping.'

Olivia slowly pulled away, wiping her tears away with her sleeve. 'What things, Mum?'

Phyllis drew in a long, suffering sigh, 'I think you already know most of them, most of it. Don't you, Olivia?'

Olivia shook her head, *no she didn't, what could her mother be alluding to? Surely, she couldn't be affirming the preposterous tales of Miriam and Hiram. Surely, not.* 'What things, Mum?' she asked more defiantly.

'How I wish you were real, my love. You are exactly as I imagined you to be, were I ever to have a baby girl. I was pregnant, once, a long, long time ago, but this is all a dream of my own making and I need it to end now. Maybe, if it can end, I can have that baby girl I imagined. But I'm lost in the dream. I've been here so long.' Phyllis looked imploringly into Olivia's eyes. 'Help me, Olivia! Help me find my way out.'

'Of course, Mum,' Olivia's tears had started afresh. Her ordinary world had shattered, as she knew it would. The real world was returning in an avalanche. Lucid though her mum was, she was still not the mother Olivia had craved for all these years. She was still a delusional schizophrenic, and no matter how good the new meds were, it didn't detract from the fact that Phyllis continued to entwine her delusion around Olivia's reality.

Olivia stood up, patting her mother's hand and then wiped away the fresh flow of tears. She glanced at the clock.

'Time I was making your tea, Mum. I'll put the TV on for you,'

Phyllis appeared to have slipped from her moment of utter clarity. Olivia could see the cloudy haze returning across her mother's eyes. The moment was gone. How long till it returned? She turned the TV on and made her way to the kitchen. She continued to wipe away the occasional flow of tears that seeped unbidden from the corners of her eyes, as she prepared tea.

She helped her mum to the kitchen table and presented her with her food. Phyllis thanked her for being such a good child and ate her meal. Pushing the empty plate from her, Phyllis spoke for the first time since starting her meal. Olivia was startled from her reverie and dabbed at a loose tear to listen to her mother.

'Time for some of my new meds, my dear. You'll find them in the front pocket of my overnight bag.'

Olivia jumped up and retrieved the bag, which she opened on the kitchen table. There was an array of pill bottles inside and she took them all out, placing them on the table in front of them. How like her father to have left without telling her which ones Mum needed when. Phyllis craned forward and pulled two tall, identical-looking tubes out from the mass.

'These ones, Olivia. One of each with water, please.'

'Are you sure, Mum?' Olivia asked, not certain she should be allowing her mother to be making her own medication decisions.

Phyllis looked sternly at her daughter, 'I may be delusional, Olivia, but I'm not daft.'

Olivia jumped at the reprimand, 'Yes Mum. Sorry, Mum,'

Phyllis smiled, 'That's alright, my dear. I understand. And when your useless father comes back, I'm sure he will get around to telling you what the full regime is.'

Olivia detected a tone of spite in her mother's voice as she spoke of her father.

The rest of the evening passed quietly. They sat on the sofa watching TV. Neither spoke. Olivia suspected her mother wasn't really watching, having drifted off into her little world. And Olivia wasn't really watching because she was so numb from her mother's return. She felt empty inside: devoid of any emotion, any thought. She just stared into the TV and waited for something to happen.

A voice drifted into her mind, *'The mountain has arrived, my dear. Time to prop you up and take a look inside. Let's see if we can't get you to come out and play.'*

For a moment, Olivia could see a blank face peering too closely into her own. She shuddered and shook her head. The image and voice faded and she realised she was looking at the clock on the wall of the sitting room. Ten past ten... time for Mum to be in bed. She could hear the news in the background. She turned to her mum who hadn't moved in all that time.

'Time for bed, Mum,' she received a welcome nod and Phyllis braced herself for the move to standing. Olivia supported her and they made their way upstairs. As Olivia bent in to say good night to her mother, having washed her and settled her for sleep, Phyllis grabbed her wrist in a vice-like grip. Phyllis pulled Olivia down so their faces were nearly touching and Olivia could see the passion in her mother's eyes as she spoke.

'I have to get out of this dream, Olivia. For your sake as well as mine. If you want to be born, to become you, it is essential you help me find the path. You're the only one who can do this now, Olivia. I am lost.' Phyllis' grip suddenly relinquished and she fell back into her pillows, her eyelids fluttering.

Olivia was stunned for a moment by the intensity of her mother's momentary insanity. With the grip lost, she leaned in once more. Smoothed the hair from her mother's brow, kissed it and said,

'Yes, Mum. I'll do anything I can to help you. Goodnight, sweet dreams, Mum.'

'Thank you, my good daughter,' Phyllis whispered from the edge of sleep, 'but no more dreams. Or I will become irrevocably lost within dream after dream. No more.'

And she slept.

• • • •

Olivia couldn't sleep. She should take one of her pills, but she was reluctant; the last time she had taken a pill she had woken up in the park. She had considered the possibility that a side effect of the pills was somnambulism. She'd looked it up; sleep walking, drugs – pharmaceutical or otherwise – could inhibit that part of the brain that prevented physical activity during the sleep cycle. True the pill would make her sleep, but it might also make her get out of bed and do something drastic while her brain had no control. She wanted sleep, she needed sleep, for the eventful day tomorrow and yet she didn't want to induce it unnaturally.

She rolled over, thumped her pillow and tried in vain to sleep. But sleep refused to come. Her mind was empty. She rolled onto her back and opened her eyes to the gloom that pervaded her room. She needed thoughts to try and find a way into sleep. She thought about her mother. About her apparent lucidity and yet there amongst it all was the delusion, constantly flitting in and out to remind them all that she was a woman with a fragile and broken mind. She thought of her father. Bloody man. How he had changed over this past week and how he had been completely the same as soon as her mother had arrived home. He had turned automatically back into the complete cunt he had always been. She thought about Rhys and Evie. Indistinguishable, part of their trio. All one and the same really when you thought about it. Rhys was a one. His antics with wooing older women and dabbling in such a variety of drugs, she wondered how he still managed to contend with real life. But maybe that was the point. He didn't contend; he used things to help him avoid real life. She couldn't imagine that his home life could be as trying as hers. So that just left boredom being his only real excuse for the way he behaved. How would he cope in the real, real world? She knew his father had expectations that Rhys would join him in the trade, once Rhys had completed school. An apprenticeship awaited him and a solid career in construction. She remembered Rhys saying proudly how his father wanted them to go into business together once his apprenticeship was complete. So, maybe that was why Rhys behaved the way he did. He knew his future was all mapped out – this was his escape. And as for

Evie, her future was all mapped out too. If her mother had anything to do with it. So, what of her, Olivia? Was her life all mapped out too? There was the life where she would stay at home and look after Mum and probably, in years to come Dad too. This was not a life she wanted. She wanted a life that included John, that included adventures, like their road trip to Birmingham and that first afternoon in John's flat. She wanted to go to university. All those things were possible, weren't they? Especially if John was there to support her. He loved her; she loved him. Anything was possible, right?

Sleep came to her unexpectedly as she was thinking about a life with John. One moment she was imagining a student's life: being picked up by her boyfriend on his motorbike, as she waved goodbye to imaginary friends. The next she was lying in a hospital room. It was the one she had seen several times before, but now things had changed. She lay on the same bed, but now she lay within a cubicle that had been constructed around her. It was silvery steel and reinforced glass. There was an airlock in the far-left corner that led into an antechamber, and beyond that lay the door out into the hallway. There was a secondary corridor-like chamber that ran the extent of the remaining cubicle, accessed through side airlocks in the main airlock chamber. She could see a man in what looked like an astronaut's bulky suit walking the corridor with a clipboard; he kept looking in at her and then scribbling notes onto the paper. To her immediate left and right there were banks of machines and wires. She could hear the heart monitor beeping. But it sounded discordant until she realised it was monitoring two heartbeats, out of rhythm with one another. She heard that infamous Star Trek door noise again, the swoosh-swoosh of a door sliding open and shut. She looked around at the noise and saw the faceless man again.

ORDINARY WORLD

She awoke in a sweat, bolt upright, the image of a faceless face still prominent in front of her. She stifled the scream and opened her eyes. Dawn's early light was seeping in around the edges of her curtains. She felt tired. She glanced at her clock, six twenty-eight. No point trying to go back to sleep. She lay back into her pillow, drawing breath and calming herself. She would get up shortly. It would give her time to prepare herself before looking in on Mum and settling her for the morning. Then discussions with Dad, assuming he was home and then preparations for the afternoon. Of course, this afternoon, she realised. It was her birthday today. Today she was seventeen.

Chapter 24

Saturday 17th April 1993

Olivia waited till seven o'clock before making her way to her mother's room. Phyllis was just stirring and Olivia sat on the end of the bed waiting to see what frame of mind her mother would be in today. Phyllis opened her eyes and smiled at Olivia when she saw her.

'Have you been sat there all night, my love?'

Olivia stifled a giggle, 'No, Mum, of course not. Just came in. Would you like tea in bed? First morning back and all.'

Phyllis stretched and yawned, 'Lovely idea, but I think I'd rather like to get up and at 'em this morning. Spent too much time at the unit just lolling about.'

And with that, Phyllis swung her legs out of bed and readied herself for the day. Olivia was amazed at her mother's sudden energy, after her apparent lacklustre demeanour of the evening before. But didn't they always say recuperation at home is far quicker than staying in hospital? She found that her mother didn't really need her help at all, so instead she went downstairs to the kitchen to begin breakfast. As she passed the door to her father's study, she pushed it open to see if he was sleeping in there, as there had been no sign of him upstairs. She wished she had knocked. Actually, she wished she hadn't opened the door. Reg was sat in his chair, trousers and pants around his ankles, his personal member firmly clenched in his hand and two young girls performing unnatural acts with vegetables on the TV, with the volume turned down.

'Jesus Christ, Dad!' Olivia slammed the door.

'Don't let it hit you in the arse,' she heard her father pant through the door. As she made her way hurriedly to the kitchen, she tried to block out the grunts she could just make out coming from his room. A shiver of revulsion shimmied its way through her and she had a momentary gag reflex. Christ alive, her dad was such a fucking animal sometimes.

Her mother joined her in the kitchen a quarter of an hour later and together they prepared breakfast. They were just laying it out on the table when a red-faced and rather sweaty-looking Reg walked in.

'I hope you've washed your hands!' Olivia demanded before he could take breath. She could see two or three small beads of sweat stuck in the furrows of his brow. She turned away from his answer, as just looking at him made her recollect her morning surprise. She felt herself gag again.

'Not that it's any of your business, but that was what I was coming in here to do,' said a disgruntled Reg. He stomped over to the sink where he proceeded to splash water all over the counter. Phyllis tutted at the mess of her recently cleaned kitchen.

They sat and ate breakfast together, like a normal family. The radio was on and, ironically, 'Ordinary World' came on. Olivia nearly choked on her toast as she looked about the table. Her parents were nominally speaking to one another. Forced politeness for the sake of the children. It was an agonisingly stilted affair and Olivia wished that they would just behave like they normally did. She brought herself up short. Here, for the first time in how long, she couldn't remember, she was in a normal scenario and she was wishing it wasn't. If that wish was fulfilled then her dad would either be in his study or not in the house at all and her mother would be catatonic in a chair or in bed. This was something she had wanted for so long. She almost had her wish and she didn't know how to deal with it. It felt too surreal.

The phone rang in the sitting room. She looked up at the clock. Eight o'clock on a Saturday morning, bit early for a call. She started to list who it could be, then realised both her parents were looking at her. They wanted her to answer it. Well, fair enough, it would be a good excuse to escape this Stepford moment. She hurried to the phone and caught it before it went dead.

'Hello?'

'HAPPY BIRTHDAY, LOVELY,' Evie shouted into her ear.

'Thank you, I think,' Olivia replied, pulling the phone away from her head to prevent permanent hearing loss.

'So, what did the grungies get you?'

'Oh, well, I don't know,' Olivia stuttered. She hadn't even thought about presents, in fact, after her unpleasant moment with her father's 'good morning' she had completely forgotten the significance of the day.

'Whaddya mean you don't know? Haven't they given you any presents yet? What about a card?'

'No, no cards. And there haven't been any in the post, not that it's been yet. Aunty Morag will bring one with her this afternoon, I suspect. But no, nothing from my parents.' The reality of this suddenly hit home. Olivia sat down heavily on the sofa and sighed. Did she ever get anything from her parents on her birthdays? Thinking back over the years, she was lucky she wasn't spending her time in the unit or a betting shop.

'Oh, honey, I'm so sorry. Well, I can understand it of Phyllis... probably not much opportunity for buying cards at the unit. But your dad could at least have remembered. He's such a selfish twat.'

'Well, he's had a lot on his mind recently what with Mum,' she had no idea why she was defending him.

'That's no excuse to forget your only daughter's birthday.'

'Maybe he's saving it for the party?' she didn't sound convincing.

'Well, you're not to worry about any of that. Rhys and I will be over for three o'clock instead of half past and we'll be bringing cards and prezzies. Although I'll get Rhys to avoid handing over an ounce of hash right in front of your parents,' she giggled at the prospect. Olivia just gasped at the thought. How like Rhys to forget social propriety! 'Do I need to bring a cake?'

'No, Aunty Morag always bakes one; she likes to make sure I get something.'

'Good old Aunty Morag. Well, I'll let you get back to your morning celebrations lovely and we'll see you at three. Oh, and I can't *wait* for you to introduce me to your lovely John.' And with that she hung up, giving Olivia no time to respond.

• • • •

When Olivia returned to the kitchen, her dad was nowhere to be seen, but her mum was at the sink washing up.

'He's gone out. Said he had some things to deal with before this afternoon,' her mother said over her shoulder, 'Hopefully he's gone to get you something nice.'

She turned from the sink and dried her hands upon her apron. She grimaced at Olivia, 'I'm sorry, my dear, I hadn't realised it was your birthday today. Don't know why or how I could have forgotten such a thing.'

She walked over to Olivia and gave her a hug, whispering happy birthday into her ear. She stepped back, holding onto Olivia's shoulders and staring intently into her eyes.

'I guess I thought it didn't matter, because it's all part of the dream. A dream we're going to be getting out of very soon. But even in dreams some things are still important, aren't they dear? So, why don't you take me into town so I can buy you something to show how much I will love you when you become a reality.' Phyllis smiled in a vague way at Olivia and she felt her heart skip a beat with melancholy as her mother's words seeped into her brain. The illness just never really went away, did it? Even in seemingly-normal moments, it came crashing in like the riot squad raiding a drug den. She smiled back at her mother and agreed with her plan.

Despite her mother's occasional sliding grasp on reality, the two of them had a perfectly lovely time in town. It was almost like a normal mother-daughter shopping trip – something she knew Evie did with her mother most Saturdays. Phyllis bought Olivia a number of trinkets from the market and boutiques. A dress here and something fashionable there. Olivia forgot all about her mother's occasional faux pas; all could be forgiven in this moment of ordinary bliss. They stopped in a café for lunch and then made their way home so they would have time to prepare for the arrival of their guests in the afternoon. Her mother said she needed to lie down for a while, as she was feeling a little drained by their excursion. Having settled her, Olivia took her bounty of goods to her room and laid them out on the bed. She stared at them, bedazzled by the last few hours. She had wished that today would be a perfect birthday. Her wish had been simple, that her mother would be able to say 'Happy birthday' to her and she had. And so much more. She grasped the dress, pressing it against her torso and danced with it around the room, until she came to the mirror on her wall and stared at it as it covered her. She swished from side to side, like a real girl, in a real, loving family and then she fell to her knees on the floor in front of the mirror and cried.

• • • •

Dad hadn't returned by the time Aunty Morag arrived, which was, perhaps, serendipitous. Morag had arrived early to visit with her sister and help prepare afternoon tea for the guests. She rather formally kissed Olivia on the cheek and presented her with a card and present, which she told Olivia to open after she had left, because Olivia knew Aunty Morag wasn't comfortable with gushing or extremes of gratitude. Olivia put the parcel in her room before joining the other women in the kitchen. Her father arrived home shortly before her friends were due to arrive and promptly made a fuss about there not being enough drinks choices. Morag pointed out that it was afternoon tea and not a shindig at one of his fleshpots, to which Dad took umbrage. To forestall a full-blown row, Olivia ushered her dad into the sitting room and suggested they could make a fruit punch, but that it needed to be virgin, as John was driving.

'Hm, yes, John. I'm looking forward to meeting this John I've heard practically nothing about. In fact, what little I do know of him I had to learn from Mrs Flint. Apparently the pair of you made quite a scene the other day.'

Olivia blushed. She hadn't said anything to her father about John and didn't even know he knew about him. Trust Mrs Flint to blab to all and sundry about the incident at school.

'Are you two shagging?' Dad's question came out of the blue. He had been engrossed for several minutes in creating a tasty fruit punch and Olivia was caught off guard. Probably as he had intended. He could be quite manipulative when he put his mind to it.

'Er, that's none of your business, Dad!' Olivia felt her cheeks warm for a second time.

'I'll take that to be a yes, then,' he hmphed, 'I hope you're using precautions… don't want you getting up the duff.'

Olivia left the room. Although, for once her dad did have a point and she realised that in their enthusiasm to discover one another she and John had not been particularly careful. *Shit!* To be honest she hadn't even considered it. She wondered if it was too late for a morning-after pill. She would ring the GP on Monday and book a nurses' appointment. The doorbell rang. She moved to answer it and found Evie and Rhys giggling in the porch. She could smell the fresh stench of skunk on their clothes and shook her head. That explained the giggles then.

Before she could bring them into the sitting room, Evie had embraced her and wished her a happy birthday. Rhys likewise gave her a hug, using it as an excuse to shove a sizeable jiffy bag of grass into her hand.

'Happy birthday, O. Don't smoke it all at once, but do smoke it. It's top-quality shit and it cost a pretty penny, I can tell you.'

Rhys grinned like the Cheshire cat and stumbled into the hall.

She was just shutting the door and gesturing for them to go into the sitting room when she heard the tell-tale roar of a motorbike. She slipped out of the front door and headed down the path to the gate to greet her boyfriend. She still couldn't get over the word and it brought a grin to her face. She saw John dismount. He pulled his helmet off as he advanced on her. The grin on her face froze and then slowly slid away. The frown John had on his own face was not what she had expected and anxiety started to worry itself in the pit of her stomach.

'Olivia,' he said with urgency in his voice. He grabbed her up in his free arm and kissed her cheek. As he did so, he whispered in her ear. 'We have to talk. As soon as possible and I need to take you away from here.'

She pulled back from him. His expression was serious and he was starting to scare her. She shook her head, more as a reaction than an outright no to his proposal.

'What? What's going on, John? I can't just up and leave from my own party. We can talk inside, but we need to be inside with the others.'

He looked at her for a moment, clearly undecided. 'OK, we need to go in anyway, so you can get your leathers and helmet. You'll need to make your excuses quickly, though. It's vital we leave as soon as possible.'

'Why? What on earth could be the matter?'

John glanced hastily about the street, 'I can't say here.' He looked over her shoulder towards the house, 'I doubt I'll be able to say anything in there either. Not with everyone else there. But I'll explain everything when we've left. We should go now.'

Olivia shook her head again, this time with more purpose. She wasn't about to leave her first ever proper birthday party in living memory, even for John. They could talk afterwards. He could explain everything he needed to explain then. But any further options as to what they were going to do were stripped from them as Evie suddenly bounded past her and grabbed John's arm.

'So, you're the elusive John, are you? Very pleased to meet you, come and meet the family, they're all dying to see you.'

She tugged on his elbow and practically dragged him up the path to the house. John looked back towards Olivia and she could see the consternation etched into his features. She could but follow; they could escape in a bit, once everyone had had a chance to wish her happy birthday. She hurried to follow and came inside to find John the focus of attention in the sitting room.

'Ah, the tarnished knight,' said her mother looking at John with what looked like a mixture of pleasure and contempt. 'Better late than never, I suppose.' And with that her mother turned her back on him and disappeared towards the kitchen.

Olivia moved over to him, 'I'm sorry about that. Mum's still not one hundred percent.'

'No need to apologise, Olivia,' he looked about the sitting room, but there was no immediate escape. So, he slipped an arm protectively around her waist and pulled her closer to him.

'Whatever happens,' he whispered into her ear again, 'just know that I love you.'

Olivia's fears washed away with those simple words and she felt herself glow. She put an arm around his waist and hugged him.

Dad handed everyone a glass of punch. He wasn't taking no for an answer, 'You'll be fine, there's no booze in it, Olivia insisted.' He threw a nod in her direction. Olivia saw the despondent look that crossed Rhys face, but it didn't stop him from having a pre-emptive swig.

'So, everyone got a glass? Good. Quick toast and then we can eat.'

He turned to Olivia, who was still holding tightly to John. 'So, it's your seventeenth birthday, Olivia. We all hope you have a grand time and wish you well for the year to come. Happy birthday.'

It wasn't the most rip-roaring of speeches, it had to be admitted, but it was also the first one Olivia could ever remember her dad giving for her. She was surprised at how emotional it made her feel. Everyone raised their glasses and chorused happy birthday.

'It's alright, O, you can probably drink some now as well,' Rhys said with a cheeky grin as he polished off his punch and went to get some more.

'Given that there's no booze in it, Mr B, that's remarkably tasty,' Rhys said to Reg as he went to the bowl. Her dad frowned at him and then went and stood by the window trying to ignore everyone. He had swapped his glass for a mug of tea. She looked around the room for her mum and saw her sat on the sofa near to the TV. She appeared to be falling asleep, her empty glass slipping from her hands. Olivia uttered a stifled gasp as she thought it would smash, but Aunty Morag was in attendance and retrieved it before disaster could strike. Olivia noted Aunty Morag then tenderly adjusted her sister's head on the sofa, propping it with a cushion. Olivia suspected that this morning's jaunt out had been too much for her.

Once everyone had had their fill of sandwiches, Aunty Morag left the room. When she returned, she paused in the doorway just out of view and bade Reg to come over to her. He dutifully accepted the summons without the slightest hint of negativity. He then switched off the lights, not that it made much difference having them on. At which point, Morag marched into the room, bearing a cake with lit candles on it. The gathering took up a ragged refrain of 'Happy birthday' and when they had all finished, Morag stood in front of Olivia proffering her the cake. She reminded Olivia of those scenes from the coronation as the archbishop presented the crown to the soon-to-be-anointed queen. She grinned with embarrassment at suddenly being the centre of attention. She looked around at the ensemble of guests, all of whom seemed to bid her to get on with it. She refocused her attention on the cake.

The candles danced and flickered before her. They were hypnotising. She found her focus started to blur as she attempted to look at all seventeen candle flames. Her head was feeling fluffy and she wondered if all the recent concentration upon her was taking its toll. Perhaps she, too, had overdone it this morning. After all, she wasn't used to such a turmoil of emotions, as she had flick-flacked her way through in the last few hours. She stared once more into the heart of the flames. They reminded her of the Indian dancers in their sarees and veils, as they weaved this way and that. Her eyes started to blur and water. She knew if she didn't hurry up and blow the fires out that she was going to faint. And how would that look?

She closed her eyes. She made a wish and blew. The lights went out.

Chapter 25

April 17th

Olivia could hear Rhys' voice, she hadn't opened her eyes yet. There seemed to be an interminable length of time between her blowing the candles out and her thinking about opening her eyes again. Rhys' voice was the only one she could hear, not what she'd expected. Wasn't there usually cheering and clapping when the candles were blown out? That's what she remembered from those few birthday parties she'd been to as a guest. What Rhys was saying didn't seem in keeping with the situation. She opened her eyes and found herself looking at a darkened room, filled with an unsavoury orange glow. The light from the street lamp was shining through the window. Rhys and Evie were sat in the gloom of the sofa and Rhys had his head in his hands.

'Rhys?' she asked hoarsely. He didn't respond immediately.

'Evie? Evie, wake up! What the fuck happened last night?' Rhys said, slowly turning his head towards Evie on the sofa. His speech was slow and slurred.

Olivia could see Evie stirring, but couldn't determine if her eyes were opening. Evie started to sit up and then made a 'whoa' noise. She fell back into the sofa. Rhys rubbed his eyes and looked around the room. Olivia spoke again, the words sounded harsh and rasping in her throat.

'Are you alright, guys?'

Rhys looked at his wrist and then about the room, 'What the hell did happen, in actual fuck? It's only eleven thirty. Where the hell is everyone?'

'I'm just over here, Rhys,' Olivia said, assuming he couldn't see her huddled in the shadowy embrace of the armchair. Evie made the attempt to sit up again. Rhys was on his feet now, unsteady, but upright. He looked confused. He walked past Olivia and disappeared from view. He came back a couple of minutes later, by which time Evie was sat upright on the sofa rubbing at her temples.

'There's no one here. No one, all gone out. Couldn't even find Olivia.'

'But I'm right here, Rhys, can't you see me?' Olivia tried to stand up, but couldn't. Something was holding her back. Something was restraining her.

'No one?' Evie replied, her words were slurred too.

'No one... it's like the Marie Celeste.' He leaned against the doorway, 'If I didn't know better, and I do, because I know my shit. I'd say someone roofied us.'

Evie looked blank, although this could just have been because she wasn't completely with it.

'Spiked, Evie. We've been drugged and then everyone else has done a runner.'

'But why?'

'Why indeed?'

Olivia started to get scared, 'I'm right here, guys. Right here, in the chair. Right next to you, Rhys,' she shouted. She closed her eyes to prevent the fear from overwhelming her. Why couldn't they see her? She opened her eyes again.

John was sat in a chair opposite her. There was a tentative smile on his face. He was leaning on a polished metal table. Behind him the walls were white. She looked about the room. It wasn't the sitting room in her house. They were sat in a large white room, which was unpleasantly bright. She was sat in a similar chair to John's, except, unlike John she appeared to be tied down. She yanked her right arm up, attempting to free it from the chair, but it remained firmly trapped. She shook her head disbelievingly and looked quickly about the room, trying to gauge her situation fully. There were no windows. There were strip lights in the ceiling that flooded the room with the harsh brilliance of false sunlight.

ORDINARY WORLD

Behind her was a doorway, and it too was white and appeared to be padded. She looked more closely at the walls – were they padded too? In the corners of the room, she could see cameras on metal arms bolted to the wall. The cameras seemed to be staring directly at her and they tracked her every movement. She looked back at John.

'Where are we?' she asked plaintively.

'Birmingham,' John replied.

'Birmingham?' she replied incredulously.

'Yes,' he cleared his throat; surreptitiously he glanced at the cameras behind Olivia and then leaned on the table. He spoke quickly in a low whisper, his hands gesticulating in front of him, masking his mouth. 'There's still time, Olivia, but we'll have to be quick. I can get you out and away. But this time we do it *now*. No waiting for another opportunity. There will be no other opportunity.'

Olivia could see John coiled behind the desk, ready to leap into action. She felt his urgency wash over her in waves. She could *feel* what he was feeling. It pulsated out from him and bathed her in an ebb and flow of cresting waves. She imagined the waves lapping against the shore and a sea breeze that tousled her hair. She could almost smell the brine in the air. She opened her eyes wider and stared at John.

'OK,' she said, 'Let's go.'

John was over to her in a flash, slicing through the ties on her wrists and grabbing her hand, pulling her with him. For a moment she felt the pulse she had received from him moments earlier, but this time she felt it course through his hands and hers. She was suddenly aware of the cameras in the room all pointing towards the floor, as if the servos in their holding arms had all failed at the same time. John was at the door and swiped a card in front of the control panel. The heavy door started to swing open.

'I'll come back for your mother another day, when things are quieter,' he said.

Olivia stopped in the doorway, 'My mother's here?'

John pulled at her urgently, trying to chivvy her along, 'Yes, but she'll be further inside the facility, probably sedated and locked down.'

Olivia refused to move into the corridor. 'I'm not leaving my mother here, wherever *here* is.'

John was getting anxious to be underway; she knew he wasn't confident in his plan to get them out. She could feel it emanating from him. She knew that if they went to rescue her mother it was very probable that none of them would escape at all. But she also knew that she couldn't live with herself, knowing she had left her mother to her fate within this facility. She didn't fully comprehend what was happening here, but she suspected enough, from all that had come to pass over this last week, to know that being here was not a good thing. As for John's involvement in it, well she had always known he worked for a powerful, clandestine organisation. Maybe this facility belonged to them and not the organisation that John Kennedy died for. It mattered not which shadow organisation's facility they were in, either one was bound to be nefarious in their treatment of people they thought might have mental powers beyond the levels of normal human beings. If she left without her mother, Olivia knew she would be condemning her mother to either a life of servitude at the hands of these individuals, or worse, a death to be dissected like some kind of lab rat. She stood her ground and stared hard at John.

'You can go if you like, John, but I'm going to go and rescue my mother,' and with that she relinquished her hold on his hand and made her way in the opposite direction down the corridor.

'Fuck it!' John responded. She heard him dither for a second behind her and then he jogged up next to her. 'Fine, but don't say

I didn't warn you.' They hurried down the corridor and reached a crossroads.

'This way,' John said, dragging them to the right, 'OK, some things you need to know.' He continued as they headed down the right-hand offshoot.

'I'm like you, Olivia. I'm the progeny of two Mentats. I have powers, but they're understated, unlike what they're hoping you will develop. I'm an empath.'

'What? What are you saying to me?' Olivia halted in the corridor. John's hand slipped its grip and he was forced to stop as well. He looked back at her. She knew all he was going to see was the stream of questions and doubt that had now washed over her face. He drew in a deep breath and reached for her arm again. She shied away from the contact and could feel the urgency that emanated from him.

'That I'm like you. We're Mentats. Like our parents, only better. Stronger and without the mental or physical failings.' He grabbed her arm again.

'Come on, Olivia! We have to keep moving.'

Olivia couldn't process what he was saying to her. And what he was saying to her was that he had known something, everything, all this time but hadn't shared it with her. He had lied to her. If he had lied to her about that, what else had he lied to her about? She was nearly pulled off her feet as he dragged her after him.

'What are Mentats?'

It was Olivia's first question of a multitude she wanted to ask, yet not the one she had intended to voice. What she'd wanted to say was, *why did you lie to me*?

'Mentats are the mentally gifted – it's just a term that's been bandied about this experiment for years, 'mental talents' - Mentats. People like your mother and biological father. My parents were the same. My father was one of the originators of the program, the chief scientist, but whatever he was working on drove him utterly insane. Killed himself, along with my mother and a number of the other patients.'

John paused as they reached a selection of doors. He raised his free arm at the cameras and they all went limp. Then he swiped his card again, this time over all the door control pads. He opened all of the doors, but ushered Olivia through the one on the left.

Olivia was in a state of shock. In an effort to regain her composure, she focused on what was happening to her now.

'I don't understand how you're affecting the cameras? Surely, if you're an empath, that means you can only affect people with emotions?'

'I create feedback in the visual cortex of the lens, it feeds back to the operators who then get a double dose of what I've sent out, amplified by the electronics. Basically, knocks them out and the cameras along with it.'

'Really?' Olivia found his explanation difficult to assimilate.

'No, not really, I have a clicker,' he said opening his hand so she could see a small black object in his hand. 'Quick in here.'

They dived in through another doorway and John hurriedly shut it. They appeared to be in a science lecture hall. Still holding her hand, he weaved between the benches until they reached the other side of the room. He opened an office doorway and they ducked inside.

'OK, we're going to wait here for about twenty minutes, while their protocols kick in. They will know I've absconded with you by now and will be searching everywhere. They'll fan out and sweep outwards in concentric circles. It'll take them about fifteen minutes to determine we're not in the building any more. At which point they'll start searching the grounds and streets beyond.' John slid down the wall to sit on the floor.

'But we *are* still inside the building,' Olivia declared, 'won't they just search in here and find us?'

'Technically, yes, we are inside the building, but I think I threw them off at the last set of doors. All the other doorways lead away from the centre of the facility. Our passage will be logged as entering one of the three before their systems shut down. It would be the most logical thing to do as well. Who, in their right minds would escape captivity only to head deeper into the prison?' John looked at her despairingly.

'But even if they don't find us now, they'll surely work out where we are because of the cameras in the rest of the facility. Even if you knock them out, they'll know something's up and send people to investigate?'

John looked at her and smiled, it was not a smile she was used to from him, it harboured none of the warmth that she usually felt and it sent a shiver down her spine. There was a Machiavellian shimmer to that smile, it was the smile of a master spy seeing his plots coming to fruition.

'I know this facility very well, Olivia. Once we enter the central hub the cameras become specific in the location. Certain doorways, certain corridors, it was designed deliberately to ensure a certain level of anonymity for the work that was going on here. Enough in the event of a security breach. I know where they are and the angles to bypass them, you just follow my lead and we can get to your mother and no one will be any the wiser.'

Olivia continued to stare at him, what he said seemed to mollify her concerns, but there was still that chill in the air between them. She felt she was missing something – something more than just John being clever and out smarting the facility. She glanced away for a moment and then back to his face. In that moment everything changed about his demeanour, once again there was that warmth and confidence to him that emboldened her. It spurred her to ask more questions, she wanted answers and they seemed to have some time for her to get them.

'So all of this,' she said waving her hands around, 'the facility, the experiments that Miriam spoke of, it's all true then?'

'Yes, it's all true,' John looked downcast.

'And you duped me into becoming your girlfriend, why? What possible gain could there have been for that?' *Other than a bit of sex*, she thought. Anger started to well up deep in the pit of her stomach.

'That had never been part of the plan, that was just an accident.'

Wrong thing to say, he realised, although he could have made it worse by saying it had been a mistake. God only knows what Olivia's reaction would have been if he had said that.

'So, that was an *accident*, was it? You sticking your tongue in my mouth and your cock between my legs? Good, glad we cleared that up.'

Olivia was suddenly fuming, any thoughts for answers were blown from her mind. She made a grab for the door handle to the office they were in. She had no wish to remain in the same room as this man.

'That's not what I meant, Olivia.'

He stood up hurriedly to prevent her from leaving. If she blundered off in a rage into the Centre now, they would be discovered.

'But it's what you said, it was just an accident, you said that, didn't you?'

'Yes, I said that. I was only supposed to guide you and monitor you. But something happened on that Saturday afternoon that no one even imagined possible. My empathy kicked in and backfired. I was overwhelmed by you, and I got the impression you were overwhelmed too. All that happened afterwards was honest heartfelt emotion, Olivia. I do love you, with such an ache that it fries my brain when you're not with me, goddammit!'

John was shouting at her in a cracking hoarse whisper. He grabbed her by the shoulders and pulled her in to him, so their faces were a hair's breadth apart. He stared deep into her eyes. Eyes that were filled with a rage that had been slowly coming to the boil for years. Olivia felt it starting to leak out of her, into him. She looked back into his eyes and saw them changing, from the lust he clearly held for her to a far more dangerous feeling. In that moment, she knew that she was feeding his emotional abilities with her emotions. In that moment, she realised she was far stronger than him, far stronger than anyone could have possibly imagined. She cut the link. The rage dissipated from his face and was replaced by his original feelings.

'Bollocks to it!' he said and kissed her hard on the lips.

She kicked him in the shin. It hurt. He continued kissing her. She kicked him again, although not as hard this time. It impacted on the first strike. It really hurt. He continued to kiss her. She responded. She bit his lip.

'Fuck's sake, Olivia, stop it! I fucking love you. I made a mistake getting to know you,'

She slapped him, 'Now I'm a mistake, thanks!'

'That's not what I said. It was my mistake to get to know you. I was only supposed to guide you from a distance. But Evie's mind is so friggin' pliable, it spun her off into a whirlwind of possibilities that sent you to ringing on my door.'

John had let her go, and was rubbing his ankle. He was pouting as well; he could taste blood.

'Evie? What's she got to do with all this? I've known Evie nearly all my life... you're not going to try and tell me she's got super powers too, are you?'

'No, far from it, her mind is a vacuous lump of soft cheese. A marmoset has more cognitive brain functioning than she does.' Olivia couldn't help laughing at this – it described Evie to a T.

'So, what's she got to do with it then?'

'One of the triplets is very good with suggestion. He infiltrated Evie's mind and gave her a few prods and prompts. We've been guiding her for years. You think her mother rules her future, it's nothing compared with the power the triplets wield, steering her to steer you in the direction we wanted you to go. Which was to awaken your abilities.'

John had withdrawn from Olivia. As he divulged more and more of what they had been doing, how they had been manipulating her life and those around her for years, Olivia became more and more devoid of emotion. Her entire life, it seemed, had been a lie. Everything, from her friends who were manipulated into coaxing choices from her, to her parents, either too stoned to be of any support or not even her real parent, just a prison guard to watch over her. Were her friends even her friends because that's how friends happen? Or had they just been convenient passers-by in her life that the Organisation planted on her to steer her in the direction they wanted her to go?

'You've done all this?' Olivia couldn't believe what she was hearing, 'But I've only known you a week.'

'I've known you a bit longer than that, my sweet. About ten years, probably. Although I was always aware of your existence. Grandfather has a tendency of monologuing when he's been drinking. But I had only seen you a couple of times before we met last week. I wasn't a prime agent in this, I had other duties and it was only when we'd overheard a conversation a month or so ago between Evie and Rhys that an idea came to Reg's handler. A cunning conspiracy to get your powers stimulated. I don't think Reg was too keen, after all, the previous plans that he had been involved in to stimulate your mother from her stupor had often left him damaged. Plus, the gig had already gone on way longer than any of us could have possibly imagined. Who would have thought it would take nearly seventeen years? Reg has lost most of his life to this work.'

Olivia was stood there shaking her head at him. This was even more unbelievable than the tales that Miriam and Hiram had woven.

'My sleepless nights? My nightmares? Were they you as well – the triplets invading my mind and plaguing me with disturbing images like they influenced Evie?'

John scoffed at her question, perhaps not the best response given her mood, 'We can't control dreams, Olivia,' he said scathingly. 'Those were entirely you.'

She noticed he hesitated as he said this, he was lying again, 'That's not true. You did influence my dreams.'

John shook his head, 'No, it's true, we can't do that sort of thing. At least, not yet. Miriam might be able to do it, she has a knack for the inner fine tunings of a person's mind. But even she wouldn't have been able to give the consistency of a prolonged attack upon your mind, like you've been suffering. No, there's only one person with that kind of power and that's your mother. Hence, our great desire for her to recover her faculties and return to the fold.

'So, as it stands, all those deeply warped and disturbing dreams you've been suffering, are, as I said, entirely down to you.' John's head tilted slightly and his eyebrow rose, indicating to Olivia that maybe she needed to look inward for some of her answers. Was her mind as fractured and damaged as her mother's? If it could inflict such heinous and horrifying images on to her sleeping mind. She veered away from the idea, she didn't wish to consider such a possibility, at least not now, not here. She looked at John and changed the focus of their discussion to her other parent.

'Reg, my father, isn't really my father, is he?' The truth of the realisation hit her like a wrecking ball. She slid down the wall, as John had done moments earlier, and sat in a stupor.

John squatted down in front of her. She could tell he wanted to reach out to her, but he didn't.

'No, he isn't your biological father.'

She looked up at him with a tremble upon her lower lip, 'Is it true, that he killed my real father?'

John looked away for a moment so she missed his immediate expression, 'Indirectly,' he said turning back to face her.

'What the fuck's that supposed to mean?'

'It means that because of his inaction, your father died. Reg should have shot someone, someone who then went on several minutes later to kill your father, several other people and himself.' John looked down at the floor, as he finished his explanation. 'But if Reg had shot that person, he would have shot my father. I suppose, in hindsight, he could have shot him to wound, rather than to kill. But if Reg had done either, your father and those other people would probably still be alive.' He looked up at her once more, a tear leaking from the corner of his eye. She felt his pain of loss, it seeped into her like rain through a broken roof tile.

'And all this, for what? Me? For some misplaced desire to improve humanity through science fiction experiments?'

John pursed his lips and nodded, 'Yup, that's about the size of it. But somewhere along the line it changed. It got warped. Maybe it never was the altruistic ideal that everyone said it was. An idea three people had had while sat around a dinner table. How to make the world a better place. In theory, it was wonderful. In practice, it's a nightmare – I've only just started to realise how much of a nightmare it really is, because I don't believe any more that the original design was ever there. I think this has always been about control.'

Olivia looked at him, her eyes narrowed, 'What do you mean by that?'

John breathed heavily through his nose before continuing, 'I mean, I think this has been more about creating a powerful weapon that a few people could use to control the world for their own ends.'

He glanced at his watch, 'Time to move. There'll be a small window of opportunity while they all look outwards. I believe I know where they will have taken your mother. But if she's not there I don't know where else she would be and we would need to abandon the search if you ever hope to get away from here.'

Olivia knew he was adamant about this. She also suspected that he was correct, but she didn't want to leave this place without her mother. She would cross that bridge if they came to it. She stood up.

'Fine, we'd better get moving then.'

Chapter 26

They exited the office through a second doorway, which led into a carpet-tiled corridor. The whole feel of the unit changed and Olivia felt as if they had stepped into a Seventies drama. The walls were panelled with faux plastic wood, the beige carpet tiles were worn and stained and the overhead strip lighting hummed, reminding Olivia of the giant hornets that had lived in similar lights within her dreams – it caused a knot in her stomach at the memory. The light cast upon the corridor with its array of office doors did nothing to enhance the environment's joie de vivre. John led them to the right, trotting down the corridor for several hundred feet until it opened out into an open plan space with cubicles for individual working. But this was no office, this was a laboratory. Olivia could see the workstations where a host of scientists had been working until very recently. She could only imagine that their escape had precipitated an evacuation in case the hunted came this way, especially if they were being pursued aggressively. John took them through the lab until they came to another corridor. As they approached, John stiffened and came to a sudden halt. Olivia slid past him, bouncing off his hip and colliding with one of the work stations. Before she could ask what the matter was, her question was answered.

Four armed men in black body armour appeared out of the mouth of the corridor they were heading towards. Olivia took in a sharp breath at the sight of them. Something she noted most about their sudden appearance was the look of abject surprise on the face of the lead soldier. The expressions of those following ranged from shock to surprise to bewilderment. The whole array caused her to glance back at John to see if he was going to react to this sudden turn of events – perhaps he could empath his way through them or just plain blag his way out of it if he was such a hotshot within the

Organisation? The look upon John's face did nothing, however, to instil confidence in her that things were about to go well.

Olivia didn't detect any sense of surprise to his demeanour at their sudden appearance and the look that crossed his face was firstly happy, a derisive smirk, followed by an expression of utter disdain for the threat that now stood in front of them.

All of them remained stationary for several seconds as they took in the situation. The lead soldier looked first at John and then at her, and she saw an imperceptible shake of his head as he glanced at John – was he disagreeing with the situation? Did he not believe that one of his bosses was in fact a traitor to the Organisation? It didn't matter, because the soldier immediately to his left brought his weapon up to his hip and shouted a command at them.

'Stop! Right there! Or we'll shoot.'

Olivia looked back at John, who was shaking his head and starting to look extremely angry. Not, it had to be said, the reaction she would have expected. She glanced back to the soldiers, but did as she had been ordered and remained leaning against the workstation that had bruised her thigh. The lead soldier finally seemed to come to his senses and advanced on them. Olivia could see he held a silver collar in his left hand, his right hand was firmly holding the pistol grip of his automatic rifle. He moved towards her and held out his left hand to her, using the muzzle of his rifle to indicate affirmation for his instructions.

'Put this on!'

She looked at the offensive collar. She remembered it from both her dream and the cut-through incident with the triplets. She may not know its true workings, but she knew enough to know that if this armed man wanted her to put it on so urgently, then it would not bode well for her. She looked back up at the soldier,

'No,' she said vehemently.

The soldier thrust the collar towards her more emphatically.

'PUT. IT. ON!' he commanded through gritted teeth.

Olivia took a step back, 'Fuck you! *You* put the fucking thing on.'

The soldier was clearly not a man used to being disobeyed and not with so much disrespect. He advanced on her, dropping his hold upon his rifle, which slid down to dangle from its strap. He lunged for her with his free hand, grabbing her shoulder and gripping tightly. Olivia kicked out at his shin reflexively, her shoe jarred on his leg, but seemed to make little impression. She involuntarily glanced down and realised his armour extended to his legs as well. Olivia looked back into his determined face and did the only other thing she could think of. She swore at him and then raked her nails over his cheek.

He flinched back, 'You little bitch,' he struck her back-handed across the face. She staggered from the impact, a lance of pain shooting through her cheek and she could taste blood in her mouth from where the inside of her cheek had cut against her teeth. She brought her hand up to her face to ward off further assaults, but it proved to be his last action towards her as John lunged at him.

'You stupid fuckhead!' John shouted at him as his shoulder drove into the soldier's abdomen.

The soldier twisted his hips, bringing his free hand down onto John's belt and using the purchase of it to lift John up and off his feet, slamming him into an adjacent workstation. John staggered from the impact, flailing over the surface, his hands grasping for purchase of their own. His hand clamped about a glass beaker, which he swung at the face of the man who now stood over him. The beaker exploded in a shower of tiny fragments and Olivia was stunned by the sudden report of a staccato burst of gun fire from the other side of the room. John fell to the floor under a hail of bullets and a cascade of glittering glass particles.

Something snapped in her head. The fuckers had just shot John. Killed John. True he was a lying sack of shit, but he was also *her* lying sack of shit. He was *also* her love – her first love, no less. And if anyone had the right to shoot him it was her. Who did these bastards think they were? She swung round to face her immediate attacker and she felt the wave of pristine light bathe her mind. The room seemed to brighten with an ambient light of its own, gaining in intensity as she drew in a huge lungful of air. The rumble started in the pit of her belly and grew in fervour as it travelled up her thorax and into her throat. The sound that emanated from her mouth was unlike anything that had ever erupted before. It was a scream, that much could be said, but it held none of the fear or horror that she had elicited in the past. This was more like a roar, not of defiance, but of utter, utter rage. Her entire being channelled into the roar, her eyes glazed and she felt, rather than saw, the path her roar would take. A clout of immense pressure hurtled into the soldier in front of her lifting him like a piece of cardboard caught in a strong autumn gale and flung him from her sight. The soldiers behind were hit by increments. The man who had fired his rifle caught the full force of her mental strike, those to his side were merely washed over by the ebb of the wave. Not that that made much difference to their final moments of life, as it was crushed from their evaporating bodies, fusing with the super-heated metal of their weapons.

The soldier who had fired his rifle at them balled up under the impact of the strike and careened into the wall behind them. He crashed through it, leaving an icky smear around the jagged hole that he was forced into it. Dust and particles of an undisclosed nature erupted out of the hole - of the soldier there was no sign. The surrounding lab was hit by a palpable wave of visible sound that washed out from Olivia in an ever-expanding disk, slicing through wood, glass, metal, plastic and brick. All that was touched by it was scythed in half and turned to dust. The final breath left her body and she staggered against the workstation she had been stood behind. She clung onto it with all her might; her vision was blurred, her head pounded and she was overcome by a soul-weary dizziness that took her legs out from under her. She landed on the tile-carpeted floor with a thud, which she barely noticed. Olivia sat. Olivia breathed.

Olivia took a moment.

· · · ·

She stood on a pinnacle of rock in the middle of the storm-tossed oceans; the smell of damp brine assailed her nostrils, chokingly strong. The cresting white horses crashed over her feet sending geysers of spray over her poorly clad body, soaking her to the skin and causing that skin to prickle and goosebump at the chill. She wondered how it was that she wasn't swept away by the waves, to drown in the endless grey and black of the churning maelstrom. The wind whipped at her, leaving strands of sodden hair to cling irritatingly to the side of her face, and yet, with the elements pounding against her frail frame she felt more grounded, more stable than she had ever done before. She was stronger than the rock upon which she stood, immoveable. Slowly she raised her head to look up into the broiling dark clouds above her. They were constantly being shredded by jagged ripping lances of lightning, that lit the shadowy masses with an unholy effervescence, scorching the skies with the powers of the universe. Her gaze lowered as a calmness settled upon her, questing the horizon, a horizon that never seemed to appear, it blended so perfectly between the sky and the sea. She felt that she stood in the centre of an orb and, as she stared out of the heart of the orb, images came to her, many images of the same instance, each one overlapping like an animator's tracing paper, each page subtly different from the one before. She could see a room and she could see her mother. She could see Miriam and Hiram; Miriam was speaking to her, yet her lips never moved. Olivia could feel the words reverberating through her bones and always the same message.

'Speak with Hiram and he will show you your path. We can all be free.'

The pages flickered past her mind's eye, speeding on and on until they were a flurried blur that became the solid wedge of a book and then they stopped. She watched as a bullet sliced through the translucent pages. She watched as it sliced through the intangible material that covered the weak flesh beneath. She watched as it pierced the skin, ripping its jagged hole into the soft flesh and she remembered the jagged rends that she had seen only nanoseconds before as the lightning had torn apart the sky. She saw the light fade in the eyes that belonged to the torn flesh. She fell into those eyes, a well of endless void now bereft of life.

Olivia gasped.

• • • •

She was still seated upon the lab's tiled floor, legs akimbo leaning against the leg of the workstation. She was staring straight into John's eyes. And they were staring back at her, not lifeless as she had thought, but with the light that only a truly horrified vision can instil. John slowly pushed himself up from the floor, tearing his eyes from hers to look to where their aggressors had once been.

'Jesus. Holy. Fucking H. Christ, Olivia! What did you *do*?'

He looked at the devastation before him, Olivia looked too, from around the edge of the workstation, as yet unable to draw the strength required to stand up. She too saw what he saw: a flattened wasteland that reminded her of the pictures of forests lying splayed across the earth after being hit by the blast wave from an atom bomb. There was nothing discernible in the carnage other than it was covered by a fine dusting of sand. *Where the hell had sand come from?* She wondered. Gripping the counter of the workstation she eventually managed to draw herself upright to stand next to John. He had as yet to say another word after his initial exclamation. He looked back at her and she knew that the expression upon his face was as honest as any she had ever seen from him. He was aghast. Horrified. Horrified by what she had done, by what she had been able to do and all with the power of her mind.

She reached out to him, placing her left hand upon the sleeve of his jacket – she meant it as a placatory gesture. He flinched, snapping his arm from her grasp. He took an involuntary step backwards. His mouth opened, but no words would come. *Strange*, Olivia thought, *how only minutes before John had wanted nothing more than for me to reach out to him. Strange how a single action can turn circumstances on their head.*

They stood for several minutes as John slowly collected himself, centring his thoughts away from the horror she knew they would have to traverse if indeed that was the way he had intended them to go.

John finally drew in a long breath. He exhaled as he spoke to her and it seemed to Olivia that he had found the strength to shut out what he had just witnessed.

'Right, we need to be moving on. It's not far now, just down that corridor...' he paused, his arm pointing to the corridor from whence the soldiers had appeared. Olivia detected a returning hesitancy on his part as the ruins of that end of the lab came back into his thoughts. He stuttered to continue, ''There'll be a door into a small lab at the end that leads to an airlock and then into the chamber I believe your mother is being held in.'

He shuddered, drew in another deep breath and then urged them both forward. He stalwartly held his head high and averted his gaze from the dripping ichor that slid inexorably to the floor from around the hole in the wall. Olivia followed, almost as hesitantly, although not for the same reason as she suspected in John. She felt calm, but tired, as if a great emotional weight had been lifted from her and in doing so it had also drained her of her normal energy. She continued to follow him and soon she found herself beyond the devastation she had wrought and back in familiar Seventies TV drama décor. After a short walk they came to the lab John had just spoken of and they slipped inside. There was the promised airlock ahead of them.

It took them into a smaller lab with a second airlock. He stepped over to the control panel and activated it. She watched as he typed on a keyboard, his speed reminded her of that day in his bedroom and a thought occurred to her.

'If you work for this organisation and not GCHQ, what was all that stuff you did on the computers at your flat? All that pursuit through the 'net... Fluffy?'

John paused for a moment before he answered. He made one final keystroke and the airlock opened.

'Stage management,' he sighed to her. He bade her enter the airlock, stepping in ahead of her.

She stared in disbelief at him, '*Stage management*? What you're telling me is that none of that was real?'

He shrugged his shoulders and beckoned urgently for her to join him.

'Don't just shrug at me, answer the bloody question!'

John visibly flinched as she spat her demand at him. She wondered if he was recoiling in fear of what she might do to him if he didn't respond.

She made no move to enter the airlock. She could tell that this was making him agitated, perhaps a good thing as it was closer to his normal demeanour and not the fearful man she had seen in recent moments. The agitation started to win through as he glanced at his watch. Time was of the essence, clearly, and she was squandering it by asking questions. He looked up at her and she saw the memory of a horror slip finally from view.

'Most of it wasn't real. There never was a secret network to invade, because it's not a secret to me and I've always had access to it. Fluffy isn't real and the chase wasn't real. It was all smoke and mirrors to coax you down the right path. I've told you about smoke and mirrors before, if you recall. Perhaps if you were more astute and less wrapped up in mundane problems you would have seen that I was warning you of what was really occurring.'

His tone riled Olivia, 'Or maybe, when you warned me about smoke and mirrors you were just having a private joke at my expense.' She stared pointedly at him. He shrugged, acquiescing the point.

'Yes, maybe I was. Knowledge is a powerful thing, Olivia, and knowing that I was pulling the wool over your eyes in that instance, maybe I was having a prod at your ignorance of the truth.' He looked at his watch again.

'Now will you come on! If you want us to get your mother out, you need to get in this airlock so we can go to her.'

Olivia was torn. She wanted to rescue her mother. But she didn't trust John anymore; how did she even know her mother was beyond this airlock? She said as much to him.

'Where are you taking me, John? Is it really to my mother, or is it just more smoke and mirrors to get what you want?'

John was clearly exasperated by her response. He stepped out of the airlock and punched a panel on the wall next to it. There were shutters over the wall above the keyboards he had just been typing at. They blended so perfectly that until that moment she hadn't realised they were anything other than a wall. The shutters opened, revealing a white-walled room beyond the airlock. Lying in the centre of the room, strapped to a gurney, was her mother.

Olivia stepped into the airlock along with John. He closed the seal and they moved briskly into the white room.

Olivia stopped almost as soon as she entered. John continued at pace over to the gurney and was surprised that she hadn't followed him. He looked back at her and realised she wasn't looking at her mother at all, but was looking over to the other side of the room. He turned to follow her gaze. There, strapped in similar gurneys, next to the wall were two other occupants in the room.

'Miriam! Hiram!' Olivia said and then turned accusingly to John. He looked as surprised and perplexed as she did.

'I had no idea they were here. They've been loose from the facility for years, abandoned by the project and for the most part ignored, I'd thought.'

'We have to rescue them too,' Olivia stated knowing how ridiculous this situation was becoming. She saw John's expression and knew he was about to point out that they weren't going to be able to rescue anyone at this rate.

'Olivia! It'll be a stretch if we even manage to get your mother out. I don't have the means to get them out as well.'

Olivia knew the truth of his statement, but it didn't prevent her from wanting to help them too. She ran over to them and started to undo their straps. She looked down into their unconscious faces; faces that looked almost normal in sleep, relaxed as they were. She undid the limb restraints but became aware of a silver collar about their necks. She looked round to where John was removing the last restraints on her mother. She noted that Phyllis also had a silver collar.

'What is this?' Olivia demanded of John, 'This collar? What is it?'

ORDINARY WORLD

John removed the last restraint and thrust his arm under Phyllis' shoulders, preparing to lift her up and pull her from the gurney.

'It's a control collar. It inhibits their natural mental abilities with a constant electrical biorhythm and if they don't behave there's a control fob that can cause the collar to discharge a high voltage shock into the neck. I had no idea they were real,' John sounded aghast at the prospect of them being a reality. 'I had been aware of the theory and the suggestion, but as far as I had been aware the notion had never gone beyond a few scribbled notes. The whole idea of them was grotesque and totally against the principles of what we're trying to do here. These collars make the wearers virtual slaves to whomever holds a fob.'

Olivia looked at him in horror, but she could feel the genuine disgust he had for these implements exuding from him, it fairly washed over her and she suddenly felt sick deep in her stomach. She knew he was telling the truth, at least about this. She reached up and tried to tug it off Miriam. It didn't budge.

'How do I get this fucking thing off her?' she cried over her shoulder.

'Without the relevant key, you can't. You need a key and I don't have it.' John grunted as he pulled Phyllis off the gurney and half-slung her unconscious body over his shoulder.

Olivia turned her attention back to Miriam; she was determined to have one last go at freeing her. She looked into Miriam's face as she felt a subtle change in the atmosphere in front of them. Miriam's eyes were open. She was looking directly at Olivia and Olivia could feel a pressure in the air between them. She closed her eyes, her thoughts whisking back to that moment when she had spoken with Hiram when she had been sat upon her mother's bed. Her mind reached out through crystal clear waters only to suddenly flounder in the murk of a brackish mire. She slowly opened her eyes and could see Miriam was smiling, she was nodding her head and then there was a click. A click of electricity that shot through her bones and set her teeth on edge.

'So you're finally coming into your own, young lady. Well done.' Miriam said in a faint whisper.

'But I thought you couldn't speak,' Olivia said out loud, 'not with that collar on.'

'I can't contact you. I can't break out beyond the halo of the collar, but you can break in. Which is what you just did, even though I don't think you realise that's what you've done.' Miriam smiled at her. 'Try responding with your mind and not your mouth, my dear. It'll speed the whole process up no end and I know time is of the essence, given the scenarios I have seen,'

Olivia frowned at her, but then remembered what Hiram had told her about Miriam and her ability to see into the possible futures. She closed her eyes and concentrated, thinking back over the few pointers Hiram had given her. Speaking with her mind still didn't come as easily to her as screaming at people did. Beads of sweat popped out of her forehead and trickled irritatingly down her face as she spoke with Miriam. She could feel the soul-draining weariness returning and it came upon her far more rapidly than it had when she had attacked the soldiers.

'There, that's better,' Miriam said. This time it felt different talking with Miriam. She no longer felt Miriam's words reverberating through her bones, now it felt more like a muffled voice was pressing against her forehead and talking through a pillow into her head. *Was this what it was like to be inside someone else's head?* Olivia wondered.

'Quite possibly, my dear, it's different for each one of us. But we don't have time for experimentation, you need to speak with Hiram.'

Olivia instinctively turned and spoke out loud to Hiram, but he didn't respond.

'No,' Miriam sounded frustrated, 'with your *mind*, Olivia. Hiram's withdrawn into himself and once again you need to initiate the contact.'

Olivia looked back at Miriam, biting her lips and nodding her understanding. Olivia faced Hiram again, but this time projected her communication with her mind. She thought it was easier than a few moments before... perhaps she really was getting the hang of this.

'Olivia!' Hiram's hoarse whisper sounded ecstatic to hear from her.

'Hiram. Miriam said I needed to talk to you.'

'Ah, yes. I needed to impart some information to you about Albert.'

Olivia interrupted him, 'Albert's here as well?' she asked despairingly. Not another soul she would ultimately not be able to save!

'No, no, but there's something you need to know before you try to get yourself away from here. It should be easy, just remember the park and when the time comes you'll finally be able to walk beyond the apple tree. Then we will all be free.'

Olivia had little time to be bemused by his comments as her mind became awash with imagery as Hiram's mind suddenly unleashed all it had to offer with regards to Albert. She found herself standing at the lip of the abyss that fell into the universe of the black hole. Flickering dancing images pounded into her mind, all with Albert at the fore.

'Hold tight,' he said, smiling his lopsided grin. She saw her bedroom, a moment of blankness then she stood in the twilit park at the end of her road, an apple tree beckoning her with a tiny green fairy door flapping in the breeze at the base of its trunk. She had a fleeting thought that she was turning into Alice, expecting to eat cake and jump into a fantastical world through a miniscule door. Her head whirled and her sight blurred.

She staggered under the weight of it all and her connections with the two allies was inadvertently terminated. She tottered backwards as she tried to steady herself. Her hands came up to her temples and pressed into them, as if by this act she could prevent her brain exploding through them. She heard John speaking to her from over by her mother's gurney.

'You alright, Olivia?'

She gurgled a response, trying to nod, but gave up as her vision began to swim. She stumbled forward and leant into the wall heavily, drawing in deep breaths as she tried to centre herself. She felt a taloned hand clasp her wrist. Was it there to support her or to draw her attention to something? She looked up from it to where Hiram still lay upon the gurney. His eyes were still shut and yet he knew where she was. It jogged a memory within the memories he had just imparted. A hope of help that would see Miriam and Hiram set free. She extricated her wrist from Hiram's hand and then stuck it into the inner pocket of her jacket. She had forgotten all about it, as her hand coiled around the butt of the tranq gun. She pulled it out, laying it upon Hiram's stomach and then placed his hand over it.

'I truly hope it helps you find the freedom Miriam thinks it will get you, Hiram. Please, be careful.'

She heard his response, 'We'll all be free.'

'Olivia, come on. We can't save them. Not now. We have to go. This instant, otherwise they will get us too.'

Olivia looked forlornly at Hiram and then back to where John was progressing across the room with her mother, her naked feet dragging behind them. They all stopped stock still when a new sound entered the room.

Chapter 27

A crisp derisive voice echoed across the room.
'He's right, of course,' the voice sounded almost robotic, coming from some unseen speaker high up in the walls. 'You can't save them. You should have gone when you had the chance, because now you're never going to be able to leave.'

Olivia heard the swish-swish sound of a door opening, she looked around the room and then became aware of two sliding doors in the opposite wall, which had blended so well with their surrounds she hadn't seen them. A swathe of individuals swept into the room, fanning out with practiced precision and suddenly she found they were surrounded by hostile individuals, all pointing pistols at them.

John spun around on the spot, Phyllis' feet and legs becoming entangled in her nightgown. Her head lolled against his shoulder, her hair falling over her face. He backed slowly towards Olivia, until he was next to her. The two of them had their backs to Hiram and Miriam, Phyllis was lowered carefully to the floor. The two of them took up wary stances to ward off the battalions of the Organisation now ranged against them. The voice continued,

'I have to say I was sceptical when John posited his plans with me. But I doff my hat to my grandson, he has a very keen mind and has done both himself and our project a superb turn. Not only has he brought in two of the malingerers that have been a constant thorn in our side these past few years, but he has also brought home the prodigal son, or as it stands prodigal daughters. Well done, John. I see a brilliant future ahead of you at my side as we complete the project and improve the world.'

Olivia's mouth opened, and then closed. She stuttered looking over at John who was no more than a foot from her.

'What?' she eventually managed to get out.

John turned to face her, a smug smile creasing his lips, 'I did warn you, Olivia, on a number of occasions, in fact not but ten minutes ago, about the concept of smoke and mirrors. But you're such a gullible dullard, you never learn.'

He brought himself up to his full height as he turned towards her, 'But you will. You will learn within the testing grounds of the facility how to be a good servant for the Organisation.'

Olivia was speechless, his tone, his demeanour had completely changed on the head of a pin. Who was this man that stood in front of her? It certainly wasn't John, not roguish John, not even lying shitbag John. This was a completely different person altogether. Self-assured to the point of arrogance. His bearing was now that of a statesman, not of an underling. He was smug, aloof.

John smiled again; he was clearly enjoying her stupefaction. All the more so as he got to lord it over her as he filled in the blanks, of which there seemed to be many.

'I had been just an observer for a long time, I've watched you for years, trying to learn your mind, to find a way in, so that I could unlock your talents. It became more evident as the years went by that some sort of external stimulus was going to be required to get those powers of yours turned on. They certainly seemed reluctant to show themselves. During one of our many case meetings about how you were progressing it became clear that a shock was required to kick start your awakening. Morag was of a mind that a trauma was the way forward, but I had my own insight, based on my own talents. What if love could trigger an awakening? Certainly, if you had ever seen your parents together and later, once you had been born, how their powers seemed to increase exponentially, you'd understand why I thought love might be the answer to our dilemma.' To ensure her attention was still rapt upon him, he blew her a kiss. Olivia shuddered.

ORDINARY WORLD

'Working on this premise I reviewed everything we had on you and there was a lot, I can tell you. Your every waking, and for that matter, sleeping, moment has been monitored and catalogued since before you were born. Seventeen years of endless, mundane tedium to wade through to find the keys to unlocking your puerile mind. But they needed to be subtle, skeleton keys, little prods and nudges bolstered with an emotional reaction, supplied by me. Can you guess what we did, how many little subliminal suggestions we slipped to you, reinforced by environment, physical representation and imagery?'

He looked inquisitively at her, head cocked to one side, 'Of course you can't, because you don't have the fundamentals of intellect to know nor understand just how much effort is involved in your case.'

He threw this at her accusingly, as if saying it was her fault that he had to make so much effort to unlock her own created talents. The suggestion made Olivia balk; the hackles on the back of her neck rose and tickled her synapses, spurring her to find the right moment to fry John's manipulative arrogant brain.

'Little things like my bike. Chosen specifically for its colour, emerald green and its power, because I knew you'd conjure a link between it and those facile romance books you used to read as you approached your teens. A little help from the triplets and it didn't take too much for you to imagine yourself as a princess being rescued by her dragon-riding knight. With that set deep in your psyche, applying my own skills to our more intimate moments made your seduction all too easy.' Olivia thought he was about to spit on her in contempt and she turned her face away from him in shame.

'But enough of you. I think we've spent far too much time considering you, as if you were the be-all and end-all of our project. A culmination, yes, but so much came before you to ensure your undeserved mental wealth, I think it's time we looked at other factors. Love has its drawbacks... for one thing who you fall in love with. Or, at least, have to pretend who you fall in love with. In my case, my sacrifice was to pretend to love a vacuous simpleton who was completely caught up in her own pitiful, self-orientated woes. Thank goodness there was a semblance of attractiveness to you, otherwise I think I would have been hard pressed to fuck you as often as I did. But it was postulated that the sexual act would be what could trigger your powers and I'm a team player. I took one for the team,' he smiled ingratiatingly at her.

'So, to other factors in your rise to full breeding potential.' He paused possibly considering how best to explain and at the same time stick the knife in just a little bit deeper. 'For instance, proof of the power of love. Your parents are a prime example of this as their powers grew, exponentially as I said, the more emotionally attached they became. And then you appeared on the horizon and they veritably blew the stack. With such an increase in their powers, your father became untenable as a test subject – leading a revolt that cost the life of my father and allowing so many of the subjects to escape, was, frankly, not to be condoned. Hence the reason Reg shot him.'

John's eyebrows rose quizzically at Olivia's sudden look of surprise, 'Oh, yes, I may have misled you a bit there, it was *your* father that killed *mine*, forcing the escape of the patients. It was *Reg*, as head of security, that brought your father down.' John flicked an acknowledging head bob in Reg's direction.

Olivia's gaze followed the acknowledgement across the room and she took a moment to register who was actually railed against her. There was her father, looking a lot less flabby than he'd appeared through her life, he was pointing an automatic pistol at her and she wondered in that moment, despite everything, could he actually pull the trigger on her? As she scanned the room she saw the woman from the bus and her compatriot who had been with her at the school. Amazingly Aunty Morag was also there, not that she had a pistol in evidence, unlike the bus woman and her friend. Aunty Morag did not look like her formidable buxom aunt any more. Now she was dressed in a formal suit and she was holding an armoured black briefcase – it looked more like a medic's box than anything. Most prominently, centred between half a dozen black armoured soldiers, she saw the triplets. The mere sight of them sent a shiver skittering the length of her spine. They looked malignant. Pale willowy corpses with shark teeth set within gaunt hollow faces, their eyes still lost to view behind silver wrap around shades.

She looked back at John as he cleared his throat to continue.

'Both Morag and Grandfather were obviously sceptical, but then neither of them could ever be described as warm, emotional people. They don't understand the power of emotion. But when you have emotion as a weapon, as a means to manipulate, then you enter a whole different ball game. It's amazingly easy to seduce a naïve sixteen-year-old girl with no life.'

John flicked a warm smile at her. She sensed him flexing and felt a pulse of intense warmth and passion wash over her. Butterflies fluttered freely in the pit of her stomach, and a hot flush radiated from there up through her torso until the tips of her ears burned. John caught her as she swooned. He leant down, brushing his lips against hers and she felt a renewed tingling in her legs, his mouth closed on hers and her desire to consume his kiss became overwhelming. As their lips parted there was a barely audible click and she felt a shiver run down her spine.

John stood back, relinquishing his hold on Olivia and she fell unceremoniously to the floor in front of him. As she opened her eyes, the warmth fading from her extremities, she caught the smile he now cast at her. The passion of moments before was completely absent. Now it was a malign smile, filled with arrogance and manipulation.

'See what I mean?' John said to her. He spun around on the balls of his feet, arms outstretched, almost dancing with his empathic prowess. His pirouette brought him back to face her, the malignant smile practically slicing his face in two, as his outstretched arms came together to point directly at her. His head bobbed to the side as he gave her an exuberant wink.

Her eyes started to focus more clearly on the moment of now and a sudden horrifying realisation struck her. Her hand snapped up to her neck and her finger tips were deflected by the smooth, cold, metal collar that now adorned it. She gasped.

John pursed his lips before replying, 'Well we couldn't have you melting people in this room now, could we? I have just witnessed the power of your talents and you have little to no control over them. That will change, of course, in time, as we train you. But in the interim best to be safe.' He winked at her again.

'It's ironic, really, when you think about it,' John continued, 'for a Mentat, you have an immensely weak mind. You were the culmination of two of our strongest test subjects and yet, from what I've seen of your total lack of cognitive prowess, your mind mirrors that of your friend Evie. How is it possible? There were one or two occasions where your powers showed minor manifestations. But even Albert in his early days could've managed more than you put out. We were beginning to despair, until the triplets enticed a little something more out of you. But, even that was awfully inadequate. Had it not have been for Albert and Hiram's intervention I really don't see that anything much would have come of it all. Your powers are pathetic. You're pathetic.' He spat this last epithet out in disgust.

'Grandfather wasn't convinced that there was anything worth gaining from bringing you in with your mother. He was all for putting you both straight into the dissection labs with the view of starting again. See where we went wrong, but I,' he turned emphatically towards her at this moment, stabbing his thumb into his chest, 'I had faith in you Olivia. I knew you couldn't have been this useless, I'd been involved in your latter development, I had encouraged you to open up, not just your legs, but your mind as well. I thought that given the correct encouragement you would achieve your potential and help me prove my grandfather wrong, prove that his doubt in you and, more importantly, in me was misplaced. We just needed to find the right incentive to get you to actually prove there was more in your mind than Swiss cheese.

'What better way to encourage it out of you than for you to think you had one final last ditch against-all-the-odds chance to save your imprisoned mum from the machinations of an evil organisation? Putting you as the heroine in some inept spy thriller to save the world. Hence, our little rampage through the facility so you could 'stumble' upon an adversary to mind control and get you to your goal. True, it didn't quite go according to plan. Certainly our security officers hadn't signed on for that particular mission to be melted into nothing, but their families will be suitably compensated for their loss. And once again, despite the colossal destructive force you unleashed, it was all very disappointing. There was no finesse, no skill or subtly employed, just the normal sledgehammer approach of a petulant hormonal teenager. Which brings me back round to – pathetic!'

John made a big show of his disappointment, heaving a forlorn sigh and letting his shoulders sag. Olivia was aware of a few in the faceless crowd that surrounded her, smirking and sniggering at John's verbal beratement of her. Once again her anger started to rise, but it was constrained not just by the collar, but also by his words. Her hand rose once more and this time gripped the collar, her flaring temper was a direct reaction to his words and the anger was born from hormonal temperament, not rational reasoned objection. She glared at him, but refused to give him the satisfaction of knowing he had wounded her.

John straightened up and slowly walked towards her, acknowledging Olivia's gesticulation to the collar, 'As we're on the subject, my love, you may be interested to know that it was *I* who came up with the idea of the collars. Although you can blame your father for my inspiration, had he not murdered my parents in front of me, I suspect I might have been more gracious to him and his kind. And by that, I mean, *you*. It was clear that not everyone from our treatments felt the same way about how they should be used; the triplets were more than happy with a role within our organisation, but not so those two behind you, and a few others.'

Olivia remained on the floor as John continued his explanations. She had been conflicted before about how she felt about John, but now it was abundantly clear to her that not only was he a lying shitbag, but that he had done nothing more than seduce, manipulate and use her for his own ends. Which seemed to be the machinations of his grandfather and his secretive organisation. She was utterly heartbroken. Despite everything up to this point, she still loved John, for his compassion, his care, the way he had been so different from anyone she had ever known, even Evie and Rhys. He had understood her and... she realised suddenly: yes, he understood her and that was how he had manipulated her. She had to know more, even though she knew it might very well kill her. She didn't care anymore; the pain of his betrayal was too deep. Her chest was tight and her stomach felt that it was going to rebel. There was nothing in her legs but jelly. She couldn't stand up. She couldn't breathe.

'But you said you loved me, only just now, back in the labs. That can't have been fake? That wasn't you playing a role, that was real.' She said it with such force as to suggest she could make it real. Even though she knew it was all a lie, he had just shown her his power of make-believe. False love cast by a spell of the mind. But she had to push, no matter what. John's response made her mind explode, solidifying what she knew to be the truth, but still didn't want to accept.

'Meh. You're a pleasant fuck, Olivia, but I've known better and love never came into it. I am detached from the emotions I use. It would make me highly ineffectual if I was influenced by my own emotions, now wouldn't it? No. I didn't love you. I *don't* love you. But all I needed to do was convince you that I did, so that I could catalyse your powers into awakening. It worked,' again he winked at her. A crowing wink that splintered her already-shattered heart into a thousand pieces.

'But I look forward to fucking you again, spearheading the breeding program, you might say. The triplets are looking forward to finally participating in that part of the program too,' John's smile sent a fresh shiver down her spine – the level of malevolence engendered within it made her mind shrivel. 'Of course, you understand we don't actually *need* to sully ourselves with actual intercourse. We have labs, you know. All we need from you are your ovaries and your stem cells. We can create a whole legion of far more malleable and obedient instruments for our grand scheme. We don't really need you after that. So it seems only fair that the boys get to have their fun before we dissect your brain to see if there are any salient points we might have missed. As for your mother, we'll do the same – not the fucking part, obviously, that would be gross,' his lip curled in distaste, ' – no, I mean remove her ovaries, her stem cells and dissect her brain.

'At the end of the day, Olivia, if you feel hard done by, you have only yourself to blame. I told you about smoke and mirrors, and with your innate powers you should have seen what I was insinuating. Although, I knew you wouldn't, hence the fact that

I reiterated it so many times. I garnered a certain amount of amusement at your inherent stupidity. If you'd paid a little more attention to what was actually going on, you could have easily blown away the smoke and shattered the mirrors.' John's lip curled into a faux smile and he shrugged his shoulders.

'C'est la vie.'

John walked away from her to join the cadre of enemies arrayed against her. Olivia continued to sit on the gleaming white tiled floor. She could feel the cold sterility of them seeping into her bones, drawing any remaining warmth she had left in her deflated psyche down into the depths of despair. She slowly raised her head, tears flowing unbidden and uncontrollably down her face. She was numb. Her mind was numb, shocked by John's revelations, secured by the collar. She couldn't speak. She could but watch as John indicated for Reg to collect her from the floor. Presumably to be taken to a lab, where they could remove bits of her anatomy for their experiments and then be dissected.

NO!

That wasn't going to be the end of her perfect birthday. The day when her mother had taken her out shopping. The day her mother had hugged her and wished her happy birthday. This wasn't real, it was one of her nightmares. How could the day start in her home and end here, in an unknown facility in Birmingham, hidden from the world? So no one would ever know what had happened to her. People would notice if she disappeared. But then, would they? With an apparently deranged mother, it wouldn't take much for it to be suggested that they had moved on, for the betterment of all concerned. But Evie and Rhys would notice. They'd know something was amiss and do something about it. Wouldn't they? John's voice rang in the back of her mind: 'A marmoset has more cognitive acuity than Evie, a brain of soft cheese'. A triplet would merely suggest all was well and then that would just leave Rhys, but a few good doses of drugs and he'd be none the wiser too. They really would just disappear, wouldn't they? Was this true for everyone in the world, someone could just take them out of existence and no one else would be any the wiser? Their parents would – they would fight tooth and nail to find them, they always did, she'd seen the shows. But the person was never found and the parents always died alone and broken. As for her, her mother was already broken, no one would miss her. And her father? Which one? The dead one or her keeper? No one to look for her, no one to care.

She continued to stare after John as her thoughts tumbled through her mind. Her attention turned to the advancing Reg, no longer her father. But then, how long had he been her father? How much longer had he just been her gaoler, her warder? There was nothing in his expression to suggest that he cared a jot for her. She was merely a job, a pay packet and a retirement bonus. She was nothing to him.

Olivia jolted as a hand was placed upon her knee. She turned to follow the hand up the arm and into the face that it belonged to. Her mother.

Phyllis had crawled over to her; she had finally awoken and with her touch they communicated.

'It is time, Olivia, for you to break the dream. Before we are both lost to it. Please, I'm begging you, release me from this enduring nightmare.'

Olivia saw the pleading expression within her mother's eyes and she felt the whispering touch of her voice within her mind. A fading zephyr that caressed the folds of her synapses. Her lips didn't move. And then the connection was abruptly broken as Reg bent down, threw Phyllis' arm out of the way and grabbed at Olivia. Phyllis tried to stand, eventually coming to her knees and reaching out to Reg, attempting to rend his grasp from her daughter. Reg contemptuously slapped at her, relinquishing his hold upon Olivia.

And then Olivia heard another voice echo across the chamber. It was a hoarse, angry whisper, like snake scales rasping across a sun-bleached rock.

'Leave her be! Or I will shoot you.'

All eyes in the room turned to where Hiram sat on the edge of his gurney, a gun pointed at Reg. By return, Reg swung to the threat bringing his own pistol to bear.

'No! Hiram, put it down!' Olivia screamed; she could see the intent in Reg's eyes. There was no remorse. She watched as his finger flexed, depressing the trigger of his pistol to send a bullet that would end Hiram.

Hiram fired first. A silver cylinder scorched across the divide and hit Reg squarely between the eyes. He staggered under the impact, as the tiny needle of the tranq stabbed into his forehead. As he staggered, his finger finally depressed the lever and there was a loud report as his pistol went off. Olivia reflexively slapped her hands over her ears because the shot was fired so close to her - it deafened her. In that moment, a memory came to her of an animator's storybook and she watched its pages flicking through their tale, overlapping the flight of the bullet as it careened through the air until it impacted with the flimsy fabric of a consultation gown. As it tore a ragged hole into the soft and yielding flesh that lay unprotected to its aggression. She watched as it sank deeper into her mother's chest and she watched as her mother's eyes flew open in surprise, as she fell backwards. To lie crumpled upon the cold tile floor, the light fading from her eyes, a smile creasing her paling lips and the words that issued forth to Olivia, 'I am free.'

Olivia screamed.

Chapter 28

Olivia launched herself off the floor towards her dying mother, clambering over the prone figure of her stunned father. She cradled Phyllis in her arms. Olivia could feel the juxtaposed sensation of warmth oozing between her interlocked fingers, counterpoint to the chill of Phyllis' palm on her arm. She looked into her eyes as the light went out and a sudden heart-stopping pain of immense loss tore through her entire being. As her mother slipped away, Olivia laid her out on the floor, pulling her hands from her and bringing them up to her face. She was unable to comprehend what had just happened; in a daze she stared blankly at the palms of her hands. They were a dark crimson in colour, covered in the arterial blood that had gushed from the gunshot exit wound in Phyllis' back. Sparkles started to dance in front of Olivia's eyes, washing the sight of the blood from her hands.

The sparkles continued to dance in front of Olivia and one pirouetted around the others until it came to a sudden and intense quivering halt right before her eyes. It vibrated there, caught by indecision. And then, it shot back towards her, drilling itself between her eyes and driving hard into the central core of her brain. There was a pause. The world stood still. The room froze. The cadre looked back at Olivia as she stood up with intent, determination fixed upon her face. She looked at them defiantly and then triggered what it was Albert wanted to share with her. They watched in disbelief as Olivia's figure vibrated into a shimmering reflection of itself and they watched as the shimmering ghost took a step forward. They watched as the silver collar remained in situ, apparently frozen in time and space, before it finally fell to the tiled floor with a clatter.

Everyone in the room looked down at the death of Phyllis, their bodies immobilised by an unseen force. Then all eyes rose as one to look at Olivia, terror etched into every one of them.

• • • •

Deep in the centre of her mind, it was dark. Dull grey-silvered pathways criss-crossed her neural highway, thousands of them, millions, billions of them. All lying beneath a dark heavy-blue sky of infinity. The sparkle brought a fleeting light to the darkness and disappeared into a node near the centre of her highway. There was a fizzle. A light flickered on inside the node and then went out.

There was another pause.

A pause that lasted the lifetime of a universe. And then the light exploded – searing whiteness tinged with gold exploded from the node, rampaging down the corridors of the silvery tubes, in all directions. As it gathered momentum, her brain remapped itself, nodes sparking into a life that they had never known before. A life they had never imagined possible for themselves. The flickering highways of her mind streamed a diffuse golden light, zig-zagging this way and that as her molecules discovered what they had originally been created for. No more were they simple neurons ensuring the basic, fundamental functions of maintaining an organic lifeform. No, now they were a lifeform in their own right, linking together to form a single entity created from a billion parts.

Olivia's mind exploded. Her memories came flooding through her mind's eye. From birth to now, every moment, every nuance, every second of her existence catalogued and stored away for just such a day. She was flooded and overwhelmed by the movie-display of images whipping in front of her. She felt all the emotions at once. She felt the pain. The suffering. The joy and the laughter. Images of her parents whizzed by. Images of Evie and Rhys. Of school and Mr Rawlinson. Of Miriam and Hiram. Dr McKenzie, Mrs McKilliecuddy, everyone. She couldn't take the emotion when Phyllis had died in her arms. Now that all the emotions of her life were intensified a thousandfold, to unload on her exposed mind in a single instant, she fled. Her consciousness disappeared inwards. Ever inwards, away from everything. Down into the darkness of before. Down there she could find peace, she could find silence.

Her consciousness rested.

But it wasn't silent down here. She was wrong; there was no peace to be found anywhere. There was a hum down here – muted, but still a hum. It was all the voices of her life, talking to her, at her, over her. All of them meshed together to make an incessant annoying hum. She swayed, first one way then another, desperate to find a way to escape. And then, somewhere deep inside her consciousness she heard another sound. It sounded like a drum beat. It was regular, it was consistent and it was very solid compared with the buzzing hum of all that chitter-chatter. And yes, as she paused to concentrate on that drum beat, she detected a second drum beat. Its tone was half an octave higher than the first drum. She focused on them, one deep and ponderous, the other light and fast. A deep intoning thump followed by several swift light taps; then the deep thump and again the swift light taps. Music of life bringing consistency to Olivia's lost consciousness.

She homed in on the drum beats and finally found a path to them. A thick, matted cord that pulsed in time with the higher pitched drum beat. Her consciousness flew down to it, tendrils from her being reaching forth to caress the cord. She felt the pulse, the drumbeat, vibrate the length of the cord and ripple through her tendrils and up into the core of her consciousness. Still entwined with the cord, she followed the passage of the beat down its length until she came to an abrupt halt. There, in a chamber, she saw the origin of the drumbeat. The pulse. It was enormous. Monstrous.

Monstrous in its size, but not in its being. A perfectly smooth, oval chamber, within which resided an embryo. An embryo that grew and matured and changed until she could see more than an opaque-skin creature with visible blood vessels and dark orbed eyes. She could see a fully-formed baby, ready for ascension to the next stage of life.

Her tendrils relinquished their hold upon the umbilical cord. Her consciousness approached the baby and now the tendrils gently rose up to stroke the face of the unborn in front of her.

'Hello,' her consciousness said with an eternal love never before realised by it. 'Hello you.'

If her consciousness had had a physical form, it would have shed a tear of utter, utter joy. Her connection was finally made as she stroked the embryo's face. She dissolved. She was at peace, at last.

She was home. There was the apple-green door she always went through to get inside. But now she understood the truth of it. The door had always been there, she just needed to find the correct key to open it, to find what lay behind it. The door separated the inside from the outside, the reality from the dream. Now she knew why she had been unable to open it so many times before. Why, when she had opened an apple green door, she might have been filled with hope or relief only for these fleeting feelings to be dashed, because it was the correct door just the wrong key. And in this endless moment she realised that she was never going to find that key until the moment was right, until she fully comprehended who she was and what she could do. She pushed open the door tentatively, glancing back briefly to say goodbye to the dream, before boldly thrusting herself forward down through the dark canal into her reality.

• • • •

ORDINARY WORLD

In the room, all eyes were on Olivia. They watched as Phyllis' body lay motionless in a crumpled heap. They watched as Olivia looked at her bloodied hands and the expressions changed across her face. They saw the single teardrop that trickled from her right eye to roll down the side of her nose and run onto her upper lip. They watched as she inhaled. They saw her expression change to anguish with the sudden realisation of loss. A life she loved ripped from her. And then they saw a sudden brightness emanate from her eyes. Her eyes literally sparkled. The light grew in magnitude, making it harder for the eyes to watch her, but they had no choice. No hands could move to cover them. No eyelids were capable of closing to protect them from the incandescent light that was getting brighter and brighter in the depths of Olivia's sockets. Their bodies were paralysed, incapable of turning away and shielding themselves from what looked like a supernova exploding inside Olivia's head. They watched as Olivia's eyes changed colour. Her pupils grew, expanding ever outwards, flooding over her irises and consuming the whites of the eyes. Her pupils gorged on the whole of her eyeballs turning them into a blackness akin to the void. And then, from somewhere in the back of those orbs, the light came again. A pinprick that grew in size and ferocity. A golden light that reclaimed the eyeballs from the pupils, turning them to complete orbs of gold.

They watched as all this happened and more. Olivia's arms were by her sides, palms to the fore, like an opera singer building towards a climatic crescendo. They rose slightly in front of her and that movement attracted attention to the lower part of her body. Her legs became bent at the knees as she raised her feet clear of the ground. Yet she did not fall. She hovered, like an angelic summoning before the faithful Host. She was surrounded by an ambient glow. Her mouth started to open, growing wider and wider. They saw her chest and torso inflate and they knew she was drawing in a great breath.

Olivia, filled to capacity, held the breath for a second that lasted an eternity and then expelled it in a scream so filled with anguish and torment that those that watched her felt their minds explode. The gurneys melted. The weapons turned to sand. The airlock door buckled and disintegrated. The shuttered windows turned to dust. The shutters disappeared. The vision of the room with all its occupants, with all its materials, froze into shards of a shattering mirror. They remained in stasis for aeons, until time no longer held sway. The room exploded. When it exploded, all the shards fell to the ground as sand. There was nothing after that.

No room. No onlookers.

No Phyllis, dead on the floor.

No Olivia.

• • • •

April 17th

There was a muted scream and a moan. It came from a woman. It wasn't loud enough to drown out the voice from the radio.

'Welcome back to the Request Show. That was Sam Fender, Seventeen Going Under, released... blimey, that makes me feel old! Twelve years ago! Well, if that made you feel old, here's something that'll turn you grey. 'Ordinary World' by Duran Duran, released in this month way back near the end of last century, in 1993...'

'Nearly there now, dear,' a woman's voice broke through the sounds of the music piping out of the radio, 'just one more push. You're over the worst of it now, dear. She's crowned!'

One more grunted scream. One more sweaty, heaving push, drawn from the depths of endurance after hours of labour and the baby was suddenly in the world for all to see. The mother collapsed

ORDINARY WORLD

back onto the pillows, drenched, beyond exhausted. She was sore, torn and bleeding. But it was all as expected. The midwife wrapped the baby in a towel and went to cut the cord. She paused and then thought better of it, a sibilant whisper in her mind commanded her to wait. There was still a pulse running the length of it, pumping last-second, vital nutrients into the new-born from its mum. Instead, she ran through the early birth checks, before finally handing the babe to its mother.

Mum cradled the gangly wee creature in the crook of her left arm. She pulled the edge of the towel back from her first-born's face with the tip of her forefinger. The baby smiled and cooed. Mum smiled back, a tear erupting from her eye to roll down the side of her nose onto her sweaty upper lip. It was not a tear of pain, but one of extreme happiness. She spoke down to her new love.

'Hello,' she whispered, 'Hello, you.'

Mum took her time to savour this moment with her new-born daughter, before letting out a resigned sigh and turning her attention to the other occupants of the room.

At the foot of her bed stood her husband, a mixture of emotions washing over his features. She looked into his startling slate grey eyes and saw the utter joy for his first born; relief upon seeing his wife awake and well from her trauma, the desperation mingling with the moment and then the anger at the realisation of what all this might mean for his family. Two black armoured men stood directly behind him; one held a metal rod that was attached to a short chain link, that in turn was attached to the silver collar that adorned his neck. His hands were unbound, clasping the bedrail at her feet, but they didn't need to be secured to ensure his best behaviour. The mere threat of harm to his wife and child were enough to keep him restrained. His captors did have the added guarantee of the collar they had slipped on him, ensuring his greatest weapons against them were neutered. Mum wore one too and balked at the fact that in her moment of greatest joy she had been unable to share every minute detail with her husband because of it.

She glanced to her left, to the bank of machines that had monitored her for the past few months and to the midwife who was finishing up with the baby's notes, before being unceremoniously dismissed by the man who stood on the opposite side of the bed, in front of the window. She looked past the short man, with his balding wrinkled head, past the greying tufts of hair on the sides of his face, over his shoulder and out of the window, to stare into the infinite void of space that lay beyond. An endless darkness that could have been their sanctuary, had *they* not intercepted her husband in their final stage of their escape plan. The vista in the window slowly changed as the room and the facility in which it was housed rolled over, and the glistening halo of Sol's rays lit up the ships that traversed the vastness of the solar system, pin pricks of light that blinded the viewer for a second as the rays washed over their bulkheads. The scene rolled onwards, always onwards, the sun's light becoming brighter as they rolled over and started to see the crescent edge of the Earth below. The window reacted to the sudden touch of Sol's caress and tinted, shading the room within, allowing light in without the harsh brilliance that would undoubtedly damage or disorientate an unprotected eye.

Phyllis sighed again as she saw all that could have been theirs, had they just been allowed a chance. She brought her vision back in to the room and the squat man by the window.

Simon smiled paternally down at her.

'So this is Charlotte, is it? That is truly splendid, my love. And we're all delighted to see that you have decided to return to our fold.' He glanced to his right, over at Stephen, 'Glad to see the old gang is back together again. It brings me great joy that we will once again be able to forge a future together.'

Phyllis saw Stephen flinch as Simon spoke to them, saw the sinews in his neck flex as he tried to disengage the collar. She saw the concentration on his face as he tried to engage his mind to slip the noose of the restraint. And then she saw the stab of pain in his eyes as the collar countered his attempts to break free. Stephen sagged, taking support from the bedrail, ever defiant – refusing even to grunt in acknowledgement at the pain that must have been fired into his brain by the collar.

She looked back at Simon; there was no reciprocating smile upon her face. She clutched her new daughter close to her breast as she spoke to Simon.

'This moment is quite mixed for me, Simon, as you can well imagine.' She noted Simon's acknowledgement.

'But what choice did you leave us, Phyllis?' Simon responded with a shrug of his shoulders and an upturn of his palms.

'The same choice you gave us, Simon – none. When our parents agreed to your program to help them with their individual ailments, a generational indenture wasn't what they signed up for. They may have been welcomed into your fold, as we were when we were young, but your intentions soon spoke of your true intent to use us as weapons and control mechanisms for your own ends. We are individuals in our own right, Simon. We are all humans and all deserve our rights to choice. You stripped us of those before we were even born. We will not serve you any longer.'

Simon smirked, 'I don't really see that either of you are in a position to gainsay the situation, my dear.' His wave took in their collars and Phyllis' bedridden predicament.

'Even if you refuse, we still have Charlotte. Although I'm inclined to call her Eve. I think the name is far more fitting, given that she will be the mother and grandmother of a whole new order of humans. We don't really need either of you now.'

And to indicate this he signalled to another black armoured soldier who had been stationed by the door to the room. The soldier stepped forward, drew out his sidearm and pointed it at Stephen's temple. Simon nodded and the soldier pulled the trigger. There was an almost inaudible phut from the muzzle and a needle shot out of it towards Stephen.

Phyllis gasped at the act, too shocked, too horrified to react. Stephen paled, but stood resolute as he saw his end had come. And then everything froze.

• • • •

'I never did like you Simon, from almost the first time I heard you speaking, I thought to myself you are not a very nice man. You're condescending, arrogant and demeaning. I certainly didn't like the way you spoke to Phyllis when Stephen wasn't around. And now that I get to finally meet you, properly, I find that all my intuitions about you were correct. You – are not – a – very – nice – man.'

Simon's mind bathed in the chill embrace of the voice that spoke to it. His body was immobilised. Where was the voice coming from? Who was speaking to him? His eyes cast across the room to see if someone had slipped inside without any of them noticing during the drama of the labour. Or were they stood outside the door staring in? As he detected no signs of another occupant to the room, his eyes shifted their quest out of the window. Was it possible that there was a spacewalker out there projecting in? But no, again he could see no one.

'For all your plotting and planning, scheming and connivance, for all your acumen, Simon, you're a bit obtuse at times.' He could detect a smile within the voice as it said this.

His gaze inexorably turned from the window to face the bed. He stared at Phyllis sceptically and then his eyes flicked down to where the babe lay swaddled in her arms, a fine tuft of ginger forelock lying slicked from afterbirth upon its brow, darker in colour because of the moisture than its true nature. The baby smiled unnervingly back at him and he visibly gulped.

'There it is, Simon. Hello, I'm not very pleased to meet you.'

'But... but how? You're but barely minutes old?'

'Ah! I beg to differ, Simon, I have already lived a life, or, at least part of one. Thanks to my mother. It was only now that I realised why Phyllis would induce a coma – it was to give me a chance. A chance she never had. I have been alive within her mind, within her dreams, within her delusion and I've had time to learn. To experience life, to make mistakes and deny my heritage. I have also had time to develop and evolve my talents. True, they're not at their pinnacle yet, but then I *am* still very young, am I not, Simon?'

The baby cooed at him. Simon was rigid. He could feel sweat trying to burgeon on his face, but it was trapped; time had stopped in the room and it would not allow something so mundane as human excretions to break its boundaries. It didn't prevent Simon from feeling a ghastly chill skitter down his spine and fill his bladder with dread.

'I hope you're proud, Simon, of what you've achieved. I am, after all, the ultimate human that you had been striving for, am I not? Perhaps, I'm just a little ahead of where you were expecting to be. Perhaps, in all your planning you should have considered a contingency where it might not go your way? Where your project might get out of hand? I think you had enough warning from my parents that things don't always go the way we intend. But, you were blinded by your greed for power and dominance. And so this shall be your comeuppance. About time too, if I may say.

'It is unfortunate that while my mental abilities far out strip anything you ever imagined in your board meetings and lab experiments, I am still but a babe in arms. My physical attributes do not fit my mental ones and that's going to be a bit of a drag for the next couple of years. But one I'm happy to play along with as it's not far akin to the sacrifice my mother has made for me in recent months.'

The baby's eyes sparkled for a moment, possibly tearing up at the thought of her mother and her sacrifice.

'So, where do we go from here, Simon?'

Simon tried to shake his head, 'You do seem to be very advanced, Charlotte, but I think you're forgetting some things yourself. One of which you've already pointed out – you're just a baby. Secondly, you're forgetting that your parents are my prisoners and their powers cannot help you, nor can they physically, because they are enslaved.' Had Simon been able to register any facial expressions, it was clear that his expression would have been smug, as he suspected even if he didn't have the upper hand, they were at least at an impasse. His eyes shifted to the right, leaving the baby for a moment. 'And I don't believe your father is long for this world.'

'My name's not Charlotte, nor is it Eve – how trite of you to even suggest it. I am Olivia. As for your enslavement of my parents. I think you underestimate my capabilities.'

Simon watched as a pudgy little hand extricated itself from the swaddling and moved up to grip the collar adorning Phyllis' neck. He watched as it shimmered, vibrating at a phenomenal rate. Olivia's hand moved away from her mother and the collar disappeared for a second and then reappeared in front of her, no longer attached. Olivia dropped the circlet, it fell to the bed and rolled off onto the floor. She then turned her angelic features towards her father. Simon watched as his restraining collar vibrated, disappeared and then reappeared with a clatter on the floor by his feet.

'As for that needle? Simon, for shame.'

ORDINARY WORLD

Simon's attention was drawn to the projectile that quivered inches from Stephen's temple. He watched as it adjusted its course, moving around Stephen, for it to end up pointing at him. The tip pressed against the liver spotted skin of his head, pressing hard enough for a droplet of blood to appear and coalesce around it.

Olivia returned her attention to Simon, 'You were saying?'

Simon tried to gulp, he tried to flinch, he tried to move. His mind was active, but nothing else in the room, in the facility, in the immediate world around them was. It was all frozen in time and space. Their own private little universe, where Olivia was god and all her subjects merely playthings for her amusement.

'So, this is what's going to happen. I will release you and your colleagues. You will, in turn, leave the room and the facility. My parents and I will collect our things and leave on a shuttle of our choosing to a destination of our choosing, unmolested. Be that Earth or off-world in one of the new colonies. We will not be followed. You and your organisation will desist all interest or pursuit of my family and you and your organisation will have a long and fulfilled life. If you pursue us, I will ensure that your end will be most unpleasant – specifically yours – anyone else will be dealt with as needs be. You have seen for yourself that your little trinkets have no effect upon me and by the time you think you've worked out a way to engage and enslave me, I will have worked out a way to counter it. I will always be four steps ahead of you, Simon. Do not be lured into a false sense of security that my current physical deficiencies will prevent me from being able to do whatever is necessary to protect my family.

'Do we have a deal?'

Simon felt the tip of the needle press infinitesimally deeper into his skull.

'Yes,' his mind gulped for his throat as he acquiesced.

'Good.'

Simon physically sagged as the room came to life around him. He raised his hand reflexively to his temple because of the tiny pricking pain he felt. The needle was still there; he could feel it vibrating with an urgency to continue its mission. His fingers gripped it and tried to throw it to the ground, but the needle remained resolute. Simon stared down at the baby that gurgled back at him.

'It's not going anywhere until your people have cleared the station,' Olivia said in reference to the needle. 'Neither are you. You will be the last to leave.'

Phyllis gasped as she watched her husband being shot. Stephen stood firm, awaiting his fate. Both were amazed and confused when they realised the needle was no longer there. The soldier who'd fired his sidearm at Stephen also appeared perplexed, his eyes questing the projectile that would have killed Stephen in a second, moments previously. It was then, as he looked at Stephen, that he became aware that the collar was no longer on his neck. He looked around swiftly towards Phyllis and noted the same to be true for her. His face paled.

'I suggest you make your authority known to your people now, Simon. Otherwise something horrible is about to happen to them.' As Olivia's voice smoothed over Simon's synapses she projected an image into his mind. He saw the baby let out a wail, a wave of sound hit the soldiers and they evaporated. Simon stuttered, preoccupied in part by the continued pressure of a pin prick of pain in his temple. He rallied, drawing himself up and turning to his personnel.

'Right, time to leave. Everyone leave now. We can come back for equipment later. Right now you all need to go. Return to our facility on Earth. Consider yourselves dismissed and stood down.'

The soldiers came to attention, as was their indoctrination, but still they hesitated. This was a clear departure from their briefing.

Simon was their leader and commander and must be obeyed without question, and yet, their entire training for months had been for dealing with this mission. This juncture when they would bring in the Mentats and return them to the facility. Yet, their leader was ordering them to desist. The soldiers behind Stephen glanced briefly at one another before marching towards the door. The soldier that had fired at Stephen dithered, his gauss pistol still pointing at Stephen. He looked at Simon, who in turn looked back at him, flicking his eyes, desperately trying to signal to the man. The soldier glanced towards the bed and saw Phyllis staring at him with ill-concealed hatred. He thought he understood. Somehow the Mentats had freed themselves of their bonds and were now using their powers to control his leader. The woman had already been declared expendable; it was the baby they wanted. He turned as quick as lightning and fired a burst from his pistol at Phyllis.

'Oh, Simon!' Olivia sounded exasperated. The baby let out a muted wail.

The needles and the gauss pistol flared with the sudden intensity of localised heat that came to bear upon them as the wail washed over them. They went incandescently white with the heat that suddenly emanated from within the core of their structures. And then they were dust, ashes floating to the ground. The soldier who had fired his weapon found himself slammed against the far wall. His armoured helmet saved his head from being crushed to pulp, but his head lolled, unconsciousness stampeding through his mind. He slid unceremoniously to the floor.

Meanwhile, Simon felt the needle point press deeper into his skull. It had cut through his skin and flesh. It was now drilling into the bone that lay beneath. It stopped as he started to scream.

'Alright! Alright! We'll go. We'll go. Please don't kill me.'

'Good boy,' Olivia's voice was as sweet as honey and but a gentle breeze across his mind.

The rest of the staff left hurriedly; they were more than happy to leave their equipment for another time. They weren't certain they really knew what had just happened, but they had seen things. Things that were impossible, certainly improbable and they had heard the abject terror in their leader's tone. Best to leave, go home, pretend nothing had happened.

• • • •

Phyllis and Stephen boarded a shuttle with their new-born daughter swaddled and nestled within the crook of Phyllis' arm. They were relieved to be getting away. They were also bemused and stunned by the sudden and unexplained turn of events.

'Best not look a gift horse in the mouth,' Stephen said to Phyllis as they were exiting the room, 'as my grandma would have said.'

The shuttle undocked from the station, bound for who knew where. Back in the maternity room, Simon finally let out a great sigh of relief as the needle fell away from his head and clattered to the floor. For such a tiny projectile, it made a horrendous cacophony of sound as it hit the floor. Simon suspected the sound was amplified by his own relief. He stood and stared at the empty bed with its blood-soaked sheets, turning slowly to take in the vista of the room now devoid of his prize, devoid of his life's work. Finally, he came to stare out of the window, at the shuttles that were toing and froing from the station. Many heading back down to Earth, but just as many heading to the liners and freight ships waiting to head off to the colonies. On one of those ships lay his life's work, disappearing to a future that he would have no say in. He gripped the sill in despair. He would find her; he would make her his tool as had been planned for so many decades. The Organisation could finally fulfil its destiny and take control of the scurrying ants that were dispersing chaotically to the corners of the universe. There would be control and order and he would oversee it all.

He pulled out his phone and called headquarters – new plans needed to be set in motion. This was indeed a setback, but he wouldn't be perturbed.

The screen flickered into life, illuminating his face in the gloom of the empty room. The screen wasn't the usual backdrop of swirling iconic clouds it usually was, instead he saw a baby.

'Oh, Simon, you just don't *learn*, do you?'

The phone fell to the floor, there was a slight groan and then a thump as a body fell to join it.

2039 – The Colonies

'Olivia is a truly remarkable young girl, Mr and Mrs Buchanan. For a girl her age, her levels of empathy are phenomenal and her intuition, well I just don't know how to describe it. She can read a situation with such a high degree of perception it's uncanny. She'll see a tragedy happen before it happens. You wouldn't believe the number of times one of the staff has been caught unawares as a child gets knocked down by another child or just falls over. But we never need worry because Olivia is there to catch them. Honestly, I don't know how she does it. One minute she's on the benches, the next she'll be on the other side of the playground holding one of her peers up.' Miss Phillips sat there shaking her head with a smile splitting her face.

Stephen felt Phyllis slip her hand into his and he squeezed it reassuringly. He felt her reciprocal squeeze of concern. Miss Phillips continued.

'There is one thing I'm a little concerned about, though.' She looked between both of the Buchanans by way of trying to engage both of them at the same time.

The hands became more tightly clenched.

'Olivia's imaginary friends.' Miss Phillips left it hanging for a moment, possibly to try and gauge the Buchanans' view on the matter. 'Lots of children have imaginary friends when they're young, heaven knows I did, when I was about her age.'

Miss Phillips took on a faraway look as reminiscence kicked in, 'Mr Fidget.' She smiled fondly as she looked at Olivia's parents. 'I'm sorry, I was suddenly taken right back. Mr Fidget, because I was a bit of a fidget. But we were discussing Olivia. She clearly has a very active imagination, but I feel she invests too much into these *friends*.'

She paused again. Phyllis spoke up for the first time since they'd sat down after Miss Phillips had requested the meeting.

'Evie and Rhys,'

'Yes, they're the ones.'

'We know about Evie and Rhys, but as you say, kids have imaginary friends. We're not worried.' Phyllis' expression belied her statement. They'd talked to Olivia about her friends recently and they were concerned that maybe there might be an underlying problem. Like the one from her own enforced delusion. She looked over to where Olivia sat in the corner. She was whispering conspiratorially, no doubt with her 'imaginary friends'.

'They're talking about us, aren't they?' Evie said to Olivia.

Olivia glanced at where her parents were talking to her form teacher. She turned back to Evie and Rhys.

'Yes.'

'Should we be worried?'

'No.'

Evie looked at Olivia and Olivia could clearly see that Evie was worried. She reached forward and took her friend's hand.

'What Phyllis said the other day could be true, y'know.' Evie said.

'What? That I'm delusional? I've taken you from my birth dream and conjured you into real people that only I can see?' Olivia looked at her friends and then shook her head with a smile on her face, 'You aren't delusions, but you are projections. For now, you are aspects of my mind that I need to interact with while I come to fully understand who I am and what I can do. Every day I discover a new aspect of my talents, a new subtle nuance. I find it difficult to constantly play the role of a six-year-old. With Mum and Dad, it's easier; they know I'm special and can explain it away as being precocious. Out here, with the likes of Miss Phillips and my class mates, it's a lot harder to be six, when I am effectively seventeen.

ORDINARY WORLD

In fact, I'm older than that mentally,' she paused for a second, 'I'm nearly 23 years old, Evie. But my body is still catching up and no one else knows the real me.'

'Why haven't you explained any of this to your mum and dad?' Rhys asked perplexed.

Olivia paused again as she contemplated the question. In those early days it was easier not to, there were quite enough awkward moments as it was. After that it became habit.

'What they don't know can't hurt them.'

'I think they're pretty able to look after themselves, y'know,' Evie scoffed.

'True, but even with their abilities they have to be careful. We are unique within the human species and, were we known about, we would be feared, hated and hunted. One reason we move around so much is to avoid attracting suspicion.'

'But we're fed up of this nomadic lifestyle, O,' Rhys continued, 'aren't you?'

Olivia looked at her friend, 'Of course I am. I'd love to be able to just settle in one place and grow up, grow up properly like a normal kid. But how long would it be before something happened and people started to question us, look at us differently? Then what? Stay and bluff it out or run? As we've had to do in the past.'

Olivia glanced over to where the adults were talking, 'It is as much my fault as anyone's. I try to rein in my powers, but I still have very little control over them. They just seem to be *on* all the time. I've never found the off switch. So I often end up acting instinctively, hence the amount of the kids in my class who don't have grazed knees or concussions.' She smiled apologetically at her friends. Evie squeezed her hand.

'All the more reason why you should speak with your parents, speak to your mum. They must have an off switch... they've lived with their powers even longer than you have. Speak with them, they will be able to help you, guide you. Trust them! You do trust them, don't you?'

Olivia sat back into her tiny tots chair, brushing her red fringe out of her eyes. She sighed and looked over at her parents, 'I do trust them, and yet, I don't want them to worry. And they've made mistakes, mistakes it took me to fix. So doesn't that mean I'm better able to look after us all, than they are?'

Rhys guffawed, 'OK, so your mind might well be that of a 23-year-old, but even so you're still young in the grand scheme of life. You have the physicality of a six-year-old and a swathe of mental talents that no one has ever seen before. Yes, your parents struggled to escape the Organisation, but they were two people running in fear from a well-organised, well-funded and highly motivated corporation with hundreds of personnel. I think they did a remarkably good job of dealing with their escape. If for no other reason than your mother managed to prepare you for what you would be entering into. She knew you would come out fully functioning, you know they both know you have and use your powers all the time. But they have the foresight to know you can go to them at any time, when you're ready. Now is that time, Olivia. Stop being a self-righteous arse and ask for help. Then all of us can have a chance at a better and happier future.'

Rhys puffed his chest out as he finished. Olivia laughed. It was a rich sound and caused the adults on the other side of the room to turn and look in her direction.

'I think that's a good example of how her imaginary friends are good for her,' Phyllis said to Miss Phillips. 'Since Olivia was born, Stephen's work has meant that we've had to move around a lot. It's not the kind of stability we would have wanted for her, but these friends are a stable interaction for her. As you said yourself, Olivia can be quite solitary, she shies away from social interaction with the children in her class and I think that's because she doesn't know how long she's going to be here for. We could have to up and leave at any time. So she doesn't bond with anyone, fearful that she will be hurt when she has to leave.'

Miss Phillips nodded her understanding, 'Yes, I can see how that would be. I've known a number of children over the years who have had to move about because of their parents. Those in the armed forces were particularly prevalent when I was growing up on Earth.' She looked at Phyllis with a serious expression, 'I do see why imaginary friends would be safer for her, but at the end of the day, it might be time, or it might need to be suggested in the next few months, for her to take that step and try and engage with children who are real. It could be detrimental for her social skills later in life, if all she's ever practiced with are figments of her imagination. But I will leave it with you. Other than this, I see Olivia as a very bright and well-adjusted child and I think she is a credit to the both of you, given that your lives may not be that stable. Which is trying for everyone.' Miss Phillips pursed her lips into a tight smile and then stood up, leaning forward to shake first Phyllis and then Stephen by the hand.

As they went over to collect Olivia from her discussion group with her imaginary friends, Stephen spoke silently to Phyllis.

'Are we going to have to move on again? Now that Miss Phillips has raised the issue?'

'Maybe. Olivia's tendency to act upon her premonitions is worrying; it won't be long before someone openly makes comment and then the whispers will start. And with the whispers on the grapevine, how long will it be before Simon hears them and comes looking?'

Stephen nodded, *'So time to pack then, shame I was just starting to like it here.'*

• • • •

Olivia watched her new world pass by in a haze through the shuttle window. It was a blur of greens and silvery-greys, all bedazzled by the glorious sunshine that enveloped the vista. It reminded her of Earth, but cleaner, newer – fresh and pristine, before humanity had had time to sully it. She laughed at herself: how could it remind her of Earth? She had never been to Earth. All her memories of Earth were her mother's and her delusion. Something triggered in her mind as she thought of this, thinking back to her recent conversation with Rhys and Evie. She let out a little sigh. Obviously it had been heard by her mother, as she then felt Phyllis' hand clasp her shoulder and give it a little squeeze.

To anyone on the shuttle looking at them, they appeared to be a young family out on a day trip to the Core, the capital city of the colony where the colonists' ships had first landed, twenty years ago. With the vast amount of investment from the corporations that financed the venture, it had taken a matter of months to establish settlements across this pleasant agricultural moon. By the end of the first decade, it was agriculturally self-sufficient and exporting the array of minerals that could be found in its crust and asteroid field that orbited it. It was a wealthy colony and reinvestment had created a boom, turning the world into a rival to Earth, so many light years away. The young family sat on their bench seat and watched the new world zip by, silently enjoying its wonders.

'Mum? Dad?'

'Yes, Olivia?' her parents both turned to look down at their daughter.

'We need to talk. A proper, serious talk and now is as good a time as any, because I know you're thinking about moving on again. I don't want to move again. I like it here. It's safe. I like my classmates, even if I do feel more like their teacher than their peer.'

Stephen took his daughter's hand in his, *'I know you* think *it's safe here, but the Organisation will find us if we stay too long. Simon* will find us; he's bound to have been looking all these years and it's only because we do move that they haven't found us yet. Until you're older and better able to hold your instincts in check, when it will be less likely that this will become such a regular necessity.'

Olivia looked up at her father and sighed again, 'It's my fault really,'

Stephen interrupted, 'It's not your fault, Olivia, you're young... it's to be expected.'

'Dad! Let me finish please,' Stephen's mind stepped back a pace, feeling the reprimand quite physically, 'It is *my fault*, Dad, not because I'm young, but because my powers are so overwhelming sometimes and also,' she hesitated, 'and also because I didn't, haven't told you everything.' She looked at her parents sheepishly, Stephen's eyebrow rose as her mother pursed her lips.

'What haven't you told us, Olivia,' Stephen asked suspiciously.

Olivia hesitated again, before letting out another sigh and pressing on, 'About Simon, to start with.'

'What about Simon, my love,' Phyllis prompted, sending a mental nudge to Stephen not to be so dominant.

'Simon isn't a problem any more. In fact... in fact, he hasn't been a problem since the day I was actually born.' Olivia was reluctant to say more as to why Simon was no longer a problem nor her part in this. 'As for the Organisation, they've had to reorganise, not having a leader to direct them. Although I would imagine six years on, they will be in a better position to look for us. They will have had time to work with those of you who didn't get away. The others within their program that were still prisoners.' She cocked her head at her mother, 'There were others, weren't there? You two weren't the only guinea pigs in their little experiment.'

Phyllis shook her head regretfully, as Stephen responded to his daughter, 'I'm not sure I like being described as a guinea pig, Olivia.'

Olivia smiled as she popped an image into their minds of an orange and white plump guinea pig with her father's face on it, eating a leaf.

'*Stop that!*' Stephen said, as Phyllis hid a chuckle, '*Stop that this minute!*'

'*Sorry, Daddy,*' Olivia smiled coquettishly at her dad, whose heart instantly relented.

'*Harumph!*'

There was a short pause as the moment passed, then Olivia addressed her parents once more.

'*There are some things I need to show you. Before I say what I need to say, it'll help me explain why I'm saying these things and why I want you to listen to my suggestions.*'

Both of her parents looked almost sternly at her, perhaps shocked by her turn of phrase and the promise of serious things to come. But then they were used to their six-year-old daughter sounding more like a wizened sage than a free-living young girl. They both nodded and watched as Olivia closed her eyes and sighed. When she reopened them she stood up, moving to the centre of the walkway of the shuttle and turning to look at them.

It took Phyllis several moments to realise what had just happened; it took Stephen maybe a few seconds more. They both gasped, Phyllis' hand rising to cover her mouth. She looked about the shuttle. The other occupants remained seated, as was to be expected, but as she looked closer she could see the clues that confirmed her realisation. The business man three seats behind them was hunched over as he expulsed a large sneeze. Phyllis viewed with disgust the spiralling cloud of misty droplets that had been ejected from his mouth. They hung motionless in the space in front of him, frozen in a moment of viral ecstasy. Behind him sat two well-dressed administrators from the Core facilities; the woman on the left was mid eating a slice of Alluvian pie, its thick blue globules of juice dripping out of a split in the pastry's seams. It hung tantalisingly, waiting to splat upon the pristine skirts of her business suit. Phyllis turned and looked at her daughter.

'I've been practicing,' Olivia said matter-of-factly, 'I've been practicing since the day I was born. A lot of it seems to be innate, like what I could do as soon as I entered the real world, but I had very little control over it. I knew I could do something and then it just sort of happened. What I've been practicing is being able to do it at will, with control over where it goes and how it happens.

'And it's not just the outside world that I can manipulate. I can manipulate inside as well – *as Simon knows all too well,*' she finished in an aside to herself. She demonstrated precisely what she meant by holding up her hand between her and her parents. The skin on her hand and exposed arm rippled, then it turned blue. Not the blue one might expect from extreme exposure to the cold, but a beautiful cobalt blue. It rippled like a mountain lake being caressed by a zephyr and then the shading changed, fading from blue to cyan, then to apple green and finally, a deep mossy green. Her fingers started to extend, becoming gnarled like the twigs on an ancient tree, leaves sprouted and unfurled from them, the nails on her fingers hinged sideways and backwards allowing tiny creatures of Fey mythos to spring forth and glide on diaphanous wings through the burgeoning jungle that had sprouted from her hand. These would land and immediately be consumed by the flesh, to once more transform into new and wondrous flora and fauna. Olivia broke her concentration upon her hand and looked at her parents for their reaction. She was not to be disappointed as they both sat stock still, jaws agape, utterly mesmerised by what she had just done. Her hand and arm swiftly returned to normal.

'As you can see, there is little I do not seem to be able to do. It just takes time and practice and as we sit here in this bubble I have created I have plenty of time, whenever I need it. It only becomes exhausting when I try to expand the bubble beyond the scope of my vision, but with practice I have discovered there is no limit to how far I can extend. At that point it is truly just a matter of time on how long I can hold the bubble for.' She smiled at her astonished parents. Stephen looked her in the eye, unnerved by her smile, a smile that invariably held the warmth of a birthing star, but not so now. Now it held the coldness of a dying star.

'Just how far is 'no limit', Olivia?'

'The solar system, the galaxy, the universe,'

'But... but... how? How is that even conceivably plausible?' Stephen was aghast.

Olivia shrugged her shoulders, 'It comes down to atoms and neurons, electrons and neutrons, quarks and neutrinos and all the other elementary particles. They are interlinked. I can see them and manipulate them. The ones inside me connect to all those outside of me. I just send the message and it ripples through till they hit the end and then they ripple back to me. It's quite simple when you know how.' Olivia sounded almost condescending when she spoke of a power that was beyond that of a god. Her mind flexed and the universe flexed with it. Stephen shuddered.

'How did we not see this, Olivia?' Phyllis interjected, allowing Stephen time to collect himself. 'How could you develop this talent and any of your others without us even having an inkling at your potential?'

Olivia could tell that her mother's tone of recrimination was aimed at herself and her husband, obviously feeling that they had been lax in the parental guidance and safeguarding of their only child. But it wasn't their fault at all, if there was any blame, it lay solely with Olivia, for she had learnt very early on based on her experiences within her birth dream that shielding was paramount. Shielding her abilities from the likes of the Organisation and later, from her parents' disapproval or abject fear, as proven by her father's reaction now.

Olivia smiled again, its natural warmth returned as her hand had also returned to normal.

'Thanks to your preparations, Mummy, I learnt to shield very early on. It's a good exercise in itself, because I never drop my guard even when practicing other powers. It means I can multitask skills, thereby learning to interlink them.

'But we digress. I wasn't totally forthcoming with you years ago when we left the orbital station. I think, because I didn't think it was all that relevant at the time – I had only just come into being, after all, but also, if I'm honest, because I didn't want any reprisals from you so soon into our new relationship.'

Phyllis was the first to respond, Stephen still coming to terms with the potentials of his daughter's previously unseen powers.

'What haven't you told us, Olivia, other than what you've just shown us?' She was aware that Olivia had opened her discourse with them, stating that she needed to show them things before she could continue. Well she had very definitely shown them some things, remarkable, fantastical things. Things that neither she nor Stephen would have ever dreamt to be possible, even for Mentats like them. Olivia clearly was becoming the sum of all the parts the Organisation had envisaged. But, had they truly envisaged such a power? And if they had, how could they have possibly imagined that they would have been able to harness it for their own ends? A nagging sense of dread began to peck at her chest, wondering what she, as a mother of a new born babe could have needed to reprise for.

'We've moved around a lot, these last few years, for fear of what Simon might do were he to come looking for us.' Olivia paused allowing for her parents' acknowledgement, 'Well, truth be told, for at least the first year there wouldn't have been any follow up to us leaving. Not just because I told Simon not to follow us. It took a demonstrative action on my part to ensure that both he and his legions understood the consequences of such actions.'

'What action?' Stephen interrupted hurriedly; Phyllis' sense of dread was starting to seep into him as well.

Olivia's head tilted to the side, mirroring its past action when she had been begging her dad's forgiveness for teasing him.

'Simon didn't listen. It was only a matter of minutes before he had already broken his promise not to look for us. I ensured he wouldn't... by stopping his heart.'

Phyllis paled. Stephen stopped breathing.

'Is he... is he alive?' Phyllis queried.

Olivia shook her head; there was a genuine sense of sadness to her action.

'He wouldn't listen. He was not to be dissuaded and, without demonstrative action, nor would the rest of the board at the Organisation. With his demise came a cessation in their projects. It is only now that I'm beginning to detect possibilities that they may have reorganised and be considering us again. It will be at least another ten years, though, before I foresee them becoming a serious issue for us. By which time we will be prepared for any encounter they may wish to try and initiate.' The confident smile that accompanied this statement once again chilled the blood in her parents' bodies. Once again, the smile held all the warmth of a dead planet.

'I like it here. Dad likes it here. I like Miss Phillips and my peers, I want to stay, so does Dad. So I see no immediate reason why we need to leave.'

Both her parents nodded, although she was uncertain whether it was in agreement about staying in the colony or if it was a more general agreement because she could detect their unease at her demonstration, or more possibly her statement with regard to Simon's demise.

'I'm not suggesting we should be idle though, while we're here. I will continue to develop in various areas, not just my practice but at becoming more than a child, which I do find a little constraining if we're being honest.' They all chuckled at this, as it suddenly became apparent to Phyllis and Stephen that their little daughter was so much older than she appeared. Older even than if you factored in her past life within Phyllis' delusion.

'Mummy,' Phyllis looked at her daughter as she summoned her attention, 'the people from your dream.'

'Yes, dear?'

'How real are they? I mean, I know you worry about Rhys and Evie, but they're sort of real to me even though I know they're just figments of my subconscious. But I find them useful for discussing problems with. But what about the other people in your dream? Were they real before that or were they just constructs of different people?'

Phyllis sat back in her seat and thought about her dream. She only had the vaguest memories of it, fleeting images of moments of extremes within an amalgam of grey mists. She shook her head as she desperately tried to remember even one of the principal participants.

'Like who, my dear?' Phyllis needed help and her daughter seemed to know more about it than she did.

'Well, what about Miriam and Hiram?' she projected an image of the two of them into the front of her mother's mind, expanding upon it so Phyllis could see the meeting the three of them had had within the underground chamber.

Phyllis nodded, 'Yes, I see.' The images seemed to unlock the sealed doors of her mind and more faces and incidents suddenly flooded her consciousness. The physical effect made her pale as she was suddenly awash with past feelings of her reality and the feelings engendered by her delusion.

'Miriam and Hiram were sort of real, others I'm not so sure about. Rhys and Evie, for instance. I've no idea how they came into my mind, maybe because I thought you needed friends - they may have been simply constructs from stories I had read in my youth. The kind of friends a young girl should have. But Miriam and Hiram are real, at least in so much as they existed within the Organisation. They were siblings, Miriam the younger and more playful of the two. I think things may have swapped about a bit within my dream.' She paused as she remembered the final confrontation and the figures that melded and blended together, trying to pick out individuals. 'The triplets, for instance, were twins in my existence, but they always seemed to be more than two people. It was one of their powers, mirroring. They could conjure illusions for people to see mirror images of themselves. It was very useful for diverting attention away from them when they were trying to do something covert.'

'And...,' Olivia hesitated before plunging on, her heart racing, fearing the answer, any answer to her next question. 'And, what of John Kennedy?' Once more she projected an image into her mother's mind. It was hazy, wobbly even, almost out of focus as she struggled with a sudden wave of conflicting emotions that threatened to overwhelm her.

Phyllis seemed to detect her daughter's dilemma with the image and placed a calming hand upon her arm. Her head was shaking even as she did so.

'I don't know this face, I don't know this man, but the image isn't clear enough for me to be certain who he might be. Who was he to you in the dream?'

Olivia felt bile rising in the back of her throat as she dropped the projection, 'He... he wasn't really anyone, just someone who was there on occasion. I don't know if he was good or bad for me in the dream.' She glanced hesitantly up into her mother's eyes and thought she detected doubt in them for her explanation, maybe also understanding as she felt her mother's grip tighten upon her arm– a gentle squeeze to let her know mum understood.

Olivia nodded, resolving to push on, push past the issue of John Kennedy, 'If we go through the people in our delusion can we work out who's real and who isn't? Who is a potential ally and who is more likely to be loyal to the Organisation?'

Phyllis nodded, mirroring Olivia, 'We can, but why?'

'Because when I said we weren't going to be idle, one of the things I want us to do is to find anyone else like you who may want out from the Organisation, if they're not already out. I want us to find them and, in effect, recruit them to our cause. Or more to the point, I want you to do it, Mum.'

Stephen stepped in, 'Even if we get to a point where we can start looking for potential allies, I don't think it's a good idea for Phyllis to do it. Far better if it was me out there.'

'Oh, Daddy! Always the protector,' Olivia smiled and reached out with her mind, giving her dad an affectionate squeeze. 'Mummy doesn't have to go anywhere to look for them, she can just reach out with her mind. She's very good at it,' she glanced at her mother as Phyllis started to shake her head, 'You *are*, Mummy, even if you don't realise it. I've detected you doing it very subtly every day I've been alive here with you. Whenever I'm out of sight, I always know you're looking in on me. That's why it needs to be you who does the searches, because your touch is so delicate. Unless you were actually looking out for it no one would ever know you were looking for them.'

'She's right, y'know,' Stephen sparked up, 'I've felt it too, whenever we've been apart. I always feel comforted knowing you're there, somewhere, looking over me.' He smiled fondly at his wife and took her hands in his. She returned the affection.

'Good, then that's settled. Mum will look for other Mentats while we live a happy and carefree life here in the colonies, away from the dangers of a questing Organisation. And it will give me time to perfect my abilities and help you two find new skills.'

It would also give Olivia time to consider what they would do if they did find and build a small army of Mentats and associated allies. The Organisation was always going to be a bane to their existence if it remained operational – for her and her parents, and anyone else like them, to live the so-called 'happy and carefree life' she had so blithely spouted about, then the Organisation would need to be eradicated. Could they do that? Could *she* do that? Yes, her powers were developing and yes, her powers were phenomenal, but could they be used to wipe out an amorphous entity like a corporation? She didn't know, but she did know they had time now to plan. She had time to plan, to consider, to view potential events, to factor and weigh billions of potential pathways towards a future where they could be free and happy.

April 2050 - Earth

'Are we sure this is a good idea?' Stephen asked of his close-knit family.

They were sat in a cafeteria run by the University of Southampton, eating a very late lunch after spending much of the day viewing the campus and its facilities.

'Of course it is, Daddy, you worry too much,' Olivia replied as she bit into her tuna sandwich. She brushed the flakes of tuna that fell from the sandwich off of her apple-green jumper; it was her favourite and perfectly suited her loosely-worn waves of red hair. She agreed with her mother that it 'drew out her eyes'.

'Someone has to, Olivia, you're too blasé, always have been. I don't like the idea of being back here on Earth and I certainly don't like being this exposed.'

Phyllis laid a comforting hand over her husband's own liver-spotted and wrinkled hand. Stephen relaxed noticeably at her touch.

'It's fine, our contacts tell us the Organisation's moved off-world and all their searches seem to have both diminished in intensity and focused towards the Colonies. We should be safe here for the few years that Olivia wishes to be here. And we will always be on the lookout for trouble.'

Stephen sighed, but Phyllis could tell he wasn't completely satisfied. This was a good thing though, because it would mean Stephen would always be standing guard against the unexpected. She tried to alleviate his tension by directing her attention to Olivia.

'So, m'dear, what did you think of the day?'

Olivia nodded, 'More informative, I think, than the Portsmouth or Leicester open days, but I think a lot can be missed in the holo-tours. I definitely prefer Southampton over the other two cities, although I did quite like Leicester, it sort of reminded me of the dream. But,'

'But what?' Stephen interjected suspiciously.

Olivia raised an eyebrow at her father and stifled a knowing chuckle, '*But*, Daddy, I preferred Exeter and they have recently invested very heavily in their AI labs. I think Exeter is the place for me... imagine what could be achieved if we were to link into AI. I've been thinking about the rudimentary systems that currently exist and connect our race across the stars. It's only a matter of time before the connections become complete and the doomsayers will have their way – humanity ruled by machines.' She smiled condescendingly at the thought, 'It is the next step I think the Organisation has been missing, integrating us into the AI complex. It's an idea I had some time ago because of my birth dream. There was an innocuous moment when John spoke of an interface between the human mind and machines.'

Olivia stuttered slightly as she spoke John's name; even now, there were residual feelings for the ghost of her dreamed first love. Difficult, mixed emotions, emotions she struggled with whenever she allowed herself to remember. She swallowed before continuing; her throat was dry and she paused to take a sip of her drink.

'Dr Saussman, at Exeter, is clearly the leading light in AI connectivity and I think he's the man who will take humanity to the next level. If I'm there learning under him, I think it won't be too far-fetched for me to be the key. Then, who knows, maybe I could become queen of the skies.' She winked at her dad and she could detect the juxtaposed consternation in his demeanour.

She was half joking, but there was the real threat that the Organisation could conceivably direct its controlled Mentats to link with the AI complex and, through it, quite literally rule the galaxy. What better way to prevent that than to pre-empt them and become the conduit herself? Imagine the possibilities of what she could achieve linked to the galaxy!

• • • •

The blinds were closed in the office, leaving it in darkness. There was a flicker of blue light from the centre of the room, briefly illuminating the walls, desk and the silhouette of a man sat behind it. The light dissipated, plunging the office back into darkness. Then the hologram fired up again, casting its diffuse blue light across the office, but still leaving the man in the shadows. The hologram of a very tall, thin individual undulated, hovering just above the carpet. Striations and pixels shimmered in and out of vision; the connection was being interfered with, most likely due to the distance of the transmission.

'What do you have to report, Jasper?' the man behind the desk commanded. His voice was a level, authoritarian baritone, used to being responded to instantly; a voice that commanded respect and fear from its subordinates.

Jasper looked towards the shadows where his CEO sat, a clear hint of trepidation upon Jasper's pale vulpine features. His report was far more positive than anything they had relayed in the last year, but it still wasn't definitive and thus, didn't prevent Jasper from feeling safe from retribution, despite light years of distance between master and servant. Not even his innate powers gave him the confidence that so readily bolstered his normal sour demeanour.

'They were here, sir. Have been for the better part of a decade. We were correct that they've been hiding in the distant colonies, but...'

'But what?' The interjection was spoken softly.

Jasper swallowed hard, 'But, they vacated their domicile about six months ago, sir. Vacated the planet shortly after that. We don't know their projected destination for certain.'

'Do you have any ideas?'

'Well,' Jasper was normally very confident and his suspicions on the current whereabouts of the child and her parents were formulated through instinct and good investigation. Even so, under the imagined unremitting gaze of his master, he feared his report would still fail to meet requirements and could all too easily meet with punitive rewards.

'Well, the general consensus after *speaking* with their friends, colleagues and neighbours is that they have moved further out to the edges of the colonies. One or two have even speculated that they were being sponsored by one of the deep ex corporations to participate in one of their long-term missions.'

Jasper paused knowing such an idea would not sit well with the man behind the desk. If true, it would take the child beyond even his extensive grasp. Damn the shadows for masking the man's face; he had no way of knowing how he was taking the news and at this distance and with the distortions in connectivity, he was unable to sense anything with his mind. Not that he could ever hope to utilise his formidable skills and talents on that man anyway, he was too guarded in his own right.

'Do you have another interpretation on the presented evidence, Jasper?'

'We do, sir. Ethan and I are in accord, for once.' Did Jasper detect a smile in the shadows?

'Your brother and you actually agree on something?' It was a rhetorical question and Jasper knew better than to answer it directly, merely nodding assent.

'If we were running and hiding and had made it this far out to the edges of human influence and were safeguarding a child, we would not be wanting to take any further risks with her safety. Embarking upon a deep exploration mission into unknown territory with little or no protection would seem to totally defeat the purpose of our current success at remaining secure and at large. No, Ethan and I both agree that if we were them we would now turn around and head back, deeper towards Earth. Among other things, it's probably the last thing anyone would expect them to do. It's been seventeen years since the child fled with her parents and we suspect that all of them will have a hankering to return to where it all began. We're confident that they are heading home. We're confident because so many people here believe wholeheartedly that they are heading away from home. It seems all too likely that if you're running then you'd lay a false trail in the opposite direction of the way you're actually going.' Jasper halted as the shadowy figure shifted his weight and a pair of clasped hands slid across the desk top, followed by a chest and the hint of shoulders. And yet, he still couldn't see his master's face, he still couldn't ascertain whether his report was being met favourably.

'What do you intend to do now then, Jasper?'

It was a test of their conviction, Jasper knew: if he said they wanted to hedge their bets and keep a force out here in the deep colonies, then his master would know he lacked confidence in their intelligence gathering; if he said they should all head back to Earth and continue the search in the solar system then his report would hold weight.

'Head home, sir. Ethan and I are confident that they have laid a false trail and they are heading back to you and the Organisation. We'll set out immediately and should be back in system by the end of the month, at which point we will link up with whatever details you've set up for looking for them.'

The arms retracted, back into the shadows. Jasper wasn't certain, but he thought he heard the man make a pondering sigh, 'Hmm.'

'We no longer have an active presence on Earth, nor on the orbital. Perhaps it's time we took some of our old facilities out of their mothballs.' Jasper was certain none of this was being directed at him. He was also certain, however, when the man spoke again that it *was* being directed at him.

'Report to me as soon as the both of you are within system. We will coordinate from there.'

'Yes sir,' Jasper responded briskly, but as the connection had been severed before he could respond, it seemed unlikely that his master had heard his final affirmation.

The figure in the chair swivelled and pushed a button upon his console. A monitor to his right sprang to life and the face of a middle-aged man with horn-rimmed glasses and a button nose ill-fitted for restraining spectacles, appeared before him.

'My apologies, Dr Saussman. The pressing nature of running an organisation as expansive as ours. I do hope you understand,' the man continued without allowing the good doctor to respond, 'I have been keeping abreast of your research in recent years, particularly your ideas pertaining to artificial intelligence and the future prospects it may hold for humanity and its colonisation of further reaching solar systems'.

While he spoke, Dr Saussman took in the man talking to him. He saw what he was supposed to see: a young, handsome confident CEO; a man in his early to mid-thirties wearing an understated suit of immense wealth. Manicured hands, a skin tone that any super model would sell their soul for, sculpted hair and teeth that dazzled the screen, leaving Dr Saussman with the afterglow of a light shone into his eyes; for a second his mind filled in the gaps in the imagery and he was reminded of those ancient 20th century black and white silent movies of a villain in black coat tails and top hat or maybe even Nosferatu as his shadow glided sinisterly up the staircase. Dr Saussman had met young ambitious businessmen before, trying to sell research ideas to him or buy his by return. The difference was that *they* were all at the bottom of their respective corporate ladders, trying to find that big deal that would give them a meteoric rise to the upper tables of the elite within their organisations. *This* man, however, had none of that to worry about. He was already there, not just among the elite – he sat at the head of the table. He was the man to whom everything was served, which meant this man's promise of research investment was assured. He had nothing to prove, he had no one to impress, his decisions were his and with that came an implicit promise that anything Dr Saussman needed to complete his research would happen. The payoff was, what did this man want to do with his research? Was it as philanthropic as he had proposed or did his ambition far exceed those that had come before him? As Dr Saussman regarded the young CEO, he knew the man had already achieved everything most others in his position had taken a lifetime to achieve. If he was going to accept the proposals that were forthcoming, he would have to think very carefully before he said yes to anything. But then it occurred to him, did he have any option to actually say no? Even over a communication screen, Dr Saussman could feel an innate power seeping from the man's pores. He could feel himself being drawn into the man's pitch; he knew he was being enthralled by the prospects of what could be. The dreams he'd had since he had first conceived of the idea of a combined human/machine symbiotic evolution. As the man spoke, Dr Saussman's reservations slowly melted away.

'It is all most intriguing,' the man continued, 'which is why we are very keen to support your continued research. We are aware that you have support from your own academic institution, which is highly commendable and also engenders faith by multiple outlets for the work you are pursuing, hence the reason our organisation would like to further fund your work, with the possibility of offering our own scientists to your cause. I believe there could be a fantastical future for the evolution of mankind if we were to combine research.'

• • • •

The call ended, the monitor faded to a blank screen, blending back into the shadows of the office. The man sat back in his chair, resting his elbows on the arms and steepling his fingers, to press the tips against his thin lips. Lips that flexed, forcing an unnatural smile to crease his features. There was no mirth in that smile, merely a coldness reminiscent of Olivia's earlier that day. All that the man needed now was the child, and humanity's future evolution would be set, with him not just master of the Organisation, but master of the galaxy. He nodded and his smile broadened, exposing the ivory fangs that populated his mouth.

Humanity ruled by machines.
Ruled by the Mentats.
Ruled by me.

THE END.

Discography

'*Come on, Eileen*', written by Kevin Rowland/Jim Patterson/Billy Adams/Kevin Archer & released by Dexys Midnight Runners, June 1982.

'*Freaks*', written by Fish & released as a 'B' side to 'Lavender', by Marillion, 1985.

'*Ordinary World*' written by Simon Le Bon/John Taylor/Nick Rhodes/Warren Cuccurullo & released by Duran Duran in the USA, December 1992; released in the UK, January 1993

'*Regret*' written by Bernard Sumner/Peter Hook/Stephen Morris/Gillian Gilbert/Stephen Hague & released by New Order, 5th April 1993.

'*Wonderwall*' written by Noel Gallagher & released by Oasis, October 1995.

'*Seventeen Going Under*' written & released by Sam Fender, 7th July 2021.

Acknowledgements

I would like to thank my editor, Steph Warren, without whom this novel wouldn't have been half as good as it now is. In particular her guidance with regard to my first ending, which, truth be told, wasn't the first rendering of the ending. But the one I presented to her, she thoughtfully then pointed out to me that, whilst it was 'very nice', it was a bit twee and something of a Happy Ever After kind of ending. Which, if you've read any of my other work, you will know isn't really my style. I went back to my original rendering and everyone was a lot happier. So, thank you very much Steph for pointing out the bleedin' obvious to me, because I'd completely missed it!

Don't miss out!

Visit the website below and you can sign up to receive emails whenever Jack T Canis publishes a new book. There's no charge and no obligation.

https://books2read.com/r/B-A-QBXX-ERJQC

BOOKS 2 READ

Connecting independent readers to independent writers.

Also by Jack T Canis

Short Tales
Going Home
Did you know the Porters?

The Weird and Unexpected World of Ronald Taylor
The Weird and Unexpected World of Ronald Taylor

Standalone
Horrific Tales for a Horrific Year
Rehashed
The Unsung Hero
Ordinary World

Watch for more at https://www.buymeacoffee.com/jacktc.

About the Author

Jack T Canis lives in South Wales, UK with his wife and three neurodivergent children. He started his professional career as an archaeologist, but through the years has also been a self-employed armourer; an administrator for the NHS and in recent years a qualified person-centred counsellor specialising in bereavement and loss, now retired. Currently he is a full-time carer for his youngest child who has additional emotional & physical needs and carer for his eldest child who is autistic. He is a part time writer. He is published in a number of publications including: *Purple Wall magazine* (honourable mention & co-champion), *Datura* & *Sledgehammer Literary magazine.* He is in four anthologies and has been longlisted in the *Cranked Anvil* monthly competition (2021) & *Bridport Flash Fiction Competition* (2021). The collection of dark short stories, 'Horrific Tales for a Horrific Year' published by Abergavenny Small Press (ASP) is available from

https://www.asppublishing.co.uk/ or
https://books2read.com/horrifictales2020
He can be found on Twitter (daily): @jackcanis.
& Facebook (rarely): @jacktcanis.
Read more at https://www.buymeacoffee.com/jacktc.

Milton Keynes UK
Ingram Content Group UK Ltd.
UKHW041823211123
432980UK00001BB/159